I0765450

BASTARD'S HONOR

Copyright 2024 by Elisabeth Wheatley
All Rights Reserved
Published by Book Goblin Books

No Generative AI Training Use

For avoidance of doubt, Author reserves the rights, and grants no rights to, reproduce and/or otherwise use the Work in any manner for purposes of training artificial intelligence or machine learning technologies to generate text, text to speech, voice, or audio including without limitation, technologies that are capable of generating works in the same style or genre as the Work, unless individual or entity obtains Author's specific and express permission to do so. Nor does any individual or entity have the right to sublicense others to reproduce and/or otherwise use the Work in any manner for the purposes of training artificial intelligence or machine learning technologies to generate text, text to speech, voice, or audio without Author's specific and express permission.

For inquiries, email support@elisabethwheatley.com

ERYMAYA
VALDAR
Istra
Otsuru
NIHAIN
REKESHI
Cursewood
HYLENDALE
Lashera
Cerin River
ILMIAR
Phaed
LIECHNABURG
LADENDELL
Iria
MYNADRA
Espa
Cibran
Trahern
DUMAL
TEMNESS
HAZAR
Yndra
ECRAN
Mandukhai

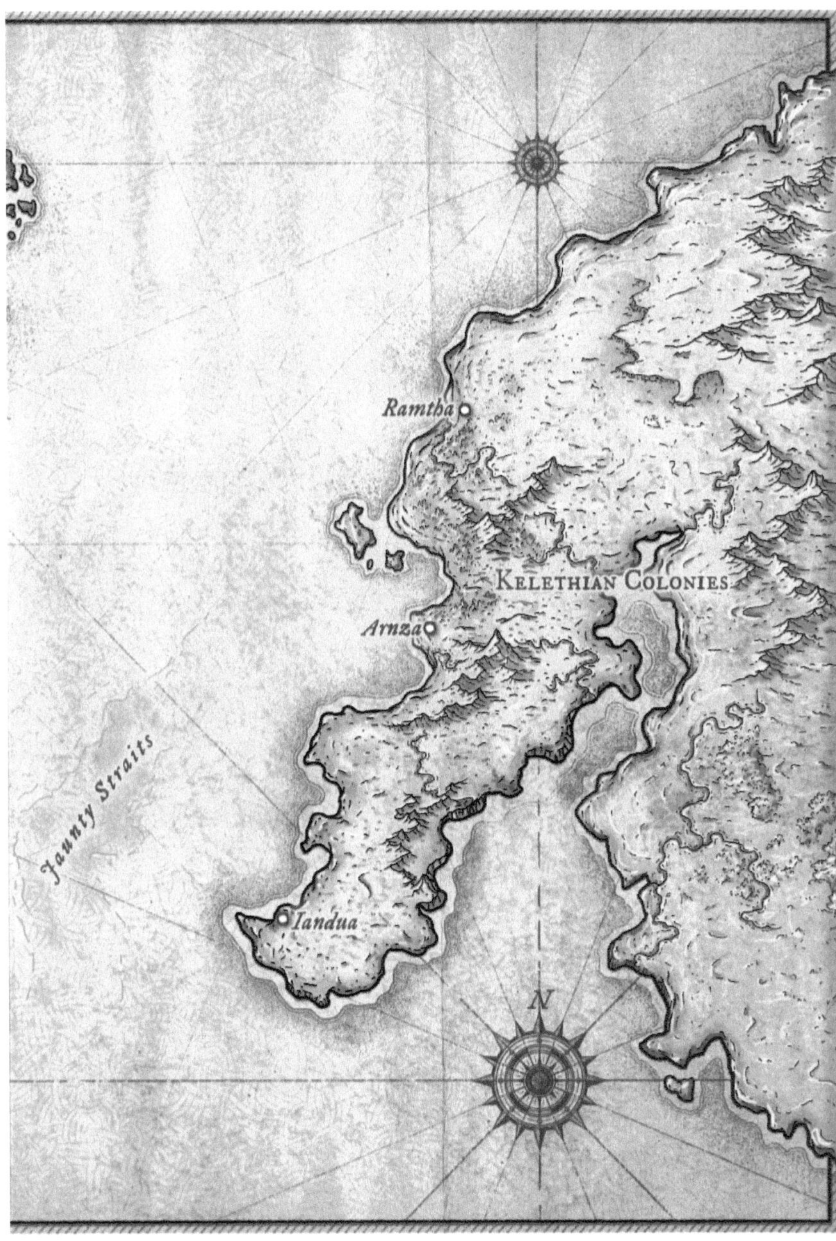

Ramtha
Kelethian Colonies
Arnza
Jaunty Straits
Iandua
N

1

THADRED

Thadred wasn't ignoring the viscountess, not strictly speaking. He just wasn't going to change his next words no matter what she said.

"So, while I appreciate His Majesty's desire to honor the empress and her people, many of us have concerns."

"Concerns, yes." Thadred leaned heavily on his cane.

Viscountess Daphne had insisted on walking in the hedge maze, probably fearing they might be overheard. She had requested an audience with the High Inquisitor under the pretense that there were possible cythraul demon sightings in her husband's lands.

Thadred's official imperial assignment these days was to make inquiries and investigate reports of the demons. However, it quickly became clear that Daphne had no concerns about the cythraul as the conversation had quickly turned to politics.

"This proclamation threatens to undermine centuries of legal precedent," added Viscount Torsten, the viscountess's husband. He kept himself firmly between Daphne and Thadred, as if he feared the knight might snatch her and run off right here.

Thadred had tumbled Daphne a few times, but it had been well before she and the viscount had married. Even Thadred knew better than to meddle with married women. Daphne now considered herself Thadred's dear friend.

As a favor to her dear friend, she had helped sway her husband, and by extension his family, into supporting the emperor through several controversial tax levies. As such, she was entitled to ask favors of her own.

Thadred just wished he wasn't the one who had to grant those favors.

"Tory has an older sister," the viscountess reminded Thadred, patting her husband's shoulder as she used his nickname. "With this proclamation, what's to stop her and her husband from trying to take our estate?"

Emperor Daindreth, Thadred's cousin, had announced his wife was expecting a child in the fall. Along with that happy announcement, he had issued a proclamation of supreme primogenitor—a fancy way of saying the crown would pass to his eldest child, regardless of whether they were male or female.

Thadred prepared to repeat the response that had been reviewed by a dozen or so imperial lawyers and advisors. "The proclamation of supreme primogenitor applies only to the Fanduillion-Brindonu house. Only those with Istovari blood will be able to make such claims."

Viscountess Daphne exhaled a sharp breath. "So your lawyers say, but if a daughter is announced as heir over a son, think of the consequences."

Thadred smiled. "My dear viscountess—"

Her husband glared at the term of endearment.

Thadred cleared his throat and started over. "Viscountess Daphne, I understand your concerns. But the fears regarding succession among the nobility have been addressed. You shall not have to fear your sister-in-law taking anything."

"But if the throne is inherited by a woman, then my sons may have to defend their inheritance from their sisters!" the viscount interjected.

Thadred schooled his face into one of empathy and concern. These were exactly the objections Cromwell and other advisors had cautioned when Emperor Daindreth issued the proclamation.

But the Istovari sorceresses had accepted this as a

compromise. They'd initially demanded a matrilineal succession—they must have known they wouldn't get it outright.

But there was still a very real possibility that the next inhabitant of the White Throne would be an Istovari sorceress. Istovari magic passed along the maternal line, so if a sorceress took the throne, that would ensure at least two generations of her and her descendants ruling over the empire.

The empire still had months until they would know if the couple's firstborn would be male or female. Thadred was content to put off these questions until then, but much of the empire was not.

The next ruler was going to have magic either way. It was just a matter of whether a woman would rule if there were male options.

"There are reasons for the rules, Lord Thadred," Daphne continued. "Order. In the days before inheritance was standardized, there were feuds and squabbles fought across the land. Second sons, sons-in-law, nephews…"

Thadred had once appreciated Daphne's knowledge of political history. Now he wished she knew a little less. Because she was right. Every time inheritance or succession was altered, especially at this scale, trouble arose.

"My lady, I understand your concerns. Truly, I do." Thadred kept his voice calm, charming, but not too charming lest he upset her husband. "But surely you have heard of the work the Istovari have done to help the people of Yndra and those affected by wildfires in the south."

"I have heard," Daphne replied slowly. From the way she said it, she would have preferred that hadn't been brought up.

"With the help of the Istovari, prosperity is fast returning to the empire. This concession from the emperor was to ensure their continued alliance."

A long silence followed.

Oddly, it was the viscount who spoke. "The Witch War left a mark on this empire." He looked down. "Many of my people have suffered. We've had an outbreak of the pox through much of the hamlets and villages." The viscount opened, then closed his mouth. A bit reluctantly, he said, "The sorceresses have helped many people in my lands."

Thadred nodded solemnly. Nearly all of the Istovari sorceresses had emerged from their protective home in the forests of the Cursewood. Dozens of them now served in rotation around the empire working to heal the land and the people who had suffered during the Witch War.

War might not have been the right word, but that was what people were calling it. What began as a series of extreme natural disasters clustered close together had escalated to a raving mob tearing across the countryside.

The late Empress Vesha had been a witch, someone who worked magic through bargains with cythraul demons from the Dread Marches. She had unleashed hundreds or perhaps even thousands of the creatures on the land, no one had exact numbers.

They had sacked cities, razed towns, and left a swath of destruction and horror in their wake. Most the cythraul had been forced back into the Dread Marches, but many had fled and gone into hiding. Thadred's primary duty as High Inquisitor was to hunt those in hiding.

All the same, the aftershocks of the Witch War continued. A particularly virulent plague here, a series of earthquakes there, droughts in some places, and floods in others. The troubles would probably end eventually, but for now everyone had to buckle down and bear it.

Torsten made a coughing sound, but that might have just been him clearing his throat. "It would…benefit us all, I think, if the sorceresses could be…allies."

Thadred nodded, deciding he might like the viscount after all.

The gods had blessed Torsten with a fine fortune, a good pedigree, and a head for land management, but not much else. He was a pudgy, toadlike man who waddled about always sweating like cheese in the summer.

But he had titles and money—neither of which Thadred had

possessed—until recently.

Thadred briefly remembered Daphne telling him, with great excitement, that she was engaged to Viscount Torsten. Thadred then remembered just what the two of them had been doing when she'd told him and felt a stab of—was it resentment? It wasn't jealousy, no, not that. Thadred didn't want her back. But it was something hot and unpleasant.

Daphne had known she could do better. They both had.

Thadred had seduced plenty of women over the years, but few of them needed much seducing. He was handsome, tall, and the closest friend of Daindreth Fanduillion, the heir of the empire.

Sometimes Thadred wondered if these women had settled for bedding him because they thought it would get them closer to Daindreth—it hadn't.

All the same, Torsten was quite the catch as far as imperial husbands went. Daphne had married well and now she wanted to make sure she would get to enjoy the benefits of this marriage.

"But we don't need them. You are a sorcerer now, are you not?" Daphne looked expectantly to Thadred.

The knight grimaced. He still thought of himself as a knight, not a sorcerer. Once, he had thought he had no ability at all, but his power had been getting stronger.

It helped that he had stopped wearing a ring of tenebrous steel that masked his abilities. He'd started wearing it to keep other sorcerers from meddling with him, but it turned out to be stifling his own talents.

He was also a Kadra'han, sworn to the emperor. As a result, Thadred's power increased in return for faithful service. And he had done a great deal of service, especially in the past year.

Magic—or at least the potential for it—was everywhere. Thadred could sense the golden threads of *ka* misting off the plants, the bodies of the two nobles, the insects, the moss under their feet, and even riding on the air.

Thadred chuckled, deflecting as best he could. "I am one man, viscountess. I fear I cannot be everywhere at once." A flicker of motion caught Thadred's eye before he felt the servant's *ka* headed in their direction.

A young man in impeccable imperial livery bowed as he reached Thadred. "My lord, pardon me."

The servant's name was Brychteinvanderwal, but no one outside his parents' tiny home province could pronounce that. Since becoming Thadred's valet, he'd shortened it.

Thadred nodded. "Yes, Brick?"

"There's a lady here to see you, sir." Brick didn't let annoyance show, he was too professional for that, but Thadred noticed how his eyes slid back in the direction he had come.

"A lady?" Thadred blinked. That did not narrow it down. Ladies were always coming to see him these days, and not for the reasons they once had.

"A sorceress, sir. She was most insistent."

That was odd. Most sorceresses in the palace would have simply sent for him or delivered a message. For Brick to be interrupting a meeting, it must be serious.

"Did she give a name?"

"Sairydwen Aulen, my lord."

The name hit Thadred like a punch. For a moment, his lungs wouldn't expand and when he finally managed to speak, his voice came out frayed. "Sair?"

A woman appeared around the corner of the hedge maze. Her hair was covered in a kerchief, and she still wore a grey dress more suited to a baker than a sorceress.

Her face was flush and windswept. Had she just gotten off a ship?

Sair locked eyes on him and began moving faster.

Something was wrong. Something was terribly, terribly wrong. Dread, foreboding, and a sick sensation formed deep in his gut.

Brick coughed at the sight of her. "I told her to wait, sir, but—"

Thadred was already moving toward Sair, turning his back to his noble guests. "I must go."

Daphne was ready to protest. "Thadred—"

"Thank you, your lordship," the viscount interrupted. "I am

sure we shall speak again later. Come along, my dear."

Thadred's full attention was already on Sair. What was she doing here? He headed toward her, cursing his injury that he couldn't move faster.

Sair broke into a run and slammed into his chest. Sobs broke out as she leaned against him.

Six months.

It had been six months since she had stopped responding to his letters. Not a word in all that time. Now here she was, disheveled, weeping, and clinging to him like a drowning woman grasping at a lifeline

Thadred wrapped one arm around her. He surveyed the empty garden out of instinct, searching for threats. "Sair, what's wrong?"

The last time he had seen her, she had been heading back to the north to help with rebuilding the Istovari there, along with her son. Sair had some of the best connections between the two and it made sense that she would see them settled in.

Thadred looked to Brick, but the aghast valet just stared as Sair sobbed into Thadred's chest. It was a horrific breach of protocol by court standards.

"Sair." Thadred steadied her, squeezing her tight. "What's wrong?"

"They took him," Sair wept. "Rhis. They took him."

Thadred felt like the ground had dropped out from under him. Rhis—Sair's son.

Thadred grabbed her shoulder and pushed her back so he could see her. "Sair, what happened?"

Sair drew in a shuddering breath. "It was Iasu, the prisoner."

Thadred's jaw clenched. Iasu was a sorcerer, if a minor one. Thadred spared a glance over his shoulder. The viscount and viscountess were well away by now.

Daphne would have probably preferred to hear the gossip, but Viscount Torsten would hardly want to deal with a weeping woman.

Iasu had sworn to serve Vesha the Usurper, Daindreth's late mother, and had made it clear he intended to keep that oath.

Empress Amira had wanted to execute him, but sorcerers were rare. It had been decided to keep Iasu imprisoned in Hylendale until they could decide what to do with him.

"I left Rhis in Lashera. The Elder Mother had moved as had many of the others." Sair fought to regain control of herself, smearing back tears and loose strands of hair.

This was so unlike her.

Thadred had seen Sair stand up to capture and torture. She had stood with Empress Amira at the mines of Mevanmar, when they had confronted Vesha and stopped the release of a fallen goddess.

Sair was brave. But now…

Thadred rubbed her back, waiting for her to catch her breath.

"Iasu Zahn escaped, somehow. He killed the Elder Mother and took Rhis as a hostage. We tried to track him, but we lost him in Phaed. He boarded a ship headed to Yndra."

Thadred grimaced. Yndra was a decently sized port along the Erymayan coast. From Yndra, one could get a ship to any of the major ports within a few days. From there, a traveler could go anywhere.

"How did the runt escape?" Thadred demanded. "Iasu was supposedly guarded by King Hyle."

"That's just it." Sair composed herself, dragging in a breath. "A man infiltrated the castle, dressed as a soldier. Then he changed."

Thadred instantly knew what she meant. "Cythraul?"

"I don't know what else it could have been." Sair pressed a knuckle between her eyes. "Witnesses said his eyes turned red and he tore the door off Iasu's cell like it was nothing. The stranger escaped with Iasu and Rhis."

That made very little sense. A cythraul? Rescuing Iasu? Not only that, but Iasu had gone along with it? As far as they knew, Iasu had been ignorant of Vesha's dealings with cythraul. Thadred tried to sort through everything he knew about Iasu, the late empress, and the monsters, but Sair was talking again.

"King Hyle was no help and the Istovari don't have the

numbers right now, and…" She shook her head.

Thadred didn't think about the logistics or practicality before he spoke. "We'll get him back."

Sair choked back another sob. "I don't even know where to start looking."

"It's alright," Thadred said, mind racing. "We'll find him. I swear to you." Despite the sliver of hurt worming beneath his thoughts, he meant every word.

But why did women only come back to Thadred when they needed something?

2

SAIR

Emperor Daindreth and Empress Amira had made it quite clear that evenings were their private time—especially now. No one was to disturb them, and no one was to try speaking to them, except two or three close advisors and family.

Luckily, Thadred was both.

Sair probably could have gotten in to see Amira herself, now that she considered it. Amira had few people she trusted, but Sair knew herself to be one of the favored. Sair had braided Amira's hair for her wedding, ridden to war with her, and served as the empress's advisor many times.

Thadred knocked on the door of the dining room with his cane, smiling at the noblewoman who passed by.

Sair refused to look, even though it appeared to be an elderly matron. Thadred's reputation as a womanizer and serial seducer was well known. The last time they'd spoken, Thadred had promised to wait for her, but that had been a year ago. She had thought he'd changed, but according to the rumors that reached her in Lashera, he hadn't. Then again, why had Sair even expected a man as wealthy and important as him to change for a woman like her? She'd set herself up for disappointment from the start.

"Who is it?" The emperor's voice filtered through the door with an edge of annoyance.

"Your favorite cousin."

"Enter."

The two guards allowed Thadred to slip through. He tugged Sair after him, holding her hand.

The dining room was small, made for informal family meals. Of course, when you were emperor and empress of the known world, there was a limit as to how informal anything could be. Gold gilt decorated the walls and a small fortune in solid silver tableware lay before them.

Daindreth occupied the head of the table and Amira sat to his right. Several empty chairs occupied the table's length.

It seemed the rest of their attendants and entourage had been dismissed. Daindreth and Amira most likely wanted to be alone right now, which probably accounted for the narrow-eyed look the empress leveled in Thadred's direction.

Amira's hair was down and uncovered, and the emperor's shirt was partly undone, which likely hinted at the couple's plans for the evening.

"Your Majesties." Thadred swept into the room and flourished a bow.

Amira's expression changed the moment she saw her friend. "Sair!" The empress made to stand.

As soon as she did, the emperor raced to help with her chair. "Darling, let me."

Amira touched his arm as she stood, but otherwise ignored him, moving toward her friend and Thadred. "Sair, I didn't know you were coming."

Sair gaped at the empress, eyes wide. Amira was alight as power radiated from her like a furnace. She had always been strong as a sorceress, but she was even more powerful now. It was beyond just the excess of *ka* typically seen in pregnant women.

Amira was a Kadra'han sworn to the emperor, just like Thadred. That meant that their magic grew based on their loyalty and service to their liege lord—the emperor.

Knowing Amira, she probably saw childbearing as a service to her husband. In a way, it was. An emperor with heirs was an emperor with power. That meant that every discomfort and inconvenience Amira experienced from her pregnancy would only make her stronger.

"Your Grace, you are glowing," Sair gasped.

Amira cocked an eyebrow with a sly smile. "I don't need flattery from you, my friend."

"No, not like that. I mean." Sair looked the empress over. "You glow with power."

"She'll be leveling mountains before we know it," Thadred said, looking over Amira with fondness.

"Woe to my enemies," Daindreth murmured, touching the hair that fell loose down her back.

Amira frowned. "Sair?" She seemed to sense something was wrong. She pulled the other woman into an embrace. Sair hugged Amira in turn. Sair had no living siblings, but she thought of Amira as a little sister.

The two pulled back and Amira looked at her from head to foot.

"What's wrong, Sair?" the empress asked.

Sair inhaled a shuddering breath. "Forgive me, Your Grace, but I bring bad news."

"Tell me." Amira's face went hard and Sair was reminded that this woman had once been an assassin.

Sair swallowed. "I fear your grandmother is dead, Your Grace. Murdered."

Amira's face gave away nothing. "I see." She inhaled slowly. "Who?"

"Iasu." Thadred growled the name.

Amira stiffened, raising her chin. "He murdered the Elder Mother of the Istovari?" The empress didn't seem upset by news of her grandmother's death. She'd always had a complicated relationship with the woman.

"Yes," Sair confirmed.

"Where is he now?" Amira looked sharply between the two of them.

Thadred cast Amira a wry smile. "It seems our dear *brother* has escaped."

Iasu, like Amira and Thadred, was a Kadra'han. Both of them had trained with Iasu at different times, though Amira had known him better. Iasu was a part of the Kelamora Kadra'han, an order of men that trained magically gifted children as bodyguards and assassins, then sold them to the highest bidder.

Amira and Daindreth exchanged a look.

Thadred thumped his cane against the ground, adjusting his grip on it. "He took Rhis."

Amira spun to Sair. "He did?"

Sair nodded, biting her lip. She didn't trust herself to speak just then.

"That whoreson," Amira spat then whirled on her husband. "I told you we should have killed him." Amira looked angry enough to incinerate a man. Coils of *ka* shimmered around the room and Sair wondered if the empress was aware of drawing power to herself.

Daindreth's attention remained on Sair. "How long?"

"A week." Sair's voice cracked. Though she had been sure she'd cried herself out, a tear slipped down her cheek. "He boarded a ship called the *Meissenfrau* in Phaed, headed for Yndra."

Amira put an arm around Sair. "He'll pay for this," she vowed. "With Vesha's death, Iasu's Kadra'han bond passes back to the grandmaster of Kelamora. He'll have no choice but to seek his master."

"Probably brought Rhis as an apology for taking so long," Thadred muttered.

Sair had considered that possibility herself. They'd destroyed the monastery at Kelamora, but many of its members had survived. The monastery had existed for generations to provide Kadra'han to those who could pay for them.

"Boys with enough magic in their blood are rare these days," Amira muttered. "They'll want him alive and unharmed."

Sair didn't bother to fight the next round of tears. "I know." She pressed a fist against her breast, trying to steady herself. "They might already have him bound in a Kadra'han's oaths. He's just a boy. He—" Sair's voice broke and this time she wept on Amira's shoulder.

That was the dark side of the Kadra'han bond. A Kadra'han was under compulsion to obey the commands of their master.

The Kadra'han bond, for all its uses and benefits, functioned like a curse. It could be broken, but it was rare to break it apart from death.

Amira had succeeded in breaking the obedience portion of her own curse, but she was an outlier. Thadred was just fortunate that Emperor Daindreth was a decent man.

"It gets worse," Thadred said.

"Worse?" Amira cocked her head, looking sharply between Thadred and Sair.

Daindreth raised one brow, probably bracing himself for the bad news, too.

Thadred glanced at Sair. "A cythraul broke him out."

Amira's eyes flashed at that. She turned sharply back to Sair.

The sorceress repeated her version of events, explaining what she knew. When she finished, the emperor and empress were silent, each watching the other.

"I would request your permission, Your Majesty." Thadred nodded sharply to Daindreth. "Permission for men, supplies, and an imperial warrant to hunt down Iasu and recover the boy."

Sair looked up through tear-stained eyes.

"I think we can agree this poses a significant threat." Thadred sounded like he had rehearsed this speech. "You outlawed the creation of new Kadra'han, as we all know. If Iasu intends to have this Istovari boy made into one in direct defiance, well." Thadred folded his hands atop his cane, not quite making eye contact with any of them. "We cannot allow this to stand."

Daindreth inhaled a slow breath, considering. "Can your duties be covered by others in your absence?"

Thadred opened his mouth and coughed, probably deciding to say something other than what he had initially planned. "This is the most certain sighting of a cythraul in months and I can have one of the reeves oversee any new reports while I am gone."

Daindreth nodded slowly, thinking.

"We can't leave Iasu and the grandmaster at large," Amira said flatly. "Kadra'han are too dangerous." Amira would know. She'd once single-handedly broken Daindreth out of this very palace through sheer force of will.

The young emperor and empress had a growing list of allies that continued to grow every day. But they had many enemies as well.

Great leaders always had great enemies. The higher one rose in the world, the more people cheered for your downfall.

There were disgruntled lords, vengeful clans, and rebellious vassal kings across the empire who would pay handsomely for their own Kadra'han. A pair of Kadra'han—Amira and Thadred—had all but established the current emperor.

What was to say that a few others couldn't establish a new one?

Daindreth exhaled slowly. "It sounds dangerous."

Thadred laughed at that. It was a sharp, genuine laugh that he quickly stifled. "Story of our lives, Your Majesty. Story of our lives."

Daindreth looked to Amira. Something passed between them.

From the way Amira gripped Sair's arm, she suspected the empress would have volunteered to hunt Iasu herself under different circumstances.

Daindreth faced Thadred squarely. "You're up to this?"

"Because I'm a cripple, you mean?" Thadred was always the first to bring up his own condition. An accident when he'd been young had crushed his pelvis and left him with a permanent limp.

Sair could sense the lines of *ka* looped and woven around the injury in a slight modification of a spell she'd taught him. He'd adjusted well, but magic could only do so much.

"Because you're a trusted advisor and I need you," Daindreth shot back. "Alive and preferably at my side."

Amira and Thadred exchanged their own significant look. The two of them had a somewhat antagonistic relationship, but they were both the emperor's Kadra'han. They had a level of understanding that Sair hadn't seen outside brothers and sisters.

Amira nodded to Thadred.

The knight turned back to the emperor. "My liege, I need to do this. We need to do this. The Istovari are our allies and they are to thank for much of the progress since the Witch War. We must make it clear that attacks on them and their families will not be tolerated. Nor will we allow blatant disregard for imperial edicts."

Daindreth exhaled slowly. He looked to Sair. "I am very sorry for what has happened, my lady. All of us here care greatly for Rhis."

Thadred offered Sair a wan smile, seeming to know he'd won.

Daindreth swallowed again. "Speak with Captain Westfall. Inform him of your departure and provide the Master of Lists with what you will need."

Thadred grinned and for a moment seemed to preen, like a cat realizing he'd caught a mouse. "Thank you, Your Majesty." His face softened when he turned back to Sair. "Get some rest, my lady. I'll prepare for us to set out tomorrow."

Sair's eyes widened. "You can do that?" She had expected to wait days before they were able to set out after Rhis.

"I'll work all night if I have to, but yes." Thadred shifted his cane to his side. "By your leave, Your Majesty. Your Grace. Lady Sairydwen." Thadred bowed to the emperor, empress, and Sair. "If you'll excuse me."

Amira took both Sair's hands in hers. "Have you eaten today?"

"No." Sair hadn't had much thought of eating or anything else these past days.

"Join us," the empress beckoned, calling for servants to set another place.

Sair took a seat beside the empress, feeling a daze of relief. They were going to help her. Thadred was going to help her.

Amira cast an apologetic look to her husband. "I'm afraid our plans for tonight have changed, my love."

Daindreth saw her seated again and kissed her hair. He squeezed her hand, their fingers lingering on each other as he took his place once again at the head of the table. There was a sweetness between them. A gentleness that spoke of a deep and abiding connection. They were perfectly at ease with each other.

Servants portioned food onto Sair's plate as her mind wandered.

She had been so focused on getting here, seeking Thadred's help, and going after her son and his abductor. For days now, that had been her only goal and only thought. Now she'd secured the aid of the empire and Thadred was seeing to arrangements, exhaustion began to overtake her.

It was all she could do to gulp down a few bites before Amira walked her to a suite of rooms for the night. The empress had her own ladies in waiting tend to Sair. They drew her a bath, washed her hair, and bundled her into a massive silken bed stuffed with goose feathers.

Amira sat on the edge of Sair's bed as the servants bustled to and fro. Outside the glass-paned window, the moon looked down on them, thoughtful and distant.

The two women had not said much, but Sair appreciated Amira's presence. There was ten years difference between them, but in many ways, Amira knew more of the world than Sair did. The younger woman had certainly seen more of it. More than that, they trusted each other.

Sair frowned, watching Amira. The empress didn't rest a hand on her belly as many expecting women did, though she was about halfway through her pregnancy, and it showed. Sair could sense the inferno that was Amira, but she could also see the secondary source of *ka* growing inside her—Amira's unborn child. It had been a long time since Sair had been able to see magic that clearly.

"After the Elder Mother died," Sair swallowed, still not sure how the other woman was taking this.

Amira looked to Sair. If she felt anything at all at the news of her grandmother's death, she didn't give it away.

"Before I left to pursue Iasu, there were reports that the

Cursewood was receding."

Amira cocked her head at that. "Really?"

Sair nodded. "I think she was the one holding the curse together."

Sair and every other Istovari sorceress who had fled the lowlands twenty years ago had given most of their power to create the Cursewood. It had stood ever since, a shifting maze of poisoned trees, mutant animals, parasitic plants, and noxious fumes that had protected the Haven. It had saved their people, but it had weakened them.

Sair had been stronger than most her people, but more than that, she had learned to make the most of what she had. Sair might not be as powerful as Amira or Thadred, but she could be creative. When she had first met the two younger Istovari, Sair had been able to outmatch them with her superior knowledge. She still had more experience, but Thadred was catching up in skill and Amira had already surpassed them both in power.

"That does explain why my mother's strength has been growing these past few days. We thought it might be a fluke." Amira looked out the window, contemplative.

Amira's mother, Lady Cyne, lived here in the palace. Nonetheless, she had a strained relationship with her daughter. Cyne was treated as more of a foreign dignitary than family.

"Do you think you might get your full power back?" Amira asked, looking to her friend.

"I don't know. Perhaps." Sair looked down at her hands, plucking the thick goose down quilt of her bed.

"Your son's power might also increase."

"Yes." Sadness squeezed Sair's chest. Rhis, like all the other children born after the creation of the Cursewood, had precious little magic. But it would still be enough to bind him in a Kadra'han's vows.

Amira reached out and clutched Sair's hands. "Thadred is leading the hunt and I have already sent word to my network. We *will* find your son." The empress looked square into Sair's face. "And the people who took him will pay."

Tears pricked her eyes again.

"No one hurts my friends," Amira whispered, brushing away Sair's tears. Her voice was calm, cool, but that belied the ferocity that simmered inside her. "Iasu can't hide forever."

"You know where to find the Kelamora Kadra'han?"

"They have stayed out of the empire for the most part, but we have one or two confirmed reports."

Sair raised her brows. "I would think you would hunt them down."

The empress had been trained by the order at Kelamora, but she had only spent a few months with them. She had never spoken to Sair of her time under their tutelage, but it seemed there was no love lost there.

Amira shrugged. "I would rather the order didn't exist, but I am content to ignore them if they don't cause trouble." Amira exhaled a long breath out her nose. "They are hardly the worst criminal organization in the empire."

"You have been tracking these things?" Sair was surprised, but realized she shouldn't have been.

"I have spies in every city from Hylendale to Ecran," Amira confirmed.

"You've been busy." Sair tried to smile.

"My advisor Cromwell has helped me a great deal." Amira frowned. "It's strange. People fear me more these days than when I used to slit throats in the shadows."

Cromwell had once been advisor to Amira's father, the king of Hylendale. Cromwell and the empress had a complicated relationship, but she had saved him from a treason charge. The man had little choice but to put his considerable talents to Amira's use.

"You have other people to slit throats for you these days," Sair mused.

"I do." Amira confirmed it almost wistfully.

Sair briefly wondered if Amira had ordered assassinations herself. It seemed likely, but a part of Sair didn't want to know.

The servants didn't give any sign they had heard, though they would have. The palace must now be used to the idea that their empress was a former assassin.

"But I will tear out Iasu's entrails myself if he hurts your son," Amira vowed.

Sair squeezed Amira's hands back. "Only if you beat me to it, Your Grace."

3

THADRED

Magical horses were not magically obedient. They also liked to bite.

As the owner of a magical horse, Thadred felt quite misled by the poems and ballads of minstrels. Though it was unclear to him if he actually *owned* Lleuad. Sometimes the kelpie seemed to think it was the other way around.

"Come on," Thadred coaxed. "It's just for a few days. And then you'll get to eat bad people. You like eating people, don't you?"

Lleuad snorted at the edge of the ramp, refusing to board the ship.

There was a high wind today, making the ship bob and sway, even at anchor.

Lleuad was a swamp horse and loved water, but *only* freshwater. The animal could play in lakes and rivers all day. He was like a cat in a bathhouse when it came to saltwater.

Thadred bristled, aware of the sailors, several soldiers, and even Brick staring at him. They knew better than to laugh, but he was sure this would be the topic of tavern jokes for months.

The docks were alive with activity this morning. Carts, wheelbarrows, and laden donkeys moved this way and that.

Through the cacophony, the crowd parted and Sair appeared on a white mare surrounded by several imperial guards. She caught sight of him and Lleuad, stalled at the edge of the ramp into the ship.

Thadred whirled a glare on the little stallion. He would not allow the animal to embarrass him in front of Sair. "Up the plank, you nag. Before I turn you into glue."

Lleuad snorted, as if daring Thadred to try.

The knight changed his tactics. "Come on, boy. Be nice. Just this once."

Sair dismounted and several of the guards followed her onto the ship while the rest returned to the palace. The sorceress took notice of them as she walked up the other side of the ramp.

Lleuad's ears flicked at that. As if he wasn't about to be outdone by the sorceress, the stallion leapt up onto the rocking boat, his whole body tense and uneasy.

"Good boy," Thadred crooned. "Easy, son. This way. Good."

The decks had been lined with sand for the horses and it crunched with each step.

Thadred guided the kelpie down the ramp into the ship's hold, leaning on Lleuad for support. A cane was just an added liability here.

The knight backed Lleuad into the narrow stall, tight so that the horse wouldn't have room to hurt himself. He buckled Lleuad into the crossties, one of the few times he dared to physically restrain the kelpie.

Lleuad snorted at him, teeth snapping.

"It's just until we get out of port," Thadred promised.

Lleuad pinned his ears and stomped as if to say, *I trusted you.*

Thadred backed away from the horse, careful not to take his eyes off Lleuad. He had bonded with the kelpie, but it was much like the bond between brothers. When there was no one else to fight, they tended to fight each other.

Thadred used the rails of the ramp to drag himself to the top decks.

Brick jogged over to meet him. "Can I help you, sir?"

"I'm fine," Thadred muttered, waving him away. He hated needing help.

"Very good, sir. Here you are." Brick extended his cane using both hands as if it was a king's scepter.

Thadred took it, not expecting it to be much help on the slick deck of a ship that constantly rocked. He'd need to rely more on magic to help him here.

A flutter of blonde hair caught Thadred's attention. Sair leaned against the rail at the front of the ship, staring out across the bay.

Fishermen's sloops, great merchants' carracks, and everything in between bobbed in the water around them. Sair's attention focused on the horizon, her cloak whipping at her back.

The ship was almost fully loaded. The horses were always added last.

Soldiers boarded the vessel with their uniforms marking them as imperial soldiers. Officially, Thadred was an escort for the sorceress Sair on an errand to Yndra—and the last known destination of Iasu.

Thadred cleared his throat. He adjusted the front of his shirt before taking a deep breath and approaching Sair.

Ka swirled around her in languid tendrils. Thadred had learned that magic did that around sorcerers and sorceresses, though it depended on how strong they were and how strong the person looking happened to be.

Thadred came up beside Sair. He was aware of Brick hovering a few steps back, waiting.

Sair's cheeks and nose were already flushed from the wind, her blonde hair flying around her in all directions. Sair looked down as he came up beside her, hands folded before her on the rails.

Thadred leaned against the rail at her side. He fought the urge to fidget, forcing himself to be still. A fluttering sensation tickled along his spine. Was this nervousness?

Since she'd crashed into him in the garden yesterday, everything had been haste and hurry. There had been men to rouse, officials to inform, and a ship to procure.

Now that they were on board the ship and waiting to draw

anchor, the rush and whirlwind of crisis was settling.

He had missed Sair. Desperately. Her voice, her laugh, the way she cocked her head with a slight smile when they teased each other. She'd made him think that perhaps he had met a woman who wouldn't leave him for someone better.

That was before.

"Thank you for helping me," Sair said, not quite meeting his eyes.

"Don't thank me yet," Thadred muttered, shifting on his arms. "We've barely started."

"I suppose so." Sair swallowed. The wind caught her hair, ripping strands out from under her kerchief like it couldn't resist touching her.

Sair was lovely. A good seven or eight years older than Thadred and used to hard work, she was leaner than he usually liked, but...soft.

That was the best way to describe her. Sair had a softness that extended into everything about her—the way she spoke, the way she moved, even the way she wove spells.

There was also a wholesomeness to her. Sair understood politics and she'd shown aptitude for intrigue, but she played no games and told no lies.

She was a good person. Kind. Decent. Everything he wasn't.

Sair looked up to him. "The captain says we'll be there in two days."

Thadred nodded. "It will be a short journey."

Sair bit her lip, staring up at him, her expression half hope, half shame. "When we get there?"

"We're going to find him, Sair." Thadred didn't doubt that.

Thadred had funds and authority to search wherever the trail led. They had no idea if Yndra was Iasu's final destination or not, but they should at least be able to pick up his trail.

It was just a question of how they would free Rhis once they found him. Iasu might know Rhis was worth a search party to the empire, or he might not. Either way, Istovari boys, or any child with enough magic to become Kadra'han, were valuable.

Sair touched his hand. "Thank you."

Her touch sent a shiver through him. Thadred tried to ignore it, but he already knew he was doomed to heartbreak on this journey.

Sair hadn't meant it romantically, at least he was sure she hadn't meant it like that, but…

Smiling, Thadred withdrew his hand. "This is what friends do, isn't it?"

Sair's face fell and she turned away. "Yes. I suppose."

It wasn't the right time to ask. As much as he was burning to know why she had ignored him for months.

A year ago, she'd headed north to sort out relations between the Istovari and their Hylendale neighbors. Thadred had thought there was something between them then. Sair had asked him to wait. She'd kissed him.

They had exchanged letters for months, but then she had stopped replying. At the time, he wondered if perhaps she had come to her senses. Maybe she regretted their attraction.

He'd written two more times to no reply. He'd been worried but confirmed that Sair was still in correspondence with Amira. He hadn't brought it up to the empress. This felt like something that should be private between him and Sair.

Either way, now was hardly the right time to ask her about it. Her son was in danger, and he was the one charged with saving the boy. It was a conflict of interest.

Movement caught the corner of his eye—Brick sneezed, despite his best efforts to be discreet. This was another reason to have Brick along. His manservant would keep Thadred from doing anything stupid.

Thadred rested a hand on Sair's back, awkward and unsure, but…well, he didn't want her to feel like he was angry with her. He wasn't.

"You should have a cabin prepared," Thadred offered.

Sair hesitated. "I'm not sure I know the way there."

"Here." Thadred hooked his arm through hers as the order was given to raise anchor. The two of them walked across the decks to the main hold of the ship.

Sailors, soldiers, and a few other servants Thadred had

brought along leapt and shouted and moved around them. This ship belonged to the imperial fleet and as such wouldn't have to be re-chartered or hired again once they reached Yndra.

Thadred had all the power of the empire at his disposal. As High Inquisitor, he led soldiers as he had always wanted to, yet it didn't look the way he had ever imagined.

Sair walked beside him, quiet and subdued. Her hair struggled to get free, strands of it rebelling from her braid and even from her kerchief to flap in the wind. Sair's plain grey dress and shawl pulled tight around her.

She was no proper imperial lady, but nor was Thadred a proper imperial gentleman. Thadred found the cabin that had been designated for her and opened the door.

"I can have your things brought here," he offered.

Sair patted the satchel at her hip. "This is all I have. I came light."

"Oh," Thadred stammered.

"I will be fine. Thank you, Thadred." That was another mark that she was from outside the courtly circles. To Sair, he was just Thadred. No title and no honorifics.

Sair's cabin was a small room with a hammock—hammocks were best for when the ship started rocking while at sea—and a dresser bolted to the floor.

Sair set her satchel down and glanced around the room. "Thank you."

Now would be a time to make his escape. He could slip away, telling her he was giving her time to get settled.

The ship began moving, sailors shouting as the massive vessel lumbered out of port.

Thadred exhaled. He pictured her alone in that room, crying quietly to herself, and it made his chest ache.

He didn't want to leave her alone. He wanted to comfort her. Hold her.

"Let me get settled and I will join you on deck," Sair said.

"Of course," Thadred agreed. He bowed humbly and stepped aside.

He made his way back to the top as the ship shifted, the sails catching wind.

He stopped to speak with Major Caiden. Caiden was not much older than Thadred, but there was a cynical edge to him that all military men developed eventually. Caiden still seemed reluctant to believe in cythraul, despite having seen them at the battle of Mevanmar Mine. But he was competent and for whatever reason had requested to remain with the Ministry of Inquiry when Captain Westfall had tried to recruit him to the imperial guard.

Thadred's Ministry of Inquiry was the smallest imperial ministry in the empire. It was comprised of Thadred, a few clerks, and the forty or so soldiers who accompanied him on investigations.

Most of the soldiers had fought in the battle of Mevanmar against the cythraul. There was nothing particularly special about them aside from their bravery. Someday, Thadred might be able to recruit Istovari to the ministry, but that was a future dream.

They wore the uniforms of the imperial army. They looked normal to an outsider.

The only unusual piece of equipment they carried were tower shields covered in tooled leather. The braided straps looked decorative, but in a fight, Thadred or another sorcerer could infuse the shields with *ka*, making them stronger. Leather had once been alive and so was easier to infuse with power than metal.

The shields themselves had a lining of tenebrous steel on the inside. Tenebrous steel was too brittle and heavy to be used by itself, but it could be used for reinforcing the usual steel and wood shields. The idea was to have leather-aided binding on the front to strengthen their formations and a tenebrous steel lining on the inside against any magic that might make it through.

Thadred had never had to use this design in battle before, but infusing shields with *ka* had yielded impressive results in the Witch War.

A part of Thadred, just a part, was excited to see what his shields might do against enemy sorcerers. If it came to an armed clash with Iasu and his ilk, they might find out.

Thadred had recruited Amira to run tests that were promising, but there was only one way to tell what would happen in true combat.

They had learned that spells, like blades and arrows, could be deflected by stone, metal, and even leather and cloth in some cases. The more things you could put between yourself and a spell, the better. Living things were the most easily affected by magic. But if a spell was powerful enough, it didn't matter what you used to try and block it. Thadred would just hope none of the Kelamora Kadra'han were at Amira's level.

Once Thadred was sure Caiden had the situating of the men dealt with, he headed to the back of the ship to watch Mynadra fade into the distance. There was not much else to do at the moment.

Brick cleared his throat. "Question, sir?"

"Ask." Thadred kept his attention on the city as the ship rocked and bobbed.

"Lady Sairydwen has brought no maids?" Brick asked, voice hitching just a little. Perhaps he had just realized that.

"No," Thadred confirmed. "No, Sair doesn't have servants."

"What is Lady Sairydwen's official title?" Brick asked. "If I may be so bold."

Thadred chewed his lip. Sair wasn't nobility. She was a sorceress, and they were entirely separate from the social hierarchy. The Istovari did things differently, but Sair was respected among them and seen as a leader. She would have surely been part of the lower gentry at least.

"You may address her as Lady Sairydwen of the Istovari," Thadred answered. "She is a dear friend of the emperor and empress. As well as mine."

"Ah, I see." Brick's tone had just a little too much understanding.

"Not like that," Thadred hastily corrected. "I never bedded her." He wasn't sure why he felt the need to defend her honor, but he did. "She fought with us in the Witch War. Her brother died protecting the empress."

Brick cleared his throat. "Forgive me, I did not know."

Brick was from Liechnaburg, a small and highly conservative nation in the central empire. Brick's family came from among the Claspers, so called because they clasped and unclasped their hands so much at prayer. They were devout, pious, and disciplined. Basically, Thadred's opposite.

Brick had been faced with plenty to offend his Clasper sensibilities since becoming Thadred's valet. All the same, he had mostly kept his shock to himself—not commenting when Thadred turned up drunk or made lewd comments.

"Lady Sair is a virtuous and courageous woman," Thadred said. "I hold her in the utmost respect, and I hope you and the others will as well."

"Of course, sir."

The admonition was wholly unnecessary. Brick was respectful to everyone, even people he probably considered to be deviants and drunkards.

"And her son?" Brick was toeing the line of decorum, but perhaps he was just too curious at this point.

Thadred sighed. "Rhis is a good kid. Way too trusting and too energetic, but…" He ran a hand through his hair.

Rhis had all but worshipped Thadred. He'd told his mother he wanted to be a knight, like Thadred, and had constantly begged to brush Lleuad, ride Lleuad, and just be around the kelpie.

Thadred had never had anyone look up to him, much less a child. Rhis had a kind of innocence and blind faith in humanity that seemed to demand the world be a better place. Rhis would be turning six soon, if he hadn't already. Still too young to know any better. As much as Thadred had grown fond of the kid, it had been terrifying. He hadn't been able to shake the feeling that he was going to let the boy down. A part of him felt that he already had by not working things out with Sair. That Rhis had been taken only added to that feeling.

Worse than that, Thadred feared he was going to fail to save Rhis, letting down both him and Sair.

Thadred didn't blame her. All women left Thadred eventually. But that hadn't stopped him from spending weeks after in a drunken haze, trying not to think about her.

All of them felt that they could do better, and they were right. Like Viscountess Daphne, they married men of legitimate birth with legitimate claims to ancestral lands and titles.

Thadred was the bastard cousin of the emperor. Raised to be Daindreth's bodyguard and protector, a single hunting accident had rendered him useless and sentenced him to using a cane for the rest of his life.

He had lands and titles now. His cousin had gladly bestowed those, but Thadred had never met his mother and didn't know the name of his father.

Of course, none of that mattered to the Istovari. All that mattered to them was that he was a man of their lineage. There was no magic in his mother's line, which meant it had somehow come from his father.

But Sair…

She was special. She had taught him to use magic. Before that, he hadn't even believed he had it.

Sair had believed in him, looked up to him. She was the first woman who had truly been in awe of him, not his reputation, his closeness to the emperor, or his charms. Gods knew he had put no effort into charming her at all.

They'd been through capture together, even torture. They had worked together during the Witch War to hunt down the empire's enemies.

And her son…

Thadred would have taken Rhis on as his squire if Sair hadn't gone back to the north. Maybe after this, he'd still make the offer.

Rhis would have the best education in the empire and have the chance to make friendships with other boys at court—the lords and ministers of the next generation. Yes, it would be excellent for Rhis.

And then perhaps Thadred could see Sair more often, too.

But first they needed to get Rhis back.

4

SAIR

Sair had heard tales of Yndra, but she never thought she would see it.

The waters of the harbor shimmered the bright blue of aquamarine. White buildings capped with domes in an array of blues and greens clustered in the mouth of the bay.

And in the center of it all loomed the palace of the city's marquis, towering as high as a mountain with gates that barred a water channel into the palace itself.

Sair leaned against the rails, one hand raised to keep her hair out of her eyes. She tried fastening a scarf over it, but her hair only seemed to take that as a challenge.

For so many years, Sair had been one of the few of her people to venture beyond their protective borders of the Haven. She sometimes fancied herself as worldly, certainly the people around her did back in the Istovari village.

Since peace had been struck with the emperor of Erymaya and the Istovari were again able to venture into the lowlands, she realized how wrong she was. The Haven, and even the Cursewood that encircled it, were tiny pieces of a much larger world.

As she gazed upon the strange and unfamiliar beauty of Yndra, Sair was struck by how little of the world she had seen. She knew only fragments of a mosaic that might be as large as the sky.

It was a humbling thought.

"We should be docking soon." Thadred's voice startled her as he came up beside her.

The knight was in a plain shirt and trousers and might be mistaken for an artisan or a merchant if one ignored the silver embroidery on his coat or the imperial signet ring and silver-capped cane he carried.

He wore no cravat, and his shirt was undone at the topmost buttons. Sair looked pointedly at his face, trying not to think on the few inches of bare skin showing at his collar.

She was a woman wedded and widowed. Thadred had nothing she hadn't seen before, and yet…

"Good," Sair said, trying to recover herself.

That manservant of his hovered not far away, keeping close by. It was like having an extra shadow.

"Yndra is a lovely place," Thadred remarked as he nodded toward the shoreline. "Over there you can see where they're still making repairs from the tidal wave they suffered during the Witch War."

During the Witch War, much of the conflict had been a string of seemingly natural disasters. Earthquakes, wildfires, floods, mudslides, droughts, and everything in between. In some ways they were natural, but the late Empress Vesha had made a pact with the cythraul demons to prevent them. That pact had held for years until recently when more than a decade's pent-up ill fortune had arrived in quick succession.

Along the shore, Sair could spot places that the docks appeared newer, less weathered. There were also large sections near the water where scaffolding encased the buildings, and a few were still missing roofs.

"I see."

As they sailed deeper into the bay, ships of every size and shape passed them by. There were small fishing vessels barely big enough for two or three men, and massive galleons that could have transported at least two hundred or more.

The ship sailed deeper into the docks, coming closer and

closer to the marquis's palace. Between gaps in the buildings, Sair spotted what appeared to be a market.

Canopies in shades of blue and green to match the domes of the houses lining the streets. Even from a distance, Sair could feel the buzz of activity and the lushness of the *ka* amongst the people.

Donkeys trundled by, laden with goods. Merchants haggled with housewives while children rushed this way and that.

It was a familiar scene in some ways. Sair had been to many markets, but it was alien at the same time. The colors, the sheer number of people. How strange.

"I take it we are going straight to the palace?" Sair asked.

Thadred followed her gaze to the market. "I was planning to have the ship dock there. They should let us in with an imperial banner."

"I see." Sair wasn't sure why her voice sounded sad. She wanted haste. Needed haste.

She was aware of Thadred's gaze on her for a long moment.

"We could…" Thadred hesitated. "We could have the ship let us off."

Sair shook her head. "I don't want to delay." Every delay was another moment that Rhis was in captivity.

"It won't be a delay," Thadred said. "They'll need an hour or so to process our paperwork at the palace. Yndrans love paperwork."

Sair shot a worried look to the knight.

"I promise, Sair." Thadred's tone softened, as if he knew exactly what she was thinking. "It won't slow us down at all."

Sair looked back to the market, with its riot of colors and life. The past two days at sea had been dull, if she was honest with herself. She wanted movement. Excitement. She wanted people walking, living, and breathing around her.

"Alright," she found herself saying.

Thadred was already calling to the captain. He shouted orders for himself and Sair to be let ashore along with Thadred's valet and a contingent of soldiers.

Sair looked down, into the pristine waters below the ship.

Water was never this clear in Hylendale, nor in Mynadra. There, the water was an endless expanse of rippling slate. Here, the water was like stained glass, crystalline and shining. It was beautiful.

The knight finished giving out his orders and returned to stand beside her. He gave orders easily and without hesitation, a man used to being obeyed. He was quite different from the bedraggled young man she had met more than a year ago—a refugee and fugitive from the empire.

"The last time I was here was with Dain," Thadred said, using the emperor's nickname. "The taverns along the docks have the best—well." Thadred cleared his throat, toying with the head of his cane. "Anyway, we had an excellent time. And the marquis is a wonderful fellow. I am sure you'll like him. Most people do."

Sair nodded, watching as the docks drew nearer.

Thadred stood close to her. Quite close to her. She hated that she wanted to touch him.

Thadred Myrani was not for her. She thought she had convinced herself of that.

Thadred offered her his arm as they stepped into a rowboat along with the valet, the rowers, and five armed guards. It seemed like a lot of trouble for a stroll through the market, but Thadred kept insisting.

Thadred helped her to a seat, and they rowed ashore.

This close to the water, Sair could make out the shapes of old ships, broken pieces of wagons, shattered pottery, and the flotsam of an ancient city below the waves. It was strange to look down and see beneath the water like this. Did the bottom of every harbor hold so many secrets?

"You can see some of the ships that were sunk in the tidal wave over there." Thadred nodded to a dark place where sand had already covered many of the hulls and masts. "Many of them have been recovered, but many have not."

Yndra was a whole new world.

They bobbed up to an abandoned dock near the market and the soldiers got out first. No sooner had Thadred helped Sair from the boat than a contingent of armed men came marching down the docks to meet them.

"Thadred." Sair squeezed his arm, reaching for *ka*. She was not back up to full strength just yet, but she could make an effort to protect herself.

"Never fear." Thadred patted her hand and stepped away. "Hello, gentlemen," he said, smiling.

The rowboat turned and went back to their ship, unconcerned. Now that Sair noticed it, the soldiers didn't seem threatening.

"Papers, sir," shouted a clerk at the head of the soldiers. He held a ledger in one hand and a stub of pencil in the other.

"Lord Thadred Myrani." Thadred nodded to Brick. "Here are my documents."

The valet presented the requested paperwork and Sair watched the clerk's eyes widen.

The clerk conferred with two of his compatriots then faced Thadred again, tone much softer this time. "Welcome to Yndra, Your Lordship. What brings you to the small docks?"

"Shopping, of course," Thadred replied, dazzling the clerk with one of his radiant smiles. Thadred was known for his charms with young women, but he had the talent for charming anyone—when he wanted to.

"I see. Your ship is headed to the palace?"

"Indeed. We will meet them there. I didn't see the point in waiting for the ship's charter to be checked. We might as well enjoy ourselves while we can."

The clerk glanced at Sair, but didn't comment again. "Very good, sir. I must ask that you report to the palace for full processing along with your main vessel, but everything is in order for now." He bowed and stepped aside and the soldiers with him.

"Thank you, my good man." Thadred inclined his head in that way of his. He bowed the same to clerks as he did to kings—in a way that implied he was truly happy to have made their acquaintance.

Thadred offered Sair his arm again. He led her down the

docks, past the clerk and the armed guards. Their own escort fell into step around them. Two guards in front, the valet, and three more behind.

"Are you going to be alright?" Sair asked, glancing furtively to Thadred's bad leg.

Thadred often grew offended when people mentioned his injury, but he responded by touching her fingers on his arm, just briefly. "It's not too far. I will be fine."

They rounded a corner and suddenly they were in the market.

It was like stepping into the center of a beehive. Voices called out, vendors hawking their wares, merchants bartering, children running this way and that.

A donkey brayed and a dog barked. A minstrel played a flute on a corner, struggling to be heard over the cacophony. Beggars called for alms on the corners, appealing to the charity of the crowds.

Sair breathed in the abundance of *ka* that filled the air. Cities were always like that—teeming with life and power. It was the one thing they all had in common.

The soldiers surrounding them made sure no one got too close. Most people made way when they recognized the armed escort.

"Everyone is on foot," Sair noticed. In the markets of Hylendale and even in Mynadra, horses and carriages often rode through the streets carrying goods and wealthy patrons.

"No horses allowed in the dock market," Thadred explained. "They took up too much space."

"Oh." Now that Sair noticed it, the streets were certainly narrower than in Mynadra or Hylendale, yet they were cleaner too.

"Pretty girl."

Sair jumped at the voice and spun.

A grey bird with black and white pin feathers watched her from its perch inside a cage. The vendor's stall was full of cages containing finches, canaries, and even a peacock in a large cage on the ground.

"Pretty girl."

Sair startled again, realizing the voice had come from the bird. "Thadred." She leaned back against him. "What is that?" she gasped, knowing she sounded insane.

Thadred glanced between her and the bird. "Oh, the parrot?"

"The what?" Sair didn't know what was happening, but embarrassment crept up the back of her neck.

The bird let off a low whistle.

"Hey, that's no way to address a lady," Thadred said, glaring at the bird.

"Lady," the bird croaked. "Lady." It let off another whistle and bobbed its head up and down. "Pretty girl."

Sair looked between the bird and Thadred. "How?"

"It's a grey parrot, my lady," said a plump man with a bandana around his bald head. "Very rare. I got him from a sailor who procured him from the southern continent."

The bird—the *parrot*—whistled at Sair again. "Pretty girl."

The vendor coughed. "I'm afraid he's still learning manners."

"Does he say anything else?" Thadred inspected the bird suspiciously, like he knew something about these things.

Until a moment ago, Sair had never heard of a talking bird at all. She'd heard of crows and ravens mimicking voices, but not one that could form words so precisely.

As if in answer, the bird squawked. "Red eyes. Watch for the red eyes. Watch the eyes."

Sair shuddered at the reminder. During the Witch War, Empress Vesha had summoned demons—cythraul—to help her win the conflict. They had possessed hundreds of people, perhaps more. Cythraul were driven mad by thousands of years trapped in the Dread Marches. They had butchered and slaughtered their way across the land until Daindreth, Amira, and their coalition of Istovari and imperial soldiers had put them down.

The vendor smacked the cage, making the bird flap and squawk inside. He glanced at Thadred and Sair with an awkward smile. "I can offer him to you half price," the vendor said, true to the nature of any market seller. "Special bargain to make up for his rudeness."

"Thank you, no," Thadred said with a smile. He made even his refusal sound like a compliment.

"What about the finches? They are quite fashionable with Yndra ladies these days. And their singing is—"

"Thank you!" Thadred called, gently guiding Sair away from the stall. "Are you alright?"

Sair tried to shake off the dark memories crowding at the edges of her mind. "Fine. I just…wasn't expecting…that."

Thadred seemed to know what she meant. "I'm sorry. I'll buy the bird and have him cooked with blackberries if it will make you feel better."

Sair laughed. "I don't think that will be necessary."

Thadred winked at her. "Let me know if you change your mind."

Sair wished his wink didn't make her heart skip a beat, but it did.

"Oh, meat skewers." Thadred was definitely trying to change the subject and it worked. "You'll love meat skewers. Brick, go get us some meat skewers. One for yourself, too."

The valet bowed and stepped forward dutifully. He carried a satchel of coins just for this purpose and set to shoving his way through the crowd to reach the front.

Several open fire pits surrounded this market stall with grates over them. Atop the grates were wooden sticks stacked with various meats and vegetables that roasted in the flames. A tanned family was hard at work with a young man chopping meat into cubes, before an elderly woman sprinkled them in spices, the children stacked them onto the sticks, and the parents and older siblings tended the cookfires.

Sair watched them work with lightning efficiency, churning out sticks of roasted meats as fast as one could. It was mesmerizing to see such cooperation.

Thadred let her watch, not interrupting. The crowd parted around them, or more accurately it parted for their soldiers.

Brick returned with three meat skewers as Thadred had called them and presented one to Thadred and another to Sair.

"These are always good," Thadred assured her. "This one at the top is chicken." He pointed to the first piece of charred meat. "This one is lamb, this one is pork, and this here is falafel."

Sair cocked her head, studying her own skewer. It smelled of unfamiliar spices and a pleasant aroma of smoke. "What kind of animal is a falafel?"

"It's not an animal, it's a plant," Thadred explained.

"What kind of plant?"

Thadred frowned. "I'm actually not sure. Perhaps the marquis can better explain it. Still tastes good." He bit a chunk out of the chicken as if to prove it.

Sair dared to take a bite. What she had mistaken for char on the outside was a seared layer of spices that burst in her mouth like a riot of flavor. Seasonings she didn't recognize with more salt than she'd ever tasted at once exploded over her tongue.

Sair coughed.

"Are you alright?" Thadred's eyes widened.

"Fine," Sair gasped. "Just a little…surprised."

Brick looked at his skewer suspiciously. "Forgive me, my lord. But it is forbidden for Claspers to eat birds."

Thadred blinked at him. "What are you talking about?"

"Only creatures that live in connection to the earth, sir." Brick sounded genuinely apologetic. "Birds fly above it."

Thadred narrowed his eyes. "How far do you think a chicken can fly?"

"It is our way, my lord. I am sorry."

Thadred rolled his eyes. "See if one of those beggars wants it. Fulfill your daily charity quota."

"It's our daily obligation of kindness, my lord. But yes." Brick actually sounded proud of Thadred. Perhaps he had been trying to teach Thadred for some time.

Thadred turned back to Sair, looking worried. "You don't like it, either?"

Sair nibbled at the corner of the chicken again. "No, it's different, but I think I'm getting used to it." The flavors took some adjustment, but she found it wasn't entirely unpleasant.

They stood to the side of the street while Brick found a beggar to gift his uneaten skewer. The valet handed it to the elderly stranger, then clasped his hands and appeared to utter a prayer. The beggar stared at him much the way Sair had stared at that parrot.

"He's a strange fellow," Thadred sighed. "But a good man, all things considered."

"So are you." Sair wasn't sure why she had said it.

Thadred chuckled, sounding nervous. "Oh, surely you haven't fallen for this façade." He gestured vaguely to himself.

"I mean it." Sair looked away then. "You're helping me. Despite everything." Even if this was in the empire's best interest.

Thadred sounded genuinely confused. "What do you mean?"

Sair swallowed. She didn't know where to start. How to tell him that she'd heard about his latest affair?

Thadred took a breath as if to ask her something, but Brick came jogging back to join them.

"Thank you, my lord." Brick bobbed a humble bow.

"Yes, yes." Thadred finished off the chicken portion of his skewer and set to gnawing on the lamb. "Let's go."

With their hands otherwise occupied, Sair and Thadred walked through the market, making their way to the grand palace.

They saw a small furry creature with hands dancing on a leash. Thadred identified it as a monkey and warned her not to get too close. Monkeys could bite, apparently.

There were snake dancers and firebreathers. People selling rugs, iron kettles, brass bells, lady's scarves, and men's buttons. Despite the closeness to the sea and the number of fishing vessels in the harbor, Sair saw no fishmongers. When she asked, Thadred informed her that fish sales were relegated to the lower docks to reduce the smell and to try to make sure they were fresh.

As they came closer to the palace, Sair noticed that the

vendors began to sell more and more expensive things. There were perfumes in alabaster jars that would have cost fortunes by themselves. Wines that were sold in bottles instead of kegs. Blown glass decorations and copper lampstands.

The clientele also seemed to get wealthier. There were gentlemen with oiled beards and ladies with parasols. Their fashions were quite similar to what one might see in the imperial court, the jewel-toned colors a luxurious departure from the motley back among the merchants, artisans, and commoners. Their skin tones also became paler, the marks of people who didn't have to work in the sun for a living.

Sair finished off her skewer—Thadred was right about the falafel, whatever it was. She licked the grease from her fingers and caught Thadred chuckling as he watched her.

"What?"

"Nothing," Thadred answered, having finished his earlier. He smiled. "Nothing, my lady."

They neared the palace, that loomed over them like a mountain, its spires rising proudly into the sky. It was not quite as large or magnificent as the palace at Mynadra, but nothing was.

They came near a clothier, this vendor selling out of a building with open doors, open windows, and goods hanging all around.

A burst of color caught Sair's eye near the window. It was a red cloak the color of ruby. When she touched it, the fabric was soft as a kitten's fur. It was out of place and unseasonal in this warm, seaside town, but back in the cold reaches of Hylendale, it would be a luxury.

"Are you looking for something?"

Sair jumped at the voice and found herself facing a stern woman with a pinched brow and a row of pins stuck into her apron—the seamstress, if Sair had to guess. "Forgive me." Sair took a step back. "You have lovely wares."

"The very best." The woman looked down her nose, taking in Sair's plain grey dress and simple brown satchel. "And priced as such."

Shame heated Sair's cheeks. She was a trusted friend and companion of the empress, but by herself, she was simply a northern peasant who had happened to be born with magic. She'd shelled her own peas, milked her own goats, and even sewn this dress. At the end of the day, she was still poor.

"Is everything alright, my dear?" Thadred was behind Sair the next moment, hovering close at her side. His cane made a thumping sound as it hit the floorboards.

The seamstress spotted Thadred at Sair's back—an obvious lord by his clothing, guards, and the valet at his side. In a moment, her whole expression lit up. "I was just telling your lady that we supply the very best."

Thadred nodded with a caustic smile. "I'm sure."

"I would be happy to have my girls give her a fitting." Sensing coin to be made, the seamstress turned a cordial, slightly apologetic look to Sair. "Let me give you proper showing around the shop, my lady."

Sair shook her head, feeling ashamed. The chiffons, silks, and brocades were lovely, but they had lost their appeal. Sair was poor and this woman had seen the truth. She turned back to Thadred. "Let's go."

"Are you sure?" Thadred glared past her, probably at the seamstress.

"Yes. The ship is probably docked at the palace by now."

"Alright." Thadred rested a hand on the small of her back.

Sair felt his touch through her entire body. He had comforting hands, warm and callused from training with a sword. As they made contact, she felt his *ka* ripple into her own. Each living thing had their own inner source of *ka* and it felt as if theirs was touching. *Ka* was not the same thing as one's soul, but it was as much a part of them as the beat of their heart. When Thadred touched her, she felt their power mingling. It was almost like sharing the same breath.

Sair loved and hated him touching her at the same time. Most of all, she wished him touching her didn't make her want more.

5

THADRED

Thadred hadn't planned a market trip, but Sair had been sad. For the past two days on the ship, she had been quiet and melancholy. He hadn't expected her to get over the abduction of her son, but he'd wanted to distract her from it. As much as it made his heart ache to see her again, it hurt worse to see her hurting.

And when she smiled, it was like the morning mist had cleared from a field of spring flowers. If only for a few moments, he had seen joy and wonder on her face.

Nothing could take away from those moments in the market, not even the aching pain in his hip, spine, and leg. Every one of her smiles was worth it.

Marquis Eben Rahl received them gallantly. The marquis was nearly as wide as he was tall, but if he was a man of generous girth, he had a generous nature to match.

Unlike the seamstress from the market, the marquis greeted Sair like a man greeting a favorite goddaughter. He bowed over her hand and kissed it and even coaxed out one of those rare smiles.

Thadred was sure he saw relief in the man's face when he realized Thadred had brought a lady with him. The last time Thadred had visited, the marquis's oldest niece had been caught sneaking out of Thadred's room.

Thadred's room this time opened onto an airy balcony overlooking the bay. It was spacious with gilded furniture and white stone.

"Brick, as soon as we go to dinner, I need you to run an errand for me." Thadred tried not to wince as the valet helped him put on his coat. Damn, his hip hurt. He'd gotten lax in applying spells to the old injury and it seemed his joints hadn't been properly supported.

"An errand, sir?" Brick looked askance, smoothing the back of Thadred's coat.

"Yes, quickly."

"I will do what I can, my lord."

"Good man." Thadred adjusted his cuffs while Brick finished buttoning up the front of his dinner jacket.

Thadred surveyed himself in the mirror, taking a quick once-over. He thought he looked fine or at least close enough. He relayed final instructions to Brick and sent the man off. He wanted to make sure the shops didn't close before his valet got there.

The knight sat on the edge of the large bed he'd been given. Bracing his hands on his knees, he focused on breathing deep. Ever since his accident years ago, the muscles in his hip, thigh, and lower back had been overcompensating to keep him together.

He could use spells to help and, most of the time, he could manage just fine. Even before he had known he had magic, he'd probably been using it subconsciously. Now he thought that might have been what had allowed him to become a jousting champion, not that he had much time for jousting lately. But after two days of being sedentary on the ship followed by an afternoon strolling through the market, he was paying for it.

Thadred drew magic to himself, pulling the natural *ka* from the air. A sea breeze drifted through the room, blowing from the open balcony.

Thadred tried to force his cramping muscles to relax. He wove the spells he'd been perfecting over the past year, supporting his injury. Unfortunately, that did little to relax the already overstrained muscles. Perhaps he'd just have to accept that he was going to hurt tonight.

He sensed shapes of *ka* in the hallway outside. Servants wandered this way and that, heading about their business.

A knock came from the door.

"Who is it?" Thadred hadn't answered his own door in some time. Brick was quite attentive.

"Thadred?"

The knight's eyes snapped up at her voice. "Sair?"

Sair cracked open the door just a sliver. When she spied him fully clothed, she entered.

She'd cleaned herself up a little. She wore a bright blue shawl over her grey dress, her hair pinned up in a simple style that exposed her neck. She had a pleasing neck. Long, white, and graceful as a swan's.

"I don't know the way around this place. You're going to have to show me to dinner." She noticed his pose, hands clamped on his knees. "Are you alright?"

"Fine." Thadred's voice came out in a wheeze that was not particularly convincing.

"What's wrong?" Sair came closer, brows pinched.

Thadred wanted to deny it, but it was hard to deny that he couldn't move. "I might have overdone it today." He had absolutely overdone it, but Sair had enough to worry about right now.

Sair crossed the large bedroom and knelt in front of him.

Despite the pain, Thadred felt an unwanted thrill at the sight. Sair on her knees in his bedroom was something he had pictured more than once.

She laid her hands on his hip and thigh. That did not make it easier. Her touch was a whisper away from the buckle of his belt and the outline of his manhood lying against his thigh.

He imagined Sair would be confident in bed and demanding, in the way of a woman who knew what she liked. He had often wondered what she liked, fantasized about it in quiet moments when he was alone.

Pain, pain, pain, Thadred silently chanted to himself. He

needed to think about the pain and absolutely nothing else.

"Is this helping?" Sair channeled *ka* into his muscles in a diffused flow, easing power into his flesh.

His muscles loosened, relaxing bit by bit. The tension eased, washed away by currents of power.

"It is." Thadred's breath came a little easier.

Slowly, Sair helped dull the pain to a faint ache.

He watched her because it would be rude not to, fighting off images of ripping out the pins of her bun and tangling his fingers in her hair. Had she always been this beautiful?

Sair looked up at him. "Is that better?" Her voice was soft, gentle. She met his eyes with concern. Sair did care for him, he could see it now. She looked at him like he was special, like he was someone important.

Then why…?

But he didn't want to know why. He didn't want to be proven right—that she had realized she could do better.

"Yes." Thadred wasn't sure why his voice came out raspy.

"Good." Sair clasped one of his hands. "Are you ready? The marquis should be waiting for us."

"Indeed." Thadred inhaled a slow breath, trying to think about anything other than the way she looked at him.

Sair fetched his cane from the end of the bed and the two of them stepped out of his room. "Where is Brick?"

"I sent him on an errand." Thadred leaned heavily on his cane as they headed down the hall.

It was lined in blue carpets, blue murals, and white tile. Wave motifs decorated the ceiling and designs of fish, squid, and sea birds decorated the walls. The marquis's family owed their wealth to the sea, and they were not shy about showing it.

"Do you think we can get access to the records soon?" That edge of anxiety was back in Sair's voice.

"We will be there tomorrow, Sair. Don't worry. The registers are closed for the day."

"Did we miss them?" Sair's eyes widened. "Did we lose time because—"

"No," Thadred quickly assured her. "They spent the whole

afternoon processing our paperwork for the ship. We would have missed the registers anyway."

Sair relaxed a little, but only a little.

The registers recorded every living thing on every ship charter that docked in their ports. Everything was recorded with the meticulousness of a miser. From the captain to the ship's cat, from the barrels of rainwater to the last thread of silk, everything had to be accounted for in the charters.

That meant that any ship that had docked in Yndra over the past weeks carrying a Nihai man and a young Hylendale boy would have been recorded. Equally, the records would show if they had boarded another ship or perhaps were still in the city.

Thadred understood Sair wanted to get to her son as quickly as possible. As an Istovari, sons were second best in her culture and even meant she was ranked lower than a woman with a daughter. But Rhis was her only child. She adored him and he had all the makings of a good man.

"We'll find him," Thadred promised, not for the first time. "We will."

Sair bit her lip. "I know." Her voice was small.

Thadred wished again that he could take away that sadness, but the only way he knew for sure to do that was to get Rhis back.

They came into the dining room of Marquis Rahl. The Rahl family were old money going back centuries, but unlike in Mynadra, the gold filigree and plating had been kept to a minimum.

The Rahl were rich, but not endlessly so. They were the kind of rich family that had remained rich through strategic frugality.

Marquis Rahl was by the balcony with his sister, several nieces, and longtime mistress Ketsia Moor.

"That is the marquis, who you have met," Thadred whispered to Sair, pointing discreetly to a man with whitening mane of red hair and an impressive blue and gold embroidered coat. "That is his sister, Lady Davena." Thadred nodded to a hearty woman with matching red hair, also streaked with white. "The girls are her daughters."

Three young ladies ranging from early teens to around the right age for marriage proposals crouched on the balcony, dangling feathers before several kittens.

"The other woman is Ketsia Moor, his mistress."

Sair swallowed. "She looks magnificent."

Thadred supposed she did, but Ketsia was not so much beautiful as she was majestic. Rahl often called her his sea goddess and Ketsia was very much like the sea—she could exude power, playfulness, passion, cruelty, or apathy in an instant.

It was clear she was the person not related to any of the others. In the cluster of red hair and pale complexions, her hair was raven-black and her skin the soft bronze of someone with mixed ancestry. While not uncommon in the upper classes, it made many people uneasy to see someone who so clearly did not come from here.

Ketsia knelt on the floor with the girls, waving feathers for the kittens. The kittens pounced and leapt between the feathers, making the entire family laugh.

Not surprisingly, it was Ketsia who first spotted Thadred and Sair's approach. Her head whipped up, dark eyes taking them in like a hawk or perhaps a snake.

Ketsia had been the one to catch Thadred's liaison with the marquis's eldest niece—who was thankfully with her new husband tonight. Ketsia watched over the marquis and his family with a zeal to rival any divine patron.

"Lord Thadred," Ketsia said, her voice like the growl of a panther. "What a pleasure."

Thadred did not miss the warning in that. The marquis might have been put off his guard this time—Thadred had his own lady with him, after all. But it seemed Ketsia would not be so easily assuaged.

"Lord Thadred! And Lady Sairydwen." The marquis came bustling to meet them, clapping Thadred on the shoulder and kissing Sair's hand again. "Come, Lady Sairydwen. You must meet my family. This is my sister, Lady Davena. These are a few of my nieces, the Honorable Ladies Willow, Fiona, and that little one there is Ebena, named after me, poor child. Their brothers and sisters could not join us this evening."

Sair curtsied and the girls curtsied in turn. "A pleasure to make your acquaintance."

"And this is my darling lady, Ketsia Moor." The marquis lowered a hand and helped Ketsia off the ground.

Ketsia wore a low-cut gown with a plunging back that revealed quite plainly she wore no corset. The black silk shimmered and flowed around her figure like dark water and a collar of topaz with matching bracelets wreathed her arms.

Ketsia took Sair's hand in hers. "A sorceress," she said as their hands brushed. It was not a question.

"Yes, my lady."

"I am no lady." Ketsia snorted as if to emphasize the point. "Not since my husband died."

"Oh." Sair swallowed, unsure of herself. "I'm sorry."

"Don't be. I killed him."

Sair's eyes widened.

"Ketsia!" The marquis laughed, wrapping the woman's waist in a bear hug. "You mustn't frighten the guests!" He kissed Ketsia's neck before looking to Sair over her shoulder. "Never fear. She just takes some time to warm up to strangers."

Thadred stepped up beside Sair, wanting to rescue her from the fearsome panther-woman. "We hope you haven't waited too long for us. Shall we sit?"

"Yes, yes!" The marquis spun to his nieces. "Girls, have the maids take those kittens back to your rooms. Cook! Let's eat, man! I am starving and our guests must be, too."

Thadred and Sair were shown to their places at the table.

As a relative of the emperor, Thadred was seated as the guest of honor beside the marquis. As his guest, Sair occupied his other side.

Lady Davena sat beside her brother and Ketsia occupied the space beside Sair. The daughters filled in the rest.

The first course, scallops in a thick cheese sauce, was served. The marquis dug in heartily and ordered his finest wine to be poured for Sair and Thadred.

The marquis asked after the health of the emperor—a

formality.

"His Majesty is well," Thadred answered. "And the empress will give him an heir in the next few months. Both are strong and healthy by all accounts."

A shadow passed across Rahl's endless smile for just a moment.

The marquis had been married briefly, but his wife and baby daughter had died within days of each other. The marquis had named his sister's eldest son as his heir and lived as a bachelor until Ketsia.

Down the table, Sair was trying to make conversation with Ketsia. "Ketsia, how did you meet the marquis?"

"My murder trial," Ketsia replied before sipping at her wine.

"Oh." Sair looked down.

"How did you meet," Ketsia pointed one long nail at Thadred, clearly unimpressed, *'Lord* Thadred?"

"Ah." Sair fumbled with her fork and spoon. "Well." Sair shot a glance sideways to Thadred. "At the time, I took him hostage."

Ketsia paused, her wine glass halfway back to her lips. "Hostage?"

"Yes. It was before the Istovari had made the alliance with Emperor Daindreth, you see."

A smirk shaped Ketsia's lips. "This I would love to hear."

Though the rest of the family seemed to have forgiven him, Thadred had impugned the honor of their eldest daughter and Ketsia wouldn't forget it. There was great irony in the mistress being the moral enforcer, but that was just Thadred's luck.

Sair told the simple version of how they had met. Sair had taken him hostage, but both of them had ended up captured by the late Empress Vesha's agents.

Sair skimmed over the parts where she had been tortured. It was hardly proper dinner conversation, but Thadred doubted she wanted to discuss it anyway. Sair told of how Thadred had bonded his kelpie, Lleuad, and how everyone had thought him dead.

Sair remembered some things differently than he did, but

that was the way with memories. Thadred let her continue and didn't interrupt.

The second and third courses came. Other conversations popped up around the table.

The marquis asked him about kelpies and if they handled easier than other horses—Thadred told him certainly not. Lady Davena wanted to know if the empress would be having a traditional lying-in—Thadred didn't know what that was.

Sair and Ketsia continued talking, both their voices keeping pleasant tones in the background. As the ebb and flow of pleasantries with the marquis and his sister continued, Thadred kept an ear out for signs Sair was uncomfortable.

At one point, both women laughed. Thadred jumped, not expecting that from either of them.

That made Marquis Rahl grin fondly toward Ketsia. Thadred suspected Sair had endeared herself to the man just by making Ketsia laugh.

The evening continued—the fourth and fifth courses coming with barely time for breath between. Wine flowed easily and conversation flowed more easily as more was poured.

The marquis told Thadred of how they were using the timber that Empress Amira had sent them from the forests of her homeland in Hylendale. The fleet of vessels in Yndra was almost back to what it had been before the disastrous tidal wave. Engineers were working to see what they could do to mitigate future waves without blocking the harbor.

Thadred thought that was probably smart, but he didn't say that he doubted tidal waves like that would happen again any time soon. It had been the result of the Witch War. Now that Vesha was gone, they shouldn't have to worry about it again.

After dinner, the women went back to playing with the kittens—it seemed the girls had not had them sent back to their rooms after all.

The marquis invited Thadred onto the balcony for whiskey and what he called cigars. They were imports from some of the scattered islands and made of the same tobacco as was used in pipes.

Thadred tried one, not particularly enjoying it. "Do these get any better?" Thadred muttered, drawing a puff of the smoke into his mouth the way the marquis had explained.

Rahl laughed. "It's an acquired taste, my boy."

"Hmm." Thadred took the cigar out long enough to take a swig of whiskey. "I might just be slow on acquiring it."

Back inside, Sair had picked up a kitten and held it to her face, making kissing noises. The kitten sneezed and Sair laughed, taking a feather from one of the girls and letting the kitten bat and paw at it.

Thadred watched her, that dull ache back in his chest. He liked seeing her happy. He wasn't sure why the sight made him sad.

"My clerk says you requested access to the records," Marquis Rahl said. It had taken him about two hours, but he was finally getting down to business.

"Yes." Thadred resisted the urge to toss the cigar over the railing. "An Istovari boy was abducted from Hylendale. We've tracked the kidnapper here."

There was a chance that they might be spoiling any potential element of surprise, but time was the most important factor here. The sooner they could move, the better their odds of finding Rhis.

By telling the marquis and his staff just who and what they were looking for, they increased the odds that word would get back to Iasu and his masters. But they also increased their odds of actually finding them.

"I don't abide slavers," Marquis Rahl said. "Unsavory, messy business. Not to mention against imperial law."

Thadred nodded. That had been an edict from Emperor Drystan, Daindreth's father. "I am sure. But this man has no concern for the law. He's a Nihainite in origin but has lived in the empire his whole life. Extremely dangerous. He once served Empress Vesha."

The marquis flicked the ash off the end of his cigar. "So this is why you are here."

"The emperor sent me to find him." Thadred adjusted the

imperial signet on his hand, the signet that gave him the authority of the emperor himself.

"We've had enough of Empress Vesha, I think," the marquis said. He glanced out across the view of the city where the dry docks were still constructing replacement ships for those destroyed by the tidal wave. "I will give you whatever you need and men from the clerk's office to personally search the records for you."

"Thank you," Thadred said. "Is there any way our quarry could have left without recording himself and the boy?"

"There is always the option by land," the marquis replied. "We do have more inconsistencies there. But otherwise, no. Unless he found a way to ingratiate himself with the Cult of Llyr."

Thadred cocked one brow. "They still mad about Ketsia?"

"They will *always* be mad about Ketsia," Rahl chuckled.

The Cult of Llyr was a more radical group worshipping the sea god. They were mostly harmless, but they held a good amount of sway in Yndra and a few other port cities.

Ketsia's husband had some important rank or other within their order. He'd allegedly been quite the pious fellow.

But regardless, Llyr had not protected him after he'd beaten Ketsia one too many times. She'd slipped him monkshood and he had met his end vomiting and shitting himself to death.

Regardless of why she'd done it, the cult had wanted her executed, obviously. The marquis had learned about the case and decided to pardon her. He'd even allowed her to stay in his home for protection.

The cult had been furious, but there was not much they could do. Religious orders had no legal authority to dispense justice.

But when the marquis had wanted to marry Ketsia, the greater churches had refused for fear of angering the cult. Marquis Rahl had tried for at least two years to get one of the religious orders or another in his city to budge, but they were quite adamant.

Thadred still wasn't clear on what religion had to do with

marriage, but he wasn't Yndran. Every city and province across the empire had their oddities that defined them. Piety and paperwork defined Yndra.

Thus, Ketsia remained Rahl's mistress, living out her days in comfort and splendor above them all.

"Honestly, she's the one thing about me that people hate." The marquis glanced toward his mistress, still a man besotted after over a decade. "It's good! Every ruler has to have a flaw. It keeps me humble." The marquis poured more whiskey from his carafe and refilled Thadred's while he was at it.

"How could this cult of Llyr be undermining your records?" Thadred asked.

"Well, a few of their members have been submitting incomplete reports," the marquis answered. "They've been fined, but the behavior continues. I haven't decided how to discipline them just yet. Meffew, my tax minister? He wants to levy extra fees on cult members' vessels. Baron Eunad, Lord Gadis, and several merchants." The marquis shrugged. "Problem is that the cult has never submitted any formal record of their members. I only know the most vocal ones."

"Hmm." Thadred couldn't think of a reason for a cult devoted to Llyr to help a group of rogue Kadra'han. Then again, anyone who wanted power might want their own Kadra'han. "Perhaps the records will show us."

"I hope so." The marquis sighed, taking another puff from his cigar. "Llyr knows I'd rather live in harmony with him and his followers, if I could."

"Fair enough." Thadred took a sip of his whiskey, which he was enjoying much more than the cigar. "I hope to get to the bottom of this as soon as we may."

"You don't think your quarry could still be in the city?"

Thadred shook his head. "I expect he wants to get out of imperial waters, or at least the mainland." The knight nodded to Sair. "She is a close friend of the empress. Our quarry knows it and will know the empire is lending aid in this hunt."

"Oh?" The marquis's brows rose.

"The boy who was kidnapped is her son," Thadred

explained.

"I see." The marquis rested his elbows on the railing, blowing streams of smoke into the night air. "As I said, we will do what we can."

Thadred nodded. "The empire thanks you."

6

SAIR

From the way Thadred and the marquis leaned together, speaking in low voices, Sair guessed they were discussing more than the small talk of earlier. She toyed with the kitten in her lap, tickling the soft fur. Its claws hooked on her skirt, and she extracted it carefully, peeling it away toe by toe.

"I think we'll name that one Ivy," the youngest niece said. "Because she sticks to everything."

The kitten mewled as Sair held a feather up before its nose. The kitten pawed at it and several others joined in.

Ketsia toyed with the only black kitten, watching as it stalked the feather in her hand. "Quite the fierce little hunter, aren't you?" For all the woman had seemed severe and stern when Sair and Thadred first arrived, Sair decided she liked her. "So fierce." Ketsia dropped a kiss on the kitten's head.

"You should keep that one, Aunt Ketsia," said another of the girls. Sair had lost track of their names. "He likes you."

Ketsia didn't respond directly, but she did smile down at the little black fur ball.

"Lady Sairydwen, do you think you could tame Lord Thadred enough for a wife?" Lady Davena asked the question conversationally, innocently.

Sair's chest tightened, feeling suddenly like she had been caught doing something wrong. "I'm sorry?"

"Well, it's just that you said you've known each other for more than a year. Lord Thadred's affairs have never lasted that long."

Something thick and heavy settled in Sair's gut, but she forced a smile.

The older girls shot looks to their mother. It was an inappropriate question, but the woman seemed not to care. Her face was bright and guileless.

"I'm…" Sair cleared her throat. "He hasn't shared his plans on the matter, my lady."

"Ah, I see. Well. Now that he is a lord, he will need to make such plans. Succession and all that. Quite a bothersome business, if you ask me." Lady Davena sniffed. "I had to provide heirs not only for my husband, but my brother as well. Though my husband gambled everything away so there won't be much left to inherit after all."

Sair tried to focus on the kitten in her lap. She was a grown woman and an emissary to the empire. Not only that, but she had to find her son. She couldn't afford to be offended.

"But as for Lord Thadred, I imagine he could have the empress arrange a match for him. Now that he's cousin to the emperor, no one should be beyond him."

Sair swallowed, head sinking lower.

"Do you suppose you'll stay on with him when he marries?"

Sair looked up in confusion. "What?" She glanced to Ketsia, but the woman was staring at Davena, lips tight.

"Your arrangement with him." Lady Davena waved her hand in the air vaguely. "At first, I tried to make my husband get rid of his, but after a time it occurred to me that she enjoyed his company far more than I did. One of us might as well find some use for him."

"Oh." Realization struck Sair. They thought she was Thadred's mistress.

That was why Marquis Rahl had been relieved when he had met her and seated her next to Ketsia at the table. It suddenly made sense.

Shame crept up the back of her neck, not so much at the

implication she was bedding Thadred, but the suggestion it was a business deal. To speak of an "arrangement" made it sound like she was just a tradeswoman.

"As I said, I don't know his plans, my lady." Sair's eyes stung and she blinked, trying to focus on the kitten in her arms. Little claws dug through her sleeve, and she focused on that.

"I'm not sure why girls think he's such a catch," Ketsia said, sniffing imperiously. "A bastard, unknown father, notable arrogant prick, and a serial philanderer." Ketsia cocked her head toward Sair and her voice softened just a little. "None of those make for a man worth a woman's tears."

Sair swallowed, trying not to let her hurt show. "But he's still a good man." She exhaled, blinking quickly. "For all he tries to pretend otherwise."

One of the nieces asked about the latest fashions in Mynadra and the topic of Thadred was dropped.

Eventually, the kittens grew tired, and the young girls scooped them up and carried them off. Lady Davena went next, saying she was tired and must rest.

That left Sair and Ketsia, just the two of them. Thadred and the marquis were still speaking on the balcony.

Sair wondered what they could be discussing. They were hardly close friends, so it must be matters of state.

Ketsia invited Sair back to the table and poured out another glass of wine for each of them. The dark woman lounged in her seat with feline grace, poised and stable.

"Now that the innocent ears of the children are gone." Ketsia pushed one of the glasses across the table to Sair. "I do think you could do better, Sairydwen of the Istovari."

Sair adjusted her shawl, suddenly aware of how plain and simple her dress was compared to the flawless silk of the other woman. "He is a good man," Sair repeated. "And…he's helping me find my son."

"Your son?" Ketsia cocked her head.

"He was taken," Sair replied. "Thadred is leading the effort to find him."

Ketsia's brows rose. "Well. I have heard worse reasons for

sleeping with a man."

Sair swallowed. "No." Her voice was small, suddenly timid for some reason.

"Hmm?"

Sair recovered herself. "We're not sleeping together." She had only ever kissed Thadred once—a year ago when she had asked him to wait for her. He had said he would and at the time, she had trusted he would. She realized now that had been foolish.

Ketsia's brows rose. "Really? Then why let Lady Davena think you were? Here I thought you were a fallen woman like me."

"I doubt anyone would believe it." Sair took another sip of wine, wanting courage.

"With his reputation? Probably not. But this is fascinating." Ketsia tapped her long nails against her glass. "Lord Thadred Myrani helping the one woman in the empire he's never bedded."

Sair looked away at that. "Surely there are others," she said, voice small.

"I do exaggerate, of course. But only slightly." Ketsia laughed. Then she took stock of Sair's posture, understanding dawned. "Poor dear. I'm sorry." Ketsia touched Sair's shoulder in apology. "Your son's father must have been quite a terrible person to lower your standards so much."

Sair shook her head. "My husband was a good man."

Ketsia went quiet for a long moment. "What was his name?"

"Rhisiart." Sair found herself speaking his name gently, like a prayer. "I named our son after him."

"I see." Ketsia thrummed her fingers on her glass. "You were married young?"

"No." Sair couldn't help the brush of sadness at the memory. "I was an old maid of twenty-seven. Much to my mother's horror." Sair inhaled a deep breath. "Rhisiart was not considered suitable. It took me some time to convince my mother to let us marry."

"Why was he not suitable?" Ketsia cocked her head. "Poor?"

"Blind." Sair smiled sadly. "His eyes were gouged out by soldiers when our people fought against Drystan the Conqueror."

"I see." Ketsia's face went pale as the words crossed her lips. "Apologies. That's not what I meant."

"It's alright."

"Continue." Ketsia poured more wine, making a waving motion to Sair.

Sair took a deep breath. Thadred and the marquis were still deep in conversation. "We knew each other from when we were children. He always said he would marry me one day."

"And he did."

Sair blinked back the sting in her eyes. "He did." The memory of her husband was like the remains of an amputated limb. She would always miss him, but the wound no longer bled, and the pain no longer crippled her. But sometimes she felt a twinge where he should have been and remembered what she had lost.

Rhisiart had been kind, gentle, but strong. On their wedding night, he had carried her to their bed and laid her down, caressing every inch of her naked body, saying he wanted to memorize every curve and contour.

Sair had loved him for as long as she had been able to remember. He'd been her first kiss when they had been barely teens, back when he still had sight. Her first everything.

When she had found out what had happened, he'd tried to hide from her. He'd asked his family to keep her away and they had locked the doors of their home but forgotten a side window.

Sair had crawled inside and gotten a look at just what the empire had done to the boy she loved. She'd cried and held him and kissed the scars, promising she would still marry him one day.

It had taken years, but she eventually told her mother that either she would marry Rhisiart, or no one.

When their son was born, Rhisiart had ever so delicately felt his face and tiny hands. Rhis had been a boy, a disappointment to Sair's mother, but Sair hadn't cared. To her, their son was perfect.

Rhisiart hadn't been able to carve the medallion Istovari fathers traditionally gave their wives after the birth of a child. Instead, he had chosen the wood by feel and Sair's brother Tapios had done the carving for him. Sair still had that medallion, though she had stopped wearing it recently when she had realized the edges were wearing off. She wanted to save as many of the details left by her brother's handiwork as possible.

When her son was just a few years old, a sickness had come to their village. The disease settled in the lungs, causing a cough and a fever as the victim grew ever weaker.

There had been a time when Istovari sorceresses were masters even over illness, but against this they had lacked the power. Sair's sister-in-law and niece had died and many others. Rhisiart had held on for days before he took a turn for the worse. He'd fallen asleep and never woken up.

Sair had been devastated but determined not to lose her son. She had ventured outside the protective commune of Istovari sorceresses and into the lowlands.

No Istovari had ventured that far south for over a decade, but Sair had been desperate. She found her way to Lashera, the capital city, and had found an herbalist. According to the old woman, the fever had been sweeping the entire country, but she had some treatments that might work.

On that trip, Sair had been caught. She was sure she would be killed, but she had been taken to Cromwell, then an advisor to the Hylendale king. Cromwell had made a deal with her for information about magic in exchange for all the herbs and tonics she could carry, a basket of bread, and a promise that she would return to speak with him again.

Sair had been desperate and reckless enough to risk it. Over time, she and Cromwell worked out an arrangement. She would instruct him, and he would supply her with the coin she needed to buy and smuggle things back to the Haven. She had never figured out why he had wanted magical instruction, but he never showed any talent for it, so it hardly mattered.

Her son had recovered along with many others. Sair had

been chastised by the leading Istovari council, but what were they to do? She had saved them.

Over time, the secrets she shared with Cromwell had set off a chain of events that had ultimately saved Emperor Daindreth, the empire, and prevented the return of a fallen goddess.

Now Sair knew that if her husband had not died, they might have lost the Witch War. It was a bittersweet knowledge.

"Does Thadred remind you of him?" Ketsia asked it hesitantly, as if she didn't know what else to say.

"No." Sair almost laughed, both at the question and the other woman's awkwardness. "Thadred is nothing like Rhisiart." Thadred was loud where Rhisiart had been quiet and contemplative. Rhisiart was pious and solemn, but tender. Thadred was irreverent and teasing, but he could also be tender.

Rhisiart had been the love of her life, but that had been a different life. She had fallen in love with him before the war, before the banishment of sorceresses from the empire.

It wasn't that she wouldn't have stayed in love with him. The person she had become would have stayed in love with him, but she wouldn't have fallen in love with him.

Sair looked down, familiar sadness creeping into the edges of her thoughts.

Some women drowned fetching water. Men were killed in war. Children might be born perfectly healthy, then die within their first year. Things could change in an instant. Sicknesses came. Accidents happened. Senseless acts of violence.

Everyone knew this. Yet there was a sense of acute injustice when it happened to you. When you were the one left to grieve, the tragedy was crueler.

Sair had been convinced it had been her fault, somehow. If she had gone to Hylendale a day sooner, perhaps she could have saved both her husband and son. Perhaps she could have saved her mother, her sister-in-law, her niece, and so many others.

It had been her brother Tapios who had talked her through it. Who had helped her see how many people she had saved, not those she had failed.

When Tapios had died in the Witch War, it had been the

memory of his words that had kept her from blaming herself. Even though she had encouraged him to take the position guarding the empress. Even though she had agreed not to go on that same scouting mission.

"I suppose it's just as well," Ketsia sighed. "Luckily for you, Lord Thadred is now the most unattainable bachelor in the empire."

Sair's brow wrinkled. "What?"

Ketsia had to swallow her next sip of wine before she replied. "Now the emperor is married, Lord Thadred is the highest-ranking man without a wife."

Sair felt the blood draining from her face. "You're right."

There were other barons, counts, dukes, and lords with more wealth and more titles, but they all had wives and the same was true for most of their sons. Thadred was not related to the Fanduillions, the imperial line. That excluded him from the throne, but he was a respected man in his cousin's court, and he did have a respectable estate. He had authority in the imperial army, the courts, and he would be effective uncle to the unborn heir. Thadred would live in fabulous wealth and so would his wife, when and if he married.

Sair was nothing by comparison. Nothing.

A sorceress, yes. A friend of the empress, yes, but little more than a retainer, really.

Sair was in her mid-thirties with a child from another man. She had no estate, no title, and certainly no dowry.

The sound of footsteps roused Sair's attention.

Thadred and the marquis came marching back from the balcony. Their cigars were discarded and both men were flushed, probably from the whiskey.

"Forgive us for ignoring you, ladies," the marquis said with a bow. "Ketsia, my dear, are you ready to retire?"

Ketsia rose gracefully, leaving her unfinished wine on the table. "Of course, darling."

The marquis took her hand gingerly, surprisingly gentle for a man as thick and broad as him. "My goddess," he murmured against her knuckles.

Ketsia's hard exterior softened just a bit. She turned back to Sair and Thadred, bowing. "Good evening, Lord Thadred. Lady Sairydwen."

Sair inclined her head back and Thadred bowed gallantly.

"Good evening, Marquis Rahl. Ketsia."

"Do have my servants show you to your rooms if you get lost," the marquis said.

Ketsia sniffed at that. "Yes, Lord Thadred. And I'll have the hall boys make sure none of the young ladies get *lost* near your rooms again, either."

The marquis laughed at that, hearty and jovial. "Ah, my dear Ketsia. You never let a man forget."

Ketsia's eyes narrowed at Thadred.

"I'm sure Lady Sairydwen can keep him in line. Come, my dear. Come." The marquis led Ketsia from the room, patting her arm gently and speaking endearments.

Ketsia said something in a sharp tone that sounded like a chastisement. The marquis nodded, laughing as he kissed her temple. Ketsia did appear to soften against him, her icy edges melting just a little in his arms.

Sair watched them go, a little puzzled.

Thadred chuckled as they disappeared through the doorway, acting more like an old married couple than a nobleman and his mistress. "So long as they are happy, who are we to judge?"

Sair watched the doorway where they had disappeared, thinking. Was Ketsia happy? She couldn't tell. She hoped so.

"Are you ready to retire as well, my lady?"

Sair's face heated at that, then she realized Thadred meant in separate rooms. "Yes. Thank you."

Thadred offered her his arm, behaving the part of a gentleman as he had been doing this entire time.

Sair took it, heart thudding in her chest. She'd met Thadred when he was an outlaw on the run from the empire. They had been equals during the Witch War, and in some ways, she had even been his teacher. She might be older than him, but that meant little when he had lived his whole life at court and fought with the army across the continent.

And now…

The two of them left the dining room as servants appeared to clean up the last of the wine glasses and sweep the floors.

Thadred led her into the halls with their flickering lamps encased in blue glass. The way was dark, but the light from the unobscured moon helped somewhat.

"Rahl is going to make sure we have full access to the shipping records," Thadred said. "He's even dispatching his personal steward to make sure we have everything we could possibly need."

"Good." Sair swallowed.

"With how meticulous the Yndrans are, I wouldn't be surprised if we're able to find the minute that Iasu brought Rhis here."

Sair nodded. "Good."

"We'll get him back." Thadred squeezed her hand on his arm as he said it, speaking the words with the force of a vow.

"I believe you." Sair inhaled a slow breath as they rounded the corner, nearing the door to the room she'd been given. "I appreciate you helping me."

"Of course." Thadred made a waving motion. "Why wouldn't I? This is important to the empire. Also, I like Rhis. A bit talkative and causes endless trouble, but still."

A smile tugged at Sair's lips. That was Rhis. Inquisitive, curious, and with boundless energy.

"Iasu better hope I find Rhis before I find him, because I swear to Eponine, if I get my hands on that whoreson…" Thadred coughed. "Sorry. I should watch my language."

It wasn't as if he'd never heard her swear. Sair gripped his arm with her other hand. "No, Thadred. I appreciate you helping me, even after I was so presumptuous."

"What?" Thadred stopped and shot her a sharp look.

They were just outside her rooms now, the hallway deserted and silent around them.

"When—" Sair swallowed as shame weighed down on her. "I asked you—" She cleared her throat and tried again. "I know I shouldn't have asked you to wait for me."

Thadred shifted, looking away from her. "Sair…"

"You don't have to explain." She shook her head quickly. "It was my fault for expecting…" Sair swallowed. The only point to waiting for her would be if he was going to marry her. She wasn't worth his time.

Thadred blinked at her. "Explain what?"

Sair swallowed, twisting pain in her chest. "It doesn't matter now."

Thadred narrowed his eyes, not letting her drop it. "I said I would wait for you, and I did." His voice had an edge to it, like he was holding back.

Sair's heart clenched, and she was struck by the desire to run.

"But you stopped answering my letters." Thadred swore and looked away. A muscle ticked in his cheek.

Sair had wanted to avoid this. She hadn't wanted to confront him about this at all until they found Rhis, if ever, but it seemed unavoidable. Sair looked down. "I heard you were spending time with a woman called Kleia Svistra."

Thadred blinked at her. "Kleia Svistra?"

Sair couldn't look at him.

He took several moments, then, "You mean the apprentice to Cromwell? That Kleia Svistra? Bloody hell, Sair, the girl can't be more than fourteen." Thadred swore again. "Yes, I've spent time with her—accompanied by Cromwell and his six or so other apprentices. Sometimes Dain and Amira, too. Are you going to accuse us of having an orgy next? Why didn't you just ask Amira? The woman has dusted the whole palace with spies, she *could* have told you."

Heat swept up the back of Sair's neck. She knew she had handled the situation badly, even at the time.

The rumor had preyed on her fear that Thadred didn't actually care for her. That he only had attention for what was in front of him. That she wasn't good enough.

She had agonized for days, weeks after hearing the tales. She had written letter after letter asking him, then torn them up instead of sending them.

Weeks had turned into months and the more time had gone

by, the easier it had been to convince herself that nothing had ever been between them at all. It was a passing fancy helped along by the fear and shared hardship of the Witch War.

But then her son had been taken and she had run straight to Thadred without thinking. There must have been some part of her that still believed in him.

"I see how it is," Thadred drawled. "You heard gossip I was rutting with some court beauty and instead of confirming it, instead of—I don't know—*asking* me about it, you decided to ignore me. Is that right?"

"I didn't know how to ask," Sair confessed. "It had been six months since we'd seen each other. We never discussed what..." She gestured vaguely between them. "What we expected."

"I didn't put a limit on my promise," Thadred snapped. "But it seems you put a limit on your trust."

Sair's eyes stung. Had she gotten this all wrong? Had she put herself through six months of turmoil for nothing? "You could have any woman you wanted," she said, her voice coming out small, little more than a squeak.

"Obviously not, because I wanted *you.*" Thadred said it like a curse, a dare, and a plea all at once.

Her heart gave a little leap at those words. But did that mean he still wanted her, or had she missed her chance?

Thadred reached for her, then snatched his hand back. "There hasn't been anyone else. You asked me to wait, and I have."

Hope mingled with shame in Sair's chest. "You have?"

"Shocking, I know." Thadred locked his hands over the top of his cane. "Notable debaucher Thadred Myrani occupied his time with something other than women. Who would believe it? Not you, apparently." His words came out sharp, but with a faint whimper, like each one hurt him.

"I'm sorry," Sair whispered. It felt insufficient. After months of circling around her anger, rejection, and heartbreak, he hadn't done anything wrong.

"I was tempted," Thadred admitted, and it was his turn to look at the carpet. "Especially after you stopped responding, there didn't seem to be a point anymore. But I…couldn't." He raised his eyes to meet hers. Pain shimmered in his eyes, like perhaps she hadn't been the only one with a broken heart these past months.

Sair bit her lip to keep it from trembling. "Do you think you could forgive me?"

Thadred exhaled a long breath. "I'm here, aren't I?" He shook his head. "Yes, Sair. You assumed the worst of me, but I suppose everyone else does." He shrugged. "I forgive you."

The words felt anticlimactic. Flat. There was still so much Sair wanted to ask, but she wasn't sure she had the right to it at the moment.

"I was wrong," Sair whispered. "And I hurt you."

"Sair." Thadred heaved a sigh. "That's…" He trailed off. He cocked his head to the side a moment before his body went tense. "Someone is at the door of your room." Thadred picked up his cane.

Sair reached out with *ka,* feeling for the source. Sure enough, she could sense a large shape big enough to be a person near the door. "Is it one of the maids?"

Thadred shook his head. "None in any of the other rooms." He motioned for her to get behind him.

Sair obeyed, though she reached for *ka* herself. She was recovering her power, but still not as strong with magic as Thadred and neither of them was as strong as the empress, but she had her own tricks.

Thadred hefted his cane by the end, brandishing the silver-capped head like a club. He pushed her back with his other hand, shielding her. "No magic." He paused for a moment, seeming to consider the space around them. "I'm not sensing bands of *ka,* so it's not a Kadra'han."

Shuffling closer, he reached for her doorknob. He glanced to Sair, making sure she was ready.

Sair swallowed, heart racing. She nodded once.

Thadred slammed his shoulder into the door. It hit something solid then a crash came from the other side. Thadred raised his cane and charged.

A scream came from inside and a heavy thud of someone hitting the floor. "Lord Thadred!"

Thadred hesitated, partly across the threshold of Sair's rooms. "Brick?"

"Yes, my lord," whimpered a familiar, miserable voice.

"Why did you go into Lady Sairydwen's rooms?"

Indignant sputtering came from the other side of the door. "You told me to!"

Sair peered around Thadred. Inside the room was dimly lit by just a few lamps.

The valet lay sprawled on the floor, having knocked over a sizable coat stand. He rubbed his head miserably, his valet's livery ruffled and askew.

"Are you alright?" Sair asked, trying to feel at him with *ka*.

"Fine," Brick sputtered, shuffling upright. He faced Thadred, chin raised and back straight. "I fetched the item as you requested, sir. I was delayed getting back in the palace as I did not have proper paperwork, but your errand is completed."

Thadred cleared his throat, glancing over his shoulder to Sair. "Yes, well. Sorry about that, Brick. Thank you. I will find a way to make this up to you."

"I am sure, sir." Brick bowed stiffly. "Can I expect you will need help undressing for the evening?"

Thadred waved a dismissive hand. "Get to your own bed, Brick. I need you to wake me up tomorrow. First light."

"Very good, sir." Brick turned to Sair. "Good evening, Lady Sairydwen."

"What item?" Sair looked between Brick and Thadred.

"His Lordship asked me to—"

"Good night, Brick!" Thadred interrupted, hands bracing against the top of his cane as if for balance. "That will be all."

Brick bowed one last time. "As you wish, my lord. I left it on Lady Sairydwen's couch, as you asked." Brick marched out in the hall.

At the same time, Sair slipped past the valet and into the main chambers of her room. Her room was not so much a room as a large suite of rooms without walls. There was a sitting area, a vanity, a garderobe, and a magnificent open-air balcony that allowed a sea breeze through the entire room.

Sure enough, Sair found a bundle lying on the couch. It was wrapped in thick brown paper with a ribbon tied around the outside. She snatched it up. As soon as she felt the quality of the ribbon in her fingers, a sick sensation pooled in her gut. "Thadred, I can't accept this."

"I want you to have it." Thadred cleared his throat awkwardly. "I wanted to." He glanced to the floor, the ceiling, the wall, anywhere but at her.

Sair slipped the ribbon off. She unwrapped the item carefully, not sure why, but loathe to tear the smooth paper. She pulled back one corner of the paper, then another.

Scarlet cloth tumbled out, as soft and sumptuous as anything she had ever touched. The fabric pooled on the couch, bright red against the deep blue of the cushion.

"Oh, Thadred." Sair's voice caught in her throat. It was the riding cloak from the market. Thadred had sent Brick back to get it. Sair shook her head hastily, her fingers caressing the soft cloth. "I could never pay you back for this."

"It's a gift. You don't have to pay me back." Thadred had gone rigid, now engrossed in studying the head of his cane. "Though I hope Brick shamed them into a discount. Serves that seamstress bitch right."

The seamstress might have been rude, but she had also been right. The quality of fabric and the meticulousness of the stitching was truly exquisite. Feeling the cloak in her hands, Sair thought she might cry. "Thadred, this probably cost more than every dress I've ever owned. This is too much."

Thadred heaved a sigh. "Look, I have plenty of money now and, as I said, I wanted to." He shrugged. "I thought you liked it."

"I do, but—"

"Then it's yours. Wear it, give it to a beggar, smother Ketsia with it, I don't care, but it's yours now."

Sair tried to breathe past the lump in her throat. "Thank you."

He had sent Brick back to the market before their conversation. Before he had an explanation for her silence and before she had asked for his forgiveness. Even this journey to hunt down a dangerous Kadra'han and a cythraul demon—all of it he had agreed to after she had left him in suspense.

Thadred nodded, adjusting the head of his cane yet again. "I hope you like it."

"I do."

"Well, then." Thadred cleared his throat. "Good night, my lady."

"Thadred?"

"Yes?"

Sair caught him before he reached the door, flinging her arms around his neck. She hugged him, squeezing tight.

Thadred stiffened in surprise then curled an arm around her, pulling her closer. His cheek pressed against her hair, his smell of shaving cream, leather, and just a hint of horse. He tucked her under his chin, like he was folding her into his heart.

Sair felt she could melt into him.

He held onto her quietly. Thadred was steady, calm, and safe.

He had the capacity for cutting words as much as violent cruelty, but never with her. Never with the people he cared about. And he had waited for her. If anything, he had shown more trust and commitment than she had.

Sair pulled away, glad the bad light hid her blush. "Good night, Thadred."

Thadred cleared his throat again, nodding. "Good night, Sair."

And then he was gone, shutting the door, and shuffling down the hall.

7

THADRED

Thadred personally considered the records hall of Yndra to be one of the wonders of the world. But people only cared about the work of bureaucrats when they did something wrong and since the records hall almost always did everything right, few people in the empire even knew it existed.

The records hall was a clerk's cathedral with shelves spanning to the ceiling. Walls filled with paper scrolls rose high with pulleys and ladders for reaching the topmost records. Over time, records were bound and sealed in wax to keep them from rotting. This close to the ocean with this much warmth, it could be a struggle to keep paper from moldering over the long term.

Thadred walked behind a representative from the head steward with Brick, four soldiers, and Sair at his heels.

Sair wore the red cloak he'd bought her. His chest warmed to see her in it. He didn't want to read too much into the gesture, but women in the empire only wore gifts from suitors if they were interested. Seeing her wear his gift reassured him that he hadn't imagined the way she had pressed herself to his heart last night.

Thadred wasn't sure she had noticed, but people didn't hesitate to bow to her or call her *Lady* Sairydwen when she wore it.

Sair looked up to the domed ceiling, stretching at least ten times the height of a man over their heads. She'd seen impressive architecture before—she had seen Mynadra, after all. But she still seemed awed by this place.

The steward's representative introduced them to the records minister. Despite being a high-ranking civil official, the clerk's sleeves were stained with ink, and he had several partially completed records in his hands.

"Minister, this is Lord Thadred and Lady Sairydwen, from the Ministry of Inquiry."

Thadred smiled and offered a bow. He came directly from the emperor himself and everyone knew it.

"An honor, sir," the minister said, bowing. "I am Minister Haffold. How might we assist you?"

Thadred flashed his cordial, friendly smile that usually did a fair job of putting people off guard. "We're looking for records of this ship when it landed." He gestured to Brick.

The faithful manservant held up the documents listing out the ship's name, day of departure from Phaed, and list of cargo.

"The *Meissenfrau*. I see. Merchant's galleon with one hundred and nineteen souls on board."

Thadred nodded in confirmation. "If we could find records of the passengers when they landed."

The minister looked to the boy at his elbow. "Have Hiletus check the records from the past fortnight. Find me records of the *Meissenfrau*."

"Yes, Lord Minister." The boy scurried off to another section of the records house. He wove and bobbed between countless tables strewn with papers with a clerk scribbling away at each one.

Tallies were taken and counts were lined up. Every bushel of wheat and bolt of cloth would have an entry and a record.

Sair came up beside Thadred, their shoulders brushing.

Thadred kept looking straight ahead. He thought back to last night, the memory of having her in his arms like a barb inside his skull.

She thought he'd betrayed her. That stung, especially because he'd put so much effort into doing the opposite.

But they seemed to have cleared that up and now…he didn't know what would happen now. He was still waiting to see.

Last night had been a test of his resolve. When she'd put her arms around him, he had wanted to put his hands on her hips and pull her against him. When she had been that soft and giving in his arms, he'd wondered if she would be that soft and giving if he kissed her.

Would she want him to?

What about if he had pushed her down on the bed? Would she want that?

The minister's voice rescued Thadred from continuing that line of thought. "If you go with the boy, he'll take you to Hiletus. He should be able to help you."

Thadred smiled to the minister again. "Thank you kindly, Lord Minister." He offered Sair his arm, as was proper. "Let's go, then."

The boy had scurried to the far end of the records hall, perhaps fifty paces off. The building was massive, but open so that one could see from end to end. Thadred noted as the boy stopped at a corner desk with a pudgy fellow in a feather cap.

Their group wove through the desks and tables, the armored soldiers squeezing carefully between the stations. The soldiers kept their halberds straight and while they might have jostled a few desks and spilled one or two ink pots, they reached the far desk without too much trouble.

The pudgy fellow was already on his feet when they arrived. He swept a bow, a scroll of parchment in his hands. "Lord Thadred. Lady Sairydwen. Clerk Hiletus at your service. You requested records for the *Meissenfrau?*"

"And passengers, yes." Thadred felt Sair go rigid at his side.

The clerk spread the paper on the desk. "Here it is, sir. One thousand and fifteen fleeces, totaling in a weight of—"

"Passengers." Thadred pointed to a list of names further down the paper. "We're looking for a man and a boy. Traveling together."

"Ah." The clerk removed his spectacles, looking down the list of names. "There were fifty-seven passengers in addition to the crew, but only four of them had children.”

Thadred’s heart sped up just a little. It was not unlike the feeling of sighting quarry just ahead on a hunt. The thrill of the chase.

“There was a Matron Glasgo with an infant.”

Thadred shook his head.

“One Carver Kefton with his two daughters, Millicent and Andria.”

Thadred tilted his head sideways, skimming down the list of names. He wasn’t sure what he was looking for until he saw it. “That one.”

“Ah. Hasdrun Sabanto with his nephew, Regalus Sabanto.”

“How do you know?”

Thadred grimaced. “Hasdrun was the founder of the Fanduillion dynasty.” Iasu had always been a fanatic when it came to serving the Fanduillion dynasty. Unfortunately, Iasu had focused that loyalty on Vesha the Usurper, not her son the rightful heir.

Sair swallowed but remained composed.

“What happened to these two?” Thadred pointed to the pair of names on the parchment. “Where are they now? We’re assuming they’ve already left the city, if that helps.”

“One moment.” The clerk Hiletus ducked back behind his desk, riffling through different ledgers. “They might be on another charter, but if they boarded another ship straightaway, I might have the records.”

Sair’s fingers dug into Thadred’s arm, her body stiff against his side. She had gone pale, her eyes fixed to the clerk as the pudgy man flipped papers and squinted at lines.

“Are you alright?” Thadred lowered his voice, bringing his face closer to hers. “Sair?”

“Fine.” Sair swallowed, not looking away from the plump clerk.

The clerk let off a little crow of triumph. “Ah, here we are.” Hiletus set another charter on the table. “It appears they departed the same day without leaving the docks. Lucky for us.”

“Where to?” Thadred leaned over, trying to get a better view.

"They boarded the *Affenwy*, headed for Iandua."

Thadred choked. "Iandua?"

Iandua had been the epicenter of the cythraul outbreak a year ago. Worse than that, it was where a certain imperial lady had fled in disgrace to marry a Kelethian count not long after Thadred had been born.

"Yes, my lord. You can see it right there." The clerk held up the parchment helpfully.

Indeed, Thadred saw the aliases listed on the ship's charter. And they were indeed headed for Iandua.

"At sailing speeds this time of year, I would expect they docked there about a week ago." The plump man nodded curtly. "Can I help you with anything else, my lord?"

"I don't think so." Thadred tried to ignore the heavy, sick feeling in his gut. "I suppose we're going to Iandua."

This whole thing had been rather simple. All they had to do now was head to the last city in the world Thadred wanted to visit.

Worst of all, he was visiting on imperial, official business. He would have to pay his respects to the head of the region and that only made it worse.

"We know where they are." Sair's voice came out so quiet, so relieved, he felt shame for being focused on his own problems.

"Yes." Thadred patted her hand. "We can be on our way before nightfall."

Sair drew in a shuddering breath. "Iandua is huge. An ancient city. How can we even begin—"

"We'll find him," Thadred promised once again, not giving her mind time to sabotage her.

Sair nodded, breathing deep. "Yes. You're right."

Thadred cleared his throat. "It's a city firmly in imperial control. We will have no trouble at all."

After they properly thanked the clerk and their young guide, Sair let Thadred guide her back through the rows of desks and tables. They had to prepare for their departure.

Perhaps their business in Iandua would be just as painless as

Yndra had been, but Thadred doubted it. He could always dream, though.

"I only hope the lord of Iandua is as accommodating as the marquis." Sair let off a little laugh, trying to make light of the situation.

"I'm not sure. The count of Iandua is eight years old." Thadred hesitated, but she was going to find out sooner or later. "He's also my brother. Half-brother." It was the truth, yet it felt wrong to say. Thadred didn't think of the foreign countess's children as his half-siblings. They were like old nail clippings. He knew they were a part of him, in a way, and yet he felt no connection.

Sair shot him a look, eyes wide. He'd forgotten she wasn't as up to imperial gossip as the ladies of the court.

"My mother—Dowager Countess Zeyna—is also his mother." Thadred exhaled a long sigh. He'd much prefer nightly ribbings from Ketsia than facing his mother and her brood of legitimate heirs. She had four or five of them. Or was it six? He didn't remember.

"Oh." Sair went quiet.

They said their goodbyes to the Minister Haffold and headed out into the streets of Yndra. Like most of the city, the administrative district had been designed to be walkable.

Thankfully, someone had the foresight to leave room for horses, which meant Lleuad and a horse for Sair could be brought along. Thadred helped Sair aboard her horse and took his own from the waiting attendant.

Lleuad was still cross with Thadred, but he allowed the knight to mount his saddle. The little stallion had calmed a bit since being fed raw ham last night. Pork was definitely the horse's favorite.

"You're not looking forward to seeing your family." It wasn't a question, but Sair said it in a way that prompted explanation.

"I've never met them," Thadred admitted. "They've never come to court, and I've never been to Iandua."

Sair kept her eyes on the streets ahead. "Will this…be a

problem?"

"No," Thadred scoffed. He would do what needed to be done. "Surely I can face some old hag and her brood."

Sair didn't argue with him.

Thadred inhaled a deep breath. "I swore to fight an order of fanatical rogues and a demon for you, Sair. I'm sure I can face my mother, too."

Sair smiled sadly but didn't respond.

8

SAIR

Sair had little to pack, so didn't take much time when she returned to her room while Thadred saw to informing the marquis of their departure and readying the ship.

When it came to matters of magic and healing, she would be useful, but for now she let him take the lead. He was the one with the imperial signet ring. It was remarkable how fast that little loop of metal could make people comply.

A knock sounded at the door.

Sair reached out, sensing the life force of only one person. She supposed an assassin wouldn't have knocked, so she called out, "Come in."

Ketsia slipped through in a dark blue dress that was almost black. It covered more skin than her dress last night, but it still dipped daringly low in the front and back. Golden earrings dangled from her ears, and she held a bundle in her arms. "You're leaving?"

Sair nodded, putting the last of her belongings into her satchel.

"I'm sorry to see you go." Ketsia inhaled a deep breath. "It's not often we have female guests who deign speak to me. Much less respectable ladies."

Sair frowned. "But you are the lady of this home."

Ketsia smiled wanly. "Eben likes to think so. He might even

believe it." She set the bundle down on the bed. "But everything I own is his. Without him, I'd be off to the hangman's gallows in moments. When he dies, I might still be hanged."

Sair blinked at the casual way the other woman discussed her own death. "You fear this happening?"

"No," Ketsia said after a moment's pause. "Eben loves me, for some reason. And the family will likely allow me to have the estate he's put aside in his will for me. But it does not change that I might lose everything in a moment." She let off a bitter little laugh. "My mother always taught me not to aspire above my own station. I thought she was narrow-minded, but now I realize she was trying to protect me." Ketsia plucked at the ribbon around the bundle she had brought, still not addressing it. "When you attach yourself to a wealthier, richer, and better-connected man, he has all the power. He might be a fair man, a good man, even. But you had best be sure because if he is not? If he decides he could have done better in five, ten years…?" Ketsia let the sentence hang, hinting at a past life that had been rife with misery. "Sometimes I wish I had married a shipbuilder or a spice merchant."

Sair looked around them, at the unadulterated splendor of the Yndra palace. "But…you have done quite well for yourself."

Ketsia laughed. "My life hangs by a thread. I have no legal claim to any of it." She grew serious, focusing on Sair. "If a man above your station mistreats you, if he seduces the scullery maids, and belittles you in front of his friends, there is nothing you can do." Ketsia looked to the ceiling and back to Sair. "People will tell you to look the other way, because didn't he lift you from a life of squalor? Shouldn't you be grateful? When he beats you, they will say you deserved it or that surely it wasn't so bad."

Sair hesitated, not sure what to say to that. "I am sorry for what happened to you."

"Can't be helped now." Ketsia blinked quickly, reaching for the bundle she'd set on the bed. "Here. One of the servants mentioned to me that you didn't have many other clothes."

Sair flushed red, heat rising to her cheeks. Was everyone

determined to clothe her now? "Ketsia, please. I don't need charity."

"A gift, then," the other woman said, voice going hard. "Friends give each other gifts. Do they not?"

"I am doing fine, Ketsia."

Ketsia rolled her eyes. "Sairydwen of the Istovari, there is no shame in being poor." She nudged the bundle meaningfully. "But there is quite a bit of shame in being proud and stubborn. You're heading to Iandua? These came from Iandua. They will help you blend in and look like a noblewoman. Noblewomen are treated better, trust me."

Sair accepted the bundle, allowing it to more than double her luggage. "Thank you."

Ketsia nodded curtly. "You and Lord Thadred should stop by Yndra again. After you recover your son."

"I would like that." And Sair meant it. The city was lovely, and she had enjoyed her time with the marquis and his prickly mistress.

"I wish you luck finding your son, Sairydwen. Your people pray to Eponine?"

"Eponine, yes. Goddess of the moon and horses."

Ketsia nodded. "I have little use for gods these days, but Eponine favor you."

"Thank you."

Ketsia looked around the room. "I suppose you're ready to be going, then?"

"I suppose so." Sair fumbled with the string on the package Ketsia had gifted her, a little anxious. She wasn't used to gifts, much less from virtual strangers.

"I'll walk you down to the harbor below the palace."

"Is that safe for you?"

"It's still within Eben's estate. It will be fine." Ketsia opened the door for Sair and the two women ventured into the hallway. "What will you do after you rescue your son?"

Sair felt a lump in her throat. She tried to make herself believe that it was inevitable that they really would find Rhis and bring him home safely. She just needed to stay focused on that.

"I will likely return to court," Sair said. "I was helping with the establishment of an Istovari village near Lashera in Hylendale, but that is all but done." Her people hadn't liked the stench and motion of the city and had wanted something quieter in the country. "We found a few outlying villages that were open to meeting with us. None that were quite willing to have us there, I'm afraid."

"Many people are still afraid of sorceresses, I expect." Ketsia was certainly blunt.

"It's true." Sair heaved a sigh. "It's worse in Hylendale than in the central empire, oddly."

"Probably because the central empire never had to deal with you in wars."

Before even the Witch War, there had been the wars of Emperor Drystan, also known as Drystan the Conqueror. Drystan had come into the crown unexpectedly—the runt of the Fanduillion litter who had somehow survived all his uncles, brothers, and cousins.

Drystan had been heir to a loose confederation of city-states and kingdoms bound by pride and common traditions that nominally paid tribute to Mynadra. He had changed all that.

Sair sometimes wondered just what had happened. Why had Drystan suddenly developed ambition where his forefathers had been content to simply maintain their borders?

Whatever the reason, Drystan had united his vassals under a single banner. He'd issued a single coinage, doing away with local currencies in favor of coins that bore his image. He stabilized the outer regions of his empire and raised troops to subdue those who rebelled. He might have stopped there, but he hadn't.

Drystan had recognized that most of the continent was just like his empire—fractured kingdoms and scattered clans. Pride and ancient feuds kept them from uniting.

So, Drystan had conquered them one by one. He had brought everyone to heel, from the horse lords of the southern steppes, to the proud warriors of the eastern coast, and the Valdarian Sea Wardens in the frigid north.

Even distant Kelethian, which had several colonies

established by his great-grandfather, was formally annexed. Kingdom after kingdom, many of them formerly great powers themselves, bowed before the golden stag of House Fanduillion.

Drystan had grown his empire across the continent, stopping only at Nihai. Why he had stopped there, no one was quite sure.

Drystan might have spread his empire across the entire world, if not for the Istovari sorceresses. They had cursed him, infected him with a cythraul demon. Sair herself had been a girl, but she had lent a portion of her power to the spell.

The Istovari had cursed Drystan, wanting to control him, but they had learned the hard way that no one controls a cythraul. Witchcraft, the practice of using cythraul for power, was like a flaming sword—no one could wield it for long without getting burned themselves.

The battle had ended in a stalemate—the Istovari sorceresses fleeing into the forests and casting a protective spell to cover their tracks. That spell had created the Cursewood, a tangle of noxious trees and mutant creatures that had protected them for nearly twenty years.

Sair thought to herself that her people were not much to fear. They might be able to help with sickness and healing even now. Many of her sistren were in far parts of the empire doing just that. Gone were the days when a single Istovari woman could tear a city to pieces.

But now that the Cursewood was receding and sorceresses were regaining their power, anything might happen.

Those days might come again, especially if Empress Amira was any indication, but for now, Sair had to rely on Thadred and his soldiers.

The marquis had his own personal harbor of sorts off the main harbor. In it were a few barges intended for feasts on the water, as well as a few merchant vessels being unloaded. The imperial ship Sair and Thadred were using sat with a ramp against it.

Thadred negotiated with Lleuad, talking to the stallion at the foot of the ramp. He patted the horse's neck and gestured up at the ship. The little horse nipped Thadred's arm. Thadred yelled in protest and yanked the horse's lead rope.

Lleuad threw his head up, glaring at the knight. Sair could have sworn the kelpie was daring Thadred to try it again.

Ketsia chuckled. "It's good to know not everyone is so easily charmed by Lord Thadred."

Sair had thought much the same. "You don't like Thadred."

"The last time he visited, he bedded Eben's oldest niece."

Sair wasn't surprised. She felt a twist of something close to jealousy, but it was not quite as bitter as it might have been yesterday. "Is it just because of that?"

Ketsia frowned as a page brought Thadred what appeared to be a ham. "In large part, that's it, yes."

Thadred held up the ham, waggling it in front of the kelpie. It looked raw, from what Sair could see. Lleuad stomped and his hindquarters shifted, refusing to look at Thadred or the offered ham.

"They call me a whore," Ketsia said. "Because I bed a man who isn't my husband. One man." The bite in her tone was hard to miss. "Lord Thadred beds a hundred women and they call him a lovable scoundrel. And he still enjoys one of the highest positions in the land and matrons still scout him for their daughters." Ketsia made a frustrated sound. "Perhaps I am just a jealous and bitter woman."

Sair touched the other woman's arm. "It's not fair."

Ketsia raised her chin and squeezed Sair's hand. "I wish you luck in finding your son, Sairydwen of the Istovari. Truly."

"Thank you."

"I hope we will meet again, but if not, farewell."

"Farewell, Ketsia."

The other woman nodded curtly and turned, making her way back into the main palace.

Sair turned her attention back to the ship that lay waiting against the docks.

Lleuad finally seemed to tire of Thadred's coaxing. He seized the ham in his jaws, opening his mouth far wider than any natural horse. Seizing the meat in his teeth, Lleuad leapt up the ramp, dragging Thadred up with him.

The knight cursed, using a creative combination of insults Sair found almost impressive.

The kelpie dragged Thadred partway across the deck before Thadred finally let go. The moment he was free, the animal bounded down into the hold below, waving the ham in the air like a trophy.

"You're going to be glue!" Thadred vowed, falling to the wooden planks. "Glue! I swear!" He let loose a maelstrom of curses that made even the sailors chuckle nervously.

"Thadred!" Sair raced up the ramp, rushing to him. "Are you alright?"

Thadred's whole expression changed the moment he laid eyes on her. "Sair." He coughed, pushing himself up onto his hands.

"Are you hurt?"

"Fine," he grumbled. The knight dusted himself off and tried to stand on his own but slipped. Choking on a fresh round of curses, he let Sair help him to his feet. "Raltor, raise that ramp before the stupid horse comes up and tries to jump ship."

Several of the sailors hopped to do as Thadred had ordered while the knight limped down into the hold of the ship.

Sair followed him, still holding her satchel and the parcel from Ketsia.

They found Lleuad in the hold of the ship. He crouched over the raw ham, gnawing on it greedily. His white eyes flicked toward Thadred with suspicion, but he didn't stop tearing off mouthfuls of pork.

Around them, the other horses had already been loaded and stood in their proper places. At least Lleuad hadn't attacked any of them. He had been known to do that with some horses but got along with others. No one had really figured out why.

"Come here." Thadred marched straight up to the kelpie. He seized the ham by the pork bone. "Get in your stall. Over there. Now." Thadred tossed the ham inside Lleuad's appointed space.

The stallion clopped into his stall, tail wringing as he did. The kelpie dropped his head and immediately set to finishing off what remained of the ham leg.

Thadred went to shut the door, but the kelpie lodged his hindquarters so it wouldn't shut. Thadred smacked the animal's rump. "Get in!" The kelpie jumped and let off an indignant whinny as Thadred bolted the door shut. "I swear, this animal is ten times the trouble of every horse I've ever owned."

Sair smiled at that. "One doesn't own a kelpie. You could just as easily say he owns you."

Thadred heaved a sigh. "You're probably right. You always are, and Eponine knows I can never make that horse do something he doesn't want to." He looked down. "Your hands are full. Can I take one of those for you?"

"Just some things from Ketsia."

"Gifts?"

Sair nodded. "I haven't opened them yet."

"I see. Let's get you settled in your cabin then." He offered her his arm.

Sand had been spread over the deck for better traction for the horses to be loaded. When Thadred had fallen down, he'd been smeared in it. Sair took his arm all the same, not caring that it left a slight dusting on her as they touched.

"How are you feeling? I'm sorry we're missing dinner, but I thought you'd want to be going as soon as we could."

"You're right," Sair said. "And I'm quite well, thank you."

"Good." Thadred reached the ramp leading back to the top of the ship. He muttered something, his free hand tracing over his bad hip. Sair sensed the ripple of *ka* as he strengthened the spells around his old injury. "Alright. Up we get." One step at a time, they began the ascent up to where the sailors and soldiers were finishing final preparations.

Goods were loaded, lines were cast off, men came rolling onto the decks, and clerks watched imperiously from the shore, taking tallies of every little detail.

"Yndra is always a pleasant stay," Thadred said. "You'll have to see it longer, sometime. It's one of my favorite places. And I'll need to take you to a singing house. Best drinking and—well, I'm sure we can find a tamer version."

Sair smiled, trying not to think too hard about her son. They were headed toward Rhis's last known destination. There was nothing more to be done in this moment. "I would like that."

Thadred faced her, not quite making eye contact. Sair wasn't sure where to go from here.

Sair braced herself. "About last night." They needed to talk about it, sooner rather than later.

Thadred looked to where the sailors were unfurling the ship's sails. "Yes?"

"I missed you," Sair said, words falling short. That was an incredibly mild way to put it. She hadn't been able to stop thinking about him.

She'd beaten herself up this entire time, hating herself for getting her hopes up, convinced Thadred had moved on without ever really giving her a chance. Her own fears had run her ragged, shame and embarrassment that now seemed to be all her own making. Thadred hadn't done anything. She'd let rumors give weight to her insecurities.

Maybe if she hadn't, she would have returned to Mynadra sooner or Thadred would have joined them in Hylendale. Either way, Rhis might not have been taken.

"I missed you, too." Thadred cleared his throat.

"Do you think you can forgive me?" Sair was almost afraid of the answer.

"I already said I forgive you." Thadred sounded tired.

Sair looked down then, afraid of how he might answer her next question. Was there still a chance for them?

Thadred seemed to sense her unease. He took her hand, his callused grip twisting through her fingers. "I want to court you, Sair. I think that's what people call it?" He still didn't quite look at her. "But I don't want you to feel like you have to."

"What do you mean?" Sair was genuinely confused.

"I'm getting your kid back. Regardless of what does or doesn't happen between us." Thadred let go of her hand. "You don't owe me…anything."

Sair thought her heart might break and explode at the same time. He didn't want her coming to him out of obligation or a sense of debt. He was probably risking his life for her son and wasn't asking for anything in return. She'd met his loyalty with silence for months and all but accused him of infidelity. Yet he forgave her and continued to offer his help freely.

He was being so patient. So kind. Ketsia and half the empire would never believe just how decent he was.

Sair's heart thudded in her chest, a sinking and floating sensation all at once. Her spine tingled and warmth bloomed through her whole body.

I love him, Sair realized. *I love Thadred Myrani.*

She opened her mouth, but all she could get out was, "Thank you."

Thadred nodded once and their ship moved, heading out of the harbor.

9

THADRED

As they rode up the avenue lined by palm trees, Thadred could count on one hand the number of people who could have brought him to this point. This was the last place he wanted to be, second only to the Dread Marches themselves. Even the inside of a boiling geyser would have been preferable.

That he was here at all was a testament to how much Sair and her son meant to him.

There were gaps in the line of palm trees where some had died, like holes in a too-wide smile. Though the whole estate was green, manicured, and beautiful, there were signs of the Witch War if one knew where to look.

When they'd docked in port at Iandua, Thadred had noticed black stains on stone buildings. Empty spaces marked where some structures had to be torn down altogether and new buildings rose to take their place. Even though Thadred had never seen this city before the Witch War, he could see it had been scarred.

When they had unloaded their horses and sent word to the Count of Iandua, Thadred had been hoping they'd get no response. It had already been late in the afternoon and with so little notice, surely the count wouldn't respond.

To Thadred's dismay, the messenger returned right as he was about to announce they remain on the ship. The count's steward had invited Lord Thadred and his lady directly to the manor as was fitting an imperial representative.

They left Major Caiden and half the soldiers with the ship. They would investigate along the docks and interview local clerks for any rumors of Iasu and Rhis. It seemed likely that Iasu and Rhis were still in the city, so the men were also to monitor all outbound ships. Thadred tried to think of a good reason why he needed to stay with them but couldn't come up with anything.

Thadred's skin crawled and he was sure he would break out in hives at any instant.

Sair rode beside him on her mare, quiet and calm. Completely in contrast to what he felt.

Sair still wore the red cloak he had given her. The color complemented her, the way a ruby complemented a gold ring. She usually wore muted colors meant to make her blend into the background, but he preferred having her stand out. He liked knowing where she was, and he wanted other people to notice her. She was worth noticing.

"Thadred?" Sair must have picked up on his unease after all. "Are you alright?"

"Yes." Thadred sat straight, trying not to dwell on what awaited them at the end of this avenue. Up ahead was the lovely home of Count Flavius—his little brother.

Worse, Zeyna was there. His mother. He didn't want to meet her. She didn't want to meet him.

If she had wanted to, she could have visited him in Mynadra at any time. He knew she'd had invitations from her sister, the late empress, but she had declined them all.

Zeyna had left her son to be raised by her sister and never shown any interest in him after that.

He'd tried to think of an alternative to staying with the region's ruler, but what options were there? There was an imperial garrison, but that would raise questions.

"I know this is awkward for you," Sair said, speaking carefully. "Is there something I can do to help?"

Thadred almost asked her if she could stab him so he could have an excuse to not see the count today. "No, I don't think so." He adjusted Lleuad's reins.

With any other horse, Thadred would have wanted to keep a little pressure in the reins, but Lleuad was still growing accustomed to things on his face. The little black stallion got cranky when Thadred tried for more. The knight had accepted he might just have to look like an idiot horseman.

They reached the front of the manor house, the servants coming forth in ranks to greet them as suited imperial guests on an official delegation. Trumpets sounded.

Lleuad's ears twitched, but he didn't jump as he might have at one time.

Brick dismounted his own pony—a calm, sweet-tempered little gelding who had never once tried to bite anyone's arm off. Brick took Thadred's reins as the knight dismounted.

Thadred flinched as the ground met his bad foot, but the little jolt was as familiar to him as the other foibles of his body. He helped Sair down as a noblewoman came floating out to meet them.

"Lord Thadred Myrani," the woman said, dropping into a deep curtsy. She had dark curls held back by a ribbon and a shimmering pale dress that would have been passable for a morning in the imperial court. "I am Lady Vespasia, sister to Count Flavius. I hope you will forgive the Lady Regent for not greeting you herself. My mother is preoccupied this morning."

Thadred winced at the word *mother*, even though it wasn't directed at him. "This is Lady Sairydwen of the Istovari," he said, presenting the lady at his side.

"How do you do?" Vespasia dropped into a second curtsy. If she was frightened or even knew that Sair was a sorceress, she gave no sign. "It is a pleasure to host guests from the empire." Vespasia smiled, but Thadred thought it looked forced. Then again, he didn't know this woman. He didn't know any of them.

"My mother has asked me to make sure you are well tended." Lady Vespasia swept aside as if to invite them in. "You shall have a whole wing to yourselves."

Thadred nodded to his soldiers. "Ratkin and Landric. Go with the servants to check it."

Vespasia seemed puzzled that soldiers would be sent to scout but made no comment.

Thadred trusted these people less for being family, not more. Daindreth's mother had tried to steal his throne and have him possessed by a demon. In Thadred's opinion, mothers were not to be trusted.

The warmth of Sair's hand on his arm made him question that for just a moment. While he hadn't had any good experiences with mothers, the sorceress was a good one.

Thadred smiled at her apologetically, though she couldn't read his mind.

"While your men inspect your lodgings, may I show you inside?" Vespasia gestured toward the house.

"How old are you?" Thadred wasn't sure why the question popped out. It was inappropriate, for sure.

Vespasia, to her credit, only smiled, if a little apprehensively. "I am twenty-four, your lordship."

Not a significant age gap, then. A few years, but not many.

Thadred nodded curtly, remembering himself. "Forgive me." He turned to Sair. The sorceress watched him with raised brows, as if to say she knew he was on the verge of a mental break.

"Shall we go in?" Sair asked, her tone completely neutral. She was guileless and straightforward and all the things women in his life rarely were.

"Yes, I suppose."

"Tea is ready on the verandah. I am sure you're exhausted after your journey." Vespasia led them into the house.

Thadred had already dispatched men to look into the last records of the *Affenwy*. Though Iandua did not keep as meticulous records as Yndra, they would still have taken note of when the ship landed and who had docked.

Come tomorrow, they should have a trail to follow. Today, they had to do as imperial representatives did and dine with the local gentry.

Vespasia remained silent until they reached the promised verandah. Tea had been set out, along with goat cheese, olives, almonds, and something wrapped in grape leaves. "Was your journey pleasant?" Vespasia asked, inviting them to sit with her.

"Very." Thadred's attention was on the garden. He sat down, Sair between himself and the strange woman in front of them.

Vespasia rearranged her hands in her lap. "Um…"

"What is this?" Sair leaned over, pointing to something on the tray. "I've never seen it before."

"Oh, those are dolmas," Vespasia explained. "A local treat. I used to eat them by the bucket when I was a little girl."

"I would like to try one," Sair said.

"Please do," Vespasia replied.

Thadred frowned at the garden, avoiding the stranger. He balanced his hands on the top of the cane.

"This is amazing! Thadred, have you tried these?" Sair offered him the plate, urging him to take one.

"Thank you." Thadred took one of the leaf-wrapped items from the plate without looking at it. When he bit into it, he found it tasted pleasantly of cheese, spices, and vinegar. It was delightful. He still didn't look at Vespasia.

"Where is the rest of your family?" Sair asked, sounding painfully polite.

"My brother, Count Flavius, is with his tutors. My youngest sister has recently taken religious orders and the other is lately married." Vespasia's voice trembled just a little at that. "My mother is busy, as I said. But she promises to join us for dinner." Vespasia hesitated. "You will be joining the family for dinner?"

Thadred almost vomited right then but managed to keep down the single bite of dolma he had eaten.

"Yes," Sair answered for him. "I believe we will."

"What brings you to Iandua?" Vespasia asked. "We often meet with dignitaries and representatives, but never someone so—well. Not since last year. When the empress came here."

"Vesha was here." Thadred remembered that abruptly.

Vesha had been the one to release the cythraul en masse. It had been assumed that most if not all of them had gone to the empire's mainland, but that was because there had been no recent reports of cythraul attacks in the colonies.

Vesha had come here, the last known place before she had been confronted by the emperor and empress and presumably killed. Everyone assumed Vesha was dead, at any rate. Though, Amira and Dain had been rather vague on the particulars of just what had happened.

Was it coincidence that Iasu had brought Rhis to the very city where his former liege lady had also fled? It might be. This was an old city, and it would be much easier to get lost here than in many others.

The colonies were firmly in the grip of the empire, but they had rougher edges and less imperialized corners. It would be a good place to become lost if that was what someone wanted.

But Thadred didn't think so. He tapped his cane against the floor, thinking.

It had been almost a week. What were the odds that Iasu and his young hostage were still in the city?

Thadred supposed they would find out.

As Thadred allowed Brick to dress him for dinner, he wondered if perhaps he should have had Sair stab him after all. It would have spared him this.

"It's dinner with the local rulers. Not a state banquet," Thadred growled.

"Forgive me, sir." Brick was unoffended, continuing his work. "I just thought you wanted to look your best to meet the family."

Thadred wanted to swear at him, but Brick wasn't the sort to swear back and that made it feel unfair. Thadred glowered at his own reflection. At any rate, they had full-length mirrors in the guest suites. A sign of wealth if ever there was one.

The dowager countess was expected at dinner along with her two present children—both Vespasia and Flavius.

Thadred would have been perfectly fine if the dowager had managed to be "preoccupied" for a few more hours. He would have been fine if she never spoke to him at all. Never saw him.

"Any word from the docks?"

Outside, the sun was fading. The men he'd sent to make inquiries should be back soon.

"None yet, sir." Brick helped him don an embroidered dinner jacket and brushed dust and hair from the shoulders. "Shall I inform you when they return?"

"Yes." Thadred braced himself on his cane, staring outside. "You can see where the shrubs were replaced." He nodded to the garden. "And where the grass is too green. That would be where the lawn was burned last year. During the Witch War."

Brick's hands slowed as he smoothed Thadred's coat. "What does that mean, sir?"

"The cythraul came here." Thadred gestured to the mansion around them. "The late empress came here."

"Well. The dowager was her sister."

Thadred chewed his lip, thinking. Was it possible that the dowager countess had been in league with the late empress? Perhaps she was the new master of the Kadra'han.

But no. The gods would never allow his mother to be a traitor. It would make him too happy.

"When we're done here, I want you to have the soldiers post a guard outside my door tonight. And two for Lady Sair."

"You already gave that order, sir, but I will see to it they heard."

"Mmm." Thadred was sure Brick had tied his cravat too tight. He tugged at the knot. "I can't wear this jacket."

"Sir?"

"It's too formal. The gold embroidery is too much."

"Sir, we agreed—"

"I want a different one." Thadred gestured his cane at his trunks. "Don't I have a different one?"

"Sir." Brick's expression barely even shifted. "I think you will be late."

"Late for what? I'm the most important person here. They'll

have to wait for me."

Brick drew in a longsuffering breath. He opened his mouth, but a knock interrupted.

"Lady Sairydwen is here to meet you, my lord," called one of the soldiers from outside.

"Damn it." Thadred ripped off his cravat. He might suffer the deplorable jacket, but he was not going to be strangled. Oddly, taking off the cravat made it no easier to breathe.

Brick collected the cravat off the sofa and didn't say a word.

Sair was the one person Thadred didn't want to keep waiting. He reached the door and flung it open.

Sair had two guards, just as he had instructed. Thadred paused on seeing her. Where had she gotten that dress? It was blue with a layered skirt and showed more of Sair's skin than Thadred had ever seen. Her arms were bare and the front dipped low in a narrow slit, as was the imperial style. The fitted bodice showed her slim waist to advantage.

"Sair." Thadred coughed. "You look well."

"Do you like it?" Sair smiled, a little unsure. She pirouetted in a charming, girlish way, making the skirt flare around her. "It was a gift from Ketsia."

The dress dipped in the back, exposing a generous amount of skin. It was a style that had been popular at court a few years ago. Thadred imagined pinning her face to the wall while he kissed all that gloriously exposed skin from her neck down to her—

"Shall I prepare another jacket for you, sir?" Brick's longsuffering voice interrupted Thadred's train of thought.

"What? No, this one is fine." Thadred did his best to recover himself. He had seen plenty of women before. Naked women, even. There was no reason that Sair's relatively modest dress should be making his heart pound. "Are you ready, my lady?"

"Yes." Sair hooked her arm through his as was proper.

Her bare arm touched his sleeve, her fingers resting lightly on the crook of his elbow. She had nice fingers—long and slender, with clean and rounded nails.

He imagined those nails clawing into his naked back before

he caught himself. She needed time. More importantly, he needed to get her son back so that she would know she had a choice. Making advances on a woman who was counting on him to rescue her child was hardly ethical, even by his standards.

The guards fell in around them. Four men just to be safe.

"Any word from the docks yet?" Sair asked, keeping her voice down.

"No." Thadred's throat remained tight. "We should have word before we go to bed."

"I see." Sair looked away.

Thadred touched her hand. "When we get back to Mynadra, I'm giving Rhis a pony."

Sair shot him a look. "What?"

"If it's alright with you, of course." Thadred kept his attention fixed ahead. "There's this little rouncey gelding back in Mynadra that shares a pasture with Lleuad. One of the few horses he'll tolerate. I was thinking that one would be perfect."

Sair remained quiet as they rounded a corner. "That's very kind of you."

"Not really." Thadred shrugged. "I just don't want him asking to ride my kelpie, is all. The damned thing is dangerous."

"I see." Sair's hand on his arm tightened.

Thadred made plans as if finding Rhis was guaranteed. He was telling her they would find Rhis safe and as annoying as ever.

"Thank you," Sair said softly.

They passed rows of portraits and paintings of people Thadred didn't know. A single suit of armor in an antique style stood on a platform, clearly important to the family somehow.

They stepped into the dining room of the family.

Servants bustled to and fro, placing dishes on the table. Carafes of wine were being filled.

Thadred glanced around, looking for anyone not in servants' livery. "I thought we were late." He glanced to the grandfather clock. "We *are* late."

"Forgive me, my lord." Immediately, a footman broke from the pack. "We don't usually start until an hour or so past."

Thadred grimaced, annoyance pricking the back of his neck.

He definitely had time to change his jacket if he had wanted to, but now he was here.

"If I could offer you and the lady drinks on the balcony?" The servant seemed genuinely apologetic.

"Fine." Thadred signaled to the guards.

Two were to remain posted outside and two were to accompany him and Sair. They stepped out onto the balcony overlooking the sea.

Most local rulers lived inside the city proper. Not so in Iandua. The home of the count had been built on the edge of the city overlooking the port from a distant hill. It was almost like the count considered himself too good to brush shoulders with the people he ruled.

"It's lovely," Sair said, though the sadness in her voice contradicted her sentiment. She rested her hands on the railing, the wind playing in her hair.

You're lovely, Thadred almost said.

"Do you think Rhis is out there?" She nodded toward the city of Iandua, sprawled across the land in a network of stone homes, shiny new cathedrals, opera houses, and insulae, buildings with smaller dwellings inside that might house a hundred families each.

"It's possible," Thadred said, keeping his voice down. He wanted to rest his hand on her back but that might be taken the wrong way.

The footman returned, bringing wine for them both.

Thadred accepted both goblets, examining them for any signs of oils, powders, or other poisons.

Sair watched him with an arched brow, that mild look of amusement. "I think if they want us dead, they'll try killing us in our sleep."

"When the guards are around us?"

Sair shrugged. "Everyone knows poison is a woman's weapon. You think your mother wants you dead?"

Thadred quirked a brow. "I don't know her at all."

"Vespasia?"

"Met her today."

"Well." Sair took a sip from her wine glass before setting it down. "Tastes fine."

Thadred didn't really suspect the family of being in league with the rogue Kadra'han. It would make things too simple. He'd force them to reveal Rhis, arrest them all, have them shipped back to Mynadra for trial, and let Daindreth pick a new count of Iandua.

Thadred sipped from his own goblet, begrudgingly admitting that it was good wine. Even Marquis Rahl would have been impressed.

"Iandua is an old city," Thadred said, wanting something to fill the silence. "It dates back farther than human memory. It used to be the seat of a great empire itself, or at least one of several city states that claimed the title."

"Oh?" Sair looked out over the coastline before them. "Lots of history, then?"

"Much." Thadred sighed.

"But then the empire came?" Sair's voice was almost hesitant.

"We can't take credit for everything," Thadred chuckled. "No, the city-states were weakened and fractured long before the Erymayans began colonizing this land." He gestured vaguely to the city below. "They had their own problems. According to legend, their last king killed every male in his own family to end rival claimants."

Thadred left out the part about the king having his brothers' wives raped by soldiers to cast doubt on the legitimacy of any children they might be carrying. He didn't think Sair would want to hear that.

"He ended up being stabbed to death by the head of his personal guards. Then Iandua and a few other Kelethian cities tried to institute democracy."

"What's that?" Sair took another sip of wine.

"It's where men with money and power convince common people that they have a say." Thadred swirled his wine glass. "Problem was, their senators told people what they wanted to hear to get re-elected, regardless of if those promises were realistic or wise." He scratched his beard. "They made a lot of bad decisions over time that added up. In the end, it all fell apart, and it was easy for Erymaya to annex them." Thadred shook his head. "There weren't even any battles. You could hardly call it *conquering* at all." He pointed to the outline of a massive structure near the center of the city. "That over there is the remains of their senate house, I think."

"We call it the amphitheater," said a familiar voice. "But yes, it is where the senate used to meet."

Thadred whirled around, cane raised on impulse.

It was Vespasia, her bouncy brown curls framing a ladylike smile. She wore a dress quite similar to Sair's, except hers was bright red and she had a shawl over it. "Forgive me." Vespasia dropped into a curtsy. "I didn't mean to startle you."

Thadred leaned against the balcony railing. "Good evening, Lady Vespasia." He glanced past her, but for now, only servants remained inside the dining room.

"My mother is preparing my brother," Vespasia said with a halfhearted laugh. "He spilled an inkwell on himself while copying letters."

Thadred's chest twisted at the word *brother*. He adjusted his grip on his wine. "Yes, well. Children will be children."

"How old is the count?" Sair asked, sounding perfectly polite.

"He turns nine this winter, my lady." Vespasia smiled sweetly.

"Do you like him?" Thadred was being rude and knew it as soon as he opened his mouth. He didn't take it back, though.

"Like him, my lord?"

"The count. Do you like him?" Thadred cocked his head to the side. "From what I understand, you're the eldest. You were heiress of this whole province until your brother was born. You're not just a little jealous?"

Vespasia flushed, eyes wide. Even if she was jealous, it would be rude to say it. That snot-nosed eight-year-old who spilled ink on himself was Vespasia's liege lord, technically.

"Thadred." Sair nudged him with her elbow. She cast him a

sharp look. "What are you doing?"

Thadred shrugged, taking another sip of wine. He might need a lot of it if he was going to get through this evening.

Vespasia drew a deep breath. "My mother should be here shortly."

"Excellent." Thadred straightened. He wondered how long this would take. Would they deny his relation this entire time? Could he stay in their house, under their roof, and not have his kinship acknowledged?

"On behalf of my brother, I would ask that you be seated." Vespasia gestured to the table that appeared just about ready. "Please. Do make yourselves comfortable."

"Wonderful." Thadred hooked Sair's arm and headed for the table.

The sorceress shot him a glare as if to say *behave*.

Thadred dipped his head in apology, fully intending to be civil for the rest of the evening.

That intention lasted until he was pulling out a chair for Sairydwen and an annoying, childish voice shrieked, "You're not allowed to sit before me!"

Thadred shot a look across the dining room to where a boy—presumably Count Flavius—had entered. The child held no resemblance to Vespasia or himself that Thadred could see. He was of average build in an embroidered coat. He had a red sash of office that was just a little too large. He wore a cap with an oversized feather that failed at making him look taller.

Sair tried to stand, embarrassed, but Thadred gripped her shoulder to keep her in place.

Holding eye contact with the child, Thadred smirked. "Then you shouldn't have taken so long." The knight leaned forward. "Slowpoke."

The child's eyes widened, anger flaring on his face. "I am *not* a slowpoke."

Thadred was feeling just petty enough to make the little boy angry. As a former little boy himself, he knew the most efficient ways to do it. "I'm not surprised. I'm sure that feather slowed you down. Fancy yourself a bird?"

The boy's mouth clamped in rage. "Mama!" He whirled to the woman behind him.

"Bet I can sit down before you!" Thadred dared the boy, reaching for his own chair.

"Cannot!" the boy shot back.

This really was too easy.

Thadred wasn't sure why he was getting satisfaction out of this, but it was delightful. "Best hurry." Thadred pulled back his chair.

Sure enough, the small count scrambled across the dining room.

The kid moved remarkably fast. Fast enough Thadred was worried.

He wove a quick spell in the air with *ka,* nothing too fancy, just enough to catch the boy's feathered cap. Sure enough, it knocked the hat off and the count stopped to grab it.

That instant's hesitation was all Thadred needed to get his bad leg and cane into his own seat.

"No!" the count cried in dismay, struggling to move his chair while servants rushed to help him. He scrambled into his seat at the head, whirling on Thadred. "Not fair!"

"You are the one who decided to stop for your hat, Count Flavius." Thadred sipped at his wine, studying the count over the rim. "I hardly think I am to blame." He wasn't sure the boy realized Thadred had used magic, but it didn't really matter.

"Mama!" the count whirled on his mother.

Finally, Thadred could avoid looking at her no longer.

Thadred wasn't sure what he had expected, but Dowager Countess Zeyna Serapio wasn't it. She was tall and must be where Thadred had gotten at least some of his height. Her arms were lean and toned, a bit surprising. She had a tan with freckles and her hair was bleached a mousy brown.

"Lord Thadred comes from the empire, Flavius," Zeyna said, looking squarely at her youngest son. She curtsied awkwardly to Thadred. "We owe him our respect."

Count Flavius sat back. It appeared they had cushions on his chair to prop him up.

"I don't like you," Count Flavius said, picking up a knife. He pointed it at Thadred.

The knight almost laughed. It was a marmalade knife with a dull edge, offering all the threat and intent of a real blade with none of the real danger.

The dowager was aghast. "Flavius!"

Thadred popped his cane up from under the table. The head hit the knife, knocking it out of the little count's hand.

Several footmen and Zeyna yelped. Sair jumped and Thadred's guard stepped forward then looked from right to left, not sure what to do.

Flavius clutched his hand, screaming. "You hit me!"

"No, I didn't." Thadred beckoned the boy closer. "Give me your hand and I'll show you what an actual hit feels like."

Flavius looked to his mother. "Mama!"

"Sit down, dowager," Thadred ordered.

"I'm leaving." Flavius had forgotten the supposed injury to his hand and tried to push his chair back.

Thadred jammed one foot behind the chair leg. "You're going to sit, and be a polite host, Count Flavius." He shot a look to the dowager. "Have a seat, countess. Lady Vespasia."

"Thadred." Sair shot him a glare.

"What?"

The sorceress grabbed his collar, pulling him over so she could whisper in his ear. "Why are you terrorizing them?"

"Flavius is the one who decided to be a terror." Thadred kept his foot jammed behind Flavius's chair as the boy howled in fury, trying to force his seat back.

"Flavius, please stop." The dowager sat beside her youngest son, patting his arm awkwardly. "That's enough, my baby. Shush."

Flavius, realizing he was stuck and his mother would not be coming to his rescue, broke down crying.

Thadred was unmoved. "Shall we start?" He smiled to the footmen around them.

Flavius made a squalling sound, pounding his fist on the table and rattling the plates.

Thadred smacked his cane across the table, making a loud crack. Several of the women yelped. Sair tugged Thadred's coat under the table.

The count jumped back, staring at Thadred in horror.

Thadred leveled the cane at the boy's nose. "Shut up and sit quietly, or we'll see if a year in the imperial barracks can straighten you out."

"You wouldn't!" Zeyna burst. "He's…he's just a child. And he has a delicate constitution."

Thadred cocked his head to his mother. "Looks fine to me. Younger boys than him serve as pages."

It would be wholly within Thadred's authority to have Flavius carted off to the mainland for a few years. Time spent being a small fish in a massive pond did most boys good. If it was up to Thadred, every nobleman's son would pay his dues scrubbing floors and polishing boots.

He looked back to Flavius. "If you want to be treated like a lord, I expect you to behave like one."

Flavius's eyes remained wide as his young mind was probably comprehending that someone was truly unimpressed by him. His little mouth tightened. Thadred waited for him to say something or make some retaliation, but the child looked away first.

"You are regent?" Thadred looked to the dowager.

"I am regent, yes." Dowager Zeyna took a shaky breath, hand trembling as she reached for her wine.

"Hmm." Thadred took in the scene as the servants set bowls of soup in front of them.

"I don't like fish soup," Flavius complained.

The servant reached back to remove the bowl, but a look from Thadred stopped him.

"Then you will sit there and look at it." Thadred had dealt with spoiled nobles back home, but he was at a point in his life where most people were more careful with him. He was the emperor's High Inquisitor, a sorcerer, a soldier, and a politician.

"Flavius, shush, darling. Just for dinner. Please." Zeyna patted Flavius's arm, but he yanked it away.

A doting, caring mother. That annoyed Thadred more than anything.

He glanced to Vespasia seated beside his mother. He noticed that Zeyna had not even addressed her so far.

The fish soup was warm and well-spiced. Nothing particularly impressive, but nothing too shabby, either.

"Thank you for your hospitality, Lady Vespasia," Thadred said. "I appreciate you greeting Lady Sairydwen and I while the rest of your family was busy today."

"Do not mention it, my lord." Vespasia avoided eye contact.

"And again, you were the first one to meet us here. Your courtesy is noted." Thadred set down his wine glass.

Vespasia cleared her throat with a demure little cough. "Thank you, sir."

Thadred should have a plan. But he didn't and he didn't see that it mattered. If the family were in league with the Kadra'han, no amount of charm would put them off their guard. If they were not in league with the Kadra'han, then they would still cooperate with him. They had to. He had the imperial signet, and he did have the power to take Flavius with him when they left.

"Dowager Countess," Sair began, trying to sound friendly. "It's a pleasure to meet you."

"This is Lady Sairydwen," Thadred said. "Veteran of the Witch War, advisor to Empress Amira, and emissary from the Istovari sorceresses."

Zeyna inclined her head with a smile that didn't quite meet her eyes. "A pleasure."

"You're a sorceress?" Vespasia sounded genuinely interested. "You can use magic?"

"I can." Sair looked to the man at her side. "Thadred can as well."

Vespasia's eyes widened. "But I thought—" She glanced to her mother.

"Magic passes along the mother's line? Well, usually yes." Thadred had already finished his soup and gone back to nursing his wine. "But it seems the goddess Eponine favored my father."

"That's how you have magic?" Vespasia asked the question cautiously.

"Yes. At least that's what she told me." Thadred said it casually, but he realized how it sounded.

"The goddess spoke to you?" Vespasia sounded just a little skeptical, which was fair.

"Yes," Thadred confirmed. "She spoke to a number of us that night. The Witch War was an exciting time. Anyway." The knight looked around the table.

"I've never met a sorceress before." Vespasia looked Sair over curiously. "Is it true women lead your people?"

"The Council of Mothers lead our clan, yes."

Vespasia's brows rose. "Fascinating."

"Among Istovari, brothers answer to their sisters." Thadred stared at Flavius as he said it.

"The empress, you know her?" Vespasia sounded genuinely interested.

"I consider Empress Amira my friend, yes." Sair gave her a slight smile.

Vespasia looked to her mother, then back to Sair. "What's she like?"

"Everything an empress should be," Sair answered. "Powerful, beautiful. Fiercely loyal to her husband."

"And the emperor?" Vespasia shot a glance to Thadred, but the question was for Sair.

"Emperor Daindreth is a good man. He wants what's best for his people." Sair smiled and this time it was genuine. "They are very happy together."

That last one was probably the least important thing as far as the empire was concerned, but Thadred agreed. His cousin was happy for maybe the first time in his life. And if anyone deserved to be happy, it was Dain.

Thadred leaned back as the servants cleared away the soup and replaced it with plates of roasted pheasant drizzled in blackberry sauce.

"I'm glad to hear it," Vespasia said. "My sister also seems to have a good arrangement." She looked down.

Sair's tone changed. She must have read something in Vespasia. "I wasn't married until I was nearing thirty," Sair said. "My poor mother was quite troubled by it."

Vespasia frowned at that. "You're married?"

"Was." Sair prodded at the roasted pheasant on her plate. "He left us a few years ago."

"Oh." Vespasia seemed genuinely surprised. "I am sorry."

"Thank you."

"We can't make anyone marry you," the count grumbled, jabbing at his own pheasant. "No one wants you now."

Vespasia glared at her little brother. "Not now, Flavius."

"Darling, that's not polite," Zeyna whispered, shooting a furtive glance to Thadred. "Not at dinner."

Thadred cocked one eyebrow, interested now. These people were trying to keep up appearances, trying to present a strong front of gentility and order, but it was fast crumbling. He couldn't imagine what might make Vespasia unmarriageable. She was the oldest daughter of a wealthy family, pretty enough, well-spoken, and clearly educated.

"You shouldn't have run off with the stable boy." Flavius waved his fork at his sister.

Thadred decided right then that Flavius would be in the imperial barracks for a year or until he learned to control his tongue—whichever came last.

"Flavius!" The dowager gasped, hand reaching for his mouth as if to close it. "Stop!"

"I don't see what the problem is," Thadred shrugged.

Back in the empire, noblewomen especially, were supposed to be untouched when they married. Most first-time brides were, but many were not. That group played pretend, their husbands didn't ask too many questions, and so long as all births were at least nine months after the wedding, everyone went along with it. Virgins were overrated in Thadred's experience anyway.

"If you need a husband, come to the court at Mynadra." Thadred allowed the servants to refill his wine, accepting his third cup. "No one will care."

Vespasia blanched at that.

"Lord Thadred, you overstep." The dowager had flushed red, trying to reassert control of the situation.

"Do I?" Thadred was a little amused. "Being a whore hardly stopped you from marrying well." He gestured vaguely to their surroundings, the gleaming tiles, the gilded frames around mirrors, and the small regiment of servants. "Why should it stop your daughter?"

"Excuse me." Vespasia shoved back her chair and fled.

Thadred paused with his wine halfway to his lips. As the young noblewoman disappeared, he realized he had said too much.

"Thadred!" Sair smacked his arm hard enough that it hurt this time.

"Ow." Thadred prepared an apology, but words fell short.

Sair stood, towering over him. She closed her eyes, opened her mouth, then shut it. She exhaled. "Good evening, Dowager Countess." Ignoring Flavius altogether, Sair went after Vespasia.

Thadred had gone too far.

Two of the guards broke off, following Sair as they were supposed to. Thadred watched to make sure.

"You are cruel," the dowager said, her voice a whimper. "You have no idea what that poor girl has been through. What we have all been through."

Thadred regretted what he had said about Vespasia, but Vespasia was no longer here. He tried to think of how to salvage the situation, but nothing came to mind. He had spiraled and they all hated him as he had known they would.

"I want to go," Flavius whined, trying to push his chair back. "Let me go!"

Thadred still had his foot wedged behind the leg of Flavius's chair. He didn't move it.

"Mama!"

Thadred looked back at the dowager. He jerked his head toward Flavius. "You let this little tyrant rule you all?"

"Flavius has been through much," the dowager said, glancing to her youngest as she said it. "He was with his father when it happened, and…well." Zeyna's shoulders trembled.

"Mama," Flavius whined, rocking from side to side. "I don't like this, Mama." When the little brat realized he couldn't force his way out, he sniffled. "I'm stuck." His lip began to tremble, and he whimpered piteously.

Thadred had never seen such a fake display of tears in his life, but Zeyna seemed convinced.

"It's alright, shush, darling." Zeyna reached for the child, crooning and comforting him.

Thadred blinked at her, hardly believing what he was seeing. Was Zeyna actually falling for this?

"So should I call you dowager?" Thadred cleared his throat. "Or Mother?"

Zeyna flinched at the word, like she had been struck. "I…"

"We've been skirting around it, but we might as well admit it." Thadred cocked his head to the side. "You know who I am. I know who you are. Now tell me what you would have me call you."

Zeyna kept one hand resting on the blubbering count, who had added snot and tears to his little act. "Dowager Countess is perfectly fine, thank you."

Excellent. Thadred didn't have to pretend their relationship meant anything. "Very well, Dowager Countess." He set his goblet down. In the back of his head, he knew he was being cruel. He knew he was acting entirely out of vindictiveness.

How often did a bastard son have the chance to wield this kind of power over his legitimate siblings? Rarely. Hardly ever, in fact.

If Thadred had been kept with Zeyna, he would have grown up in their shadows. He would have been shuffled to the side and forgotten.

But no. Zeyna had chosen to abandon him. She'd left him to become a knight, a Kadra'han, and now a sorcerer. Far from being forgettable and dismissed, Thadred was the emperor's High Inquisitor and one of the most powerful men in the empire.

Thadred had every intention of taking his siblings back to Mynadra. Flavius could use the discomfort and Thadred could have Vespasia married off in a few months to any man she wanted.

Zeyna shook her head as tears filled her eyes. "What do you want?"

Thadred didn't like women crying, but he wasn't about to be manipulated, either.

"What do you want!" Zeyna screamed, her voice cracking.

What did he want? Thadred considered it. He wasn't actually sure.

He didn't wish he'd been raised by his mother. Looking around him, that wouldn't have been a blessing. He didn't want her approval. He didn't want her affection. And yet…

"I don't know." Thadred cocked his head to the side. He knew he was being childish and petty, but a part of him just couldn't stop.

By the door, Brick looked on, mouth pressed into a hard line. He was disappointed.

Sair was, too, otherwise she wouldn't have left.

"I'm not a good man," Thadred said. "Effective, yes. Useful, most definitely." He exhaled a long breath. "But I'm not good. Not at all."

Zeyna looked to Flavius, who was still blubbering impressively.

Rhis never acted like this. Sair's son was younger than Flavius, but one would never know it. Rhis was mischievous, curious, boundless in energy, and always getting into trouble, but he was good at heart. So full of his own goodness, in fact, that he found it hard to understand badness in others.

Rhis was depending on Thadred. Rhis needed him to keep it together. Sair needed Thadred to keep it together.

But Thadred couldn't keep it together. This woman in front of him was the embodiment of everything he had always hated about himself.

"You're right to be afraid of me, I suppose," Thadred mused. "I am dangerous." He glanced to Flavius. "You should be *more* afraid of me, I think."

Thadred moved his foot from behind Flavius's chair.

The chair shot back, and Flavius scrambled free, rushing into his mother's arms.

"Shush, darling," Zeyna murmured, folding Flavius into her embrace. "It's alright. It's alright."

Thadred turned away, both disgusted and ashamed. "Good evening, Dowager." He rose from his seat at the table.

Brick fell into line behind him and his guards, too. No one spoke, and no one stopped him.

Thadred marched out into the hallway. He reached with *ka*, feeling for the telltale sources of life that would lead him to Sair.

He owed her an apology.

10

SAIR

Sair didn't know what had gotten into Thadred. That was a side of him she had never seen. He harbored resentment for his mother and jealousy toward his siblings, that much was clear.

The young count had behaved horridly, but Thadred's reaction hadn't been much better. Sair didn't even know what she would say when she saw Thadred again.

Lady Vespasia had rushed out of the room with tears in her eyes. Sair barely knew the girl, but she had been polite enough. She'd been kind and seemed the only one of the family willing to do the unpleasant things here. And Vespasia's mother had hardly done anything in the girl's defense. Someone had to.

Sair raced out into the hallway, catching a flash of red skirts around a corner. "Lady Vespasia!" she called, holding her own skirt in fistfuls as she ran. Her two guards came after her, their armor clanking as they followed.

The young noblewoman paused, about to head into a residential wing of the palace. "Lady Sairydwen." Her voice was strained, but still trying to be polite. "Forgive me. I lost my appetite at supper. You must excuse me."

Sair caught up with her beside a portrait of a grand elderly couple in a garden setting. "Please forgive your brother." She caught Lady Vespasia's hand. "He will apologize to you, I know it." And Sair fully believed that. She might not even have to tell him to do it.

Lady Vespasia let off a little laugh through her tears. "You mean Lord Thadred."

Sair swallowed. "Forgive me." She glanced to the side.

"It's alright." Lady Vespasia nodded, daubing at her nose with a kerchief. "Someone might as well say it. Lord Thadred is my illegitimate older brother. Yes?"

Sair nodded. "Everyone…it's common knowledge back on the mainland. It never occurred to me you wouldn't know."

"I did." Lady Vespasia forced a smile. "As of about a year ago." She shook her head. "The empress said something when she was here, and I found out. Flavius and the other two girls might know by now, but I'm not sure. A whole brother we never knew about. And a quite a famous one at that."

"He's a good man," Sair said. "I promise he's a good man, he's just…" She tried to think of how to explain it. "He's an imperfect man. And sometimes his sharp edges cut deep."

"You love him?"

Sair felt her chest clench at the words. "Yes," she confessed. "I'm afraid I do." She could only hope the soldiers wouldn't repeat her words back to Thadred, though he might already know.

For some reason, Vespasia laughed at that. "I think I understand." She glanced around the deserted hallway. "Would you like to talk?"

Sair looked to her guards.

The one on the left nodded to her. "The whole manor is secure, my lady."

"The verandah is over here. Come." Vespasia beckoned.

There was a significant age gap between Sair and Vespasia, but the other woman seemed ready to take her into confidence. Perhaps she was just that curious about her brother or sorceresses or both.

Vespasia led Sair through a door that had been left open, the entrance blocked only by a thin veil to allow better airflow. The garden outside was in bloom with peonies rising in fluffy hedges. The sun was still out, casting an amber glow over the garden.

Vespasia took Sair to a metal bench beneath the porch, one of many porches outside this house. She folded her hands in her lap, still holding her kerchief.

"What is it you want to talk about, Lady Vespasia?"

Vespasia inhaled sharply. "I confess I hardly know. I've just been so alone since…the Witch War, you called it?"

Sair nodded, thinking she understood. "That's what most of us call it."

"I have barely seen anyone outside my own family since. Everyone knows it started with the empress. Everyone knows we hosted her. The other families in the city we used to socialize with have avoided us. And then my middle sister married and the youngest left for a convent and that left me."

"With your mother and Flavius."

"We could be considered traitors. At least that's what my mother fears."

Sair began to see things from this family's perspective and several things abruptly made sense. "You thought Thadred and I were sent to make inquiries into your family?"

Vespasia nodded. "When we heard that an imperial ship with the High Inquisitor was here, we assumed it was to deal with us." She cast a sidelong glance to Sair. "But that's not why you're here. Is it?"

Sair smiled, not sure it was safe to divulge the whole truth.

"I see." Vespasia seemed to understand. "You finding out what a mess we are was incidental."

Sair shrugged, not able to tell the whole truth just yet. "What happened a year ago? With the empress?" Sair was reminded of her conversation with Thadred.

Vesha had come here, to Iandua. Now one of her most loyal subjects had also come here. It might be coincidence, but it probably wasn't.

"A great deal," Vespasia said. "The empress arrived much as you did. No warning, no messages. She was just here one day." Vespasia frowned. "I am not sure what's useful."

"Tell me." Sair rested her hand on Vespasia's arm.

The girl seemed willing to cooperate and Sair would take as

much advantage of that as she could.

"She seemed…well, a lot like Lord Thadred. Angry."

Sair thought back to just what had been happening to Vesha at that time. The late empress had just suffered a crushing defeat and had been desperate. She probably had the greatest reasons to be on edge of anyone.

"She got upset with my mother and mentioned him."

Sair looked over the other woman. Vespasia had said she was in her mid-twenties and had just a year ago found out she had an older brother?

"My mother went out with the empress into the city. My mother came back, saying the empress had stayed. She just *disappeared.*" Vespasia shook her head. "For days, we heard nothing. I thought perhaps she had left, but her servants remained. And then those *things* came."

"The cythraul," Sair said.

Vespasia nodded, studying her hands. "People changed. Their eyes glowed red and they became stronger. Crueler, too." Vespasia shuddered. "Most the servants ran. I don't blame them. My father was lost. I found out later he became one of them." Vespasia hesitated, as if struggling with herself. "I had a…Galen. His name was Galen, and he was a stable hand."

Sair felt empathy growing as she recognized the way Vespasia said his name. "I'm sorry."

Vespasia scrubbed at her eyes. "He took me and my sisters into the country. To his home village two-days' walk north. We thought we'd be safe there. His grandfather was upset that he brought three more mouths to feed, but we were desperate. I did my best to earn my keep and my sisters did, too." A fresh flow of tears fell and Vespasia covered her face with her hands. "I was happy. It sounds awful to say it. The city had burned, I had no idea what had become of our parents, or our little brother, but I…"

Sair rested a hand on Vespasia's back. She felt that human urge to say something, but after losing her husband, she'd found nothing people said ever made it better. Quite the opposite.

Vespasia recovered herself enough to keep going. "We were

able to pretend. Just for a few weeks, we were able to pretend that I was simply a shepherdess, and we would be able to spend the rest of our lives together. We made love in a meadow at sunset and bathed together in the brook and…I was never so happy."

Sair put her arm around the younger woman.

"The soldiers eventually came for us. Men sent by my mother. I tried to explain, but they accused Galen of kidnapping us. I tried to say he'd saved us. I tried." Vespasia's shoulders shook as she leaned against Sair. "They wouldn't listen to me. They hanged him." Vespasia broke down into sobs.

None of this would help Sair find her son, most likely, but compassion got the best of her. She held onto Vespasia, stroking the other girl's head. She doubted that Vespasia's own mother had done this.

"It was my fault," Vespasia gasped between choking breaths. "All my fault. If I hadn't asked him to take us to his village—"

"No," Sair said. "It's not your fault, child. I promise."

Vespasia whimpered, doubled over in Sair's embrace.

They stayed like that for some minutes.

"We've all made mistakes, Lady Vespasia," she said quietly.

"I've ruined my life," Vespasia whimpered. "That's what my mother says."

From what Sair knew of the dowager's own life, that sounded supremely hypocritical. But the strictest and most judgmental people always had the most shame, didn't they?

"But what I did cost Galen his life, so maybe I deserve to be ruined."

Sair shook her head gently. "You did the best you could. It was soldiers who killed Galen, not you."

Vespasa buried her face in her hands, still doubled over. "I'm sorry. I'm so sorry, I just…need a moment."

"Take your time." Sair sat patiently while Vespasia recollected herself.

It must be a terrible thing—to have the guilt of your first love's blood on your hands. Yet the dowager was more worried about her daughter's reputation. Not the boy's life, not even her daughter's grief.

Vespasia swallowed, pulling a handkerchief from her pocket.

"Sair?" A familiar voice called from the hallway with just a hint of sheepishness. "Sair?"

"Ah." Sair had been expecting that voice at any moment. "Here comes Thadred to apologize." If it turned out he wasn't here to apologize, she planned to make him apologize.

Vespasia sat up, scrubbing the tears from her face. "He seemed rather angry."

"He probably was," Sair admitted. "But he will get over it."

"Sair." Thadred pushed aside the curtains onto the porch, his own pair of guards in tow. He spotted Sair with Vespasia and drew up short. He took a deep breath. "Forgive me, Lady Vespasia. I did not mean to upset you this much. Or at all. I was careless with my words, I shouldn't have said what I did, and I apologize. It will not happen again."

Vespasia cleared her throat. "Thank you, Lord Thadred."

"Sair…" Thadred adjusted his grip on his cane before he rubbed the back of his neck. "I'm sorry."

Sair extended a hand to him. "Come join us." He'd apologized without her having to say anything. Yes, there was definitely a decent man in there somewhere.

Thadred bowed his head, adjusting his grip on his cane. He shuffled to sit beside her, keeping a breath of space between them, facing straight ahead so he didn't have to look at Vespasia.

Sair hooked her arm through his. "Your sister tells me that the former empress disappeared into the city for several days when she was here."

Thadred's head snapped around. "What's that?"

Vespasia swallowed, looking to Sair.

The sorceress nodded, encouraging. She imagined Vespasia didn't want to discuss the other topics with Thadred.

"Yes," Vespasia said. "I can ask my mother's servants where exactly. But the empress—former empress—went to a brothel in the city and we didn't hear from her for days."

Thadred's brows rose. "That's…surprising."

There were rumors, of course. Rumors that Vesha had

orgiastic parties and sometimes bedded dozens of men at once. But those sorts of rumors always surrounded women in power. This was the first time Sair had heard anything concrete on the matter, which made it seem likely this wasn't about the brothel at all.

"The next thing we knew, the monsters came." Vespasia's voice hitched.

"Can you have the location of the brothel for us tomorrow morning?" Thadred glanced to Sair as he asked it.

Vespasia's cheeks flushed. "I can."

"Tell them I asked, if it helps," Thadred said. "No one will be shocked I'm asking after a brothel." As soon as he spoke, Thadred cleared his throat again and turned away.

Silence descended on their small trio. The guards' armor clinked softly at their backs.

They were an odd bunch—all of them outcasts in their odd little ways. Vespasia had made an indiscretion that might affect her life for a time, though Sair doubted it was as serious as she seemed to think. If Vespasia did come to the continent, no one would care.

Thadred had been born a bastard. He'd had no control over that, yet it would define his life. Oddly, if he had been a woman, he could have married well and earned respectability that way, but as a man, the world expected him to make his own way, forever trying to outrun his parents' shame.

And Sair…well. Sair was an Istovari of no great power. She had no land, no titles, no fortune to her name. She might be respectable in the empire now, thanks to Amira, but she was still a nobody.

Thadred looked to Sair in the corner of her eye, a silent question in his face. He wanted to know if he was forgiven.

Sair squeezed his arm. Forgiving Thadred was easy for her. She wasn't sure about his family.

"It has been a long day," Sair said. "I think it's best if we retire now."

Thadred nodded quickly, probably glad someone else had thought of the excuse.

Sair stood first and Thadred used her arm to help him stand.

Lady Vespasia stood and dropped into a shallow curtsy. "I wish you good evening."

The sun was still setting, bathing the garden in an amber glow. It was probably still early in terms of most people, but Sair didn't think it was a good idea for them to stay out and about tonight.

Thadred cleared his throat and bowed his head. "I apologize again, Lady Vespasia. I shouldn't have said what I did."

Lady Vespasia offered a smile that looked forced to Sair. "Think nothing of it."

Thadred let off a sigh that ended in a groan. "Now I will think about nothing but that for the rest of tonight." He shot another sideways glance to Sair. "I will find a way to make this up to you. I promise."

Lady Vespasia's brow wrinkled. "That's…quite kind, sir."

"I don't know how I'll do it just yet," Thadred admitted. "But I will."

Vespasia looked away. In that moment, Sair saw the slight resemblance between them. There was something in the jawline and the mouth, and the way their eyes slid sideways. Vespasia was a curvier, softer echo of her brother, even if they only shared one parent. "Thank you, sir."

Sair thought it best to end this audience while the siblings were on good terms. "Thadred, I'm tired. Escort me to my rooms?"

Thadred nodded. "Yes, of course."

They said their goodbyes and good evenings to Vespasia. It felt abrupt to leave like this, but it still seemed best.

The sun had slipped below the horizon, so they had to find their way by lamplight as they ventured back into the mansion, their guards following after them. Guards gossiped as much as anyone, so the details of this encounter would probably be shared before too long.

"I know I handled that badly." Thadred looked straight ahead, leaning on his cane with every other step.

"You did," Sair agreed, keeping her tone mild. "You'll do

better next time?"

"Yes."

"Good."

Thadred let off a long exhale. "I don't understand why I care so much. She's just some noble. Plenty of them hate me and I've never been bothered by it. But her…"

They weren't talking about Vespasia, Sair realized. "She's your mother," Sair said quietly. "It's alright."

"Why should that make a difference? I'm nearly thirty. She left me as soon as she could." Thadred made an exasperated sound. "Couldn't wait to leave me behind."

"You don't know that." Sair tried to keep her voice steady. "You don't know what she felt."

Thadred made an incoherent grumbling noise.

"Your mother was a girl caught in the middle of a huge scandal. Her sister was being courted by the emperor and the whole empire would have been sniggering about it. I don't think we can judge her for leaving you with your aunt."

"She could have kept me."

"Would that have been best for you?" Sair gestured vaguely behind her. "Would you be better off now if she had? If you'd grown up in this house? A bastard stepchild instead of a sorcerer and a knight?"

Thadred grimaced. He might have a grudge against his mother, but he was pragmatic enough to see the truth.

"Your mother did the best thing she could do for you," Sair said. "I don't know her reasoning. I don't know for sure why she kept you secret from your siblings. But whatever the case, you have a good life now and you wouldn't be here at all if not for her."

Thadred glared at the ceiling. Sair was sure he would argue, but he didn't. He remained silent as they continued down the hallway, past paintings of strangers in sumptuous gowns and luxurious robes. There were even a few marble busts of stern men and ethereal women, no doubt idealized by the artists' hands.

"You wouldn't give up your son," Thadred said. The words

were fierce, almost accusatory. It wasn't a question.

"No." Sair didn't have to think about it. Her heart ached at the thought. "But I've never been in her position. And I won't condemn another woman for doing the best she could." Sair tried to focus on her breathing. Thoughts of her son, of where he might be right now, threatened to overwhelm her. She forced them down, reminding herself there was nothing she could do right now.

Thadred tapped his cane against the ground. "I suppose it doesn't matter. I'm not the dowager's judge."

Sair didn't think Thadred and his mother would ever be close. But maybe someday they could be civil. Perhaps Thadred might one day even be friends with Vespasia. There seemed to be the most hope there.

"You're better than all of us, my dear." The endearment slipped out Thadred's lips like a habit, as if he had called her that a thousand times before. "I should take you as my moral advisor everywhere I go." Thadred snorted. "Between you and Brick, you might be able to convince the empire I'm a decent man."

The thought of going everywhere with Thadred, of staying with him, brought to mind a host of images. Some of them were innocent. Most were not.

They reached their designated wing of the mansion and Thadred dismissed the guards. There were already men posted to patrol the outside and two more stationed at the wing's entrance.

Thadred insisted on having them guarded, but he only had so many men. He had to make sure the ones he had were rested.

"Good night, Lord Thadred," Sair said. "I hope to see you early in the morning."

"Let me show you to your room," Thadred said.

It was just a few doors down the hall from his, but Sair relented. They didn't touch as they walked this time, but Sair was glad to have him close.

They stopped just outside.

"Good night," Sair said for the second time. She reached for the handle of the door.

"Good night." Thadred didn't bow or move to leave.

"We'll meet at first light?"

Thadred nodded. "If not before. Hopefully, Vespasia can find that location for us." He rested his cane against the wall, freeing both hands to take both of hers. "We'll find him," he whispered. "I swear to you."

Sair tried not to let the tears come. She kept them under control fairly well these days, but they still threatened from time to time. "I know," she whispered back.

Thadred looked into her face earnestly. Though there was a grating to his voice, as if it was hard for him, there was no sign of his earlier sardonicism. "I promise to behave if only for you. For Rhis."

Sair forced her mouth to shape a smile. "I appreciate it."

Thadred cradled her cheek in his hand. "Don't cry, Sair." He brushed his thumb across her cheek, wiping away a tear she hadn't noticed.

Sair swallowed a lump in her throat. "I believe you." And she meant it. She had faith in Thadred that he would rescue her son or die trying. And that was where the worm of fear wiggled its way in.

The Kadra'han had no qualms about killing. They'd kill Thadred and her without a second thought. Then Rhis would be left to their mercy, perhaps never knowing how far they had come for him, how hard they had tried.

Sair hadn't wept in days, but the fear and the talk of giving up sons had chipped away at her. It was always easier to focus on other people's problems than her own and now that the evening's emergencies were past, Sair was left with her own fears once again.

"Dearest." Thadred pulled her against him, wrapping his arms around her and folding her against his chest.

Sair had lost her parents, her sister-in-law, her niece, her husband, and her brother all in less than a decade. She had no one left except her son and now he had been taken, too.

Sometimes she felt like a tree that had been hacked down to the stump and forced to grow back from the roots over and over. She might survive, but her heart had become misshapen, full of knobs, knots, and tangles.

And then there was Thadred.

He was broken, too. Like her, he'd lost people over and over, except nearly all of them had chosen to leave him. Now she wondered if that was what had drawn her to him, unknowingly.

Thadred was imperfect. Incredibly so. He had a past that would have made her mother gasp in horror and rough edges that sometimes cut before he realized it. He could be charming, devilishly so, but Sair was starting to realize that the more he trusted a person, the less charm he slathered onto his words.

But he kept his word. He was loyal and brave.

Thadred held her, stroking her hair. He kissed the top of her head. It was a chaste kiss, so soft she barely felt it.

Sair wept quietly against his chest. She'd been on her own for so long, the center of her son's world and the entire weight of it on her shoulders.

And now here was Thadred, self-proclaimed scoundrel, the first person to share the burden. Even after she had shunned him.

She held onto him, the one sure thing in the world right now. Thadred slid his arm around her, but he must have forgotten her dress didn't have a proper back.

His hand touched her bare skin. Shivers of warmth rippled through Sair and her fingers seemed to clench the back of his jacket of their own accord.

Thadred went rigid. "Sair." His arms tightened around her.

Sair's heart pounded as she looked up to him. His gaze smoldered, pupils dilating in the lamplight. He stared at her with surprising softness and something akin to fear, like he was afraid of what might come next.

Sair rested her hand on his chest, feeling his *ka* and how it thrummed and sparked through his body. His magic rippled and skipped, responding to his emotions.

Sair pulled at his power, not directly from him, but at the stray wisps that shimmered off him. She traced a line from his collarbone down his sternum, channeling a harmless spell. A normal man wouldn't have felt anything, but Thadred was a sorcerer, he would feel the magic tingling warmth through his skin.

Thadred shuddered, head bowing over her. "Damn it, Sair. What are we doing?" His voice was low, choked with…something.

Thadred leaned down slowly, almost hesitantly. He stopped, mouth barely a hair's breadth from hers. He hovered there for what felt like forever.

Sair's heart pounded in her ears. What she wanted warred with the fear of what she knew would happen if she closed that distance. It would change things. She knew it would, even if she wasn't sure exactly how. If they did this, there would be no going back.

Thadred seemed to know it, too. He shifted, pulling away. "You don't have to."

"I want to." Sair caught his face in her hands. "Please." She wasn't even sure what she was asking, but her voice came out in a broken whimper. "Thadred."

He kissed her hard and deep, his tongue sweeping into her mouth like he couldn't possibly taste enough of her. His hands gripped her waist, gripping tight as he pulled her body flush against his.

Thadred kissed her fiercely, stealing her breath. He kissed without propriety, without restraint. He kissed her like he'd never wanted anything more in his whole life.

His mouth broke away from hers and he kissed her cheek, her jaw, moving down the side of her neck. His teeth brushed her skin as he nipped her, just enough that she felt it.

Sair gasped and clung to him, stroking the back of his neck, his shoulders, his chest. She gripped his bicep, barely able to encircle his arm halfway. His muscles bunched and flexed under her hands.

"Mmm." Sair tilted her head back to give him better access. She gasped as he sucked lightly on her shoulder, just where it joined her neck.

They were still in the hallway, where anyone could come

across them. That should have given her pause, but she couldn't seem to care about anything but the sensation of Thadred's lips on her skin.

"Tell me to stop," he whispered, voice coming out ragged and hoarse.

"I don't want to." Her shaky voice betrayed how her own heart skipped and throbbed.

Thadred brushed her wrist and *ka* tingled warm and silky where they touched. "Is this how you did it?" He traced his fingers up her bare arm, sending shivers and sparks of *ka* through her skin. It was just the lightest flutter of magic, something only another magic wielder would feel, but it rippled through her in delightful shivers.

Sair shuddered. "You're a fast learner."

Thadred grinned at her, devilish and smug. "So I've been told." He stroked down her back, sending power in sparks through her whole body. "Do you like this?"

Sair gasped, choking back a moan. "Yes." Sair realized she had made a mistake. He was already gorgeous, seductive, and irresistible, but now—

He wrapped one arm around her, pulling her flush against him. "What else do you like?" He kissed the top of her ear, his tongue stroking the outer shell. "Do you like it when I touch these?"

One finger traced the outline of her breast. Clothing was a small barrier to magic. Thadred sent tendrils of warm power into her breast, his finger tracing a delicate spiral down to her nipple.

"Thadred," Sair moaned. She felt it through her whole body, waves of heat that were only partly from his magic. "Thadred, please."

"Do you want me to stop?" His voice held a dare, a challenge. His hand slowed, but still threaded magic into her, stroking the curve of her breast.

"No," Sair gasped. She buried her face against his shoulder, trying not to scream. "More. I need more." She wanted to get him on the other side of the door and lock it so they could get out of these clothes. Sair wanted his hands on her bare skin and to feel him inside her when she climaxed. She reached for the door handle, but Thadred stopped her, pressing her back against the door.

"More, you said?" His devilish grin widened, showing that he was willfully misunderstanding her.

"Thadred, please." Sair didn't know what would happen if he kept dragging this out, but she didn't think she could last much longer.

"I will give you more," Thadred whispered against her ear, and it sounded like a threat.

He began stroking her other breast the same way, spirals and sparks of magic shivering through her—pleasure so intense it was almost pain. Sair's back arched and she gripped his arms, sure her nails would leave marks.

Heat pounded between her legs as he kept on playing with her breasts, like he was trying to see how much she could take. "Thadred," she whimpered. "Please!"

Thadred kissed her temple. "Already screaming for me, darling?" But his hands stilled on her, resting on her sides. He breathed deeply of the scent of her hair, nuzzling her neck. "Tell me what you want," he whispered, brushing back her hair.

"You," Sair gasped. "I want you." She wanted him so badly she thought she might weep again.

"I can give you that." Thadred kissed her neck, reaching past her for the door handle. He didn't turn it. His whole body stiffened and the playful smile left his face.

A long heartbeat passed.

Thadred dropped his hand from the door. He looked back to her and swallowed. "Someone is inside."

Crushing disappointment, anger, and frustration all marched through Sair's mind before she settled on the correct emotions of surprise and alarm. "It's not Brick?"

Thadred shook his head. "There's no reason for it. There shouldn't be any servants here, either."

"My lord?" called a hesitant voice from behind. "I heard Lady Sairydwen cry out. Is everything well?"

There was Brick, standing in the hall in his formal livery. He took in their disheveled hair and flushed faces without the slightest hint he knew what he'd interrupted.

Thadred looked back to Sair. He swallowed. "We should call the guards."

11

THADRED

Thadred was oddly relieved at the same time he was infuriated. Bedding Sair right now was a horrible idea and one he apparently lacked the self-restraint to avoid.

He signaled to Brick to fetch the guards, pulling Sair away from the door.

She came to his side, not looking at him. Her cheeks were tinged red, her neck flushed and marked where he'd nipped her skin. The need to take her rattled through him, but he knew better than to sleep with her while her son's life depended on him. Truly, he did. It would be unfair. He wanted Sair to lie with him because she wanted to, not any other reason.

He knew better, but he still wanted her. She was unlike anyone he had ever entertained before and something about being desired by an objectively decent woman was exciting. She was wise, experienced, and a good person. If she wanted him, then there must be something about him worth wanting, right?

But he could sort that out later.

Right now, there were several human-sized shapes of *ka* in Sair's bedchamber, and he had no way to account for it. How had they gotten past the guards?

"Brick, fetch the—"

A pulse of *ka* jolted through the air. All the lamps went out at once like a single snuffed candle.

"Shit." Thadred grabbed Sair by the arm and shoved her farther behind him, then drew the sword from his cane.

It was dark, but he could sense the figures beyond the door moving toward them. *Ka* swirled around them, too much to be just normal. These were sorcerers. Worse, he could sense the bands of their curses around their necks.

Kadra'han. Delightful.

At Thadred's back, he could feel Sair drawing magic to herself. Brick was close, but he could only sense the valet by his *ka*.

"Sir?" Brick called.

"Kadra'han," Thadred warned.

"What should I do, sir?" The valet's voice shook a little.

"Alert the rest of the men like I said. Three Kadra'han attacking." Scrambling came from the dark and Thadred sensed the shape of his valet fleeing down the hallway. "Sair?"

"I'm not leaving." Sair sounded almost aggressive, like she was ready to fight him along with the rest of the rogue Kadra'han.

"You—" Thadred had wanted to say that she would be in danger. His magic was stronger, he had a weapon, and the Kadra'han were most likely here for him. But he didn't get the chance to argue.

Sair was already weaving magic. He saw the golden lines from her threading across the doorway in a mesh of just a few threads at head and shoulder height.

The door smashed open and three figures leapt out—or tried to leap. The first one hit Sair's web of *ka* across the door and let off a cry. The mesh wrapped around him like a trussed bird and he went down.

"You're welcome," Sair muttered from behind Thadred.

The fallen man struggled against the spell, blocking the way for the two men behind him. One of the Kadra'han's arms moved, throwing into the dark. Something thudded farther down the hall, probably a knife thrown after Brick.

Thadred didn't hear a scream, so he hoped that knife had missed.

One of the Kadra'han cocked an arm again. Thadred grabbed Sair and jerked her down. A thud hit the wall behind them as a knife buried in the wood.

"Missed!" Thadred yelled.

Sair grabbed something off the wall, and it smashed into the advancing Kadra'han. That had been a reasonable action, but now they'd be fighting on broken glass. Not the most stable footing.

The Kadra'han barely slowed, coming closer.

Thadred and Sair faced down two Kelamora Kadra'han. Soon to be three since the one on the floor was almost free of Sair's spell.

Thadred lunged to meet the first one, jabbing his sword in the dark. The Kadra'han hadn't expected it and Thadred's sword hit something solid.

The man yelped and jumped back, *ka* leaking down his arm. Thadred had struck his shoulder, and he was bleeding, but not too badly.

"Ha!" Thadred sneered.

"You are arrogant," growled a gravelly, harsh voice with a foreign accent Thadred couldn't place right away. "It's going to be your downfall."

Thadred didn't reply. He grabbed something small off the wall—it felt like another mirror—and hurled it down the hallway. It crashed in the dark.

As Thadred had hoped, the assassins leapt, facing that direction. Thadred used the distraction to charge again, slashing for what he thought should be the other Kadra'han's neck.

The man skirted back even as the second circled around them. Thadred withdrew, pivoting to lash out at that man. The second assassin ducked.

Screaming echoed through the mansion. Were more Kadra'han attacking, or was that just the natural chaos and confusion caused by the darkness?

Another Kadra'han dashed for Thadred. He twisted around, blocking the attack, swinging his sword.

The Kadra'han hovered back. Even if they could sense *ka,*

his sword wasn't made of living material. They couldn't see his sword any more than he could see their weapons, but if he had to guess, he was the better armed.

"What's wrong?" Thadred smirked into the dark, facing down all three Kadra'han in front of him. "Scared that mine's bigger than yours?"

The Kadra'han didn't respond.

The newly freed Kadra'han hurled something and Thadred ducked, hearing the knife hit the wall at their backs again. He should probably stop talking. That only helped his enemies take aim.

Sair was close at his back, not touching, but her magic frothed now as she drew power to herself in great gulps. He had been told many times that her power was to his what a thread was to a rope and that had been true once, but Sair had spent a lifetime practicing with that thread—and she was getting stronger lately.

A single whisp of *ka* struck out from her and the Kadra'han jumped as it connected with them. It didn't appear to do much, but it was enough to unsettle them. Sometimes, that was all it took.

Thadred jabbed his sword, catching something fleshy on the end. One of the Kadra'han growled in response, but instead of flying back, this one charged straight for Thadred.

The crazy son of bitch barreled straight into the knight, knocking Thadred over even as his sword speared the man's shoulder.

Roaring in pain and fury, the Kadra'han smashed Thadred against the wall. Tiles cracked and paintings crashed to the floor. Thadred grabbed the front of the man's leather jerkin, surprised by how bulky this one was. With his sword stuck in the Kadra'han's shoulder, he had to resort to fists.

Thadred preferred to avoid grappling since he had only one good leg, but this Kadra'han had only one good arm.

Sair screamed in the dark.

"Sair!" Panic rose in Thadred's chest.

Thadred slammed his fist toward the *ka* shape in front of

him. His knuckles connected, shooting pain up his arm even as his opponent's head jerked back.

Thadred anchored himself against the wall for balance and thrust out, both palms striking the man's shoulders, forcing the other man back.

"Thadred!"

Then he became aware of Sair screaming. The Kadra'han had reached her. In the dark, his eyes had adjusted and he could make out her shape along with the outline of *ka*. One of the Kadra'han grappled with her, trying to catch hold of her. Sair fought back with spells, far better versed than they were.

Her magic snapped out, but like with any weapon, she had to aim. The Kadra'han could see her spells and dodged with surprising speed.

The wounded Kadra'han staggered back toward Thadred, blocking his path to Sair. Something gleamed as the man drew a long knife.

A crash like a thousand vases breaking boomed in Thadred's ears. The door to Sair's room screeched open, ripped off its hinges. A massive black shape barreled through and a keening, blood-curdling scream rent the air. White eyes flashed in the darkness and pale teeth sparked in the light of the stars through the windows.

The Kadra'han heading for Thadred whirled around in time to have the shadow chomp down on his sword arm. The man yelled as he was ripped off his feet and slammed into the ground. The Kadra'han cried out, struggling in the dark.

Hooves pounded and flesh squished. Tile cracked when the pony missed and struck the floor.

Lleuad was here. Thadred had no idea how.

One of the Kadra'han tried to get behind the little black horse, drawing his weapon.

"Lleuad!" Thadred shouted. "Watch out!"

Whether Lleuad had heard his warning or not, the next moment, the second man was airborne. A kick from Lleuad's back hooves hit with a meaty thud and the assassin launched into the air, disappearing back into Sair's room.

Something ripped and tore in the dark. *Ka* splattered in all directions—blood.

Lleuad's dark hulk spun around to face the remaining man. The kelpie stood beside Thadred, possessive and protective.

Fear spiked through Thadred. Lleuad had just saved his life, but he didn't know who the horse might consider a threat. In this state, breath heaving and the blood of a dead man on his muzzle, might he think everyone was an enemy? Would he hurt Sair?

The Kadra'han had gotten close to her, within striking distance.

Glass slid underfoot as Thadred tried to reach her. "Sair!"

"Thadred."

"Kelpie," a gravelly voice gasped. "The kelpie knight."

Voices came from down the hall. Torches flared and the tramp of boots was coming.

Light flooded into the room as soldiers came charging with torches and swords drawn. The kelpie in stark silhouette, tail lashing and ears pinned. Lleuad was spoiling for another fight.

Thadred saw Sair turn, stepping to the side, away from the Kadra'han and toward the wall.

The Kadra'han dove for Sair, not with his weapon, but grabbing for her arm.

Sair ran, heading straight for the left of the kelpie.

Lleuad made that keening, eerie shriek.

"No!" Thadred yelled.

The Kadra'han dove after Sair as Lleuad's ears pinned back, flat against his skull. The kelpie charged.

Sair ran straight for him.

The kelpie swooped for her, then swerved at the last moment. The Kadra'han ran face-first into the open maw of the waterhorse.

Lleuad smacked the man down. Bones crunched and the man screamed. The kelpie was on top of him the next moment, smashing hooves into his chest, face, head, and ribcage, over and over.

"Thadred!" Sair crashed into him, broken glass crunching

under her feet. "Are you alright?"

Thadred grabbed her arm. "Sair!" He groaned, pain beginning to throb through him. "Are you alright?" He'd been sure he was about to see her beaten to death by his kelpie.

The horse stood over his latest kill, kicking and pawing at the corpse as if to see if he could make it move again.

"I'm fine," Sair assured him. "Are *you* alright?"

Torches flooded into the space as the soldiers took in the scene. They advanced and Lleuad squealed, stomping. The kelpie pinned his ears again.

"Stay back!" Thadred yelled.

The men stopped. At his voice, Lleuad's ears twitched.

"Come here, boy." Thadred limped toward the kelpie, holding Sair's hand.

Lleuad faced down the soldiers for just a moment too long. Thadred feared the little horse might try attacking the men after all. The kelpie was intelligent, but definitely not human.

Then the horse snorted, backing up one step, then another.

"My lord?" One of the armored men called out.

Thadred couldn't recognize them in the dark with their visors down. "Search the grounds," Thadred ordered. "And search the other rooms. See if there are any more assassins. One of them fled." He had been distracted, but he no longer sensed the man who had been launched back into Sair's room. Kicks from a horse could be deadly, in theory, but that Kadra'han must have gotten lucky. "Find him."

The men rushed to obey.

Thadred glared at the mutilated corpse of the man who still had Thadred's cane sword embedded in his shoulder. The knight pulled it free, glad to see Lleuad hadn't bent it while smashing the dead man against the floor.

Lleuad nosed at Thadred's sleeve. He chuffed, mouthing at Thadred's shoulder. It was just lips, no teeth. Lleuad sometimes did that when he was nervous or just fretting over Thadred.

"Easy." Thadred touched the kelpie's nose and the animal winced. Thadred peered closer.

The kelpie's coat gleamed, not just from blood, but from bits of broken glass embedded in his head, neck, and shoulders. Lleuad had crashed through one of the windows to come rescue them.

Thadred figured the stable hands here hadn't known about his door-blocking technique and the horse had been able to escape. Lleuad must have heard the commotion and come to protect his rider.

"He's covered in cuts," Sair gasped.

Lleuad's tail swished as he stood beside them. It appeared the Kadra'han hadn't been able to do much harm to him, none actually. There was still plenty of broken glass in the stallion's skin.

One of the guards came jogging down the hall toward them.

Lleuad stomped, ears pinned in warning.

"Stay back," Thadred ordered, raising a hand. "Where's Brick?"

"Here, sir!" The valet called from the end of the hallway. "Are you well? Lady Sairydwen?"

"Fine." Thadred leaned against Lleuad's shoulder. He had no real injuries, but his hip ached, protesting at the abuse of the past few minutes. Thadred looked to Sair. "Are you sure you're not hurt?"

He sensed dark pools of *ka* on her arms and shoulders, bruises, most likely. Her skirt was torn, and hair mussed, but she appeared fine otherwise.

"Yes," she said, voice small. "I...don't think they wanted to kill me."

Thadred touched her arm. Whatever these rogue Kadra'han wanted with her, they would have to go through him and Lleuad first.

"My lord?" Brick approached, lantern in hand. "Shall I fetch some ham, sir?"

Thadred looked to Lleuad. The kelpie was still agitated, watching Brick suspiciously. "No," Thadred decided. He would rather not give the kelpie raw meat while he was in this state.

Lleuad was a small horse, but these hallways weren't meant for horses. He took up most of the space, shielding Thadred.

Thadred remembered Lleuad going for the Kadra'han instead of Sair. Maybe the kelpie was getting used to her. Maybe he'd smelled Thadred on her.

The little black horse nosed at Thadred's back, nickering.

"I'm fine, boy." He patted the kelpie's neck, careful to avoid the many cuts on the horse's coat.

The kelpie shifted, broken tile and broken glass crunching underfoot. These damages would be fun to explain.

Outside, Thadred heard the soldiers securing the exterior of the mansion. It didn't sound like they had found the remaining Kadra'han.

"Well, this is encouraging," Thadred sighed.

"Encouraging?" Sair's brows rose. "That's a strange way of looking at it."

"Think about it." Thadred gestured to the corpses of the two Kadra'han on the ground. "If they sent men to stop us, that means we're close." Thadred smiled at Sair, his lip stinging. It must be split.

Sair swallowed, looking over the two dead men. "Why would they want to capture me?"

A memory tugged at Thadred, one from what felt like a lifetime ago. A Kadra'han of Vesha's had said something about boys with the right bloodlines being in short supply. He shoved that aside along with its implications. "I'll be sure to ask Iasu when I catch the little rat."

12

SAIR

Sair had expected to be exhausted today. She'd stayed up late with Thadred, holding the lantern as the knight picked shards of glass out of his horse's coat. Lleuad wouldn't let anyone else touch him. Danger seemed to make the animal revert to a wilder state.

It was a good thing, too. The little horse had saved their lives. Even if there was now a huge hole where a window had once been, half the furniture in Sair's room had been struck, the door had been kicked off its hinges, and the tiles of the hallway were smashed.

Thadred had taken reports from his men while working, though none of them found the escaped Kadra'han. They'd tracked him to the edge of the estate and the main road where the trail had gone cold. Sair had hoped to take one of the men for questioning, that was why she had started out with a non-lethal spell. It seemed they were not so fortunate.

"Do you suppose there's a spy in your mother's house?" Sair asked.

The two of them had taken a carriage today, something with solid walls and a roof. Guards circled them all the way around and Thadred had several spells over the doors and windows. Lleuad was still recovering, even with the help of Thadred and Sair's combined magic.

"I don't know," Thadred grumbled. "Maybe? Perhaps Vespasia."

"Why her?" Sair cocked her head to the side.

"She's the one I like the most. Seems reasonable she'd be the one to stab me in the back."

Sair fixed him in a long stare.

"What?"

"I am willing to consider she played us both for fools." Sair was also fond of the girl, but she had just met her. "However, I need a better reason than the fact you like her."

Thadred shrugged. "Preparing for the worst, is all."

Sair watched the city of Iandua pass outside their windows. It was an old city, new portions layered like plaster over ancient foundations. This was a city that had been eroded, rebuilt, and revived many, many times, perhaps over thousands of years.

Bright curtains fluttered from weathered stone windows and flowering vines tangled up the sides of pockmarked walls. Children chased doves in the shadows of crumbling statues.

Well-dressed women and men chatted beneath a massive stone arch. The arch displayed a massive frieze depicting some manner of battle. The details had long since worn away, sentencing the artist's subjects to anonymity.

All around were echoes of an ancient time—mostly in the stone works. But mixed with those were the signs of modernity, opera houses, theaters, horse stables, and what appeared to be academies and houses of scholars.

Thadred had been quiet the whole morning, skipping breakfast despite the dowager's invitation. They had the location of the brothel from Vespasia, so despite suspecting her, Thadred was following her directions.

"Are you alright?" Sair asked, looking him over. His *ka* appeared healthy. A mesh of power braced his bad hip and thigh, the spells at full strength today.

"Fine." Thadred didn't look at her.

"Is something wrong?" Sair leaned over, trying to get a good look at his face. They sat side by side and he had been staring out his window since they left his mother's mansion. "Thadred?"

He finally faced her. "I'm sorry." His expression was a mix of frustration and regret and…something else. Something she couldn't quite name.

"What for?"

Thadred raked a hand through his hair. "Last night. I shouldn't have done that."

It was easy enough to know what he meant. Sair turned back to her own window.

"It's just as well that Kelamorans showed up, because…" Thadred heaved a sigh. "That would have been a mistake. What happened *was* a mistake."

"I'm not sorry," Sair whispered, not sure he heard her over the clatter of hooves and the creak of the carriage.

"Sair," Thadred sounded chiding. "It wouldn't be right."

Sair bit her lip.

"I don't want to hurt you," he said.

Oh, he had already done that. Many times over. But it was in large part her own fault.

"I don't want you to do something you'll regret because you're depending on me."

"What does that mean?" Sair narrowed her eyes at him.

"You need my help right now," Thadred said.

"You think I'm just using you to find my son?" That stung her heart and pride in equal measure.

"I said I want to court you, and I do. But not until we sort this out. Not until we get Rhis back."

Was he afraid she'd change her mind about him as soon as she had her son?

"I'm not *good,* Sair. I'm not decent. I terrorize my family at dinner parties. I drink too much. I have at least thirty ex-lovers scattered across the empire."

That number was actually much lower than Sair and most people assumed.

"Once we have Rhis back…" Thadred exhaled a long breath. "Well, then you can decide."

"I've already decided." Sair looked out the window as she said it, afraid of what he might see on her face.

After Rhisiart had died, she'd expected to spend the rest of her life as a widow. She had a son to raise and there weren't many eligible men left in the Istovari village. She'd filled her life with caring for her people, her son, and her family. She had been content in her small world with its small pleasures and tenuous peace.

Then Thadred.

They'd met in a stranger's house. She'd taken him captive as a hostage. He'd cursed at her, sworn his revenge.

But when they were caught by Vesha's Kadra'han, Thadred had spoken up for her. When he'd gotten the chance to escape, he had come back for her. She was alive because of him several times over.

Thadred might think what he wanted about himself, but bad men didn't risk their lives to protect their enemies.

Thadred was bold, outspoken, and chaotic. Stuffed into corners and compelled into decorum his whole life, he seemed to rebel against it at every turn.

Thadred groaned and flopped against the back of the seat. "I still shouldn't have done it."

"I wish I was younger."

"Why?"

Sair cursed inwardly. She regretted the words as soon as she said them. "It's nothing." She hoped he would drop it, but he didn't.

"Sair?"

Sair locked her arms across her chest. "You like them younger." And childless, she thought to herself. But she didn't add that out loud.

"Sair, don't be stupid. I go for younger women because by your age, they've all outgrown me." While that wasn't the most tactful statement and he had unnecessary emphasis on *your age*, Thadred sounded sincere.

"You are a sorcerer, a knight, a war hero, and a powerful imperial official," Sair clipped. "You have no right to be as insecure as you are."

"I'm not insecure," Thadred countered, defensiveness

creeping into his tone.

"What would you call it, then?"

"Realistic," Thadred said. "I am a bastard of unknown paternity. I have no father, no family. I was raised on the charity of my aunt in the hopes I might one day be useful."

"You're a fool," Sair shot back, bristling. Now wasn't the best time to argue, but they weren't at their destination yet and he had brought it up. "You still see yourself as the poor abandoned child, don't you? Maybe all those women outgrew you because you refused to grow out of that."

"Look." Thadred's tone had a stern edge, like he was asking her to be sensible. "I'm trying to do the right thing for a change."

Sair appreciated the sentiment, at the same time it grated her with frustration. Why was it acceptable for everyone to have him except her?

The carriage rattled. Voices called outside as cloth merchants and fruit sellers hawked their wares. The horses' hooves clopped.

"I love you," Sair whispered, not looking at him. "When I thought you'd found someone else, it broke me."

"Sair." Thadred's tone changed, lowering as if he was about to share some terrible news. He shifted beside her, and she was sure he moved away. "You are making this very difficult."

He didn't say that he loved her in return, but she didn't want him to say it unless he was ready. Sair been the one to dig the chasm that had stretched between them in the past months. It seemed fair that she be the one to reach back across it. But she had never doubted that they were important to each other, even in those dark days of silence.

There were things between them she wasn't sure anyone else would understand. Sair had been the one to teach him to use his magic for the first time. There had been an intimacy in that, a closeness she'd never experienced before or since. Their souls had touched in that exchange, and she didn't know how else to describe it.

And he had saved her. Even when they had been enemies, he had proven himself a man of honor.

Thadred closed his eyes, mouth pinched as if in pain. When he opened them, he seemed much sadder and more tired than before. "Sair…" He spoke her name like a plea, almost like a prayer.

"I love you," she repeated, just in case he had any doubts about what she had said.

Thadred opened his mouth, some thick emotion shining in his eyes.

Sair pressed a finger over his lips. "I didn't say it because I want to hear it back," she whispered. "I said it because I want you to hear someone say it." As much as she wanted to hear it back, Thadred needed to hear it more. "I've seen the worst in you," she whispered, "and I still love you."

Thadred shook his head. The dear fool was determined to mark himself as unworthy.

Nagging thoughts had arisen into her mind these past days. Despite their differences in station and the problems they both had, she kept wondering if maybe this was the gods' way of giving them a second chance.

They probably wouldn't have seen each other again without this. Amira had wanted Sair to stay on as one of her ladies in waiting, but Sair had wanted to get away from Thadred.

If she had just returned to Mynadra, Rhis would have been protected by hundreds of guards within the palace. He would have become a squire or a cup bearer to someone important and had a place at court. He wouldn't be wherever he was now.

"I don't think I deserve you, Sair," Thadred admitted. "I'm not sure I ever will."

"Not with that attitude, you won't," Sair clipped back.

Thadred huffed, almost sounding amused. "You are stubborn."

"A match for you, then." It might be a little presumptuous, but she was at a point where she was willing to risk it.

Thadred inhaled, but Sair never heard what he had planned to say. The carriage rocked to a halt and the coachman called out that they had arrived.

Brick opened the door, looking at their destination with a

look of morbid curiosity. "We have arrived at the den of iniquity, sir."

Despite herself, Sair almost laughed. Brick said it like it was a proper title, the obvious thing to call such an establishment.

"Thank you, Brick." Thadred exited the carriage first. He reached back a hand for her.

Sair tried not to read anything into it. He was being courteous, was all.

Still. His hand lingered on hers outside the carriage, just a little longer than necessary. Or maybe he was making sure she had her balance. It was hard to know.

Sair had donned her humbler attire for today. She suspected that it might make her more approachable to the women they were about to meet.

She paused at the sight of the building. "Are you sure this is the right place?" She glanced to Thadred.

The knight frowned. "It should be."

The building in front of them was perhaps the oldest one on this street. It dominated one side, more a compound than a simple building.

The front doors were open, showing a central courtyard filled with workmen. The men had shovels, pickaxes, and wheelbarrows. They were hard at work digging up the central courtyard of the compound. Someone was undertaking massive renovations to this structure.

A lean man with squinting face met them at the front of the establishment. He looked them over uneasily, glancing over his shoulder.

"Hello, my good man," Thadred called, lathering on the charm. "I am Lord Thadred Myrani, head of the Imperial Office of Inquiry. Brick, show him our credentials."

Brick marched up to the strange man with perfect calm, showing the papers and the imperial seal. They were hardly necessary, any man with eyes could see they were accompanied by imperial soldiers.

"I'm Xander, foreman here." The lanky man jerked his head over his shoulder.

"We are looking for a Mistress Hawthorne," Thadred said. "Is she here?"

"The whore? No. She sold the place and packed up."

Thadred and Sair shared a brief look.

"Baron Prisca owns it now." The foreman jerked his head toward the building. "Has been having us work on the place for a few weeks. Did you want to speak to him? He's not here today, but he might be able to tell you where she went."

Thadred considered that for a moment. "Where might I find Baron Prisca?"

"He should be at his ministry office today."

Thadred arched one eyebrow in response.

"He is the Minister of Coin, sir." The foreman nodded slowly as if Thadred should have known that.

"I see."

Sair looked past the foreman. It was hard to know exactly what the men were doing, but whatever it was, they were tearing up entire chunks of the courtyard. It appeared to be less of a renovation and more of an excavation. She was no expert on building projects, but this didn't look like one. What was going on?

Thadred exchanged a few more questions with the foreman before consulting with their driver. It seemed that the Minister of Coin was fairly well known.

Sair wondered if Vespasia had known the man had bought the old brothel. Probably not, but she wondered. Sair and Thadred climbed back into the carriage.

"I wonder if Iasu is trying to find Vesha," Thadred said as the horses took off.

"Why do you think that?"

Thadred shrugged. "It's what I would do."

"I don't think Vesha was to him quite what the emperor is to you." Sair could understand Thadred's loyalty to his cousin. Daindreth was the only family he knew. They were as close as any brothers she had ever met. Maybe even closer than she and Tapios had been.

"No," Thadred agreed. "But he had nothing else." Thadred

heaved a sigh. "Iasu was sold off by his family as a boy. He's a man who made perfection his goal for years. He has nothing to strive for anymore."

"He needs a cause."

Thadred nodded. "The late Empress Vesha might be that cause."

"I thought his bond to her was broken with her death."

"We don't know for sure," Thadred said. "Dain…he told me what happened to Vesha. It doesn't make sense."

"What do you mean?"

"I'm honestly not sure she's dead," Thadred admitted. "None of us are."

Sair's nostrils flared. "You mean she could be out there somewhere?"

"I didn't say that." Thadred frowned, chewing on his lip. "Amira's not worried about her coming back, if that makes you feel better."

That did make Sair feel better. Amira was as paranoid and thorough as anyone. If she was satisfied, Sair was as well.

"She's in another place," Thadred said. "The way Amira explained it…"

Sair shifted as the carriage hit a stone. "You're not making sense."

Thadred exhaled. "Amira says she saw Emperor Drystan. Dain agrees with her."

Sair took a moment to respond. She hesitated, trying to make sure she hadn't misheard. "Drystan the Conqueror? The man who lies buried in a tomb in Mynadra?"

"The very same."

"That makes no sense."

"It doesn't, does it?" Thadred shook his head. "But they both agreed it was him. Different, but him. He took Vesha with him."

"Took her where?"

"Alshone."

Alshone was the home of the gods. It was the eternal land where the blessed souls went.

Sair bristled at that. "They think Vesha went to Alshone?"

"They do."

"I can't believe that."

"Why not?"

"If anyone deserved to be left in the Dread Marches, it was Vesha."

Thadred shrugged.

"She caused the deaths of thousands!" Sair wasn't sure why, but indignation rose in her chest. "Those villages that were razed by the cythraul, you saw them."

"I did." Thadred looked out the window.

"All those innocent people, those soldiers, my brother…" Sair's voice hitched, and she looked away. There had been so much to keep her attention the past year. She had been busy with negotiating the peace between Hylendale and the Istovari. There had been work to do helping those affected by floods in Hylendale, and to stave off the diseases that had cropped up last summer.

She thought she'd mourned her brother, but perhaps that had fallen down her list of priorities.

"Sair?" Thadred touched her shoulder. "Are you alright?"

Sair smeared back her tears. "Fine."

"I didn't mean to upset you."

Sair cleared her throat. She was weepy these days. Fear for Rhis paired with this whole *thing* with Thadred ate at her. "Forgive me. But if Vesha is in Alshone, then the gods have no sense of justice."

In the corner of her eye, she saw Thadred shrug. "Injustice and mercy often look alike. I'm not sure I know the difference anymore."

"That makes no sense."

"They're both about not getting what you deserve." Thadred rubbed the back of his neck. "Humanity's sense of justice is one of our crueler traits, I think." In a quieter voice, he added, "Especially toward ourselves."

Some part of Sair felt perhaps that he was stumbling on something bigger, that he was trying to tell her something she wasn't seeing. She composed herself, taking deep breaths. "Where are we headed?"

"The Ministry of Coin is near the docks." He leaned against the back of the carriage. "The minister isn't expecting us, but I have my signet ring, so he should make time." The knight thumped his cane against the floor.

"Why would Iasu be here looking for Vesha?" Sair asked, going back to Thadred's earlier words. "Do you think there are others here? Kadra'han who were sworn to Vesha?"

"That's what I can't understand either," Thadred groaned. "It doesn't make sense."

The carriage rattled through the streets of Iandua. A laden donkey waddled past them outside the window.

Sair adjusted her shawl, a blue one that had been another gift from Ketsia. "Are the Kadra'han trying to free Vesha or trying to rebuild their order?"

Thadred exhaled a sharp breath. "I have no idea. Maybe both. Maybe something we haven't even considered yet."

Sair felt blind. Like she didn't know what she should be looking for. Her son was somewhere in this damn city, and she didn't know where. Any building, any warehouse could be hiding him. And she would ride by without ever knowing.

As if he had read her mind, Thadred spoke and repeated his promise to her. "We're going to find him, Sair."

13

THADRED

This whole puzzle spread out before Thadred, a riddle daring him to solve it. Iasu was a Kadra'han, sworn to Vesha. But the last they'd checked he had still been bound in vows to someone. The golden band of his curse was still detectable to sorceresses in Hylendale. Was his liege still Vesha? Or someone else?

Allegedly, the order at Kelamora had sold all their Kadra'han with the stipulation that if the buyer died, the vows would pass back to the grandmaster of the order.

Thadred wondered how that would work. The only transfer of vows he'd ever actually seen himself was when Amira's vows had been passed from her father to Daindreth. In that case, Amira had been ordered by her father—who hadn't realized what he was doing—to serve Daindreth *as you have served me*. It was a common thing fathers said to brides, but in Amira's case, that had been enough. In an instant, Amira was Daindreth's second Kadra'han.

And was Rhis just a hostage? Had Iasu snatched him in order to escape the Istovari or had he planned something more sinister? Rhis had enough magic that he should be able to make a Kadra'han's vows stick. That was all the Kelamora sect needed.

Their carriage pulled to a stop in front of the large municipal structure. Like many public buildings across Erymaya, it was designed with being impressive in mind. Many colonies made use of old palaces and temples for their bureaucratic centers and Iandua was no different.

Thadred held out his hand for Sair as they alighted outside. Tucking her hand under his arm, he faced the large building.

"My lord," Brick's concern came through clear. "Would you like me to find another entrance?"

No less than thirty steps led up to the entrance to the municipal building. Clerks, messengers, and simple people here to pay taxes and file documents rushed this way and that.

Thadred inhaled a deep breath, taking in the expanse of steps. They were shallow and not the most prohibitive he had encountered, but there were a lot of them. Still, he wasn't about to let this Baron Prisca hide behind stairs.

"I'm fine, Brick." He glanced over their guards. "Are we ready, then?"

Ivo, the head of his guards today, nodded, and they began the ascent.

"Brick, run ahead and inform the proper authorities I am here to see Baron Prisca. Bully them if you have to," Thadred said. Though, the idea of Brick bullying anyone was laughable. Brick would as soon kick a puppy as be anything less than courteous.

"Yes, my lord. I will, my lord." Brick sprinted lightly up the steps.

"You can lean on me if you need it," Sair said as they mounted the first step. Her voice was low, barely audible, probably to keep the guards from hearing.

Thadred was almost offended, but he stuffed the feeling down. She didn't mean it that way. "I will be fine." He hoped he wouldn't make himself a liar.

They scaled the steps, the flow of traffic parting around them. Thadred wasn't sure what to expect when he arrived. He'd never heard of this Baron Prisca, but there were thousands of nobles, their relatives, and landed men of means who might buy titles. Iandua was a colony and that meant some of the imperial rules were interpreted differently.

A few unethical viceroys had been granted the right to bestow titles on the locals who served them well. A few had realized "service" was open to interpretation and had begun granting titles to anyone who could pay the fee. The crown had put a stop to it, but it had been easier to allow the "penny lords," as they were called, to keep their titles. Kelethian was now scattered with penny lords and Thadred had a sneaking suspicion that Prisca might be one.

Who better for Zeyna to install as a minister? He'd probably be indulgent and eager to please.

It seemed to take forever to reach the top of the steps, but Thadred finally entered the main building with his guards, Sair, and dignity. His leg and hip ached, but he focused on his mission here instead of the discomfort.

Brick met them amid the bustle of clerks and the lines of waiting petitioners.

The whole place buzzed like a beehive. Everything whirled with the chaos of bureaucracy. Despite the seeming madness, there was an order to the proceedings. People seemed to know where they were supposed to go. Clerks worked studiously at their assigned booths. Many of them were guarded by iron bars.

"The minister's office is right this way, sir," Brick said. "He's expecting us."

"Lead the way."

Brick led them through the halls and passages of the ministry complex. The building was set up on a grid system, but they had to dodge the racing clerks every few steps. Thankfully, Brick guided them to a quieter portion of the ministry building. Guards stood posted at the entrance to a broad hallway and Brick nodded to them before leading Thadred and their group past.

Brick wasted no time. He took them straight to a broad set of double doors, currently swung open, and bowed to the clerk outside. Pleasantries were exchanged, and the clerk verified their credentials before asking them to please follow this way.

That was perhaps the best thing about being a high-ranking bureaucrat himself—Thadred rarely had to wait for anyone these days.

Baron Prisca's office might have been any minister's office in the empire. The floors were black and white checkered tile. The walls were aligned with impressive mahogany shelves stocked with neatly organized rows of records.

"Thank you, Brick. While we're here, see what you can find on that Mistress Hawthorne."

The Ministry of Coin would handle all the tax records for the province. Hawthorne might have nothing to do with Vesha or the Kadra'han, but they would perform their due diligence.

Brick nodded, lips pressed into a tight line. "I'll see what they can give us, sir." The valet offered a bow before marching off to hunt down a clerk.

The baron might prove to be cooperative, but Thadred didn't want to give him the chance to cover anything up if that wasn't the case. Besides, this would save time.

Beside the large central desk at the middle of the room, smaller tables were placed around it and teams of clerks worked at each one. Baron Prisca was certainly an industrious man.

The man himself stood at the center wearing a cravat and jacket that were of the imperial style but less practical for the warmer climate of Iandua. His head jerked up when they entered. He wore his sash and chain of office proudly displayed on his chest. It was hard to tell his age. He might have been a dour thirty, or a well-preserved fifty. Either way he had the look of a man who had risen far above his station and was determined to stay here. Thadred immediately disliked him.

It wasn't that Thadred had anything against men who rose above their station. Several such men had proven to be quite useful in the new empire. But there were the ones who rose above their station and owned the role. Then there were the ones who were always afraid that people didn't give them the respect they deserved.

The latter group were always trying to prove themselves, always trying to earn respect from people who would never give it. They still felt like imposters no matter how successful or how respected they became. They raised their accolades, honors, and achievements like shields against public opinion, as if that could protect them from scorn.

Despite his personal assessment of the man, Thadred bowed and politely introduced Sair. The baron looked Sair head to foot with something like alarm, probably wondering who this strange woman was and why a sorceress had been brought into his domain.

"Baron Prisca," Thadred sprinkled the necessary amount of charm and charisma into the name, "we apologize for the short notice. We have just a few questions and then we will be on our way. We would have given you better warning, but the needs of the empire do not wait."

"Of course," said the older man in a voice that was a little too polished to Thadred's ears. His accent was a forgery of a nobleman's. One that had been made too perfect by too careful study. Men who had been born into money didn't spend this much effort on looking like it.

"We come on urgent business." Thadred looked around at the scribes and clerks hard at work around the room. "Is there somewhere we could speak in private?"

"Here is quite well." Baron Prisca clapped his hands twice, and the clerks, scribes, and various workers left their projects where they lay and filed out of the room. The baron called to an attendant in the hall and the doors were shut after them.

Efficient. Meticulous. With a taste for order and excellence. Begrudgingly, Thadred could see why this man had been chosen as Minister of Coin.

"May I offer you a seat, Lord Thadred? Lady Sairydwen?"

Thadred's hip, lower back, and upper thigh ached, but he feared if he sat down, he might not be able to stand up. "No, thank you."

Sair surveyed the room mildly, with a lady's polite interest. Thadred trusted she was surveying the nearby documents for anything of suspicion.

"We are here in pursuit of a fugitive," Thadred explained. "A man of great interest to the empire. We believe he arrived here two weeks or so past. On a ship arriving from Yndra."

"I believe you already made inquiries at the docks, is that correct?" The baron broke eye contact. "Were the dockyards uncooperative in providing you with the charter?"

"They did provide us with a charter. But you see it was incomplete. And the two passengers of interest do not appear on the rolls."

When he had received the news this morning, Thadred had momentarily feared that perhaps Iasu and Rhis had suffered a mishap on the ocean and were now somewhere at the bottom of it. People did fall overboard or ill or suffer any number of accidents on the sea. But as Thadred had told Sair this morning, Iasu was not going to be killed that easily. And last night's attack by the Kadra'han seemed to prove that there was still something to find in the city and someone didn't want them to find it.

"I'm afraid they weren't able to help us. But I was hoping you might be?"

The baron bowed stiffly. It looked forced. "Yes, of course. However, I may. What was the name of this fugitive? Or any other information you might be able to provide?"

"We have several possible aliases, but his name is Iasu Zahn." Thadred saw something flicker over the baron's face. He wasn't quite sure what it was. There was nothing around the room to indicate danger and the only sources of *ka* were those expected.

The baron recovered himself quickly. "I'm afraid not."

Thadred smiled again. "No worries. We do think he might have some connection to a former brothel in the red quarter."

Prisca swallowed. It was almost imperceptible, but Thadred caught it. "A brothel, my lord?" His voice strained.

"Yes." Thadred locked eyes with the other man. "We were told by the foreman you were the new owner. Massive renovations underway. What exactly are your plans for the place? A new summer home, perhaps?"

The baron glanced between Sair and Thadred. "A business investment."

"I see. And have you invested in many brothels?" Back on the continent, this would hardly have been a scandalous question. At least not in the central empire. Plenty of nobles owned brothels. Not many other people could afford the heavy taxes imposed on them by the imperial government.

Prisca spluttered. "No, I…I am holding the land."

Thadred hadn't been too suspicious before, but this man wasn't making any sense. "I see." He tapped a finger on his cane. At his side, Sair stood rigid and alert. She must see that the man was hiding something, too. "Anyway, would you be able to help us search your records for several other names? These are known associates of the fugitive."

Thadred wrote down the names of several other Kadra'han who had also come from Kelamora, like Iasu. Thadred wasn't sure those men would still be alive, much less using their real names, but it would keep the baron talking.

"Yes, of course." Prisca recovered himself, though Thadred wondered if he wasn't just a bit paler than he had been. "Would you mind waiting here a moment? I believe this calls for my personal clerks, and they are next door."

"I'll come with you." Thadred adjusted his grip on his cane.

"No, sir. Please don't trouble yourself." The baron offered a half bow to Thadred. "It is just next door, and I wouldn't want you to waste the effort." That was a polite way of saying he didn't want the cripple to have to limp into the other room.

It rankled Thadred a little, but he was sore enough to agree. "Whatever you think is best. We will wait here."

The baron gave one of those bows again and marched past Thadred, Sair, and the guards, stepping out into the hallway and closing the door after him.

"You think he will be able to help us?" Sair hovered close to Thadred's arm, even as she looked over the various papers on the desks around the room.

"As well as anyone," Thadred said. "For whatever reason, the Kadra'han have chosen to stay in the city. Someone is helping them. Someone has to be footing the bill for their food, lodging, and whatever else it is that you need as a member of an warrior cult."

It made sense that their sponsor might be someone like the

baron. How brothel renovations fit into this, Thadred had no idea.

Sair shook her head. "I just…"

As the baron exited into the hallway, there came a rattle and jostle from the other side. The guards spun around at the same time Sair and Thadred did.

"Did that son of a bitch just lock us in here?" Thadred blinked at his guards, half in shock, half in outrage.

The nearest man reached for the door and tried to yank it open. He got only a rattle in response.

"Get out of the way." Thadred raised one hand toward the door and summoned *ka*. This was a spell that Amira had taught him. Thadred wasn't quite as good at it as the empress, but he was still quite good. Thadred drew a burst of *ka* to himself and released it outward, snapping free.

The doors ripped open. Thadred spared a moment to hope that no one innocent was on the other side.

The hinges tore, and the doors sagged outward. Thadred looked to his guards and back to Sair.

She looked on with amazement, appearing to be just a little impressed. Thadred very much enjoyed that look on her face. He would love to impress her all the time.

"Catch that weasel and bring him back to me." Thadred readied his cane sword and glanced to Sair. "I'm afraid I'm going to have to leave the running him down to you, my dear."

Sair bolted out of the door. The guards took off after her, closing around in tight ranks.

"Be careful!" Thadred didn't think he needed to say that to Sair, but it couldn't hurt to tell her anyway.

Two guards stayed behind with Thadred. He looked around the room, toward the large desk at the head. He approached it and found all the desk drawers had locks. He pulled one, and then another, but none of them gave.

"What an interesting fellow you are, Baron Prisca." Thadred yanked a few more drawers and heard something rattle inside.

It occurred to him then that the drawers might be trapped. He would rather not have to deal with poison and stabbing today. Thadred focused on the papers on top of the desk, trying to get some sense of just what Baron Prisca chose to give his personal time to.

The baron would have plenty of clerks, and various underlings meant to help him with the day-to-day running of his ministry. Thadred found you could always learn a great deal about a man by what he chose not to delegate.

There were only so many things a single man or woman could directly control. People who rose through the ranks to become successful knew this. A man like Baron Prisca would have carefully chosen what he kept within his personal purview.

As Thadred looked over the papers on the desk, he found nothing particularly alarming. They were exactly the sort of records that one would expect to see in a Minister of Coin's office. There were charter requests, and various proposed contracts for local mercenary companies, and shipping route changes. It seemed that several major trading companies were in negotiations with Prisca to make Iandua their new port of provenance. Mercenary companies provided security for wealthy families as well as many cities in the colonies. When able-bodied men willing to serve in the military were rare, oftentimes you had to ship them in from other places. It wasn't uncommon for peasant boys down on their luck to join mercenary companies in Erymaya and then come to the colonies to earn their fortune.

Thadred flipped through the papers, trying to take note of any names that he saw. There were several documents from the Taredicci bank, assurances of payment plans, and questions about future payments.

Thadred eased down into the seat at the head of the table. He kept looking through the papers, the sounds of footsteps continuing outside in the hall. He heard shouting and running. The baron was putting up a struggle, but what did he hope to gain? It wasn't like he could outrun the empire in these halls.

Thadred sensed the shapes of *ka* coming towards him and his men. It sounded like two or three people, and the amount of *ka* was consistent with that. He sensed magic gathering around one of the figures and looked up expecting to see Sair.

Instead of Sair, three men in dark clothing came through the door. In an instant, Thadred realized his mistake. Golden bands circled the men's necks, the telltale sign of a Kadra'han curse.

Thadred had never seen these men before, but that meant nothing. He hurled a counter spell and blocked the magical attack, but he was already too late.

A flying knife struck one of his guards in the neck. The second guard, stood to block the men's access to Thadred, but two of the figures charged him, descending on him at once

"No!" Thadred shouted, but it did no good. The spell he hurled back was blocked, and two highly trained assassins descended on the imperial soldier.

The soldier slashed one of them across the arm before they came within striking distance with their short knives. He turned and hacked at the other. Their knives slid off his armor, and he managed to beat them back for just a moment.

It was enough time for Thadred to get his cane sword out and hurl another defensive spell toward the strangers. He did a repeat of the blasting spell, heading straight for the third Kadra'han.

The Kadra'han blocked the spell, hurling it off to the side. Thadred's spell burst through the window, sending a rain of stone, glass, and wood onto the street below. People screamed, and a donkey cried out.

The third Kadra'han then joined in, heading straight for the soldier. Thadred blasted again, though sweat was beginning to bead on his forehead. His spell was weaker this time, but it caught one of the Kadra'han as the man was attacking his soldier from behind. The Kadra'han shot backward and hurled out the window.

Thadred lashed out, feeling with his power again. One of the Kadra'han remained, facing off the soldier. The other veered off, heading straight for Thadred.

The knight dropped into a ready stance with his sword, but magic was still his best chance at surviving this. He prepared a spell, but then the Kadra'han had a chain out.

The Kadra'han swung it, catching Thadred's sword and

tangling it in the links. Thadred had been expecting a strike, not a grapple.

The sword ripped out of his hand, flying across the room. The Kadra'han wasted no time. Thadred might have been able to put up a better defense if he hadn't been tired, sore, and caught flat footed.

The Kadra'han closed the distance between them. Thadred legitimately expected to be stabbed. He had one moment where he was sure he was about to be skewered, and that he would die right here, right now.

Instead of stabbing him, the Kadra'han came in close and lashed something around Thadred's neck. Thadred was yanked off balance, something that wasn't hard to do in his state.

He ended up on the ground with the Kadra'han. The second Kadra'han appeared, grabbing him and slamming him to the ground. What had happened to his last guard? Thadred couldn't see from his place pinned behind the desk.

The third Kadra'han came up and grabbed Thadred's legs when he tried to kick. Something metal cut into his arm—he thought it was a knife, until he felt it going around his wrist.

He thrashed under the weight of the three Kadra'han. They weren't large men, most of the Kadra'han were small. But they were tough little pricks. Thadred fought to throw them off, but it was pointless.

The Kadra'han locked something around his wrist, and his awareness of *ka* winked out. Tenebrous steel. They had made sure he wouldn't be able to use magic.

Thadred fought, but the three Kadra'han chained his hands behind his back and tied his ankles together. He'd never felt quite so helpless, or quite so angry in his life. They tied a bag over his head that smelled sickly-sweet.

He cursed at them and delivered threats and promises alike. The Kadra'han didn't respond.

The sweet smell filled Thadred's nostrils and made his head spin. It became hard to think straight, and despite everything, he felt himself becoming drowsy.

He struggled to stay awake, and attempted to hold his breath, but that didn't do anything. He felt himself being dragged across the floor. There was a sudden drop, and the noise of the street became louder. He tried to yell. He tried to fight back, but everything was muffled inside the bag.

His last conscious thought was fear for Sair.

14

SAIR

Sair and the guards chased Baron Prisca through the bureaucratic building. Clerks rushed out of the baron's path, ducking aside at the sight of imperial soldiers.

The baron did not seem to be a particularly athletic man. Sair was a little hampered by her dress, but she was fit enough, and the soldiers around her certainly were.

Sair wondered if the baron would attempt to call for his own guards, but he didn't. Where *were* the guards of this building? It was not a palace, or a treasure house, not in the strictest sense, but government buildings still needed protection most of the time.

They chased the baron through the halls, and away from the main business areas. He led them up a flight of stairs. The guards stopped Sair at the foot, pulling her back.

"Lady Sairydwen, he could be leading us into a trap."

Had the baron known they were coming? He couldn't have had more than a few hours' notice that they were headed this way. Maybe someone had been watching them? They themselves hadn't known that they were going to come here until about an hour ago.

"Then he will be committing treason. I am here on imperial authority. As is Lord Thadred. If Prisca would assault me, he will face the empire's wrath."

"With all due respect my lady." The guard nodded to Sair with just a hint of a smile. He was a young man, with a pleasant face and dimples that deepened when he smiled, a lieutenant. "We will face Lord Thadred's wrath if anything happens to you. Please let us go first."

They were wasting time. Prisca was guilty of something, and he might very well know where her son was. She waved the guards ahead of her, more annoyed at the delay than anything else. She wondered why a man with such authority wouldn't have called for help. Why wasn't Prisca summoning his guards? Why had he run away like a little boy caught stealing pies?

They followed Prisca up the stairs, which were only a few flights. They burst out onto the roof. It was flat with several potted plants and a pergola meant for shade. The stone was whitewashed, probably an effort to help with the heat. The guards surveyed the roof then gestured for Sair to follow up after them.

Baron Prisca stood on top of the low wall that circled the roof. They were only three floors up. The bureaucratic building was large, but it was not as towering or magnificent as the buildings back in Mynadra.

The baron stood facing away from them, hands fisted at his sides.

"Prisca?" Sair looked between the guards. "I'm not sure what you plan to gain by running away from the empire. Will you come peacefully and answer the questions we have for you?"

Prisca turned around, looking at her for a long moment. "I fear them more than I fear you."

"Who?" Dread clenched Sair's stomach. She could think of only one *they* who might incite such fear. "Who are you talking about?"

The baron shook his head. "It doesn't matter. I'm finished anyway."

"We can help you," Sair promised. "Whoever is threatening you, Lord Thadred and I can help."

The baron shook his head, looking back over the city. "You can't. It's too late."

Sair surveyed the surrounding roof, trying to find some threat, some explanation for this man's behavior. But there was none in sight.

The bureaucratic building was the largest building for many blocks. From here, they could see much of the city in the fading light of the afternoon. People moved about the ground, riding by on the streets with horses and donkeys or with burdens slung over their shoulders. Sair saw nothing to indicate the presence of shadow men, but that didn't mean that they weren't there. Kadra'han were remarkably good at what they did. Amira, the empress, had been trained at least in part by these Kadra'han. She was possibly the deadliest woman alive.

A crash came from below them. There was the sound of breaking glass, screams, and a sound like a rockslide.

Sair fought the impulse to rush up to where the baron stood to see the street below.

The baron nodded sadly. "That will be them."

Fear gripped Sair's chest. "Thadred?"

The soldiers looked to one another. Sair had brought six of them with her. They surrounded her in a protective huddle. It occurred to her then that they had left Thadred with only two.

"We need to get back to Thadred," Sair said. "Now!"

"But the baron…" The young lieutenant gestured with his spear to where the baron stood atop the wall, facing the street once again.

Sair was already back to the stairs. "Come on!"

The baron jumped.

Sair saw him dive headfirst toward the street below. Her heart jolted, that instinctive reaction to seeing another human fall.

She rushed up to the wall along with the soldiers. They looked down to see Baron Prisca's broken body on the cobblestones. He had struck headfirst, and blood splattered around him in a gory display.

In the street, she saw the source of the explosion they had heard. Glass, rock, and bits of wood had spilled out into the street. Three figures crawled out of the gash in the building, dragging a limp shape with them.

If Sair's heart had been in her stomach, she felt it hit the floor then. "Thadred!" Sair's scream ripped out of her before she thought about it.

He couldn't be dead. He couldn't be gone. She needed him. *Needed* him.

Sair beat the soldiers back to the stairs. The lieutenant asked her to wait, but this time she didn't. The soldiers clanked after her, moving as fast as they could with their weapons.

Back inside, there was chaos. Word must be spreading of the baron's suicide. People were gasping, screaming, crying, and many more just looking around in confusion.

Sair shoved past them, elbowing and shoving her way to where they had left Thadred in the baron's office. They found it in shambles. Both guards they had left behind with Thadred lay dead on the ground. Sair rushed over to the ruined window, where the three figures had escaped dragging their captive.

There was no sign of them now. Sair's first instinct was to rush into the street, but one of the soldiers grabbed her arm.

"Lady Sairydwen! Please get away from the window." The lieutenant pulled her back into the relative safety of the ruined office.

"They took him." Sair buried her face in her hands.

The young lieutenant studied her. "I don't think they'll hurt him, madam. They seem to be wanting a hostage."

Sair took a shuddering breath. The two bodies of the soldiers were beyond saving. Blood spread around them in dark red pools. The Kadra'han had not taken any chances. They had wanted those men dead, and they'd made sure that Sair wouldn't be able to help them.

"What do they want?" Sair paced in a tight circle. "What good is he to them? He already has a liege lord. It's not like they can make him take a Kadra'han's vows over again."

"I am not sure, my lady," the lieutenant answered calmly.

Sair looked around the ruined office. What was she supposed to do now? The Kadra'han would make their demands, surely. But only if they actually wanted a hostage. They might have some other use for Thadred.

Another option occurred to Sair. Istovari blood was powerful. All bodies were rich in *ka*. *Ka* was the life force that bound all living things together. *Ka* was richest in things that were alive, but some dead things kept residual *ka* over time. Many wooden items retained *ka*, and some leather items too. But blood was by far the most concentrated source. Blood was almost pure *ka*.

The blood of an Istovari had been used to unleash Caa Iss years ago. What if, the whole purpose of the Kadra'han coming to this city where Empress Vesha had unleashed her cythraul armies, was to do the same thing over again?

"Lady Sairydwen?" Brick appeared, his white-gloved hands held awkwardly in front of him. He looked around at the ruined room, holding a scroll of papers. "I found the…" He gasped as his eyes fell upon the dead men on the floor. "What happened? Where is Lord Thadred?"

Brick paled as he stared at the bodies on the floor. The soldiers had covered the faces of the dead, arranging the bodies of their fallen comrades.

Brick stared with wide eyes. "My lady…"

Outside, the commotion had drawn the guards of the administrative center. It seemed that they did have a security force after all. Sair mentally prepared herself for questions, and what exactly she would say when the Ianduans came and made their demands.

For a moment, she worried that she was a sorceress without the backing of Thadred, the Minister of Inquiry. But she couldn't show fear. Men were a lot like dogs in that way, they sensed who had authority and who didn't.

Sair straightened, preparing herself for what was to come. Baron Prisca had known something. He was involved with the Kadra'han in some way.

From the look of this room, there had been quite a struggle. Tables had been knocked aside, and the residual *ka* of a powerful spell still lingered in the air. Sair would guess that Thadred had used magic to defend himself. She found Thadred's cane and the sword that went inside it. They appeared to be undamaged, so the Kadra'han had probably found a way to get them away from Thadred during the fighting.

The chair near the desk at the head of the room had been knocked back. If Sair had to guess, Thadred had been behind the baron's desk when he'd been attacked. Sair ran up to the desk and searched the top. She found a series of letters, accounts, a few sharpened quills, and sealed bottles of ink. She reached for the topmost drawer, and yanked. It didn't open. She looked down and realized that every single drawer on the baron's desk was locked. It wasn't uncommon to have *a* locking drawer, but seven of them? That seemed a bit excessive.

Sair reached for the drawer and yanked harder. She suspected that the drawer was intended more as a protection against tampering than actual security. Sair levered Thadred's cane, using the silver head on the bottom of the center drawer. She was able to smash through the thin layer of wood. From there, she was able to lever against the lock, and smash the drawer open.

Brick was at her elbow along with the lieutenant.

"Lady Sairydwen? What are you doing?" The lieutenant asked her the question, but his eyes were on the doorway. From the sound of it, they would soon be joined by any number of bureaucrats and guards, asking questions.

Sair yanked open the mutilated drawer. Inside, she found a collection of papers. There were none of the used wax stubs, old pen nibs, bits of string, and other odds and ends that one found in most top desk drawers. Instead, there were rows of papers, neatly stored, and beautifully organized.

Sair prodded the papers with Thadred's cane, not wanting to touch them just yet. They appeared to be no different from the papers on top of the desk. There were charters, debt reports, tax revenue sheets, and the odd documents that one would expect in the office of an administrator.

But why were these locked up? And none of the others?

Motion at the doorway interrupted Sair's line of thought. A small army of clerks crashed through, followed by screams, shouts of accusations, and a cacophony of voices demanding just what had happened, where the baron was, and what the witch had done.

"What did you do?" That was a man Sair recognized as having been in this office just a few minutes ago.

"Who are you?" Sair made the question as businesslike as possible, not wanting to sound offensive, but also wanting to sound like someone who was owed a response.

The clerk took just a second to respond, not having expected that response apparently. "I am Scribe Edwin. Personal secretary to Baron Prisca."

"My condolences." Sair inclined her head. "I need you to fetch whoever is in command of the guards here. At once. We have been attacked by enemies of the empire. This calls for a formal investigation." Sair fought to remain outwardly composed while her insides writhed.

The Kadra'han had taken away her son, and now Thadred. She couldn't lose them both. She had lost so many people. It seemed that death touched everyone she loved. She had lost, lost, and lost.

Dread and a sense of fear filled her that it was about to happen again, but there was also rage. A cold, jealous rage. The kind of rage that simmered and iced over instead of boiling. It was enough to keep her composed—for now.

Scribe Edwin glanced out the ruined window, the lines of his face deepening as he peered out. "What happened? Where is Baron Prisca?"

"He is dead." With the man's body lying mere paces away, there wasn't much Sair could do to soften the blow. "I am very sorry. Please fetch the head of the guards at once."

The lieutenant at Sair's side interjected. "Will you obey Lady Sairydwen? In the name of the empire?"

The small crowd at the doorway of the office sprang to life, and several figures rushed off, presumably to fetch the needed authorities.

Out in the street, people screamed and cried out as clerks from inside the building and people from the street realized just what had happened. Or at least part of what had happened. It didn't seem that anyone had realized that Baron Prisca was the body lying on the cobbles.

Sair cast about the room, brain scrambling. If the Kadra'han or Baron Prisca had any accomplices in whatever he was trying to conceal, then leaving this room might mean permanently giving up whatever was important within it. Sair had the authority of the empire, but right now, it was limited to a few men and sheer force of will. Her power was effectively a bluff. She had no idea who might be working with the Kadra'han. If Baron Prisca had been involved with them, anyone might be.

"Brick, come here." Sair gestured over the valet.

Brick was even paler than usual, his already ghostly complexion reaching a deathly shade of white. He pointedly refused to look at the bodies of the three dead men scattered about the office and outside in the street. But he came when called. "Yes, my lady?"

"Do you have your bag?"

Brick carried a bag for errands, and messages that he ferried for Thadred. "Yes, I do." To prove it, Brick pulled the satchel from his shoulder, opening the top.

Sair didn't think she was going to get a better opportunity than this. The clerks were standing just across the room, but for now they were distracted by the horror of Baron Prisca's body, and the two dead guards within the office. Using Thadred's cane, Sair pried open the rest of drawers.

All of the drawers had been designed with subtlety in mind. They had not been designed to keep people out, so much as to show when people had tried to get in. That was the way most drawers on desks functioned and things that truly needed to be locked away were kept in vaults. Perhaps that meant the papers inside this desk were not all that important, or perhaps Baron Prisca had simply assumed that no one would dare break into his personal desk.

Sair broke into the first two drawers of the desk and dumped the contents into Brick's bag before anyone said anything.

By the time Sair got to the third drawer, the guards had

arrived. They demanded who Sair was and on what authority she was here. The lieutenant ran interference. Without Sair having to say anything, he stepped up, and began demanding a report from the guard.

Unfortunately, the guard had called attention to Sair and now the head scribe remembered she was there. He came storming over to her.

"What are you doing?" The scribe demanded. "Those are confidential! You have no right!"

"I have the right of the empire," Sair shot back. "You may obstruct me under pain of treason."

"What are your credentials?" This man was a scribe, he was used to clerical technicalities and paperwork.

Sair realized with a pang that Thadred had the imperial signet that gave them authority. That meant the Kadra'han had it. Was there a way that they could abuse it? Fear sliced through her, realizing just what the Kadra'han might have acquired besides the Minister of Inquiry.

Even as those thoughts rolled through her head, Sair faced Scribe Edwin with composure. When she had been a lone woman in the markets of Lashera, there had been many times when she'd had to face down aggressive, hostile, or even predatory men. She faced this one the same way. No fear, no challenge, but with firmness.

"I am collecting evidence for the imperial investigation. I am working in cooperation with the Minister of Inquiry. Baron Prisca is currently suspected of dealings with enemies of the empire."

"That is preposterous," Scribe Edwin exclaimed, "Baron Prisca was a loyal imperialist."

"I truly hope the evidence will prove as such." Sair didn't see how that was possible at all. The man had killed himself when it had seemed apparent that he would be caught. And right after he'd killed himself, Thadred had been captured. Sair generally liked to assume the best of people, but the case for Baron Prisca looked bleak.

Scribe Edwin backed down, looking uncertain as another

soldier stepped up beside Sair, clearly communicating who he and the other armed imperial soldiers answered to.

Sair continued breaking open the drawers of the desk and shoveling the contents into Brick's bag. By the time the guard responsible for the Ministry of Coin arrived, Sair had already emptied out the desk of all its contents. That was the first task completed.

Now she just needed to begin a citywide search for Thadred, Rhis, and a cult of master assassins.

Sair desperately wished to have Thadred with her in that moment. He would know exactly what protocols to follow, and exactly which imperial officials needed to be contacted. He would also likely have the knowledge of the imperial officials, their personal relationships, their histories, and their alliances to help sift who could be trusted and who couldn't.

Thadred was better suited for this in every way. It truly would have been better if she had been the one kidnapped, and he had been the one left behind.

Perhaps if the Kadra'han had kidnapped her instead, she might be closer to finding Rhis. But that wasn't what had happened.

Now Sair needed to get things together, and Sair needed to hunt down the Kadra'han. Where to start?

She stepped away from the ruins of the gutted desk and faced the commander of the ministry guards. "Hello, Commander. I am Lady Sairydwen of the Istovari, and I am here with the Ministry of Inquiry with the authority of the empire. Now send for the head of the city watch and lock down this building."

15

THADRED

Thadred had woken up in strange places before. Prior to his hunting accident, he had frequently gone out for nights of debauchery with other young men from the lesser nobility and soldiers from the barracks.

Once, he had woken up under a tavern bench with a woman's corset over his face, naked from the waist down. He still wasn't quite sure how he had ended up there, but he'd never wanted to wake up that way again. He had been cold, hungover, and had to walk back to the palace.

Thadred wasn't sure how that incident compared to this current moment, but his hip was on fire and his head throbbed with the lingering effects of something that felt a lot like a hangover.

Except, Thadred hadn't been drinking. He remembered that much. There had been a fight, he had been slammed to the ground, and then he had been dragged out into a wagon. Thadred did remember the wagon starting to move, and then everything was darkness.

Thadred saw the light filtering through his vision. He blinked, and shifted his head, and the light no longer shone in his eyes.

Thadred shifted and felt a pinching in his wrists. He was bound. Of course he was. Chains rattled, and he remembered why he couldn't feel *ka*. He was locked in tenebrous steel.

"Is he awake?"

"I thought he was dead."

"He isn't dead, idiot. Why would they chain up a dead man?"

"I'm not an idiot. And how would I know? Maybe he died while he was lying there."

The voices were odd. Not quite right. Kind of whiny, and high pitched.

"Thadred?"

Thadred's head lifted at his name.

Pain rocketed through his entire skull and he winced, laying carefully back down. His head felt bruised, and he wasn't sure if it was the effects of the drugs the Kadra'han had used, or perhaps he had hit something while unconscious.

"Thadred?" the small, hesitant voice repeated. "Are you alright?"

Thadred opened his eyes slowly this time, tilting his head to get a view of his surroundings.

They were in a stable of some kind. Old stone rose around them, and light filtered through the ventilation slots near the ceiling. Wooden beams arched overhead, and piles of straw rose here and there.

The doors were missing from the animal stalls, leaving behind empty iron hinges.

Shingles were missing from the roof letting in a constellation of sunlight. Sunbeams pierced down from above, shining in Thadred's face. For all that the roof had holes, the walls appeared solid stone.

His hands were shackled in front of him, but his captors hadn't bothered to chain his ankles. It didn't make much sense to shackle the legs of a crippled man, he supposed.

Thadred was missing his signet ring, as well as the extra knives he had stashed in his boots and belt. He was helpless. Without magic, weapons, and any way of reaching the outside world.

A few paces away, out of reach of his short chains, was a giant metal cage. It looked much like those cages that were used to transport large beasts from the southern continent. The cages were expensive, and certainly attributed to why such animals were so expensive. But this one looked as if it had certainly seen better days. A few bars were missing from the top and the hinges had fallen off. The door was now held in place by a coil of chains.

Inside the cage, were children. Six of them. They were grungy and dirty. Five of them were boys, but one was a girl in a tattered dress with long brown curls.

The oldest of the children, or at least the tallest, stood with one hand on the bars, staring at Thadred.

It took a moment, especially in Thadred's partially drugged state. But he recognized the boy. "Rhis?"

The kid had to be at least a head taller than when he'd last seen him and looked like he'd been living in that cage for months instead of weeks, but it was him. Rhis hopped up and down with excitement. "Is Mama here?"

Thadred hesitated. He wasn't sure who might be listening in on this conversation.

The moment after he felt the rush of excitement at having found Rhis, he experienced a crushing sense of despair.

Yes, he had found Rhis. But who was going to find him? The Kadra'han had taken them both captive, and definitely not for anything good. There was nothing positive about this situation.

Thadred wasn't even sure what had happened to Sair. Had she been attacked? The Kadra'han might have sent a second group of men after her.

Sair might be dead. That thought threatened to double him over, so he forced it deep, deep down. Sair was alive and safe. He needed to believe that for now.

"Yes, your mother is here and she's going to find us." That was safe to say, if only because the Kadra'han already knew Sair was here, and if she was alive, she was already trying to find them.

"She's here? Mama is here?" Rhis's voice held so much hope, and childlike faith, but it still wavered, a hint that he was being brave despite being very, very afraid.

"Are you alright? Have they hurt you?" Thadred wanted to reach out with his power and see if he could sense the golden band of *ka* around the boy's neck. That band would be the sign that the children had already been bound in Kadra'han's oaths. Once that happened, there wasn't much to do aside from killing everyone who held their oaths. "Have they forced you to say anything? Repeat any words?"

"No, not yet." Rhis was young, but there was something in his voice that said he knew what was coming. Maybe the Kadra'han had told him what was going to happen.

"You know him?" asked one of the other children. It was a grimy little boy with pale hair and a pug nose. His tunic was belted at the waist with a golden cord that looked far too fine for a child as grungy as him.

"He's my friend. He's my mama's friend. And he rides a kelpie, a magic horse from the goddess Eponine herself."

Something about the way Rhis spoke of him, filled Thadred with a sick sense of inadequacy. He had known he was an idol to Rhis, but to hear the boy talk of him this way, like he was a hero of legend, was more painful than he was prepared to process.

Rhis was too young to realize that Thadred was a charlatan. Thadred made his way in the world through bluffs, deals, and the good graces of the emperor. If it weren't for Daindreth, Thadred would be nothing. Nothing at all. He had no virtues to recommend him as a person except stubbornness, cleverness, and charm.

Once, he might have become a great knight, but a tumble on a horse had changed that.

Thadred opened his mouth to argue with Rhis, to tell him he wasn't someone to look up to. To tell Rhis he was only going to disappoint him if his hopes were that high. But one look at the expectant, hopeful child's face and Thadred couldn't do it.

He had the feeling that Rhis hadn't been this hopeful in a long time. He suspected that the boy had been near breaking.

Even though Thadred and Sair had been searching for Rhis without ceasing, there was no way for the child to know that.

Seeing Thadred would be the first breath of hope he'd had thus far.

Thadred forced a smile, even though moving his face made his scalp twitch ever so slightly, which upset the bruise on his head. "Hang in there, kid."

Rhis turned around, looking at the other children. "I told you we're getting out!"

Thadred truly and thoroughly hated himself in that moment. Here were half a dozen captive children, counting on him. And Rhis, a boy who was barely six years old, was the one keeping them together. He was even the one encouraging Thadred right now.

"How long have you been here?" Thadred's guess was that they were still somewhere in Iandua. He didn't think the Kadra'han could have brought him very far in the amount of time that had passed.

"I don't know," Rhis said. "Days and days."

Thadred knew roughly when Rhis would have arrived in Iandua. "Were you kept anywhere before this? Have they moved you since you arrived in the city?"

"We stayed in a fancy house for a while. There was better food there and it wasn't quite so cold at night. But then something happened, and they brought us here."

Thadred's mind moved slowly, almost like his thoughts were responding to the physical pain in his body. "A fancy house? Were people living there? Or was it abandoned?

"There were servants and everything," said the pale haired boy. "I'd never had servants before."

Thadred wondered at that. "Can you all use magic?"

"I can't," said the pale haired boy. "But Rhis says he can and Vynn says he does too."

"Maëlys has the strongest magic. I heard that one man say so." That came from one of the other boys, a stout little fellow with ruddy cheeks.

"Maëlys is a girl," said the pale haired little boy.

"Girls can have magic," Rhis insisted. "Girls can have more magic than boys."

The girl in question remained crouched, like she was trying to avoid being seen. She hovered close to Rhis, cowering like a frightened little rabbit.

Rhis stood in the middle of them, back straight and looking out the bars. There was a stubbornness about him that would have set him apart even if Thadred hadn't known him.

"My mama is going to come for us. And she's going to bring the emperor and the empress with her. And they will rescue us."

Thadred didn't want to correct Rhis. He glanced around the stable. The doors of the stalls were gone, but the musty animal smell of goats remained. Whoever had lived here before the Kadra'han hadn't been gone for long.

"You're a knight?" queried the pale haired boy.

"Yes," Rhis said. "The greatest knight who has ever lived."

Well, damn, kid, Thadred thought to himself. *No pressure, right?*

"I'm a knight. Not sure if I'm the greatest, though." Thadred decided that children were terrible. Especially when they thought you were infallible.

Thadred himself had never thought adults were infallible. His whole life, for as long as he could remember, the adults around him had been there to control him, to tell him what he was doing wrong.

This blind faith coming from Rhis was completely alien to Thadred. It gave Thadred the sick sense that he was going to fail them all.

Why would the Kadra'han want Thadred? It couldn't be good. He might not know exactly what it was, but he knew it couldn't be good.

Thadred would have loved to indulge in some hearty cursing. If there was ever a moment to swear, it was when one had been abducted, assaulted, chained in tenebrous steel, and locked in an old stable.

Unfortunately, the Kadra'han had left him with an audience of children, so he was denied even that luxury. Thadred put on a brave face and glanced around. He tried to find something he had missed before, something that might stand out, something that might point him in the direction of escape.

If Thadred had been the magnificent hero that Rhis so firmly believed him to be, he would have been able to break himself free, probably using a wood splinter or something. He then would have broken all the children out and walked them back to his mother's estate without incident. Sair would return to the manor to find him and all six whelps drinking mulled wine.

But Thadred was a cripple, he was in chains, and everything hurt. Thadred wasn't sure that he could fight a house cat now, let alone a Kadra'han.

The door at the far end of the stable creaked.

Thadred forced himself upright. Not that it did much good. It wasn't like he was any less vulnerable sitting up versus lying down. He was still chained.

A shape stepped into the stable. Thadred squinted against the light, then recognized the man. He didn't bother to hold back his cursing then. "You son of a bitch."

"Always the charmer, aren't you, Sir Thadred?" Iasu spoke with a flawless imperial accent. It was a little disjointed to Thadred's mind, hearing an imperial education speak out of a Nihainite face.

Thadred had never made an effort to adopt the mannerisms of the empire. Not perfectly, anyway. He'd picked up the accent of his nurses and tutors, and by the time Dain had come along, Thadred had his own accent. One he had refused to drop despite living in the central empire surrounded by people who spoke like refined, civilized human beings.

Iasu on the other hand, had completely adapted to the empire. From all appearances, he had utterly abandoned his roots as a Nihainite and integrated himself.

Iasu swaggered toward Thadred, his small frame roped in muscle. One would have hardly believed he had been captive in Hylendale for over a year.

"How is our honored guest?" Iasu purred the words. He had a singular talent for making respectful statements sound mocking, even vindictive.

"Delightful." Thadred smiled up at Iasu. It was perhaps the only time Thadred would ever look *up* at him.

Most people made the mistake of assuming Iasu was not a threat because of his height. Most people tended to be more cautious around big men—men who overshadowed the people around them. But all the tall men Thadred had met tended to be gentle giants rather than large brutes.

On the other hand, Thadred had met far crueler short people. Thadred had a theory that it was because the rage had fewer places to go. Being a small person did not mean you were a small threat, it just meant that all your hate and anger had to be condensed.

Iasu crouched before Thadred, inspecting him like a cat discovering a downed eagle. "I wasn't expecting you. Well done. I am not often surprised."

"What? Your friends didn't tell you that they were picking me up?" Thadred tried to grin roguishly up at Iasu.

"Oh no. I didn't expect you to come after the boy. I suppose his mother must have been very convincing. How many times did she have to suck your cock before you agreed?"

Thadred smiled up at the man. "I'd say I'll kill you for that. But since I already plan to kill you, that seems a bit redundant."

Iasu smirked. "You care about this woman? She must have done a very good job indeed."

"Really, Iasu? Are you trying to make me angry? You drugged me, chained me up in a random barn, and have been holding my friend's child hostage. I'm already pissed off. I am already trying to think of a way to strangle you in your own intestines. So why don't you skip the pleasantries and ask me whatever it is you want to ask me?"

Iasu studied his fingernails, pretending to be bored. But there was a purpose to everything the man did. "How much do you know? What does the empire know?"

"Everything, obviously." Thadred winked at Iasu. "That's why I'm here. And the empire, of course, knows all your plans, too. They're sending reinforcements right now. As soon as word reaches the mainland that I'm missing, this whole land will be crawling with soldiers." Thadred adjusted his chains, trying to get it so that they didn't dig quite as painfully into his wrists.

"Your order survived the empire because the last empress saw fit to let you exist. But do you really think the emperor will be so charitable when you kill his only living family member? Amira has very few friends, and she jealously guards those she does have."

"Our sister has made her choices." That was an interesting statement. Being a Kadra'han meant something to Iasu. More than just defining the trajectory of his life, it defined his identity. "She killed my liege lady. As such, we are enemies."

"Oh, you didn't know. Fascinating."

Iasu's eyes darted sideways, fixing Thadred in a hard glare before he caught himself. "Do share." There was an edge of cynicism to the words. Iasu might want to know just what Thadred knew, but he was not going to easily be fooled by lies or deceit.

Thadred noticed the six children had gone quiet. The moment Iasu entered, they had withdrawn to the back of the cage, huddling into the corner. Rhis sat beside Maëlys, holding her hand while she leaned against his arm, her face buried against his shoulder.

Rhis was being strong for them. At his age, he shouldn't have to be strong at all, much less for other children.

Thadred made the bold decision to tell the truth. "Vesha never died."

Iasu went deadly still. Whatever he had expected, that was not it.

Thadred shrugged, feeling just a little satisfaction that he had caught the other man unawares. "Your curse was supposed to pass back to the grandmaster upon Vesha's death, wasn't it? So you wouldn't have known the difference. If you thought she was dead, it would have the same effect on you as if she was."

"I'm supposed to believe that she is holed up somewhere?" There was a sneer in Iasu's voice, something dangerous. Thadred wouldn't be able to tell him lies. It would be hard enough to tell him the truth.

"No, it's a bit weirder than that." Thadred smiled ruefully. "According to Dain and Amira, she ended up in the Dread

Marches. And the late emperor came for her." As he said it, Thadred realized how ridiculous it sounded. Unfortunately for Thadred, it was the truth.

"The man who's been dead for twenty years?" Iasu's hand wandered to the dagger at his belt.

"It's the Dread Marches—land of the living dead. It stands to follow that the dead and the living can both enter." Thadred shrugged. "I'm not sure I believe it myself. But what matters, is whether you believe it."

Iasu's eyes narrowed. "My vows have transferred to the grandmaster. Regardless of where Her Majesty is."

Well, it had been worth a shot. "So, your vows did transfer back to the grandmaster?"

Iasu didn't answer. "Are there any other sorceresses with you? Besides your whore?"

"Don't talk about my mama like that!" Rhis shouted. His act of defiance made the others cower.

Iasu glanced over his shoulder to the cage and the six children inside it. Thadred didn't see his face, but the other little ones huddled back, as if they were trying to get as far away from the Kadra'han as possible.

Thadred shook his head. "Kid, let me handle this. I already told you I'm going to be killing Iasu here, so just know that I'm already dealing with it."

Iasu swiveled his dark eyes back to Thadred. "You're going to kill me?" There was amusement in the small man's voice. Like Thadred had just told a great joke.

"I am thinking that, yes. Though, I might be willing to forgive you if you apologize."

Iasu didn't seem amused at that. "The grandmaster wants to know how many sorceresses you brought with you."

"Thousands. I have a whole legion of sorceresses trained by Amira herself. They'll be here any moment."

"There are not thousands of sorceresses left in the whole empire." Iasu's lip curled.

"Well, then it sounds like you could have answered the grandmaster's questions." Thadred tapped his good foot against the floor, making the chain rattle. "Let's play a game."

"I am not interested in playing games with you." Iasu sounded as if he meant it. He drew one of his knives and began toying with it. "It does occur to me, that your people stabbed me to the point I was a cripple for months."

"In fairness, they took me captive at the time, too."

"And then they kept me captive for months after. A whole year." Iasu studied Thadred. "I have been wanting to repay that."

Thadred interrupted him, not wanting to continue this line of conversation. "I was thinking we could play answer for an answer. I give you an answer, and you give me an answer."

A long time ago, before Thadred or Dain had been born, the Emperor Drystan had met an enemy ruler for negotiations.

The emperor had asked the general a series of questions, and the general had replied with questions. So the emperor had suggested that instead of trading questions they traded answers. *Answer for an answer* had become a kind of code among generals and nobles in Erymaya.

"I don't play games with my captives."

If there was anything good to be said for Iasu, it was that. He might be heartless, but he wasn't sadistic. He was too pragmatic for revenge.

Thadred decided to change tactics. "Alright, how about this? Do you like being bound to the grandmaster?"

"He is my liege lord. And I am a Kadra'han. To serve is my purpose." Iasu's tone was flat, not defensive in the least.

But the fact that he was answering at all was interesting.

"Well, I suppose it's best that way. I'm not sure you'd know what to do with yourself without a leash around your neck. Most dogs are like that. They might strain at their collars, but as soon as you take them off, they come right back to their masters. See, I don't think most dogs really want to be free. They wouldn't know what to do with themselves."

Thadred didn't know Iasu very well. But the smaller man wasn't moving. Not that he was prone to fidgeting, or shifting, but his whole body had gone very still. He barely seemed to be breathing. Iasu glanced over his shoulder to the cage. "We'll be training those soon. You and your friends almost destroyed our order, but we do have friends of our own."

"Baron Prisca? Is he one of your friends?" Thadred had guessed as much, and it didn't bode well.

"Less of a friend. He was just a tool."

"Was?" Thadred cocked his head at that.

"He will no longer be of use. Thanks to your woman."

Thadred wanted to ask about Sair, but if anything had happened to her, Iasu would have rubbed it in his face by now. "What exactly is your plan? What do you hope to gain from this?"

Iasu studied the sky through one of the holes in the roof. "The bloodlines have become weak. We were hard pressed to find just those six." Iasu gestured to the cage. "The late emperor did an excellent job of purging sorcerers from his lands. We have started looking in other lands, but this continent seems to be the richest in magic. At least the kind of magic that can be used to create Kadra'han."

Was Iasu volunteering information?

"The order is probably finished either way. It can either die, or it can transform." Iasu did not look at Thadred. "The new grandmaster would see it transform."

"New grandmaster?" Thadred's interest piqued at that. "Tell me about him."

Iasu ran a hand over the sparse stubble on his jaw. Thadred noticed bandages on the other man's forearms. What had happened there? "He fetched me from Lashera."

Thadred took a moment to consider that. If that was the case, then the new grandmaster was a cythraul, or could at least be possessed by one. Shit.

Something else caught Thadred's attention. *Fetched* was an interesting word. Iasu could have just as easily said *rescued* or *freed*. It might be nothing, but when Kadra'han tried to speak around commands, they had to be subtle.

"If you stay in the empire they will find you, eventually," Thadred said. "I am just the first of many. You and the order have to leave. Go far, far away. You can do whatever you want.

Take up fishing. Maybe become brewers. Hell, walk off a dock for all I care. But if you and the order want to choose your own end, you're going to have to leave and you're going to have to get rid of this grandmaster."

Iasu opened his mouth, then shut it again. He flinched. It was slight, but Thadred caught it. The other man was trying to speak around his curse. "None of us get to choose our ends. Not really." Iasu rose to his feet. "But I don't fear mine."

Great. Thadred and the six children had been taken captive by a suicidal madman. "Well, I've already promised to kill you if I can."

"We'll see." Iasu smiled and it was like seeing the fangs of a snake.

16

SAIR

Sair returned to the manor house of Thadred's family as the darkness descended. She had spent what remained of the daylight hours sending word to Thadred's soldiers, particularly Major Caiden, and trying to convince the city watch that they should search the whole of Iandua for any sign of Thadred or his kidnappers.

There was also the matter of Baron Prisca's suicide. The city watch had wanted to take Sair into custody, but Major Caiden had shut that down. Lady Sairydwen was above reproach, he said.

Sair had a fear in the back of her mind that the imperial soldiers didn't actually want to work with a sorceress. Whether that was true or not, they didn't hesitate to take her side now.

They went with Sair to the late baron's personal residence. According to his servants, he was a widower who had lost his wife a few years ago. She had been from the continent and the couple had a daughter, but the girl was very young and shy.

The servants, with some pressure, allowed Sair into the baron's study. There she had found his ledgers for his personal finances and confiscated them all.

The stacks of bound documents rode in boxes on the carriage seat across from Sair. She didn't have any real authority to do that, but she'd ask for an imperial pardon if it came down to it.

Thadred's life was at stake.

Caiden was much better qualified to lead this search, but he lacked the authority to make the city officials obey him. They might be able to bully these men into listening, but it would take time. Time wasn't something they had.

Brick rode outside the carriage and when they arrived at the manor house, he opened the door for her. He stepped aside, hands clenched tight in front of him.

Sair wanted to comfort him, but she needed comforting herself. Just what was she supposed to do now? This had gone from being a fox hunt to a bird hunt. No longer were they looking for tracks and signs, hoping to find where their quarry had gone to ground. Now they were charging through vast swaths of land, buildings, streets, and the buzz of daily life searching for whatever they might scare up.

The Kelamorans would not have taken Thadred unless they had a plan. They were not impulsive. Everything they did was premeditated.

Just what did a displaced order of warriors want? One of their order had abducted a child and come here, but that did not necessarily mean that the grandmaster had wanted Rhis.

The Kelamora Kadra'han did not have a quarrel with the empire, or at least they hadn't. Daindreth, though he had outlawed the creation of new Kadra'han, had been content to ignore the existence of the Kelamora order.

The order might have been allowed to continue as they had for who knew how long. But no. They had first tried to assassinate Sair and Thadred, and then abducted Thadred outright.

There was no coming back from this. They had made themselves enemies of the empire. The level of this insult would require a full-on retaliation from the emperor. This would call for eradication.

Which begged the question, why? Sair didn't think that Iasu was important enough to the order for them to jeopardize everyone for his sake. That meant the order either thought they were already enemies of the empire or had plans that would make them enemies of the empire. It didn't bode well.

These men were backed into a corner and convinced that they had nothing to lose. No badger fought more fiercely than when trapped in its burrow.

What could the Kelamorans be planning that would make them so willing to become enemies of the empire? No demands had been made yet, and while it was possible that would come tomorrow, Sair was not so optimistic.

They had abducted Thadred because they had a purpose for him. Their own purposes.

Sair had wracked her mind over it a thousand times. What could they need him for?

One of the late empress's Kadra'han had once mentioned that it was hard to find boys of the right bloodlines to become Kadra'han. That was thanks to the extermination of the sorcerer bloodlines wrought by the last emperor.

Thadred had magic even though his mother didn't. Somehow, his father had passed magic to him. What if the order wanted to use Thadred to make more sorcerers?

That thought made Sair sick, for more reasons than one. But if that was correct, then they would need to keep him alive and relatively unharmed.

Sair rubbed her forehead, her whole head aching. She gave instructions to have the late baron's documents sent to Thadred's suite of rooms, that seemed the most secure place. Guards flanked and circled her as she headed up into the manor.

Brick marched beside her, following just a few steps behind. Like her, he seemed to be wanting something to do. Sair didn't blame him.

Sair had barely entered the main doors of the mansion when Vespasia burst out to meet them. Vespasia still wore a day dress despite the late hour, and her hair was disheveled as if she hadn't bothered to prepare for dinner tonight.

"Lady Sairydwen!" Vespasia rushed up to the other woman, grasping her hands as if they were old friends. "What happened? We heard the most alarming news. Mother hasn't confirmed it yet, but—"

"Baron Prisca is dead." Sair didn't see the point in trying to soften the blow.

Vespasia held her hand to her mouth, a small gasp escaping. "We heard something had happened to him, but I didn't think…"

"It is quite unfortunate." Sair meant that wholeheartedly. Baron Prisca's death was incredibly inconvenient. Sair had tried to find someone who might have helped with his personal accounts. The servants they had been able to talk to claimed that those who would know anything had been somewhere in that ministry building. It was maddeningly unhelpful.

Come morning, she would have quite a few people to question, and reason with. She would see just how far she could wield and flex her power without Thadred backing her up.

"Where is your mother?" Sair didn't want to see Zeyna, but the dowager was regent. She needed to be informed that an imperial official had been abducted in her province.

Sair would need her cooperation. The dowager couldn't outright refuse to help an official of the empire, but she could slow them down if she truly wanted to.

"She is with my brother." Vespasia glanced past Sair. "Where is Lord Thadred?"

Sair hesitated. She thought about what Thadred had said. Perhaps Vespasia and the rest of the family were in league with the Kelamorans. But so far, they had no evidence of that aside from the fact that Thadred had liked Vespasia. Sair would assume that the other woman was innocent for now.

"The men who attacked us last night took him." Sair's chest wrenched as she said it, but she kept her chin up and her voice steady. At this point, she should be an expert at how to lose people with grace. But it never got any easier.

Vespasia didn't seem to register the words. "What do you mean?"

"I believe they took him as a hostage. He is most likely still alive. We are conducting a search now."

Sair was only here because Major Caiden had assured her

that he would continue the search through the night. She needed to get her rest since she was the only sorceress they had. There was also precious little to be done in the dark.

Most of the men were equipped with shields reinforced with tenebrous steel, having expected to meet sorcerers eventually. All the same, they were right. There wasn't much more she could do tonight.

Sair wished she were more like the empress. If she had been like Amira, no one would have been able to touch her child in the first place. She would have been able to hunt down and kill Iasu, freeing her son long before Thadred ever had to become involved.

If she had just been a little stronger, a little more vigilant, none of this would have happened either to her son or to the man she…

Sair had lost them both now. What were the odds she would get them back? Unharmed and unhurt?

It was wishful thinking even to consider it. But if she could only choose one of them to get back, which one would she choose?

No, she couldn't think that. She wouldn't give the gods any ideas.

"I need to speak with your mother," she said to Vespasia. "Would you mind showing me to her? I think she would appreciate that. Not having to see me alone, I mean."

Vespasia nodded, still visibly shaken from the news. "Of course." She looked at the soldiers around Sair, and even to Brick, as if one of them might offer some explanation. As if one of them might reveal this was all just a sick joke.

If it was, then it was a joke on Sair. She was the one who had dared try to have something more with Thadred. Perhaps if only she hadn't taken the chance, then at least she couldn't have lost him.

The memory of last night, his hands on her, his breath in her ear and his lips on her skin was enough to make her chest crack. She missed him with a painful intensity that threatened to drive her to her knees.

She missed her son too, but in a different way. Like the difference between being stabbed and being branded with a hot iron.

It occurred to her as they walked that she might never know what happened to Thadred or Rhis. So far, the Kelamorans seemed to be very good at disappearing. What if both Thadred and her son vanished forever? What if they were never heard from again?

"Is there anything I can do?" Vespasia held onto Sair's arm, that pressure grounding Sair in the here and the now. "Anything at all? I will do it."

"I will let you know if I think of anything." Sair was so tired. Not just from speaking with city officials, and not just because of the late hour. Her soul was exhausted. She'd been fighting so hard this whole time to rescue her son. And for a short time, Thadred had taken the bulk of that burden onto himself. For the first time in she didn't know how long, Sair had someone else carrying the weight of the world beside her.

Now Thadred was gone too. And the weight of saving him fell on her as well. The whole empire might soon be looking for Thadred, but he was only here because of her.

Sair found the dowager where Vespasia said she would be. Zeyna was in the parlor, reading to her son beside a brazier that crackled and popped.

At least fifty candles were also lit, casting the room in so much light it seemed almost day. The footman announced their entry, saying that Lady Vespasia was here. He neglected to mention Sair, either because he didn't think she was important, or for another reason Sair didn't understand. Either way, she was too tired to be offended.

"Mama," Vespasia entered the room first, pulling Sair after her. "There's something very important we need to discuss."

The young Count Flavius lounged on a nearby settee, his shoes off, and his toes digging into the plush cushions. "Mama is reading me a story."

"Countess," Sair bowed her head, "I am afraid I have bad news."

The dowager lowered the book into her lap, her hands fluttering over it anxiously. "What is wrong?" She looked nervously at her son, fear in her face.

Sair could only guess at what the woman might be thinking, but she was quick to put Zeyna out of her misery. No one should have to fear for their child when they didn't have to. "Baron Prisca is dead. I cannot tell you more than that at this time, but there is an investigation underway with the city watch and the local constables."

"Yes, I have been told. Thank you. You may go." The words were rude, discourteous, but they came in a timid, pleading tone. It was like the dowager was trying to prevent bad news from coming by virtue of ignoring it.

"There is something else, I'm afraid." A weight settled in Sair's chest, so heavy she felt she might bow under the weight of it. "Lord Thadred is missing."

The dowager looked up to her, then to Vespasia. There was something in the older woman's face, something hard to read. Sair didn't know her well enough to understand what that look meant. Was it regret? Sadness? Or maybe relief?

Zeyna cleared her throat. "Missing in what way?"

"He was abducted in your city." Sair added that phrasing, because she wanted to remind the dowager that an imperial official had been attacked in her province. If nothing else, leadership over the province would be removed if they did not do everything possible to save the emperor's cousin. Daindreth would not take kindly to this news.

"Abducted? Surely you are mistaken."

"I hope the monsters got him," said the horrible little boy on the couch. "I hope they rip off his fingers and eat his insides."

Sair didn't have time to deal with bratty children on top of everything else.

"Not now, darling," said the dowager, making a frantic shushing motion, then turning back to Sair. "But surely, he is simply wandered off? I heard he was asking after a brothel. Perhaps he is…?"

Vespasia ducked her head, looking away from Sair.

"I was with him at the brothel," Sair said. "He was taken after we left."

"You went with him?" the dowager sputtered.

As soon as she said it, Sair had a vague sense of how it must sound to be put that way. Regardless, she had bigger things to consider. "The important thing is that I saw him taken. I don't know the men who did it, but I believe that they are associated with the men who attacked last night."

"Well," the dowager said, "in that case, you must inform the head of the city watch."

"I have," Sair said. "They have not been cooperative."

"Did you or your soldiers speak to Sheriff Telis?"

Sair's jaw tightened. "Yes. He was not helpful, either."

Telis was a gruff man who had been displeased when Sair demanded to personally speak with him. He had been dismissive toward her but had at least bothered to answer Major Caiden's questions. When the major had pressed for particular counts of available men and protocols to search the city, Telis had found a way to end their audience.

"He never has liked people interfering with his work." Zeyna looked back down to the book in her lap. "I am sure he will handle it."

Sair tried not to let her frustration show.

Mothers of child rulers could be incredibly powerful if they so chose, and the late empress was true proof of that. Of all the women who had risen to power in the continent over the centuries, most of them had done so as regents.

But Zeyna seemed to leave the actual management of the province to her ministers and officials. That was a problem when the officials appeared to be either corrupt or uncooperative.

"I shall send word to Telis. Informing him that this is of the utmost importance." Zeyna went back to looking down at the book in her hands, implying that it was something she would save for tomorrow.

Didn't she see that every second counted? Sair might be able to search the city herself by the time this woman and her officials thought to act.

Sair forced herself into calm. "I know your husband maintained a garrison on this estate, and I would ask for twenty of them to help me search the city."

Zeyna quailed at that. She looked to her daughter, but whatever the dowager saw there, it must not have been what she was hoping for. She looked back to Sair. "I cannot spare men, especially if you are right and there are assassins on the loose. I will need them to protect me and my children."

"I have no reason to think that you or your children are targets." That was a lie, Sair realized. Thadred was very much a target.

"All the same…I will not risk it. I will not put them in danger."

"Lord Thadred is your child." Sair wasn't sure what she expected to accomplish by saying the words. The dowager knew it as well as all of them, and she had already made it clear that she didn't want to think about that relationship. "And he is in danger."

"I…" the dowager looked to her little boy. "Darling, I think it is best you go to bed now."

"But I'm not tired." The boy sat upright, glaring defiance at his mother.

Rather than argue, Zeyna set the book aside and rose to her feet. "Let us continue our conversation in the hall." She said it with a forced smile.

"Very well." Sair allowed the dowager to lead them into the hall, while a nursemaid appeared to care for the protesting little boy.

Not for the first time, Sair thought that perhaps Thadred being raised by the late empress had been a good thing. Neglected he might have been, but Thadred had grown up with discipline, a sense of honor and duty. Come to think of it, for all her flaws, and her many, many mistakes, both the boys raised by the late Empress Vesha had grown up to be quite decent.

In the hallway, the dowager closed the door and shooed away the servants. Obediently, Brick and the others retreated, presumably out of earshot.

Sair didn't understand the effort at secrecy.

"I am afraid I cannot give you soldiers," the dowager repeated. "It is quite beyond my capability. You will have to do with the city watch."

"The city watch are barely staffed as it is. They have not yet recovered from the Witch War. But you already knew this—as regent." Sair was growing weary of this pretense.

The dowager looked to her daughter, and this time Sair looked as well.

To her credit, Vespasia did not quail under scrutiny. "Lord Thadred is a minister with the empire, Mama. It will not look good to the empire if anything happens to him on our watch. It is already shameful that he was abducted, but if any harm befalls him…" Vespasia glanced to Sair.

To these women who had never met the emperor, perhaps the thought of his wrath was a fearsome thing. Many people had found their heads on stakes after defying his parents. Many had lost their titles, land, and holdings, their sons impressed into military service and their daughters cloistered or wedded off to imperial men.

Daindreth was not a petty man or a vengeful emperor, but none of them knew that.

"I need your help," Sair looked straight into the eyes of the dowager. She grabbed the other woman's hands, softening her voice. She tried to appeal to the thing that they had in common. "Lord Thadred was helping me find my little boy. My only son." Sair didn't have to feign the desperation that crept into her voice at that. "Please help me. From one mother to another."

The dowager held Sair's gaze for barely a moment. Then she looked away. She shook her head and pulled her hands free. "I am sorry. Truly, I am. But I…"

Appealing to the woman's sense of goodness had failed, appealing to her fear of the empire had failed. That left one thing—shame.

"You carried Thadred. Birthed him." Sair blinked at the other woman. "He is your firstborn child. How can you just leave him like this?" Sair's voice broke on the question.

"I don't know him." There was a fierceness to Zeyna's words, vehemence that hadn't been there before.

For just a moment, Sair could see that this woman was indeed of the same blood as the late empress. That same ferocity was there, if buried deeply, and if relegated into an obscure corner. Where the former empress had nurtured her ferocity, fed it like a flame and let it blaze like a furnace, this woman had diminished her own spirit, smothered it in ribbons and starved it with frivolity.

"He is still your son. Do you feel nothing?" Sair shook her head. "I have crossed a continent and an ocean for my son. Will you not let your men cross a city for yours?"

Zeyna shook her head, refusing to meet Sair's eyes. "I mourned him well and good for years. I am well practiced at it by now."

Sair had imperial authority on her side, that much was true. But if this woman chose to defy her, it would take soldiers to force compliance. More soldiers than Sair had.

While this would have long term consequences for the dowager, by the time Sair could send word back to the mainland and help could arrive, it would be too late for Thadred—and Rhis.

Fists at her sides, Sair raised her chin. She was shorter than Zeyna, but only by a few inches. "You may be content to abandon your son, but I am not. And if I have to tear apart your city, your home, and your entire life with my bare hands, I will do it."

Sair stormed away, leaving the dowager and her eldest daughter behind. Sair caught Brick at the corner of the hallway and gestured for him to follow her.

As she walked away from the other woman, she wasn't sure if she had been speaking of her own son, or of the dowager's. Both, she supposed.

"What can I do, my lady?" Brick asked nervously. He hovered at her shoulder, his satchel still swinging at her side.

"You can read?"

"Of course, my lady. Though, I am not much for writing."

"That is all I need. Come. We are going to go through Baron Prisca's documents." Maybe, if they were lucky, they would find something that would help them to locate the Kelamora Kadra'han.

Sair walked through the mansion, back to the wing that she and Thadred had been sharing. Night had long since fallen, and the estate was mostly quiet.

Carried on the night breeze, Sair could hear the whining keen of a kelpie. Lleuad was upset. The little stallion must know that his master was missing.

Sair and Brick camped out in the room where Thadred had been staying. It had been secured the night before and was probably the safest room in the mansion.

Brick didn't say anything when she took a coat from Thadred's wardrobe and wrapped it around her shoulders. It was warm and surrounded her with his scent of leather and spices. She could almost imagine it was him holding her—almost.

Sair lit another candle as she and Brick settled in for a long night of work.

17

THADRED

As Thadred sat on the floor, the cold gnawed at him with icy teeth. In their cage, the children huddled together. Rhis sat at the center of their little pile, several of the smaller children close to him including the girl.

Thadred was exhausted, but he couldn't sleep. The discomfort chewed at him relentlessly. The tenebrous steel shackling his wrists prevented him from reinforcing the spells that kept his hip and thigh supported. His joints ached, and his hip throbbed on top of the pain of being on the hard floor.

Thadred wondered when he had gotten so old. He remembered a time when he had been able to sleep on the ground and wake up refreshed. Not so anymore. Perhaps it had been the accident. He couldn't remember sleeping comfortably since then. Not really.

Thadred closed his eyes and tried to think. He had exhausted himself trying to consider ways that he might be able to get out of this. But unarmed and defenseless, he could do little more than wait for rescue.

Sair. Sair would come for him. She would come for both him and Rhis. Definitely for Rhis.

Sair was strong, determined, and brave. She would find a way. He had every confidence in that. He had to. He was beyond the empire's reach, and the only person who cared about him on

195

this side of the sea was Sair.

I love you, she had said. And he had tried to talk her out of it.

If he had just married her a year ago instead of waiting, they wouldn't be here now. If he had become Rhis's stepfather, Rhis would have been safe. Which meant that Sair would have been safe and none of this would have happened.

Sair loved him. It seemed undoubtable and impossible at the same time.

And he loved her too. He had loved her for a long time. He thought he might have fallen in love with her when she had taught him to use magic. Maybe even before then.

In that cold, and dark forest, when they were both wounded and vulnerable, they had seen each other at their worst. Sair wasn't impressed by him, not the way other women had been.

But she revered him in a way that they didn't. He wasn't a shiny bauble or a toy to her. He was something valuable, something she didn't want to live without.

He was still sure that he wasn't good enough for Sair. Who could ever be good enough for Sair? But she made him better. Maybe she could make him good enough.

Thadred didn't remember falling asleep, but he must have because the next thing he knew, he was being kicked awake by Iasu.

"Get up. Unless you'd like to piss on the floor."

"Unmatched courtesy, as always." Thadred sat up, hiding a wince for his creaking joints. "Have you thought any more about what I said?"

"The grandmaster wants to see you."

"So soon?" Thadred blinked away the last vestiges of slumber. He had no idea how he had been able to sleep.

Two other men stood in front of the cage with the children. They were in the process of undoing the many chains that seemed to be more a means of holding the door in place than securing the small captives.

Thadred made eye contact with Rhis. The little boy looked up at him, childish determination in his face.

"They do this about the same time every day. We get to go

outside to make water and eat before they bring us back here."

The order had routines. Not surprising.

"No talking," snapped one of the Kelamorans.

Rhis bowed submissively, but he winked to Thadred.

Indeed, that child's faith in Thadred was terrifying.

Thadred considered resisting as Iasu unchained him from the center brace. But it wasn't like he would be running away.

Thadred resigned himself to being a captive for now and let Iasu lead him out of the warehouse. They followed the children, Rhis looking back frequently as if he expected something to happen. Iasu must have noticed because he tightened his grip on Thadred's chains.

Outside, Thadred was disappointed as he found walls blocking most of his view. If there were other buildings nearby, he couldn't see them.

The small courtyard had tended flowerbeds and vines snaking up the walls. The building was old, but not unkempt.

Listening, he couldn't hear much over the wind and the distant squawking of seagulls. If they were near the docks or the outskirts of the city, or in an entirely different city, he couldn't tell.

The children were taken off in one direction, and Thadred was led in another. Thadred tensed as the children were pulled out of sight, jerking back on his chains.

"You'll see them again." Iasu sounded annoyed. "Not like they're getting sacrificed or anything."

"That would be funnier if I hadn't seen your grandmaster participate in child sacrifice." Thadred turned a harsh glare on the other man.

In Kelamora, Thadred had seen Vesha try to summon a demon with the help of the grandmaster and his ilk. They had sliced the arms of a little girl to do it and it had taken the combined power of Thadred and Amira to save her.

Iasu shrugged. "They're no good to us dead, are they?"

Thadred supposed he was right. If he should be worried for anyone, he should be worried for himself right now. He still wasn't sure what the Kelamorans wanted with him.

Iasu led him to what appeared to be an outhouse. It was a series of seats with round holes opening over some kind of drain. Beyond it was a midden heap that looked and smelled fresh, so they must be inside the city still.

"Can I trust you not to stab me while I piss?"

Iasu responded with a flat expression.

Thadred pissed and shat and did his trousers back up, supposing that he should be grateful his captors were so generous.

Iasu led him back through the old complex. The smell of woodsmoke caught Thadred's attention along with the smell of something cooking. The grumble of his stomach reminded him that he hadn't eaten since yesterday morning. Iasu led him around to the source of the woodsmoke, a large fire with a stew kettle over the flames.

The children sat in a row, carefully guarded by their captors but untouched. They sat with bowls in their hands, slurping the stew and mopping at it with pieces of bread.

There was not much they could do to resist, but Thadred's heart sank when he recognized what was happening. The children were being trained. It was the same thing that happened in the barracks with young squires. It was one of the first things a boy learned, how to sit and eat.

The children were being broken. It was not the beatings and harsh punishments one usually thought of when they thought of breaking a child's will. But it would be more effective in the long term.

Rhis might shelter the other children for now. He might protect them and look for a way out, but give it a few weeks, months, and years, and Rhis would become as hard and soulless as Iasu and the others. They all would.

Thadred didn't have much time to think on that dark line of thought as Iasu pulled him back through the barn. A door at the opposite end was open, and Iasu led him straight toward that.

Thadred wasn't exactly looking forward to reaching the other side, but he was eager for the suspense to be over. Perhaps the grandmaster would kill him. That would be delightful. That would mean the full weight of the empire's judgment would crash down on this small order of renegades.

Kadra'han were not gods. They were stronger, and in most cases better trained than average soldiers, but they were very much mortal. They could be killed as easily as other men.

On the other side of the barn was another courtyard, much larger. Men who appeared to be masons were hard at work, tearing up the stone courtyard and hacking away at the earth.

A large crater already lay in the center of the courtyard. The men hauled out buckets of dirt and wielded wheelbarrows.

Thadred spotted the foreman he had spoken to yesterday outside the former brothel. Thadred looked around hastily as a jolt of realization went through him. They were inside the former brothel, the same one that had been purchased by Baron Prisca. Except now the entrance to the courtyard was barred and the masons worked with heads down, avoiding eye contact.

What Thadred guessed to be another Kadra'han oversaw them, watching with arms crossed. Were these workers being forced to do this? What were they doing, anyway?

Thadred recognized the grandmaster at once. He was an older man, though he wasn't what Thadred would have considered frail. He might be past his prime, but the bulge of muscles still stood out through his sleeves.

Beside him stood a younger man, hands behind his back and facing the workers.

Thadred smiled at the grandmaster. "It has been a long time. But not long enough. How do you do, grandmaster of Kelamora? Do you have an actual name? Because I've only ever called you the grandmaster."

"Senru is no longer the grandmaster." The young man beside the former grandmaster spoke, and the voice was wrong.

Thadred did not consider himself the bravest of men. But he didn't consider himself a total craven, either. Either way, the sound of that voice made him stumble backward, his chains yanking in Iasu's hands.

He had heard that voice before, if only a few times. But he would never forget it.

The young man turned around, and Thadred was greeted with the flaming red eyes of a cythraul.

The creature grinned, though everything they did in their stolen bodies never quite seemed right. "What? You, the High Inquisitor seeking me across the continent, are surprised to find me?"

"You were sent back to the Dread Marches."

Caa Iss shook his head. "No. My witch may have chosen to betray me in the end, but when she broke her side of the pact, I was freed."

This had suddenly gotten much, much worse. Never in all of his imaginings had Thadred imagined this.

Caa Iss looked to the former grandmaster at his side. "Senru has graciously stepped aside. He continues as my second, but he understands that for the Kelamora order to survive, it needs someone more powerful at its head."

Everything had just changed. Thadred tried to compose himself. Cythraul could be killed in these bodies. At least if their physical forms were destroyed, they could be banished from the world of the living.

"Javen volunteered for this. He was the one to kill the Elder Mother, thus ending the contract that bound me to the Fanduillion bloodline. After that, I was free to take another host." Caa Iss flexed his hands, the hands that weren't really his, admiring the way the tendons and muscles flexed.

So Iasu had not been the one to kill the Elder Mother after all. Thadred shot a glance to the other man to find Iasu staring straight ahead, not at Caa Iss, but past him.

The demon continued. "While I was there, I couldn't resist taking back my perfectly good Kadra'han." Caa Iss motioned to Iasu. "And the boy crossed our path on the way out. So fortunate."

It hadn't been a plot. It hadn't been planned. Iasu's escape and Rhis's capture had all been about opportunity. Then again, Thadred was less sure by the moment that Iasu had escaped anything.

"I suppose I can expect soldiers from Daindreth if anything

happens to you. Closest thing he ever had to a brother. I do remember how you always helped him fight me." A note of menace crept into the creature's tone. "In fact, without you, I would have taken him over long before he met that Istovari bitch."

By *Istovari bitch*, Thadred assumed that Caa Iss meant Amira. She had been the original sacrifice offered to Caa Iss to bring him into this world, but she had survived. Unbeknownst to anyone at the time, because her blood had bound Caa Iss to this world, she had been able to silence him. Like a net sprung over a caught boar. Because of Amira, they had ultimately been able to free Dain of the demon altogether.

Caa Iss had been exorcized and nearly twenty years of the demon's careful planning had gone to waste in a single moment.

Thadred had never had to face the monster directly. He had seen it take over Dain twice or thrice, but never for long. The demon had clung to his cousin like a malady for most of his life. Any strong emotion had always made the demon stronger.

Dain had lived a secluded, calm life. He had done his duties as heir to the empire, but there had always been a wall between him and the rest of the world.

And now the creature was unleashed. Now it was standing in front of Thadred inhabiting the body of a young Kelamoran. At least the man looked young. He might be in his twenties or thirties. It was hard to tell.

In the center of the courtyard, the workers continued to dig, hacking at the stone, and carting out massive pieces of it in chunks.

Thadred wasn't quite sure what to think of this. They were digging? There didn't seem to be any real focus to the digging. They hacked and clawed at the earth, taking up huge blocks of it and carting it away. What looked like construction yesterday looked more like indiscriminate destruction today.

Thadred fixed his attention on the workers. "Are you looking for something?"

Caa Iss glanced to the side, hands still clasped behind his back. "Oh, that? No, we are not looking for anything. We are destroying this."

"Destroying what, exactly?"

"This is a place of power. So long as that well exists, I will always have the risk that one of my other brothers or sisters at large in the world may return here and release others."

There were several implications in that statement. Demons could lie. They did it all the time, but it seemed an odd lie to tell.

Thadred considered his next words carefully. "You don't want the portal opened?"

"No, foolish boy. While that portal is not strong enough to let my mother through, it is more than large enough to release several others. Araa Oon, Maak Kess, Saan Thii, and the other demon princes would be all too eager to get a piece of me. No, my only goal is to keep out of the Dread Marches and to do that, I must reduce my risks of being hunted by my own kind."

"You could offer your services to the emperor," Thadred suggested, stalling. "He might actually help you if you helped us hunt down the rest of your kind that are loose in the world. That would be easier to do if you kept me alive of course."

Caa Iss threw back his head and laughed. At least Thadred thought it was a laugh. It was a cackling, rasping sound that reminded Thadred of broken glass. "I am almost tempted. For the irony of it. There is a certain kind of pleasure in hunting down my own kind. A singular pleasure. You never hate anyone the way you hate your own brothers and sisters." Caa Iss peered closely at Thadred. "I hear you recently had a family reunion. You must have felt it."

Many people spoke of the rivalry between siblings. History was splattered with the blood of brothers spilt by brothers, sometimes sisters too. But even if the dowager's children might be his half-siblings, it was Dain that Thadred considered his brother. Thadred had never truly hated Dain. He might have resented him when they were younger, but that was the past. They had suffered together for years—Dain with his demon and then Thadred after his accident.

After his fall, Thadred had lain in agony for weeks. He had begged Dain to let the physicians overdose him with nightshade and be done with it. Dain had refused. Thadred had cursed him for it, but Dain had stayed at his side. Dain had been there when Thadred had learned to walk with a cane, to ride again. Thadred had never thanked the emperor, but he was grateful now that his cousin had forced him to live.

If the hate for a brother was unlike anything else, then the love for a brother was also unlike anything else. But that last part was the part that demons seemed to be missing.

Caa Iss made a purring sound a human couldn't have made. "As I said, I would get great pleasure from killing you, but I think it is in my best interest to keep you alive for now. You are much more interesting than these." Caa Iss gestured around the Kelamorans vaguely. If they were offended by the accusation, they gave no sign.

Thadred glanced over his shoulder in the general direction of where the children were taking their morning meal. "What exactly do you plan to do with the children?"

"I always have uses for the blood of sorcerers." Caa Iss pulled a knife from his jacket. It was an embroidered jacket, made of velvet. It was the kind of clothing that might have been fashionable in the winter court of the empire. It looked a bit warm for this climate, but again, cythraul were not rational creatures. Not in the slightest.

The demon played with the knife. It was bright silver, with a jeweled hilt. It seemed that Caa Iss was a creature who appreciated luxury. What a stark contrast to the rest of the Kelamorans around him. "Hold him for me."

Well, that didn't sound good. Thadred was fairly sure they didn't plan to kill him, and probably didn't mean to cut out his tongue just now—how else would he entertain the demon?

Regardless, there wasn't a whole lot Thadred could do. He was weakened, sore, outnumbered, and had no access to his magic.

Two Kadra'han, a pair of the larger men, grabbed his arms and dragged him forward. Thadred managed to kick one of them and rammed his elbow into the mouth of the other. All that got him was a fist to the gut that doubled him over, driving the air out of his lungs.

They dragged Thadred over to a stump and forced him to his knees. That sent a flash of pain through his hip and shooting up his spine. He gritted his teeth to keep from crying out.

They grabbed his arms and stretched them over the top of the stump. Were they planning to cut his hands off?

It had long been common practice to mutilate one's enemies so that they couldn't take up weapons. Thadred wondered distantly if that was what was about to happen to him. Already he was trying to separate his mind from his body, trying to witness this as an outside observer to lessen whatever they were about to do to him.

With his arms stretched over the stump, palms up, two more Kadra'han came from behind and pinned his shoulders.

Thadred let off several choice curses, and bit the bicep of a man who came too close. That earned him a curse, and another elbow to the nose. Thadred went blind with pain for a moment and saw stars.

"Did I ever mention how much I love it when you fight?" That came from Caa Iss. The ghastly creature grinned down at Thadred. He played with his knife, grinning. He slit Thadred's right sleeve, exposing his forearm.

Thadred tried to struggle again, but against four Kadra'han, he didn't stand a chance.

Caa Iss drew the blade from Thadred's elbow down to his wrist. Pain sliced into him, and Thadred grunted. Blood welled to the surface.

Caa Iss stared down at the blood, slitted pupils dilating. His nostrils flared just a little as he studied it. "Blood is as close to pure *ka* as we can possibly get. Filled with all the things that keep living things alive. And the blood of sorcerers? That is just distilled power." Caa Iss licked Thadred's blood off the knife, making a growling sound as he did.

Thadred spat. "I hope your mother turns you inside out."

Caa Iss wagged a finger in Thadred's face, grinning at him. "Be careful. Or I might turn you inside out first."

Caa Iss clapped his hand down over the wound on

Thadred's arm, fingers digging painfully into the cut. The blood rushed up in crimson tendrils like a nest of snakes. It slithered up Caa Iss's arm. The red lines slid underneath the velvet sleeve of the cythraul's jacket, instead of staining the fabric. Was he absorbing it somehow?

Thadred didn't understand what he was seeing. He was a sorcerer, but he was no expert in magic. He had less than a year of proper training. He didn't know just what a cythraul could do.

"I cannot access *ka* in this form. That is where you come in." Caa Iss patted Thadred's cheek. "Like I said, I can always use the blood of sorcerers." Caa Iss held up his hand and though Thadred couldn't see *ka* in this state bound with tenebrous steel, he was able to see the flicker of flame that sparked on Caa Iss's fingers.

Caa Iss raised his eyebrows and looked back to Thadred with delight. "So much power. You have served your master well, have you not? Of course, I'm sure being bonded to the kelpie has helped."

Blood kept welling from the cut. The wound was shallow but long. Red soaked his forearm and the stump below.

Caa Iss seemed to notice. "Get that bandaged. I would hate for my new toy to die just yet."

It was Iasu who brought a linen strip to press against the cut. The pressure hurt, but Thadred gritted his teeth, and this time didn't struggle.

Iasu made eye contact as he held the bandages against Thadred's skin. The smaller man looked down and Thadred followed his gaze to Iasu's forearm. He remembered then that there was a bandage there too. What appeared to be several. Looking up, he realized that all of the Kadra'han had bandages visible on their bodies. Was Caa Iss bleeding these men for power?

Somehow, the thought of being tapped like an ale keg to give a demon power sounded like the worst fate he could imagine.

Was Caa Iss using the children like this? Was he using their power the way he appeared to be using the grown men?

Just when Thadred understood how terrible and evil cythraul

were, he learned something that took their awfulness to a whole new level.

Iasu wrapped Thadredn's forearm in a snug bandage. It pinched, and his blood soaked through the linen in moments. Why did Iasu have a roll of bandages to hand? Was this truly such a regular occurrence that they carried around clean linen?

The two Kadra'han holding him down, hoisted him up and dragged Thadred back through the complex. They took him straight back to the old stable where he had been chained previously. They didn't bother to feed him, but he didn't want to eat anything they might offer him anyway.

The two Kadra'han chained him while Iasu leaned against the doorway, overseeing.

The cage was empty.

"Where are the children?" Thadred demanded. He wanted to ask where Rhis was but didn't want to draw more attention to the boy.

"They will be back soon," Iasu said. "We don't hurt children, knight."

"Not for lack of trying," Thadred shot back.

"That incident you witnessed in Kelamora was the will of the empress." Iasu's expression didn't change, but he glanced away for just an instant. He meant Vesha—Daindreth's mother, the former empress, and Iasu's former liege lady.

"She's not dead." Thadred looked straight at Iasu as he said it. The smaller man didn't react.

The other two Kadra'han glanced to Iasu, who did not choose to elaborate.

Iasu folded his arms across his chest, moving away from the doorway. "Rest well, knight. Giving blood to him is exhausting. And I expect you will be doing quite a bit of it."

"You can't want this. None of you can." Thadred wasn't sure just how Caa Iss had convinced the grandmaster to let him become grandmaster instead, but no one could have planned on being used as that monster's magical wine cellar. Though their vows might keep them from actively working against the demon, Thadred knew as well as any other Kadra'han that there were ways around your vows.

The three Kadra'han did not respond to him. They did not even look back as they marched out of the barn.

Thadred had known that sorcerers had power in their blood. He had seen sorcerers use the blood of animals and people to work magic.

Like the demon had said, blood was almost pure *ka*. It was the easiest thing to harvest power from, and it was how weak sorcerers usually got power, leading to rumors of blood magic.

Thadred was now strong enough that he could harvest it from the air, using the excess that wafted off all living things. But for a creature like Caa Iss, he had to tap it directly from living things. And not even just living things, living sorcerers. Though bodies retained their *ka* for some time after death, so Caa Iss could probably work with the recently dead, too.

It occurred to Thadred that perhaps two nights ago had not been an assassination attempt at all but an abduction effort. Perhaps Caa Iss had wanted both him and Sair alive.

If there was anything to be grateful for in this situation, it was that Sair was beyond the demon's reach—for now, at least.

18

SAIR

A yelp jolted Sair out of sleep. Her bleary eyes came into focus on Brick, scrambling to his feet.

"Forgive me, my lady," Brick stammered. "I didn't mean to…forgive me. I have never been this improper in my life and I swear it will not happen again."

"Brick, what's wrong?" Sair winced, her back and shoulder reminding her she was too old to be sleeping on the floor.

Brick gestured to the piles of documents surrounding them, the spent candles, and the general disarray of the room. "I didn't mean to fall asleep, my lady. I certainly didn't mean to sleep in the same room."

Realization came to Sair and she had to stifle a chuckle. "Brick, I'm a widow. I believe that widows can do as they please."

Brick cleared his throat. "If word gets back to Lord Thadred…" Brick shot a glance to the door, as if suddenly remembering that guards had been posted last night and the guards would know.

"Nothing happened," Sair sighed, rubbing the bridge of her nose as she tried to focus on the document before her. "And Thadred won't care. Now would you mind seeing about breakfast?"

Brick nodded hastily, probably grateful for something

proper to do. He retreated out the door, leaving Sair in the middle of Thadred's rooms surrounded by a dead man's papers.

Baron Prisca's papers were frustratingly mundane. There were receipts detailing different transactions with various other merchants, guild fees, and all his taxes down to the last copper. There were totals of usury, and records of how much was owed to various bankers. It seemed that he owed an impressive amount to the Taredicci bank, but it should have been entirely manageable for someone in his station. It wasn't as if the bank was demanding payment.

There was nothing here to indicate what had been worth killing himself.

As she looked through another report that appeared to detail yearly grain shipments to and from a local merchant, Sair was ready to give up.

A knock sounded from the door.

"Come in, Brick."

"I am not Brick. But I hope I am allowed in all the same."

Sair looked up. "Lady Vespasia. You will forgive me if I do not rise. How might I help you?" Sair did not have time for pleasantries.

"I came to see if I might be of some assistance. My mother has left for a council meeting this morning. I believe she will be speaking to them about Lord Thadred's disappearance."

Sair tried not to feel too much hope at that. "Do you think she will call for assistance in our search?"

"No more than she promised yesterday." Vespasia looked down, her hands clasped before her. The girl's hair lay straight, not curled by hot irons. She was still dressed like a noble woman, but her usual jewels and finery were missing. She was dressed for work, or at least a gentlewoman's idea of it. "Is there something I can do?"

"I wish there was." Sair heaved a sigh, the letters on the document swimming in her blurry vision. "Unfortunately, I do not know where to begin myself."

"Well, what are you doing now?" Vespasia looked hesitantly at the documents scattered around the room.

"I am trying to figure out just what the late baron was hiding. It seems quite a bit of harmless drivel. As far as I can tell, Prisca was a perfectly competent minister and businessman. I can see why he rose so high as a respected steward and a bookkeeper. I cannot see what he had to do with Thadred's abduction, or what he had to do with these Kelamora Kadra'han. But there must be a link. Somewhere. But either the man hid it so well that I cannot find it, I am simply blind to the clues, or this entire thing was a misunderstanding." Sair dropped the papers in her hands and leaned back against the couch. "So short of communing with the dead, I do not see how you or I could help."

Vespasia stepped into the room, moving carefully around the strewn papers. "Mama has left a contingent of soldiers here to guard me. Some thirty men."

Sair stifled a curse at that—one she had learned from Thadred.

Zeyna had the soldiers. She just refused to use them for anything other than protecting herself and her legitimate children.

"Another thirty are to remain here and guard Flavius." Vespasia exhaled a slow sigh. "But…I did ask the lieutenant. They do not have orders to keep me here."

"Yes." Sair felt her patience wearing thin. She wanted to be done with this conversation and move on to more important things—mainly finding her son and the man she loved.

Vespasia glanced to the side, then back to Sair. She straightened just a little, like she was making up her mind. "If I was to go searching for Lord Thadred, they would have no choice to come with me."

Sair froze, not sure she heard right. "What?"

Vespasia shrugged. "They have orders to guard me. They do not have orders to keep me here. I can't make them defy Mama, but…" Vespasia grimaced.

Sair ran her hands over her face. "Thank you, Vespasia. Truly. If we knew where Thadred was, that would be of immense help." Sair tried not to sound angry, she *tried*, but her voice rose as she spoke. "But we do not know where he is. We have no way of finding him. So, unless you can think of a way to have your men assist with the search…"

Another keen from the kelpie stabbed through the air.

Sair fell silent, her sleep-deprived mind putting first one piece in place, then another. Sair turned from Vespasia, looking past her to the doorway.

A knock sounded and Brick stepped through, carrying a tray of fruit slices, warm bread, and steaming bacon. Sair's stomach twisted with hunger, but she didn't have time for that.

"Brick, I'm going to get dressed." Sair still wore her dress from yesterday, but she would need something different for what she had in mind. "Can you send word to the city and have the major meet me in the courtyard?"

Brick barely had time to bow to Vespasia before he set down the tray and rushed out, not questioning Sair for a second.

"What do you have in mind?" Excitement sparked in Vespasia's eyes, a glint of something akin to mischief. She might be Thadred's half-sister, but Sair caught herself noticing their kinship more and more. Vespasia certainly shared her brother's daring.

"I need…" Sair considered it for a moment. "I need my riding dress." She fled out the door and into the hall, back to where her trunk was kept.

"I'll join you. Shall I have our horses saddled?"

Sair grated. Ladies took forever to prepare for riding. It was as much an event as going to the salon or a friend's for tea.

"I can be ready in a trice," Vespasia promised. "Mama even taught us all to ride bareback."

Well, Sair wouldn't have guessed that. "I don't know if what I am planning will work," Sair said. "I might not be able to do it."

"You need my soldiers, whatever the case." Vespasia raised her chin, daring Sair to argue.

"Very well. Quickly." Sair nodded, tearing back into the room she'd been given yesterday.

Vespasia gave a little grin of triumph before whirling away and racing back down the hall.

Sair had no maidservant, but she had been dressing herself for her entire life. She pulled off her frock and outer surcoat. She lashed her hair back under a kerchief, the way married women did in Hylendale. It was intended for modesty, but it also served quite well to keep hair out of her face.

Sair donned her riding boots and her riding dress along with wool leggings underneath. It was warm for the sultry climate of Kelethian, but this early in the morning, Sair felt fine.

By the time she made her way to the courtyard, Brick was already waiting with the major. Trusty Brick. After this, Sair would tell Thadred to increase his wages, no matter what they currently were.

From here, Lleuad's squeals of outrage sliced through the air like the howl of the wind.

Sair carried Thadred's coat, the same one she had worn last night.

"Lady Sairydwen," the major bowed. "Brick said you have a plan?"

Sair swallowed. "I do." She nodded to the stables.

The major shook his head. "My lady, the creature has been rabid since yesterday. No one can get near him. It's been a struggle for the stable hands to keep him contained. All the other horses had to be moved out because he was making them anxious."

"Do you have a better idea?" Sair demanded.

The major inhaled very slowly, like a man dealing with a petulant teenager. "My lady, we were unable to track Lord Thadred with dogs. He has no scent trail."

"Lleuad doesn't need his scent." Sair didn't know that for sure, but the bond between a kelpie and his rider was a thing of Eponine. It went beyond understanding, beyond logic. Kelpies were wild, untamable, and vicious by nature, but with their chosen riders, they were the fiercest protectors.

"He might attack you," the major said. "He's attacked everyone else who has tried to get near him."

Sair nodded. She had considered that. "I'm willing to risk it."

"If I lose both you and Lord Thadred, the empress will have

my head."

"Nonsense, the emperor will save you." Sair stepped toward the stable, but the major blocked her path.

"Ma'am—" He grasped her arm, just above her elbow.

Sair yanked herself free on instinct. "I am not a child, major." Her nostrils flared. "Nor am I one of your recruits. Now stand aside and let me try the one option we have left, or I will remove you."

Motion from the corner of Sair's eye told her that Vespasia had arrived with her contingent of soldiers. The lady sat astride a sleek rouncey with lean muscle, the signs of a horse used to being ridden fast.

"Prepare your men to follow us," Sair ordered the major. "I will come out of that stable with a willing kelpie."

"Or you won't come out at all," the major hissed, his voice dropping low as he leaned down.

"In that case, I trust you will find another way to save Lord Thadred." Sair stepped past him, and he didn't stop her this time. She didn't look back, that would show a lack of confidence, but she was sure Brick and Vespasia stared as she entered the stables.

As the major had said, the stalls were empty. Lleuad's distress had been contagious. They'd had to remove the other horses from the stalls and even the barn cats had fled.

Sair dragged the great doors of the stable aisle closed, barring them after her just in case. If Lleuad tried to bolt, there was no telling what might happen.

In the enclosed space, Lleuad's screams were even louder. He snorted and pawed, hooves batting at his stall door.

Sair ventured carefully down the aisle, taking slow breaths to steady herself. Lleuad was panicking. She needed to be the calm one, the anchor in his tempest.

The other stall doors had also been shut, but there was no mistaking which stall held the kelpie. Even if Sair hadn't been here the other night, the extra boards nailed around it were a giveaway. Canvas had been spread around Lleuad's stall in an early effort to shield him from the other horses.

Inside, stomping hooves and the kelpie's keening continued. His hackamore bridle had fallen from its hook at the front of his stall. His slamming against the doors had probably knocked it off. Sair picked it up.

"Lleuad?" She called his name quietly, not sure if even he could hear it over his own squeals. "Easy, boy." Another shriek. "It's me. Remember me?"

Sair carefully removed one of the bars over the top half of his stall door. "Easy—"

The top door smashed open and Sair barely managed to duck in time to avoid being hit full in the face.

A shaggy black head thrust through, white teeth snapping, white eyes rolling. Spittle and blood rained down on Sair's head and she crouched out of his reach.

"Hold," Sair ordered, her voice shaky as her heart thundered in her chest. That door had been smashed open with enough force to throw her across the aisle. It was pure luck she hadn't been hit. "Easy, boy." She adjusted her grip on the coat and the hackamore.

Lleuad lunged for her, ears pinned and teeth flashing.

Sair raised Thadred's coat, smacking the kelpie's face.

The horse clamped down on the sleeve and pulled back, then seem to think better of it. He let go, snorting.

Lleuad's ears swiveled forward. He nosed at the coat, huffing.

"Good boy," Sair said, voice low. "Good—"

The kelpie squealed, ears flicking down. His lips curled, and he dove for Sair's arm.

"No!" Sair popped her elbow straight into his nose. "None of that!"

Lleuad jerked back. That must have caught him by surprise. His ears flicked, the dark slits of his pupils focused on her intently.

He studied Sair, sides heaving, finally standing still long enough for her to get a good look at him.

The kelpie looked awful. Blood splattered the inside of his stall, probably from the many cuts and scabs now ripped open and bleeding on his head, neck, and forelegs.

Where he wasn't bleeding, he was covered in a sheen of sweat. The little animal had worked himself into a frenzy. Deep ruts had been gouged in the floor of his stall from pawing and teeth marks scored the inside of the door. It was a miracle he hadn't broken a leg from kicking the walls or gored himself on a wooden splinter.

This animal looked the way she felt—desperate.

"Easy." Sair spoke calmly, keeping the coat raised between them.

Growing up, kelpies had been semi-mythical. Sair and her brother had been raised on tales of Istovari who had tamed them, blessed by Eponine. Despite knowing those many stories, Sair was no longer sure how much of her people's lore was fact.

According to some, kelpies could only be ridden by their masters. But according to others, kelpies could be ridden by anyone once tamed.

Sair's grandmother insisted that anyone who truly loved a kelpie's rider could earn the horse's favor. *They can smell love*, her grandmother had said. *It has a perfume to them.*

"You miss Thadred?"

Lleuad cocked his head. The kelpie might have recognized that name or it might have been the sound of her voice.

Sair took a step closer, coming within the kelpie's reach. The little horse didn't move, though his snakelike eyes watched her intently.

Thadred was an imperial knight. He had trained Lleuad using imperial commands. Sair raised her right hand and stepped forward, clicking her tongue.

Lleuad stepped back, obeying.

Sair's heart leapt, just a little. "Good," she crooned, voice low and soft. "That's it." Not taking her eyes off the kelpie, she removed the bar from across his stall door.

A little tremor went through Lleuad as she did. He tensed, like he was about to bolt, but she kept her hand up and he didn't test it.

"Back," Sair urged, pulling the door open. She stayed to the side, so that if Lleuad did decide to bolt, he wouldn't trample her.

Lleuad took a step forward.

"No. Back, young man."

Lleuad snorted, then obeyed a third time.

Sair dared to step inside the stall. "You're doing well." Her heart hammered, half with excitement, half with the knowledge that the kelpie could still kill her at any moment.

She reached out, Thadred's coat draped over her arm, hackamore in both hands. "Come here. Good boy." Sair sidled up to stand at his shoulder. "Here you go."

She eased the noseband over his muzzle and slipped the buckle behind his ears. The hackamore had no bit, leaving the kelpie's mouth free to bite. Moving as fast as she could without startling him, she buckled it in place.

Lleuad raised his head, yanking against the reins. Sair knew it was unsafe—she couldn't win a tug of war with a horse—but instinct told her to hang on. Sair pulled, dragging his head back down.

As soon as he felt the pressure, Lleuad dropped his head. He made a chuffing sound. His sides heaved in a huge breath, almost like he was…relieved. Like he had been waiting for someone to step into this stall and tell him what to do.

"Good," Sair whispered, stroking his shoulder. She fed *ka* into the many cuts and scratches on his coat.

The little horse's body absorbed her magic greedily, soaking it up. The kelpie nosed at the coat hung over her arm.

"Do you know where Thadred is?"

This time, the kelpie's ears definitely twitched at the name.

"Thadred?"

The kelpie's eyes rolled and his ears twitched again. He wrung his tail, but he didn't try to pull away from her.

"Can you take me to him?"

Lleuad panted, still catching his breath.

"This way." Sair led the kelpie forward.

He followed her obediently, if not quite placidly. There was still something tense and rigid through his whole body, like he might snap back into his frenzy at any moment.

Sair led the kelpie to the doors barred at the stable entrance. She pulled on Thadred's coat to free her arms. It wasn't like the coat would fool Lleuad, but it might make them both feel better.

The kelpie watched her, nostrils flaring, but he didn't resist or try to pull back or charge ahead.

With one hand on the kelpie's reins, Sair removed the bar. Slowly, she opened the door.

Lleuad gave a little jump at the sight of open sky. He hopped in place once.

Sair put pressure on his reins, tugging his head down. "Not yet, son. Not yet."

Lleuad snorted, hooves scraping at the ground.

Sair led the kelpie out to the surprised and relieved stares of Brick, Vespasia, the major, and all the soldiers. The major closed his eyes for just a moment, as if thanking his patron god for her survival.

Brick grinned, looking between her and the kelpie with a wide smile. Vespasia stared, mouth open.

Sair would have felt more triumphant if she hadn't known the kelpie could still bolt or attack at any second.

Lleuad gnashed his teeth at the other horses, ears pinned. Sair suspected there would be no getting close to the other animals, at least for right now.

"What next, my lady?" the major asked.

Sair hadn't been sure she would get this far. "Follow us." She assumed Thadred had to be somewhere in the city, so she turned in that direction.

"Are you planning to walk to the city?" the major called.

"My lady, that's miles away!" Brick protested.

"Just follow us." Sair had walked much farther when she had made her journeys to Lashera and from the Haven.

Lleuad walked after her, ears forward, focused on the road ahead.

The major mounted his own courser to lead the imperial soldiers. Vespasia and her guards followed them at a safe distance. Brick mounted a small pony and rode beside Vespasia.

It occurred to Sair then just what she was doing. She was leading some fifty men and Vespasia, an inexperienced noblewoman, directly into the hands of the Kadra'han. This could end very, very badly.

Awareness of just what she was risking pressed down on her like a weight. There was so much at stake, and she had no plan, not really.

But Thadred and Rhis were depending on her. Saving them fell to her. And no one had any other ideas.

"Do you know where he is?" Kelpies were said to be clever, nearly human in their intelligence. Sair didn't think Lleuad could understand whole sentences, but maybe a few words. "Thadred," Sair whispered.

The kelpie snorted.

Sair looked to the road before them, snaking far down the hillside. This would go faster if she wasn't on foot, but Lleuad wouldn't let the other horses near him in this state and it wasn't as if she could allow him to just gallop ahead.

An idea occurred to her then. A crazy idea that would have made Thadred proud.

Sair glanced to the kelpie, then to the road. She swallowed a lump in her throat.

Lleuad was allowing her to lead him. She'd pushed him this far. Maybe she could push him a little further?

Sair stopped, waving for the soldiers behind her to keep their distance. Lleuad snorted, stomping once as she did.

"Is something wrong?" the major called, standing in his stirrups.

"No," Sair answered, heart in her throat. "It's fine. Just a moment." It took a valiant effort to keep her hands from shaking as she lifted the hackamore's reins over Lleuad's head.

This animal could rip her arm off. He could stomp her to the ground. One wrong move, and he could crush her before she could even weave a spell to counter.

The kelpie snorted, attention still on the road. He was impatient to reach Thadred. Sair got the impression the horse was only complying with her because he somehow knew that was the best way to reach the knight.

Sair swallowed. It was a risk. She wasn't sure someone besides a kelpie's master could mount them, but she had already established she had nothing to lose.

Sair faced the kelpie, gathering his mane in one hand. Lleuad rolled an eye in her direction, a silent challenge.

Sair waited, heart pounding, aware that if he decided to turn on her, she would be in mortal danger.

Finally, Lleuad snorted and lowered his head. It might have been her imagination, but the kelpie seemed to be granting permission.

Sair pulled herself up the kelpie's side. It was awkward without stirrups or someone to boost her up. Thankfully, Lleuad was a small horse.

She half-scrambled, half-flopped her way onto his back. The kelpie let off a derisive snort and shifted. He raised one hoof, lashing at the air.

For one horrible instant, Sair was certain he would buck her off and run. Then all four of the kelpie's hooves came to rest on the ground.

Sair adjusted the reins of his hackamore, fixing her skirts and straightening. She hadn't ridden bareback since she and Tapios had been children, but she managed.

Taking a deep breath, Sair looked over her shoulder. Triumph glowed in her chest, and she couldn't help smiling.

Only Brick looked properly impressed, mouth open and eyes wide.

The major and Vespasia appeared a little confused, and the soldiers stared blankly from behind their helmets.

"Alright then." Sair cleared her throat, but one could only be so dignified after having crawled like a crab onto the back of an animal. "Follow me but be sure to give him some space."

The kelpie lowered his head, reaching for light contact with the reins. Thadred had been training him well.

"Let's go, son," Sair whispered. "Thadred. Take us to Thadred."

The kelpie's ears twitched. Sair nudged him lightly with her heels.

Lleuad took off into a brisk walk. Once she was sure he wouldn't bolt, she let him step up into an easy trot. The rest of their party trotted after them, armor clanking and hooves clopping on the ground.

When they reached the end of the avenue, Sair nudged Lleuad again. The little kelpie snorted, tail snapping. He tossed his head, like he might throw her off after all. Sair braced herself, but the kelpie hopped once and loped into a smooth canter.

Sair looked back once to see the guards and soldiers urging their mounts to keep up.

Lleuad huffed, pulling at the reins as if to tell her he still wanted to go faster. The little animal probably wanted to barrel top speed to wherever Thadred was being held. But that would only endanger them all.

Sair patted Lleuad's neck, thanking him for his restraint.

If only her brother could have seen her now—riding a kelpie bareback across a strange land. Tapios would have been awestruck.

Under her, Lleuad snorted. Small black ears pinned with determination. They were going to find Thadred.

19

THADRED

Thadred leaned against the wall, counting the dust motes that floated through the sunbeams. He hadn't realized how much he had come to depend on magic until he was cut off from it.

The tenebrous steel around his wrists had worn them raw. He'd tried not moving to minimize the chafing, but it wasn't helping all that much.

Tenebrous steel worked by soaking up *ka* before a sorcerer could use it. Thadred had theorized there had to be a limit as to how much a single piece could soak up. But if there were such constraints to tenebrous steel, neither he nor anyone he'd spoken to knew of it. Another reason he'd made sure his men had shields lined with the stuff.

The sounds of the city buzzed in the distance. He considered shouting for help, but it would do little good. He'd be silenced by a boot or a knife from one of the Kadra'han before he ever got anyone truly useful to come to his aid.

This reminded him of the days following his accident. He had been trapped in the broken shell of his body. Dain had been at his bedside, as had a flurry of physicians and servants, but he had felt alone. Alone with the pain, alone with the crushing helplessness.

Thadred's mind turned to Sair. The Kadra'han hadn't

captured her. Caa Iss would be sure to taunt him with that if they had. That meant she had to be safe.

He closed his eyes, remembering her warmth. Her softness. She loved him. He loved her.

Why hadn't he said it back? Why had he been too coward to—

The doors at the far end of the barn swung open. Thadred straightened.

In marched his fellow captives with a group of Kadra'han herding them. Rhis caught Thadred's attention first, the small boy dirty and a bit pale, but head up.

The kid looked straight to Thadred, like he had been afraid he wouldn't see the knight when he got back. Thadred tried to force a smile, but couldn't, not quite.

Iasu entered at the back of their small column. He swaggered with the confidence usually reserved for street thugs and tavern bouncers. The small man stopped at a brace a few steps from Thadred's and leaned against it with his arms crossed. Muscle bulged under his sleeves and rippled under the bandages of his forearms.

Iasu watched as the other Kadra'han herded the children back into the cage. "They're learning well," he said. "Especially that boy of yours."

Thadred forced himself not to react. They already knew Rhis was important to him. Best not to give them any more reason to hold the boy over his head.

"They should be ready to take their vows by the end of the year." Iasu studied the children like they were a flock of pullets prepared for autumn roasting.

Thadred knew better than to take the bait. "Is your new grandmaster treating you well?" He looked pointedly to the bandages on Iasu's forearms. "From the look of it, things could be going better."

"It is not for me to question." Iasu didn't make eye contact with Thadred.

Thadred didn't have much hope in his odds of befriending Iasu. Even if Iasu was open to turning against Caa Iss, he was still bound in a Kadra'han's vows. All the same, Thadred had no better plans.

"Did you know the Empress Amira broke her Kadra'han curse?" Thadred shifted on the floor, trying to adjust his bad hip. Without magic, a sharp ache had settled into his joints.

"So I have heard," Iasu sneered. "The story told again and again by my Istovari captors."

"It wasn't just a story," Thadred said. "I was there."

Iasu flicked his eyes to his fellow Kadra'han who had just finished locking the cage with the children inside it. "Leave us."

The men looked askance, but they didn't argue. The two Kadra'han nodded, half bowing to Iasu on their way out. So Iasu was a higher rank than the rest. Interesting.

In the silence, Iasu turned back to Thadred. It was entirely possible that Iasu was under orders from Caa Iss to report anything Thadred said to him. But it was unlikely that Caa Iss would be able to use this against any of them.

"How exactly did she break her curse? I see no evidence of it. Amira Brindonu has remained close to the emperor. She will be giving him an heir soon if the reports are to be believed."

"Oh, that's correct. My cousin is most eagerly awaiting the arrival of his firstborn. But everything that Amira has done for him, fighting against Vesha, convincing her own mothers to ally with him, going into the depths of Kelamora to rescue him, braving the Dread Marches themselves, even bearing his child— she did that because she wanted to. Not because he ordered her."

"Nothing you described has convinced me she broke her curse." Iasu's nostrils flared. It was the first real sign of anger from him. Iasu was a man who lived in a state of constant control. The curse might keep him on a tight leash, but it was not nearly as tight as the one Iasu kept on himself.

"Vesha was planning to have Daindreth possessed by Caa Iss. You might have heard of this."

"Caa Iss may have mentioned something about it," Iasu snapped. The man was as trapped as Thadred and chafing at his invisible chains.

"Daindreth ordered Amira and I to leave Mynadra. Both of us. To leave him to his fate." Thadred watched Iasu carefully.

He was taking a risk. He had no idea what kind of commands Caa Iss might have placed over Iasu or what might trigger them. Unlike Amira, Thadred was not particularly practiced at speaking around his curse and defying it in a thousand subtle ways. He'd never had much reason because Daindreth had never tried to control him. His cousin had only outright commanded him a handful of times and quickly regretted after.

"But she didn't," Iasu said. "So he must have given her commands before then."

"No," Thadred corrected. "She defied her curse."

"What does that *mean?* How did she do it?" Thadred wondered if he didn't imagine the note of desperation in Iasu's voice.

"Daindreth ordered her to leave him. But because she defied him in order to serve him, the curse made her stronger at the same time it tried to punish her. A snake eating its own tail is how we think of it."

Iasu seemed to consider that for a moment.

"Amira used the curse to break itself."

"That does not help me." Iasu's voice broke on that sentence, like his own curse had acted up at the traitorous words.

"There might still be a way." Thadred knew he was tossing wishes into a well.

Even if Iasu could free himself from his Kadra'han curse, Thadred wasn't sure that Iasu would be on his side. Iasu had served Vesha with a zealous fervor. He had been truly loyal to her, beyond his curse. There was no way of knowing what he might do now that she was gone. He might try to seek vengeance against Daindreth. Or he might become the emperor's most zealous supporter as Vesha's heir.

Either way, whatever Iasu might or might not do, Thadred was in a place to risk it. He was trapped, helpless, and he had six young sorcerers and a sorceress to think of.

Not to mention the demon prince that was currently at large in the empire.

Today was not a day to be picky about allies.

Iasu huffed. "You are maddeningly unhelpful, knight."

"I try." Thadred shrugged. He looked to Rhis, who sat leaning against the bars, grubby fingers clutching the iron.

Rhis had so much faith in Thadred. It was terrifying.

Iasu straightened. "I hope that woman of yours is cleverer than you."

"Touch her, I dare you." The words came out sharp and aggressive, more like a growl.

Iasu quirked one eyebrow, seeming amused. "It's not *me* you should worry about," he said, voice laden with implication. "Rest well. You'll need your strength for whatever happens next."

Iasu marched out of the stable.

Thadred looked to Rhis. "Are you alright? They didn't hurt you?"

From what Thadred could see, none of the children had fresh wounds. Caa Iss probably wasn't using them for their blood just yet. Why bleed children when you had full grown adults? Adults whose magic was stronger after a lifetime of service.

Rhis shook his head. "They've just been teaching us to use magic. Having us practice with spells. Easy things."

So, the Kadra'han were testing the amount of skill and talent the children had. Not a great sign, but it meant that they were probably going to be kept alive. Ever since Daindreth's father had banished sorcerers who refused to take Kadra'han vows to him, it had been difficult to keep the Kadra'han ranks replenished.

Children had been brought in from across the continent, sometimes kidnapped, sometimes found in orphanages, sometimes even sold by their own parents. Poor families could live for years just by selling off one of the extra mouths from their table.

"Is there a plan?" Rhis sounded confident that Thadred had a way to get them all out of this. It was naïve. Adorable, but naïve.

"I'm still working on it." Thadred forced a smile.

Rhis nodded solemnly.

Thadred closed his eyes, trying to push down the stabbing pain throbbing in his hip and the base of his spine. How had he ever thought he didn't have magic? That was the only way he had been able to function. Consciously or not, magic had been helping him even before he'd learned to use it.

Thadred looked back up to the dust motes floating through the sunbeams. He thought about praying, but he didn't know what there was left to say. He had said every single thing to the gods that he could think of—bargains, pleas, and threats.

Thadred exhaled a long breath and went back to waiting for whatever would come next.

20

SAIR

Sair wasn't entirely certain Lleuad knew where he was going.

She gave him as loose a rein as she could and let him choose the path. Lleuad headed rather confidently toward the city, but that might not mean anything. Lleuad may just be heading toward the last place Thadred had been seen, or he might be seeking out the ocean—the largest body of water.

Both were questions she asked herself and questions that the major called out from behind her as they headed closer and closer toward Iandua. But Lleuad had not been there when Thadred had last been seen. And he hated saltwater.

She kept her face straight ahead, not letting herself dwell on any of her questions for too long. Where would Thadred be? What would they do once they found him? Was he still alive? Of course he was still alive. He had to be.

As they came near the city, Sair pulled Lleuad back into an easy walk. He resisted at first, but she was able to ease him down from a canter to something more suitable for the narrow city streets.

Sair glanced behind her as they clopped down the cobbled lanes. The soldiers were watching the roofs and the side streets for any sign of a threat. The major voiced several times that he didn't like her leading the way. She was out in front, with several horse lengths of space between her and her guards. She would make a perfect target for any of their enemies, or even just random street toughs.

Sair wasn't worried about street toughs. In his current state, Lleuad would rip their faces off before they ever laid a hand on her.

What concerned her was that the Kelamora Kadra'han might be watching. An arrow to the neck or the heart and this whole thing would be over for her.

That was her greatest fear. That she would fail Thadred and Rhis.

Lleuad turned, taking them into a dead-end street. He snorted, frustrated as he pawed at piles of refuse and kicked at discarded pottery.

That was oddly exciting to Sair. It meant that Lleuad was following something other than the streets. He had some way of knowing where he was supposed to go.

Sair steered him out of the alley and back to the main road to the befuddled stares of passersby in the street.

"Assuming we find whoever it is who took Lord Thadred," Caiden said, "they will see us coming."

"As I said before, major," Sair responded sweetly, "I am open to suggestions if you have a better plan."

He fell silent, stewing at her back.

Thadred had surrounded himself with good soldiers. The empire had been at peace for nearly a generation. Twenty years had passed since the last true conquest.

While Sair would not wish a war under any circumstances, it meant that a certain type of man now filled the Erymayan military. They had developed a taste for predictability and security. Though they still engaged in the occasional skirmish and put down the odd rebellion here and there, their ranks were dominated by men who had been taught to value stability and caution above all else. But caution was a luxury. It was something you could practice when you were the dominant force in the continent, when you had the full force of the empire behind you.

Sair had been an outcast, a refugee, forced to work in the

shadows, taking risks because it was the only way left to her.

Caution was one luxury the Istovari had not had in a very long time.

Lleuad rounded a bend in the road, ears forward, head up. He knew where he was going, wherever it was.

The little horse nipped at a laden donkey that came too close. Sair had to pull his rein, muttering apologies to the owner.

The buildings around them became worn. They appeared to be in an older portion of the city. It was not so much that the buildings were not maintained, but the signs of age were more apparent. Curtains and banners decorated the upper windows in an effort to hide the crumbling stone. Paint peeled and lacquer cracked, revealing even older murals fading underneath.

Shapes that had once been statues, stripped of their identifying features by wind and rain, lined the walkways. Sair had been to this part of the city before. She recognized with an odd twist in her chest that this was the red quarter.

She came here yesterday with Thadred. Perhaps Lleuad really was retracing their steps.

Sair glanced back to Brick and the major behind her. The major grimaced as he had been doing this entire time. Brick looked around with wide eyes at the mostly empty streets.

A painted sign featuring a nude woman with her legs spread hung over one of the buildings. Brick blinked at it for several seconds as if he didn't realize what he was seeing, then looked away, cheeks flaming red.

The streets were deserted, even more so than yesterday. Faces peered at them from windows, and behind doors. They seemed frightened, but that might have been the case yesterday, too. Sair had been inside a carriage and hadn't had the best view.

Perhaps it appeared that the soldiers were a raid here to clean up the criminal underbelly of the city. That wasn't too far from the truth, but at the moment, they weren't interested in enforcing brothels or policing opium dens.

Behind Sair, a snort and squeal rose from the other horses. Sair turned to see that the major, Brick, and Vespasia's horses as well as those of the guards had stopped, pawing at the ground.

"What's wrong?" the major asked.

"I don't know, sir," a soldier answered. "The horses won't go any further."

A sick sensation swelled in Sair's gut at the same time she felt a spike of excitement. She knew what this was.

Most animals refused to go near a cythraul. It had made it impossible to use cavalry in the Witch War.

"Major." Sair looked to Caiden.

The man nodded, grim understanding on his face. "There's a demon close." The major swung down off his horse. "Two of you stay here with the horses.

One by one, the men dismounted. Vespasia swung down without hesitating and her guards followed stiffly. They singled out a few of their number to stay with the horses after securing the animals in lines.

Sair only hoped the animals wouldn't flee. That had been a problem before.

"Lead on, my lady," Caiden called, one hand on his sword.

Now the only mounted member of their party, Sair nudged her heels into Lleuad's sides. The little horse headed on, snorting his impatience.

Lleuad's nostrils flared, his ears twitching. Sair tightened the reins just a little bit, feeling his body tremble with excitement. Whatever he was following, he was getting close.

Lleuad led them up and around a seemingly empty side street and stopped. He halted alongside an exterior wall of a large building. The sloping roof made it hard to see what might have been on the other side. Narrow slits for light were cut into the stone ten or fifteen feet up the wall, out of sight.

Lleuad stomped. He nosed at the stone wall, scraping his hoof against the brick.

"Easy, boy." The last thing Sair needed was for Lleuad to break his leg kicking rocks. "What is this place?" Sair looked back to the major and Vespasia, anyone who might have an answer. They were in the red quarter, but Lleuad had taken them around to the side of one of the buildings.

The wall appeared to be part of some compound. It looked

almost like an old temple or some kind of religious structure.

"No idea." Caiden looked around with a hard glare, almost like he was trying to intimidate the stones into giving up their secrets.

"Pardon me, my lady, but do you hear that?" Brick raised his hand tentatively. "Can anyone else hear that?"

"The seagulls?" The major didn't even bother trying to hide his annoyance.

"No, sir, the…listen." Brick pointed toward the building.

Sair listened, trying to make out anything over the anxious pounding of her own heart. She strained to hear, past the seagulls and the stomping of Lleuad's hooves, and the rattle of the soldiers' armor. She held her breath, though that did little to help.

At first, she didn't hear anything. But as she waited, she caught the faint scrape and rumble of metal on stone. There was the jangle of chains, and Sair thought she even heard the voices of men.

"What is that?" Vespasia looked to Sair as if she might have an answer.

Sair shook her head. It sounded like digging. Or stonework. Or…

The major frowned, leaning toward the wall. "It sounds like some sort of construction."

Sair's eyes widened. "Baron Prisca."

"What about him?" The major shot a look back to her.

"He purchased a former brothel and was having it renovated." Sair's pulse sped just a little. "I…I think this is the same one we visited yesterday.

The major didn't argue this time, turning to the other soldiers. "Scout this building," he ordered. "Assume everything is a threat. We don't know what's inside yet."

Several soldiers separated, jogging off in pairs and trios to obey.

Sair's magic was still not quite what it had been, but she reached out, past the wall. She could feel the faint shimmer of lichen and mold on the stone. She'd forgotten it was possible to feel those things, it had been so long. But as she stretched her awareness into the space beyond the stone, Sair felt shapes. She wasn't strong enough to make out the exact shapes, but she could sense their *ka.*

"There's something alive on the other side of this." Sair looked back to the major. "I think..." Sair couldn't be sure. Her magic was still weak. But she could swear that the figures on the other side of the stone had too much power to be just normal people. They had magic.

Sair's heart hammered in her chest. Thadred was inside. She knew it.

"He's here." Sair forced herself to take deep breaths. She had been so helpless, so desperate, and now she knew with certainty Thadred was just a few steps away, separated only by stone. She whirled on the major, careful to keep a snug grip on Lleuad's reins lest the kelpie start kicking at the stone. "Lord Thadred is here."

This time, the major didn't ask her how she knew. Caiden nodded and cast a grim look to Vespasia. "Have your men ready to—"

"We answer to the dowager countess. Not to you, sir," the lieutenant in command interrupted crisply. It seemed that Thadred's aggression toward his youngest brother had not won him much goodwill with the household staff.

"Lieutenant." Vespasia's voice was sweet, polite, the perfect timbre of the perfect lady. "Either you help the imperial soldiers rescue my brother, or I will walk straight into this brothel, and you can protect me or not."

The lieutenant seemed surprised at that. He probably hadn't thought she'd be willing to put herself in danger, but he had underestimated her, as it seemed quite a few people did. "My lady, I cannot allow that."

"Then I suggest you help the major and Lady Sairydwen. Because you will either have to drag me out by my hair, or you will have to help the major of your own accord."

Yes, most people underestimated Vespasia.

After a moment of pained silence, the lieutenant acquiesced.

"Do as she says."

Vespasia looked to Sair, no hint of triumph, just concern.

Sair swallowed. She had no idea how well defended this structure might be. Worse, she had no idea what might be waiting for them inside.

Sair padded Lleuad's neck as the little horse stomped, shuffling his feet. He snapped at the air, teeth clacking as he did. He was impatient.

Sair kept reaching out, trying to feel through the stone. Something stepped into Sair's awareness. Something she had not felt for over a year. Even though she had expected it, nothing ever quite prepared her for the noxious life force of a demon.

She sensed more *ka*. More figures came into the barn or whatever was the space beyond this wall. Most of them had to be sorcerers. Sair recognized that right away.

But one of them…

Sair inhaled a sharp breath, her hands clenching around Lleuad's reins instinctively. The little stallion seemed to sense it too. He pinned his ears and squealed, stomping at the cobbles beneath his hooves.

"What is it?" Caiden gripped the sword at his hip.

Sair managed to choke out her answer. "The cythraul is with Thadred."

21

THADRED

Thadred was hearing things. He had to be. He could have sworn he heard Sair's voice.

It had been faint, but he had been sure…

"How did they find us?" Caa Iss smashed open the doors of the stable.

"I don't know, my lord." The speaker was one of the Kadra'han Thadred didn't know. He wasn't the grandmaster, but appeared to be close to the older man's age.

Caa Iss whirled on Thadred. He bounded to the knight, faster than any human would have been able to, and grabbed him by the front of his jacket. The demon hauled Thadred to his feet with inhuman strength, slamming him against the wall.

Thadred had never felt so small and helpless, not since being a child.

"How did you do it?" Caa Iss's nostrils flared, bright red eyes burning into Thadred's like hot coals. "How did your bitch find us?"

Thadred glanced past Caa Iss. It took a great amount of will. Something primal told him not to look away from the demon. Not to take his eyes off it. But he forced himself to look to Iasu hovering in the doorway.

Iasu's arms were folded across his chest. He met Thadred's eyes with one mildly raised brow. It was impossible to read the man, but he was still the closest thing to an ally Thadred had in this place. If nothing else, Iasu hated Caa Iss as much as Thadred did.

Thadred shook his head, looking back to Caa Iss. "I don't know. For all I know she's not even here." Thadred knew that was a lie as soon as he said it. Sair was here. He hadn't imagined her voice.

That realization came with no relief, only fear. Thadred wanted Sair as far away from this *creature* as possible. Rhis was one thing, but Rhis was valuable to Caa Iss. Sair had fought in the Witch War. She had played a large role in his failure to free his mother, leading to his current state of exile.

Caa Iss liked to hold grudges, and he was definitely holding a grudge against Sair.

"My lord, there's at least fifty of them," one of the Kadra'han reported, rushing in from the courtyard. "They have surrounded the temple."

"It doesn't matter." Caa Iss dropped Thadred.

Thadred slammed to the ground, his bad leg buckling. His chains rattled and yanked taut as he scrambled to catch himself.

"Thadred!" Rhis pressed up against the bars of his cage, watching the knight with terror.

"My lord." It was Iasu. "We must retreat. The work to destroy the well is nearly completed as it is."

"They outnumber us two to one," said the former grandmaster, speaking over Iasu. "But they may also call for reinforcements, so we must withdraw to a more defensible location."

"Why were there no scouts?" Caa Iss roared. "How did they catch us unawares?"

"Forgive me, my lord. We did not count on the sorceress." The former grandmaster seemed to be trying to focus the demon's anger elsewhere.

"That bitch," Caa Iss roared. "That whore. I will make her suffer. I will make her beg!"

Thadred's heart raced. He had to keep Sair away from the cythraul. He looked to Rhis. The boy looked back at Thadred with wide eyes, expectant. Damn it, why did the kid have to have so much faith in him?

Voices clamored from outside the stable. A horn blew.

Someone shouted, sounding official and just a little threatening.

One of the Kadra'han standing in the doorway of the stable turned to relay the message. "They are telling us to allow them entry. Under the authority of the emperor."

Caa Iss swore, not in any language that Thadred knew, but the tone was recognizable enough. The demon spun on Thadred. "You will tell them to stand down."

Thadred arched an eyebrow. "What if I don't want them to stand down?"

Caa Iss snarled and reached for Thadred, then seemed to think better of it. "Bring me the boy."

The other Kadra'han seemed confused. "Which one, my lord?"

"That one!" Caa Iss pointed straight to Rhis.

Rhis took a step back, seeming to realize for the first time that he truly was in danger.

Caa Iss had been caught flat footed. And he was desperate.

Thadred struggled to stand, chains rattling as he balanced against the wall at his back. "Leave the kid out of it. What do you want?"

Caa Iss whirled on Thadred, teeth snapping with a loud clack. Human teeth were not meant to slam together like that. "I tried being reasonable," the demon said. "So now I shall be unreasonable."

"The kid doesn't have anything to do with this."

"Oh, but I think he does."

A Kadra'han brought Rhis to Caa Iss.

No, no, no! Thadred's whole mind screamed, but he was powerless.

Caa Iss grabbed Rhis's shoulder, hard enough that the boy yelped. Caa Iss dragged Rhis to stand in front of him, one hand wrapped around the boy's throat. "Shall we see how your whore likes her son in pieces?"

Rhis whimpered.

This was all happening too fast. Thadred had no idea what Sair and the others might be planning, but Caa Iss was unraveling in his panic. Thadred needed to deescalate this. He needed to stay calm.

Thadred looked to Rhis and tried to give him a reassuring smile. "Steady, kid."

If Caa Iss was allowed to escape, there was no telling what horrors he might wreak across the continent. But if Thadred didn't do as he was told, it would cost Rhis's life.

Rhis was innocent. Rhis was counting on him.

Thadred looked back up to Caa Iss. "What do you want me to do?"

Something like triumph flickered in the demon's eyes. Caa Iss singled out Iasu and three of the other Kadra'han. "Take them to the gates," he ordered. "Hold off the imperials for as long as you can." Caa Iss pointed to Thadred and Rhis. "See them both dead once the imperials break through, then return to me."

Iasu and the others bowed, not hesitating. They were Kadra'han. They had no choice.

Caa Iss turned back to Thadred. "If you try to warn them or speak a word out of line, my men will kill the boy. Do you understand?"

"Perfectly." Thadred raised his chin.

One Kadra'han held onto Rhis and the boy shook in the grip of his captor.

How could Thadred save Rhis? If only one of them could live, it should be him. Thadred would have traded himself for the kid in an instant, but there wasn't a trade to make. Caa Iss had them both.

Caa Iss whirled to the other Kadra'han. "Get me out of here." There was an edge of command in the demon's words, but also an edge of panic. Caa Iss was afraid. The goddess Moreyne might haunt the nightmares of children and fuel the imaginations of holy men, but Thadred doubted anyone feared her more than her own offspring.

Caa Iss ordered the other children to be hauled out of the cage. It seemed that despite everything, he still hoped to keep these future Kadra'han.

Thadred tried to think of something that would keep him and Rhis from being utterly buggered. Iasu and the others had orders to kill them as soon as their diversion stopped working.

It meant that Thadred's only option would be to kill all four of their guards first.

Iasu glared at him when he made eye contact. Would Iasu enjoy killing him?

Thadred moved slowly with his bad leg, stiff after hours and hours on the hard stone. His arm ached where Caa Iss had cut him, and his head pounded from dehydration. Everything hurt. It was a struggle to keep his wits about him, but he tried all the same.

Iasu and the others marched them up a flight of stairs. They took Rhis up first. The boy tried fighting but received a twisted ear for his trouble.

Behind them, Thadred heard the rumbling as the stone workers were rounded up. Was Caa Iss planning to kill them all? Did he have time?

Thadred stumbled up the uneven set of wooden steps to the arch that ran over the front gate of the brothel. *Gate* was a generous term—it was a pair of thick doors barred by an iron rod. The Kadra'han with Rhis was already at the top. Thadred was brought up the rear with a guard on either side, and Iasu slunk behind them, crouching low out of sight. It seemed he was acting as back-up, in case the other three failed to kill Rhis and Thadred on time.

Thadred was outnumbered four to one, injured, sore, and the shackles around his wrists kept him from using magic. What exactly was he supposed to do?

Thadred looked up to the sky, but the midday sun blazed across it. Could Eponine even see him right now?

Thadred had long ago accepted that he wouldn't have a warrior's death on the battlefield. But being used as bait then summarily killed was too anticlimactic for his tastes.

Down below, a number of imperial soldiers already blockaded the front on foot. One of them blinked up at Thadred, head cocking in recognition.

"My lord?" It was a young, enlisted man, a fellow named Erhard Landric. He was a good soldier, stayed out of trouble and did his job well.

"Hello, Landric. As you can see, I am in a bit of a situation." Thadred tried to stay calm. In this moment, the only thing he could really control was himself. He glanced to Rhis. He forced another smile at the boy.

Immediately, Rhis seemed to relax. If Thadred looked like everything would be alright, then Rhis assumed everything would be alright.

Doubts tangled Thadred up in knots. He had the worst feeling that he was about to see this kid slaughtered.

"We found him!" the soldier shouted in excitement. "We found Lord Thadred!"

Most of the soldiers were smart enough to stay in place, keeping the brothel surrounded. But several figures appeared around the corner of the building, trotting into sight. Thadred was glad to see they carried their reinforced shields.

First came Major Caiden, on guard with his sword unsheathed at his hip. Next came a pair of soldiers, and finally came a little black horse. Lleuad had seen better days. His coat was bloody, and he looked up immediately to Thadred with wide, wild eyes.

But Sair was on his back, riding him without a saddle. Even at this distance, Thadred could see the relief and fear mingled on her face at the sight of him. Instantly, her gaze was drawn to his left, to the boy at his side, held just out of reach.

"Rhis!" Sair's voice cracked. She trembled on Lleuad, and the little horse stomped and pawed at the ground at her agitation.

"Mama!" Rhis pulled against his guard, but the Kadra'han pulled him back.

Thadred considered shouting to Sair that Caa Iss was inside this building, even now escaping. If it had been just himself, he would have, damn it all. But he had Rhis to consider.

Sair had lost everyone she'd ever loved. She didn't need to have her son killed in front of her on top of everything. She didn't deserve that, and neither did Rhis.

"Are you alright?" It was hard to know if Sair was talking to him or her son.

Thadred answered. "We might be worse in a moment."

Sair looked between him and her child, then to the Kadra'han standing behind them. This was bad. She had to know this was bad.

"What are your demands, men?" the major got straight to business. "You must have demands. You're obviously holding them as hostages."

The Kadra'han had been ordered to create a diversion for Caa Iss, and they set to doing just that. The one holding Thadred's right arm took a deep breath. "We would demand safe passage from the city in exchange for the inquisitor and the boy."

"Starting your demands high, I see." The major sounded skeptical. He looked to Thadred, probably searching for some signal from the knight.

Thadred would have loved to give him a signal, but there was no signal for a demon prince about to escape.

He considered the possibility of just throwing Rhis over the wall. But even if he could reach the boy, and wrestle him away from his Kadra'han guard, the fall was too far. It wasn't worth it.

Behind him, Thadred was aware of the flurry of motion as the Kadra'han tried to get Caa Iss and their abducted children out the back.

"There are more of them," Thadred said. "A lot more."

"We're working to contain them, sir," the major responded.

"Careful, or they die." The threat was delivered in cool, cold tones from the Kadra'han beside Thadred. The knight seethed in his chains, thinking.

Thadred looked down to Sair. He and Rhis were about to die in front of her, less than a stone's throw away. Thadred hadn't come this close to saving her son to only come this close.

There had to be something he could do.

Major Caiden seemed to be thinking the same thing. He conferred with his officers, speaking in clipped tones.

Thadred kept his eyes on Sair. *I'm sorry,* he wanted to tell her. *I'm sorry it's come to this.*

Sair looked between him and her son. She was keeping remarkable control. On the outside she appeared perfectly composed, but she had to be stewing in fear on the inside.

The imperials and the Kadra'han stayed locked in a stalemate, for several torturously long moments. No one knew how to break it. No one was quite sure what to do next. The imperials had crossbowmen with them, but there was a risk that the archers might hit Thadred and Rhis instead of their captors.

A sharp squeal broke the silence. Lleuad bucked, snapping his entire back and dumping Sair to the ground.

"Sair!" Thadred jerked against his captor on impulse.

"Mama!" Rhis screamed.

Sair crawled onto her hands, wincing, but appearing unhurt.

Lleuad charged straight for the barred door at the front of the brothel. Over one thousand pounds of pure rage bent on destruction.

The kelpie hit the door hooves first, hard enough that something crunched. Lleuad screamed, kicking and pawing and slamming his shoulder into it.

It seemed that the little horse was going to get to Thadred if he had to tear apart the whole brothel to do it.

The Kadra'han holding Thadred and Rhis looked to each other. The one holding Rhis pulled out a knife, looking to Iasu.

Iasu frowned, shaking his head.

The doors to the brothel had been designed to keep out unruly patrons, and the occasional crowd of disgruntled rivals. They had not been designed to keep out a pissed off kelpie.

Thadred heard the first boards give way with a loud crack. Seeming invigorated by his success, Lleuad struck harder. Wood splinters flew in all directions.

The kelpie was going to hurt himself.

"Lleuad!" Thadred shouted. He meant to stop the animal,

but it seemed to have the opposite effect.

Lleuad body slammed the doors once, twice—one of the doors buckled completely. It smashed inwards, and Lleuad charged through.

"Persistent little freak, isn't he?" Iasu muttered. "Hold them off if you can," he ordered the others, drawing a short sword from his belt. "You know what to do." Iasu jogged back down the steps to face the kelpie, sword drawn.

Lleuad found the bottom of the staircase only to be blocked by Iasu with a drawn weapon. The kelpie made a growling, snarling sound that not even Thadred had heard before.

The Kadra'han holding Rhis jammed a knife against his neck. "Stay back!" he shouted to the soldiers below.

Several men had already made ready to follow the kelpie. The major raised a hand, motioning for them to wait.

Sair was on her feet now, looking between Thadred and Rhis. She said something, but it was lost at this distance.

Iasu faced down the small horse at the foot of the stairs. He slashed at the kelpie's head with his sword. Blood flew, and a piece of Lleuad's ear sheared off.

Lleuad squealed, but it was hard to tell if it was pain or rage. He dove straight for Iasu. Iasu slashed again and this time cut a gash in the kelpie's neck. Lleuad flinched, but it didn't stop him.

Lleuad's jaws clamped around Iasu's sword arm. There was one stunning moment, where Iasu's eyes went wide, and Thadred smiled despite everything.

The kelpie had just won, and they all knew it.

Lleuad wrenched sideways, spinning a half circle as he did. Iasu went flying across the courtyard. He slammed into the stones, rolling several steps, his short sword skittering out of reach.

Thadred didn't think—he acted.

Thadred shoved his full weight into the man on his left, the one closest to Rhis. The Kadra'han on his left hadn't been ready for it and stumbled back, knocking into the fourth man holding Rhis. Both the Kadra'han and the boy went down. Rhis was a quick thinker and scrambled away from his captor, wriggling free like a fish.

The Kadra'han on Thadred's right recovered, drawing a long dirk. It seemed that the Kadra'han were ready to enact the "kill them" portion of Caa Iss's instructions.

Thadred raised his fists, though his hands were still shackled. The Kadra'han stabbed for him, and Thadred swung his hands together, using the loose chain between them like a flail.

The Kadra'han wasn't expecting that and flinched back. Thadred saw his opening and shoved. He slammed the man straight over the rail. The Kadra'han hit the cobbles with a thud and laid still.

Thadred barely caught himself in time to keep from pitching over the wall before the second guard was on him, also with a dirk. The knife sheered over Thadred's forearm as he blocked.

"Thadred!" Sair cried from down below.

Thadred gritted his teeth. He wasn't going to let himself be killed in front of her.

The Kadra'han bellowed, jabbing for Thadred's ribs.

Thadred couldn't move out of the way, so he was forced to catch the blade on his forearms again. He felt the pain distantly, a vague awareness. He shoved the blade wide and charged.

Thadred and the Kadra'han landed in a sprawl on the ground. The Kadra'han tried to bring his blade up, but Thadred caught his hands between them.

The two men strained, each one fighting to angle the knife toward the other. The Kadra'han was strong, fit like they all were, but Thadred had the advantage of size and gravity.

Lleuad shrieked, apparently trying to ascend the steps, but the wooden stairs had been designed for humans, not kelpies. The steps cracked under Lleuad's weight, but the little horse kept trying to step up them.

Grunting with the effort, Thadred shoved the blade down, seeing the fear in the other man's face as he realized who was winning.

After smashing the bottom four or five steps, Lleuad had nothing left to step on. He squealed and hopped angrily at the foot of the ruined staircase.

"Stop!"

Thadred jerked his head up.

"Stand down or he dies." It was the fourth Kadra'han, the one who had taken Rhis. The man had retaken the boy and held Rhis in a tight grip, a knife pressed under his ear.

Thadred didn't let go of the knife in his own grip, didn't lessen the pressure down, but Rhis—

The Kadra'han holding the boy jerked. His throat ripped open. The knife stabbed for Rhis in a final act of defiance, but the boy dropped and scrambled free.

Thadred spun his attention back to the Kadra'han pinned underneath him. Roaring with effort, Thadred shoved.

The Kadra'han's resistance faltered for just an instant and that was all the opening Thadred needed. He punched the knife down, straight into the Kadra'han's throat.

The dirk speared into the boards under them. The Kadra'han's eyes went wide as blood bubbled out his throat. His hands flailed up and Thadred remembered that the Kadra'han had been ordered to kill him—the man would keep trying as long as he was alive.

Thadred rolled to the side, out of the Kadra'han's reach before a blast of magic shot at his head. The spell wasn't particularly strong, but it left shallow cuts in the railing at their backs.

Thadred kicked the man aside with his good leg, panting. The dying man gasped and twitched, his blood soaking between the boards and dripping down below. Caa Iss wouldn't be pleased to see how much sorcerer's blood had just been wasted.

"Rhis?" Aching, bleeding, and gasping for breath, Thadred looked to the boy. "You okay, kid?"

Rhis crashed into him. Small arms flung around Thadred's neck. The boy trembled, holding tight.

Thadred held onto him, watching to make sure the stabbed Kadra'han actually died.

Down below, the imperial soldiers breached the walls of the former brothel. Lleuad stood guard at the foot of the stairs, not letting anyone near. The imperial soldiers and men in the livery of Count Flavius poured into the former brothel, but too late. Caa Iss was already gone. Too many men had been diverted by the hostage situation at the gates and from the shouting, Caa Iss and his denizens had gotten through the weakened ranks at the back.

There wasn't much Thadred could do about that at the moment, but somehow, he and Rhis had survived.

The imperials found the surprised masons and stone workers, who were being ordered to lie face down with their hands in plain sight. The major would sort them out, as would the city guard.

It seemed there was no sign of Iasu down below. He must have fled with the others. That wasn't good.

Caa Iss had escaped. They needed to hunt him down as soon as possible. As long as he was at large, he would be a threat.

Rhis shivered, clinging to Thadred.

"It's alright." Thadred exhaled, holding onto the kid until he stopped shaking. "Let's go see your mother, all right?"

"Mama!" Rhis jumped up as if he just remembered. He ran to the railing, peering over the edge. "Mama?"

Sair was nowhere to be seen outside the walls. Another woman stood there, surrounded by guards. It took Thadred a moment to realize it was his sister, Vespasia. What was she doing here?

"Thadred! Rhis!" Sair's voice came from below.

"Mama!" Rhis almost vibrated with excitement. He ran to the stairs, where Sair and Lleuad waited at the bottom.

Lleuad had allowed Sair in close, but he pinned his ears at any of the soldiers who tried to get near them.

At the sight of them, Sair's eyes welled with tears. "Rhis!"

If Lleuad hadn't smashed the last few steps into oblivion, Sair would have probably run up to meet them. Thadred would be annoyed with the kelpie later but seeing as how Lleuad had probably saved his life, he would try to find it in his heart to forgive the horse.

Rhis and Thadred made their way to the last remaining step. "Come here." Thadred beckoned Rhis over and gripped the boy under his arms. Kneeling, he lowered Rhis down to Sair.

Sair caught her son, straining under his weight. He had grown too large to be casually carried on the hip, but she caught him. Sobbing, Sair wrapped her arms around the boy.

Rhis clutched her, wrapping his arms and legs around her and clinging tight. "Mama, you rode a kelpie!"

Sair's sobs cracked into a laugh. "Yes, I did."

"Does that mean Lleuad is your kelpie too?"

"I think Thadred is still his favorite." She looked up, meeting the knight's gaze. "You're hurt."

Less than an hour ago, he had feared he'd never see her again, but there she was. He ached to touch her, to hold her, but she was still out of reach.

Thadred shrugged one shoulder. He felt terrible, especially as the rushed haze of fighting for his life wore off. "You should see the other guy." He nodded to Lleuad, who was still keeping the soldiers back. "Do you think you could persuade my kelpie to let the soldiers help me down?"

Stairs were difficult for Thadred on the best of days. Without his magic, bleeding from a series of wounds, and the last few steps smashed to oblivion, it was impossible.

Sair caught Lleuad's reins. She spoke softly to the kelpie, and led him to the side, Rhis still held against her hip with her other arm.

The kelpie allowed himself to be led a few steps away. Several of the soldiers immediately stepped forward. Thadred might have been embarrassed another time, but under the circumstances he was willing to indulge in a little bit of helplessness.

Two men held his arms as he carefully eased down the last few steps to the ground. Thadred groaned, pain shooting up his leg and the base of his spine.

As soon as Thadred touched earth, Lleuad jerked free of Sair, charging straight for his knight. The kelpie pinned his ears at the soldiers, daring them to get in the way.

Thadred held out a hand, intercepting the kelpie before he took a bite out of anyone. "Easy. I'm alive, you vicious nag."

He caught Lleuad's reins and pulled the kelpie around to face him. Lleuad smashed his muzzle into Thadred's side, and inhaled a massive breath, like he was confirming that it really was Thadred.

The kelpie nosed at Thadred's bandaged forearms. He lipped lightly at the shackles, almost in question. The kelpie inspected Thadred from head to foot like he was taking an inventory of parts.

Thadred did much the same thing, taking note of where Iasu's sword had slashed the kelpie's neck. Part of Lleuad's ear was missing, but the kelpie didn't seem to notice for now. Thadred touched Lleuad's neck, chains rattling as he moved his arms.

"Good boy. That's a good boy."

Lleuad chuffed, nuzzling Thadred's arm.

"Good work, son." Thadred patted the kelpie's shoulder.

Lleuad snorted and heaved a massive breath.

Thadred rested his forehead against the kelpie, smelling sweat and horse. The kelpie chuffed, tail swishing.

Lleuad had found him. Crazy little stallion had smashed his way through a door to get to his knight. Without the horse, Thadred and Rhis would probably be dead.

"Thadred?" Sair sounded almost hesitant.

"Yes, love?" Thadred looked to her. Gods, she was beautiful. He'd been afraid he would never see her again.

"Are you alright?"

Thadred shrugged as Lleuad nosed at the bloody bandages on his arm. "I've had worse."

Sair's eyes welled with tears.

Thadred wanted to wrap her in his arms, but wanted to give Lleuad a few more moments to calm down first.

"Lord Thadred!" Brick came bounding through the gates. He skidded to a stop a few paces off when Lleuad pinned his ears. "My lord! It's good to see you."

"Thank you, Brick." Thadred rattled his chains. "Can you find a way to help me with these?"

"Oh, yes, sir."

22

SAIR

Thadred had resumed command almost as if nothing had happened. He spoke with the major, giving orders and taking reports while Brick worked to remove his shackles.

Lleuad gnawed at his shoulder, hovering over Thadred. The kelpie snarled at anyone who came too close.

Sair held onto Rhis, squeezing him to make sure he was real. He was grimy, and smelled as if he hadn't bathed since being taken from her, but he was in one piece. And he seemed relatively unfazed by his ordeal.

After a few moments, he began squirming in her embrace. Sair's arms were growing tired, but she didn't want to put him down just yet.

"I'm fine, Mama." Rhis twisted in her arms. He tried to see to the far side of the courtyard, where the soldiers were rounding up the stone masons. "Did they catch the bad man?"

Sair looked toward the soldiers. "You mean Iasu Zahn?"

"No. The cythraul. The one who controls them."

Sair squeezed her son tighter on instinct. She looked to Thadred. He must have overheard what the boy said, because he cast her a grim look and nodded. Sair had felt the demon's presence. She had known but hoped to be wrong.

"Caa Iss," Thadred confirmed.

Sair gasped as her stomach tightened painfully. She pressed

a hand to her middle, willing herself not to be sick. Caa Iss was here? Caa Iss was the demon the Istovari mothers had summoned from the Dread Marches decades ago. Sair was a young girl at the time, barely in her teens. But she had helped.

Sair gripped her son's shoulder, pulling him around to face her. "Are you sure? Are you sure it was Caa Iss?"

Rhis nodded. "That's what they called him. He's the grandmaster."

Sair spun on Thadred.

Thadred nodded again, only once. That was all the confirmation she needed.

Sair squeezed Rhis against her, suddenly needing to hold him tighter than she had before.

"I'm all right, Mama."

Sair squeezed her eyes shut. Her son had been taken by Caa Iss? She was glad now that she hadn't known.

Thadred exchanged low words with another one of the officers, giving orders for them to seal the building, and organize a search.

"Where are the others?" Rhis kept twisting in Sair's arms, looking around the courtyard.

"Are there other children?"

"Maëlys. And the other boys."

"How many are there?" Sair looked at Thadred, but he was already giving orders to another one of his officers. How many of them were there?

Lleuad seemed to feel the same way and pinned his ears at the strangers. Thadred gripped the kelpie's bridle to keep him from lashing out.

Rhis thought about it for a moment. "There was me, and Maëlys. The twins, Grub, and also Holt."

The Kadra'han had been making an effort to replenish their ranks? They'd done it before. Vesha's Kadra'han had once raided the Haven looking for children to take. They'd tried to take Rhis, but Thadred and his friends had stopped them at the time.

"Sair?" It was Thadred. He leaned against Lleuad for

support. He was drawing magic back to himself.

Sair could see the golden lines of *ka* coiling around him as he used them to ease his wounds. He also was focusing a great deal on wrapping spells around his bad hip and thigh. He usually had quite a mesh of spells there, but the Kadra'han had locked him in tenebrous steel, cutting him off from his magic for the past day and a half.

Thadred straightened, as if to come toward her, then winced.

Sair didn't need to be prompted twice. She went to him, a little surprised when Lleuad didn't pin his ears at her.

Thadred reached an arm for her, and as soon as she came within reach, Thadred drew her and Rhis to his chest.

Sair pressed her cheek against him. He was warm and solid and real. She wanted to curl against his side and stay there forever.

He tucked Sair under his chin, stroking her back. "The major says I have you to thank for finding us."

"Mama rode a kelpie!" Rhis squealed.

Thadred chuckled. "She did." He kissed the top of her head. "She's an impressive woman."

Sair choked back a laugh, emotion too thick in her throat for her to speak.

Rhis didn't seem to mind being partially squished between her and Thadred. He put an arm around each of them, patting awkwardly like he wasn't sure what the big deal was.

He got to be heavy in her arms, and Sair let him down, though she held tight onto one of his hands lest he run off.

Rhis tugged at her lightly, probably trying to see what was on the other side of Lleuad. But he didn't interrupt as Sair leaned closer into Thadred.

The knight looked down to her right hand. He studied her fingers, noting the dried blood coating them. "You learned some tricks from the empress, I see."

Sair shook her head, looking away. Using a dead man's blood to power spells was a crude, but effective method. "I haven't used that spell in years, but I didn't know what else to try. The archers couldn't do anything, and you were outnumbered."

After Thadred had thrown that one Kadra'han over the rail, the dying man's blood had seeped onto the cobblestones. With the one Kadra'han threatening Rhis, Sair had remembered a spell she'd used in the war. A spell that could cut through flesh like it was butter.

Offensive spells could be challenging. There was very little danger in channeling power into a person, because any excess *ka* would flow into other parts of the body or out of the body entirely. *Ka* tended to be ephemeral. It would flow in and out of forms as it saw fit. But it was possible to force *ka* to cut through a single point like a blade, if one had the concentration and if one did it quickly enough.

Sair might have enough strength to cast that spell on her own now, but there had been no time and she had needed to be sure.

"I didn't want to hurt him." Sair shook her head. "I just…"

"You did what you had to do." Thadred kissed the back of her hand.

Sair's chest tightened. For just a moment, she forgot that she had killed a man. She forgot that Caa Iss was here somewhere. She even forgot about the other five children.

Rhis was safe. Thadred was holding her hand, with his arm around her, and looking at her like…

"Marry me. Please."

For a moment, Sair was sure she had heard wrong. It hardly seemed the right time or the right place for this conversation.

They were both covered in blood. Thadred appeared to be beaten within an inch of his life. There were soldiers all around them, and Rhis was already pulling on Sair's arm, trying to reach Lleuad.

But Thadred was staring at her as if she was the most important thing in the entire world. There was a feverish intensity in the way he looked at her. Tension rippled through his whole body as he held his breath, like he was bracing for a blow. Like he wouldn't be able to breathe until he heard what she said next.

"What?" Sair wished she had said something else the next

instant.

"I love you, Sairydwen Aulen. I've always been sure I would die in service to the empire, and I was at peace with that, until yesterday when I realized that would mean never having a life with you." Thadred swallowed. He looked sideways. He was afraid. Afraid she would reject him like so many others had. Like his mother had. "I know I said we'd have time. I know I told you we could wait, but I don't want to wait anymore. I love you, and I want to marry you. If you'll have me."

Sair's lips parted in surprise. Her heart skipped a beat. Her whole body seemed suddenly weightless. She had been waiting for the right time to bring it up. She hadn't thought he was ready.

Among the Istovari, it would have been her place to ask him. But Thadred was an imperial lord, and while this was still not strictly proper protocol, Thadred had never been particularly proper. Sair doubted he ever would be.

Thadred misinterpreted her silence. "I understand it's a large decision. I know that the emperor and empress will have to give their approval before we can announce it publicly, but I'm confident that they will approve. I know I'm not the most desirable suitor, given my assorted flaws. But all that I am and all I have… I offer it to you. I hope…that you will consider." Thadred inclined his head a little, a shadow of a bow. He shifted, as if to pull away from her.

Sair gripped the front of his shirt to hold him in place. "Fool," she whispered, pressing closer to him. "Beautiful, beloved fool."

Thadred looked back to her, intently, hope blazing to life in his eyes. "Sair?" He spoke her name like a supplication, like a condemned man before a judge, begging for an end to his torment.

She granted mercy. "Yes. Yes, I will marry you."

Relief flooded Thadred's face. Silly man. Had he really thought she would turn him down after all this?

Sair stood on her toes to reach him, and he leaned down to kiss her. It was a chaste kiss, probably because Thadred was aware of Rhis. But the gentle kiss was full of a thousand promises of more to come.

Thadred smiled down at her, looking boyish and devilish all at once.

"Mama?" Rhis looked between the two of them.

Sair looked at her son. How was she supposed to explain this to him? She didn't think he'd ever seen her kissing someone before.

Rhis frowned up at them, looking confused.

"Rhis…" Sair cleared her throat. Where to even begin?

"Lady Sairydwen?" Vespasia interrupted, headed their way. She looked entirely out of place in this former brothel turned demon's lair. One couldn't ignore the embroidery on her sleeves and skirt, or the peacock feather stuck in her cap. She was quite clearly a lady, and a lady had no place somewhere like this. "Lord Thadred, I'm glad you are well." Vespasia bowed.

"In large thanks to you, I hear." Thadred inclined his head to his sister.

"Who are you?" It seemed that Rhis's manners had not been improved by his captivity among the Kadra'han. The boy looked up at Vespasia, curiously.

Vespasia smiled down at him. "I am Lady Vespasia. You must be Rhis. I've heard so much about you."

Rhis smiled back, almost bashful. He leaned closer against Sair, studying Vespasia from half behind her.

Another officer came, ready to speak with Thadred. "My lord, it seems that the Kadra'han have escaped. There is no sign of the cythraul."

"Did you find any more children?" Thadred glanced sideways to Sair as he asked the question.

"Yes, my lord. We found a girl and four other boys."

"Are they well?"

Sair could hear the unasked question in Thadred's words. Caa Iss and the cythraul had been known to engage in child sacrifice. If they could not keep the children as Kadra'han, they might try to keep the children from being rescued.

"A bit frightened my lord, but appear to be unhurt. What shall we do with them?"

Thadred looked at Sair, but Vespasia spoke up.

"We can bring them back to the palace. At least until we decide what should be done with them." Vespasia looked to Sair, and then back to Thadred. "There's plenty of room."

Rhis was tugging on Sair's arm. "Can we take Maëlys with us?"

"She's coming with us," Sair promised.

"Where is she?" Rhis tugged on her arm again.

"Patience, son."

The soldier was still giving a report to Thadred. "There are some thirty masons and stone workers here, sir. They were tasked with digging it seems. Though it's not clear what they were digging for. None of them seemed to know."

Thadred nodded, adjusting his hold on Lleuad. "It's all right. I know what they were after."

Vespasia offered to have soldiers sent back to the palace alongside Sair, Rhis, and the other rescued children. Sair considered it. Rhis and the others were definitely in need of baths and though they hadn't been starved, they could all probably do with a hot meal.

All the same, Sair didn't want to have to deal with the dowager countess alone. She'd already tried that, and it hadn't gone well.

More than that, she didn't want to be separated from her son and Thadred. Not when she just gotten them back again. Caa Iss had suffered a humiliation, but he was still out there. And though the city watch had been alerted, no one had anything to report. It was like he had vanished into thin air, along with Iasu and the other Kadra'han.

It was unsettling to think that the demon had been hiding in the midst of a major city and no one had noticed. Or perhaps someone had noticed and that was the problem.

Thadred and Vespasia dealt with the stone masons, sent for the constabulary, and instructed the soldiers, while Sair stood watch with Brick over Rhis and the other children.

Brick looked after the small ones with the same long-suffering patience he gave to Thadred. Sair thought to herself once again that Brick would need a raise, no matter how much Thadred was currently paying him.

"I want my mama." One of the children, a little boy with brassy blond hair said, looking up at Sair.

Sair touched his shoulder, trying to smile reassuringly. "We'll do what we can, all right? You're safe now."

"I want to go home." That was the first time the girl had spoken.

Her voice was small, so quiet Sair almost missed it.

"We'll do our best to get you home." Sair had her hands full, trying to keep all of them occupied and calm. She squeezed the girl's hands.

Maëlys was in a simple dress, but even under the dirt, stains, and numerous rips in the fabric, it looked like she came from money. Sair could see the tiny flowers embroidered on her cuffs and collar, the quality of the dress was exceptional, even if its state left something to be desired.

"I want my papa." Maëlys's eyes filled with tears.

"It's alright, darling." Sair wrapped the girl in an embrace, holding her tight. "Everything is going to be all right. You're safe now. Do you hurt anywhere?"

Maëlys sniffled, shaking her head against Sair's shoulder. Rhis patted the girl's back delicately.

Sair could see that her son was quite fond of this little girl. Under different circumstances, it would have been adorable. But Sair couldn't help but wonder what horrors these children had endured together.

"The monster told my papa that I could go home as soon as the hole was finished," Maëlys whimpered.

Sair tried not to react to those words. "Was your father a stone mason?"

Even as she asked the question, Sair knew it wouldn't be the case. The girl's clothes were too fine, and she sounded like a child raised with imperial tutors.

"No, my papa sent them here."

Everything clicked into place with that sentence. Sair tried to ask her next question delicately, already fairly certain of the answer. "Is your father Baron Prisca?"

"Yes. Do you know him?"

Sair forced a smile. This was why the baron had become a traitor. Caa Iss had taken his daughter and held her hostage in exchange for cooperation.

The whole tragedy suddenly made sense.

The baron had been forced to become an accomplice to a demon to protect his only child. Then the imperial inquisition had shown up, and he had chosen to take his own life rather than risk the anger of Caa Iss coming down on the girl.

Thadred and Sair might have been able to rescue Maëlys if they had known what was happening. Either way, the baron had done the best he could and now his daughter was safe. But it was still tragic.

This child was an orphan. And it made Sair's heart bleed.

She stroked the girl's back, not wanting to lie, but not ready to burden her with the truth yet.

"You're safe, child. You're just going to stay with us for a little bit longer, all right?"

23

THADRED

Yesterday, Thadred had thought saving Rhis was the best he could possibly hope for. Now he couldn't stop smiling, even as he gave orders to his men.

Sair had agreed to marry him, and he thought he might explode with happiness.

Lleuad was a little worse for the wear, but he probably didn't need a whole ear anyway.

Rhis was safe, the other children were safe, Thadred was alive, and they were all free. And somehow, Thadred was betrothed to the most incredible woman he had ever met.

It was almost enough to distract him from the reality that Caa Iss was still on the loose. There was also the matter of the Kadra'han who still gave Caa Iss allegiance. Not to mention the small matter of his mother wanting to leave him for dead.

Thadred would have preferred to go anywhere but his mother's estate. He tried to think of a reason to go somewhere else, but in the end, the palace was the one place they knew was secure.

Thadred had to think of what was best for Sair and Rhis. Not to mention Brick, Lleuad, and the soldiers.

Thadred stalled for as long as he could. He questioned several of the masons, informed them that they were under arrest. Gave orders for the foreman to be placed in the city jail, then thought better of it and ordered that they be put in the prison tower on the count's estate. Who knew if Caa Iss might try killing them to keep what they knew from getting out.

Thadred half suspected that the workmen would have been killed wholesale if Caa Iss had the time. The demon wanted nothing more than to avoid going back to the Dread Marches which meant he had to stay in a living host. He had to disappear.

How the mighty had fallen. Once, Caa Iss had been on the cusp of ruling the empire through Daindreth. Now he was scurrying away like a bedraggled fox, barely managing to stay one step ahead of the hounds.

They returned to the palace as the sun was sinking toward the west. Notably, Vespasia had not sent word home as to where she was. Thadred had also not sent anyone ahead to warn his mother of their return. Warnings were a courtesy. And he wasn't feeling particularly courteous right now.

Sair took Rhis and the children inside the palace, herding them like a flock of ducklings. She cast him one lingering look before she disappeared inside. Thadred watched her go, feeling…strange. There was deep longing mixed with excitement and something else he couldn't name.

He loved her so much. She felt like a piece of him. They were two separate people, but when they were together, things worked. Life made sense. His place in the world made sense.

He still couldn't believe she'd agreed to marry him.

Thadred headed to the stables, to see Lleuad tended. He cleaned the animal's wounds as best he could, and used *ka* to heal the wounds that were more serious. Lleuad's ear had stopped bleeding, and the gash in his neck mended, albeit with a scar. Brick helped him best he could, staying out of reach of the kelpie's hooves and teeth.

Thadred finished speaking with his soldiers then, finally, he ran out of excuses. He was sore and tired, and even his will to avoid his mother was wearing thin. He would have to face the woman eventually, so he might as well get it over with.

Thadred approached the palace, with Brick at his side. Though his magic was aiding his injury again, it had been a trying day, and he braced his cane as he limped up to the mansion.

Brick hovered at his back, quiet, and solemn.

They entered into a flurry of activity. Servants raced through the halls as they saw to the clothing, bathing, and feeding of six children.

"I shall prepare a bath in your rooms, sir," Brick said.

"Excellent, thank you." A warm bath sounded splendid. "I will be there shortly."

Brick frowned, opened his mouth to say something, then closed it. He proffered a half-bow and scurried off to the west wing of the mansion.

Thadred reluctantly headed to the east wing of the mansion, the one devoted to his mother's family. He was still covered in dirt, blood, straw, and whatever else had been in that barn. He looked terrible, but he wasn't going to bother cleaning himself up for his mother. No point in sanitizing what had happened.

He worried he might have to ask for directions from one of the servants, but luck proved to be on his side. Thadred heard raised voices—female voices—from upstairs. Bracing himself, he followed. It took him a few extra moments to limp his way up one faltering step at a time.

He ignored the twisting dread in the pit of his stomach and marched toward the women's voices and the sources of *ka* up ahead. As he drew closer, the voices coalesced into words, then full sentences.

"You left the estate!" the dowager cried. "Do you have any idea what a risk that was?"

"I did what needed to be done," Vespasia said.

Thadred encountered several maids hovering outside a door to one of the private rooms. The women glanced to each other, then hesitantly to him.

"My lord—" One of the maids tried to stop him as he reached for the doorknob.

"Don't worry," Thadred said with a wry smile. "I'm family."

Before any of the maids could stop him, Thadred opened the door and limped inside. He shut the door quietly, finding himself in a sitting room.

He followed the sound of the shouting match to the open door of a bedchamber. He would guess the room was Vespasia's, judging by the dresses strewn here and there. His mother and half-sister faced one another across the room like two knights ready to charge across the lysts.

"I am the parent. *You* are the child," the dowager barked. "You will obey me!"

Thadred paused in the doorway, somewhat impressed. He hadn't thought his mother capable of that much venom.

"Are you?" Vespasia demanded. "Are you the parent?"

Zeyna drew herself to her full height, which was impressive, but comparable to her daughter's. "Young lady, if you try to defy my authority—"

"*You* didn't save me and my sisters when the demons came," Vespasia screamed. "*I* did."

That set Zeyna back, just a little bit.

Thadred wondered how long it would take for the two women to notice him.

"Whatever that boy did to you…" Zeyna cleared her throat, smoothing back her hair. "He paid for his crimes. The rumors will abate eventually, and no one ever need know—"

"He never raped me!" Vespasia shouted. "I wanted everything he did to me."

From the way Zeyna flinched, Thadred guessed no one had actually said the words.

"I *wanted* it. Did you hear that, Mother? He didn't rape me any more than I raped him." Vespasia shook her head. "I…I loved him. And your soldiers killed him."

It seemed that scandalized Zeyna more than anything thus far. "You don't know what you're talking about."

"What don't I know, Mother?" Vespasia demanded. "I know your men murdered my lover on your orders."

"I will not allow you to ruin your life," Zeyna insisted. "You will not repeat my mistakes. You will not—"

"If you expected me to let another man die to let you save face, I will not." Vespasia stared down her mother and Thadred saw the family resemblance then. Vespasia had played the part of a gentlewoman. She had played the part of the dutiful daughter and perhaps part of her was, but deep down, she was just like him. Defiant, strong-willed, and lacking all tolerance for hypocrites.

"What are you talking about?" Zeyna shifted her weight, almost as if she expected a blow.

"You were hoping Lord Thadred would die, weren't you? You were hoping he would just go away and put an end to the scandal that has followed you for twenty-eight years."

"Vespasia…"

"But here's what you don't understand, Mother—no one cares about the scandal more than you." Vespasia's nostrils flared. "You are dowager countess, now regent of this province, perfectly respectable. No one *cares* you had a bastard son. Just like no one cares I swyved a stable hand."

"Your reputation, Vespasia—"

"Damn my reputation! My dowry is more than sufficient to compensate."

Speaking from experience, Thadred knew Vespasia was right. Premarital celibacy was by no means a requirement if a woman's dowry was large enough. Lords and noblemen cared far more about fidelity after marriage than chastity before. Though, if a woman's landholdings were large enough, some men were willing to overlook even that.

Thadred had bedded plenty of young noblewomen in the imperial court. A few of them had no previous experience, but many did. Yet all of them had ended their affairs when they had been offered the hand of some nobleman.

"You will not shame our family." Zeyna shook her head, voice cracking on the verge of tears. "You will not shame me!"

Thadred decided this conversation would get nowhere. "I was thinking of what to write to Emperor Daindreth."

Both women jumped, whirling on him.

"Though I might just speak to him in person, I suppose." Thadred met Zeyna's shocked stare.

"You have no right to be here," Zeyna said, indignant. "It's indecent."

Thadred barked a laugh. "Really? You think I'd try to seduce my own sister?"

Zeyna visibly cringed at that title. Well, Vespasia was his sister whether anyone liked it or not. They all might as well get over it.

"I was thinking of suggesting Count Flavius spend a few years in the imperial barracks." Thadred leaned against the doorframe, staring at the ceiling as if deep in thought. "Squiring for a few years would do him good, I think. Not for me, of course. I haven't the patience. But I do have a few friends in need of staff."

"No." Zeyna looked to him, aghast.

"You're free to visit him any time," Thadred said. "The court is always open to the mother of the High Inquisitor." Zeyna would be welcomed at court as the emperor's aunt, but Thadred couldn't resist getting in that last barb.

"Lord Thadred." Her voice turned pleading—fearful.

"You made your choices, madam." Thadred cast her a bitter smile. "And I am the consequence." He turned his back on her before he was overcome with the temptation to harass her further.

Zeyna called after him, but he ignored her.

Thadred had wanted to reconcile with her or at least become amicable with her—for Sair's sake. Perhaps for Vespasia's sake, too.

He could admit his part in getting them off on the wrong foot, but he could not reconcile with someone who had no desire for reconciliation. Zeyna wanted to be rid of him. In her eyes, he wasn't her son, he wasn't even a man. He was the product of a mistake that had ruined her life.

Thadred felt drained as he shuffled out into the hallway. Like an oil lamp burning the last dregs.

Thadred limped down the stairs and back to his chambers. From the hallway, he heard Sair's voice over the clamor of a half-dozen children's voices. It sounded like his betrothed was wrangling her son and his small compatriots.

Their voices overlapped and clashed, a cacophony of

questions and Sair's long-suffering answers. Judging by the servants bustling in and out of the chambers, she had plenty of help.

Thadred hobbled into his assigned room to find papers stacked throughout the sitting area. He arched one eyebrow, taking in what appeared to be the flotsam of a clerical madman.

"Brick?" He could sense the valet's *ka* in the other room.

"In here, sir!" Brick called.

Thadred shuffled into the bedroom to find Brick filling a tub before the hearth.

"Almost done, my lord." Brick poured another bucket of hot water in, stirring a few times before he turned and began picking papers off the floor.

"What happened here?" Thadred gestured around the room.

"Lady Sairydwen and I worked in here last night, reviewing the late baron's ledgers."

Thadred looked around the apartment. The stacks and piles were orderly, but it was clear that this had been the site of a feverish effort through the night.

"She worked in here?" Thadred looked around the room, a little confused.

"She wanted to work here, sir." Brick cleared his throat awkwardly. "I didn't protest, but if you'd like me to keep her out of your rooms in the future—"

"No, Brick. Lady Sairydwen is free to enter my rooms as she wishes. I just wasn't expecting this."

Brick nodded in a way that was partially a bow. "As you wish, sir. Shall I help you undress?"

"Yes. Please." Thadred was still stiff after a night on the hard ground without his magic.

Brick helped him shed his coat, shirt, boots, and trousers and carefully sink into the tub.

The water was hot at first, but Thadred leaned back into it with a long exhale. The heat seeped into his taunt muscles, soothing away the knots and aches.

"Is the heat good, sir?" Brick glanced at the hearth. "Too hot? Too cold?"

"It's perfect, Brick." Thadred closed his eyes. "You're a damned saint."

"Should I be so blessed." Brick cleared his throat a little awkwardly. "Shall I fetch your dinner? I don't suppose you would want to join the family for the evening meal?"

Thadred barked a laugh. "Fetching it is fine."

"I shall see to that at once." Brick bowed again and swept out of the apartment.

Thadred leaned back into the hot water. How long since he'd had a proper bath? Probably Mynadra.

He savored the pleasant warmth. With his eyes closed, it was easier to focus on *ka* in the world around him.

Thadred drew power from the air, spinning it into golden coils and soaking it up into himself. He felt his body slowly mending, healing the bruises and sores of his imprisonment.

He coiled loops of magic around his bad hip and thigh, reinforcing the supports on his injury. The muscles around it had tried compensating and locked tight. Thadred thought it might be a day or two before they loosened again. The warm water helped, but it wouldn't be a cure.

Reaching out, Thadred sensed the *ka* of the bodies around him. He could feel the servants and their hustling up and down the hallway. There were the guards on the perimeter of the mansion, outside the house.

Thadred could feel no telltale golden bands that marked Kadra'han or the toxic, miasmic presence of a cythraul. He was safe.

More importantly, Sair and Rhis were safe. He could sense them a few rooms over.

Thadred tilted his head back, arms resting on the tub, and let the warmth of the water soothe him.

He hadn't intended to fall asleep, but he jolted awake at the sound of a door opening. Thadred groaned, finding the water had gone lukewarm and his muscles had cramped after staying in one position for too long.

He shifted, sensing a shape of *ka* entering his apartment. Brick must have returned from fetching his dinner.

"Brick?" Thadred rubbed the sleep from his eyes. Overall, he felt much better. The *ka* had been doing its work and his hip and thigh no longer throbbed.

"Not Brick." Sair slipped in through his bedroom door. She glimpsed his bare chest above the water line then looked away, but didn't retreat. "Do you want me to come back later?"

Thadred's mouth was suddenly dry. It took several tries before he was able to speak. "Stay."

Something flared in Sair's eyes as she stepped inside, but then it was gone. "Do you need help?"

Thadred could probably manage, but he had the feeling she wanted to help. "Yes."

Sair adjusted her skirts to crouch beside him. "What do you need help with?" Her voice was soft, gentle, but Thadred could swear it was just a little husky.

"Help me wash my hair?" It was the first thing he thought of.

Sair nodded. "I can help with that." She found the oils and soaps Brick had left. She slipped behind him, skirt rustling as she crouched down at his back.

Thadred was naked, in a bathtub, with her at his back. His soldier's training told him he was completely vulnerable, and yet…he trusted Sair. He would trust her even more than this.

Sair poured the oils over his head. She massaged his scalp, her nails scraping pleasantly against his skin.

Thadred closed his eyes, stifling a groan. He was going to melt in her hands.

Sair pulled gently, kneading the muscles he hadn't even known were sore.

"What are you going to tell Rhis?" Thadred asked the question softly, not wanting to spoil the moment.

Sair inhaled a slow breath. "I am not sure yet." Sair moved down his scalp to his neck, massaging where his skull met his spine.

Thadred leaned into her ministrations. How did she make this feel so good?

"It helps that he already knows and likes you."

Thadred flicked the surface of the water. "I don't know how to be a parent. I've never done this before."

Sair worked her way down to his shoulders. "No one knows how to be a parent, love. Not really."

Thadred chuckled at that, shifting under her touch.

"You simply do the best you can." Sair kneaded his shoulders, her fingers digging into the tense muscles of his upper back. "And hope your children forgive your mistakes."

"Should I have waited to ask you in private? Not in front of him?"

He felt Sair shrug. "Perhaps. But I still said yes, didn't I?"

Thadred tilted his head back to look up at her.

Sair smiled gently down at him, pure affection in her eyes.

What had he done to deserve her? Quite simply—nothing. There was no possibility that he had ever done anything worthy of her.

Thadred opened his mouth to say something about what they would need to do to find Caa Iss, but what came out was, "I love you."

Sair's smile widened and she kissed the top of his head, breath tickling his ear as she did. "I love you, too." She shifted around to the front of the tub, crouching at his side. "Let's rinse you."

Thadred ladled the now tepid water over his head, scrubbing out the soaps and oils, but leaving behind their clean scent. If not for the marks on his forearms, it felt as if he'd washed away the whole ordeal.

"What's this?" Sair paused, looking at the long pink marks where his cuts were still healing.

"Caa Iss can't use magic," Thadred explained. "Not without Istovari blood, it seems."

Sair shuddered. "He used your blood to work magic?"

Thadred nodded, wishing he could forget how helpless he'd felt, how weak. "He's using all the Kadra'han, I think. Iasu and several of the others for sure. They aren't strong enough to heal themselves, so they all wore bandages."

Sair grimaced, fingers tracing gently along the marks.

Thadred shouldn't have scars once the wounds healed properly, but for now his magic had still left behind tender pink veins. "It's somewhat good news, I suppose. To hear that he has no power without blood."

Thadred wasn't sure about no power. The cythraul was still freakishly strong and could heal too fast, but Sair was right.

"The Kadra'han don't want to serve him. At least, Iasu doesn't." Thadred exhaled. "I didn't figure out how to use that to our advantage, but it might be helpful yet."

Sair's thumb traced the marks on his skin. She touched them gingerly, almost fearfully. Her hands shook.

"Sair?"

When she met his eyes, hers were full of tears.

"What's wrong?" Thadred shifted toward her, sloshing the water as he did.

"You could have died. You could have…" Sair's voice broke, and she looked away. She blinked several times and took a shuddering breath. "I'm sorry."

"I'm not dying, my dear," Thadred said. "Lleuad would never allow it."

Sair rolled her eyes, choking on something that might have been intended as a laugh, but came out as more of a cough. "I see."

"Sair." Thadred's hands were wet, but he touched the side of her face. "I'm not going to leave you."

If nothing else, he refused to let her lose another loved one. She deserved to be surrounded by the people she cared for, the people who cared for her. He was determined to love her for a long time yet.

Sair leaned into his touch, nuzzling his palm.

Thadred drew her around to him, close enough that he could feel her breath on his face.

She watched him intently, leaning closer until only the barest distance separated them. She was offering, letting him choose.

But Thadred had chosen her a long time ago.

He brushed his lips over hers. Sair returned his kiss with a sharp inhale, her mouth parting to let him in.

Kissing her was like drinking liquid sunlight—all warmth and brightness.

Thadred had never realized how much he kept his guard up with women until he found himself letting it down with her.

Sair touched his shoulder, his chest, just the barest brush of her fingertips. She didn't use magic this time, but Thadred felt shivers of warmth all the same. She was skirting boundaries, asking permission.

Thadred cupped her face in his hands and kissed her deeper, pulling her toward him. Much farther and she would be toppling into the tub on top of him.

Sair's breathing quickened, her chest heaving as she gripped his arms, her nails digging into his biceps.

Thadred found the knot of her kerchief at the base of her neck and tugged it free. Sair let out a surprised gasp as he pulled the pins from her carefully arranged bun.

He paused. "Was that alright?"

In response, Sair finished pulling out the rest of the pins for him, shaking her hair free.

Thadred smiled as the dark gold strands fell like a curtain around them. It fell below her shoulders and smelled of the apple blossom perfume she usually wore.

He inhaled the scent of her hair, enjoying how soft it felt against his face. He'd wanted to do this for so long.

Sair shook her head, the ends of her hair tickling his bare shoulders. She smiled at him, girlish and playful, if a little shy.

Thadred grinned back at her, sliding his hand up through her hair, close to her scalp. He curled his fist into her locks and pulled her head to the side to expose her neck.

Sair gasped but let him. Her breathing sped up and she pressed toward him, urging him on.

Thadred kissed her throat, starting at a spot along her jaw, just under her ear. He sucked lightly along the vein in her neck, and she moaned.

"Thadred."

"Mmm?" Thadred kissed lower on her neck, more careful this time.

Sair whimpered, shifting closer.

"Should I stop?"

"No," Sair gasped. "Don't stop."

Thadred smiled against her skin, kissing a line down her neck to her collarbone. She tried to turn her head, but he held her in place, raking his teeth lightly against her flesh.

He ran his tongue back up her neck. He traced the shell of her ear, making her squirm in his grip.

Thadred moved slowly, deliberately. Sair shook in his grasp, tension running through her whole body. She moaned as he tugged on her ear lobe with his teeth, pressing closer against the side of the tub.

"Please," she rasped. "Please, Thadred."

Thadred couldn't help the wicked grin that came to his lips at that. "Please what?"

"Please," Sair whimpered.

"What is it, pretty girl?"

Sair ripped out of his grasp. She spun on him, all her former hesitance gone. Sair caught his face in her hands and kissed him—deep and hard. It was a hungry kiss—ravenous and insatiable.

She pulled away from his mouth to kiss the stubble along his jaw, his neck. She moved lower, kissing bare chest, his shoulder then back up to his mouth.

Sair kissed him like she wanted to consume him, like she would never get enough.

The water splashed as Thadred moved to grab her waist, pulling her closer. He left wet handprints on her bodice, but she didn't seem to care. She touched his side, her hand barely dipping beneath the waterline.

Thadred's heart raced as her hands slid over him, her mouth skimming a path along his bare skin. He loved her mouth. Visions of things he wanted her to do with it flashed through his head.

Sair reached to kiss his opposite shoulder and overbalanced. She slipped, landing awkwardly on top of him. The water splashed, and Thadred jumped. He caught her, but she still fell partway into the tub, soaking her dress.

He winced as her weight pressed into him, jostling his bad hip.

"Are you alright?" Sair looked at him in alarm. "Did I hurt you?"

Thadred breathed deep a few times. "It's fine."

Sair studied him for a moment longer. Her gaze flickered back to his mouth.

"Sair." Thadred's voice came out thick and hoarse. Beneath the water, he had gone painfully hard. He wasn't sure Sair could tell or not, but he had a feeling she knew.

"Is something wrong?" Sair searched his face.

Thadred drew deep breaths, trying to collect his thoughts.

Sair's breath began to slow, concern replacing her arousal. "What's wrong?"

Thadred pressed his forehead to hers, eyes squeezing shut. "I'm going to take you in this bathtub if you don't stop me."

He heard Sair swallow at that. "I want you," she whispered. "I love you, Thadred."

Thadred loved her, too, that wasn't the problem. Or maybe it was.

"I don't want to wait anymore either," she said. "I've waited so long. I wanted everything to be perfect, to have the empress's blessing, Rhis's approval, and all the messy details sorted out, but…" He felt her shake her head. "Things are never going to be perfect. I realize that now. I don't need perfect." She touched his cheek, her fingers brushing through the stubble along his jaw. "I just need you."

Thadred looked up to her. "No bastards."

Understanding dawned in Sair's face. "You mean…"

Thadred nodded tightly. He'd always taken what precautions he could and, to the best of his knowledge, he hadn't fathered any himself. But there wasn't time for precautions right now. What was more, he didn't want Sair to have a child out of wedlock.

As an Istovari, she probably wouldn't care, but Thadred would. Not to mention Amira would be furious. Daindreth would just be disappointed.

Sair looked down. "I see."

A stirring came from the other room. *Ka* in the shape of a man entered through the apartment, accompanied the delicate tinkle of porcelain on a tray.

"Terribly sorry about the delay, sir," Brick said. "The kitchens are a bit astir with the day's excitement, not to mention feeding all the children. It seems that—oh!" Brick opened the bedroom door and immediately flushed red at the sight of Sairydwen. "Forgive me, I didn't…" Brick coughed. He looked back to the door. "Shall I fetch food for Lady Sairydwen as well?"

"You're fine, Brick."

Sair flushed, looking down at her soaked dress and disheveled hair. She began fumbling to find her kerchief on the ground.

Thadred realized with a little twist of surprise that he had done the right thing. If Sair was embarrassed being caught by Brick, one of the least judgmental people there was, the judgment from the imperial court would have hurt her.

Even if she did want him. Even if she did love him.

"You said you don't need it to be perfect." Thadred cleared his throat. "Do you mean that?"

Sair hesitated, but when she answered, her voice was firm. "Yes."

Thadred nodded, thinking he was about to do the single most impulsive thing that he had done in his life. "Alright, then. Can you find Vespasia? And the household lawyer? I'm sure they have one on their staff here. All my clerks are still with the ship. Can you have them meet us somewhere private?"

Sair shifted back, cocking her head at him. "What are you thinking?"

Thadred smiled at her. "Neither of us want to wait." He nodded to the door. "Brick? Can you set down that tray? I need you to help me dress."

24

SAIR

"Why am I here?" Vespasia perched on the settee beside Sair. "You said you needed something?"

"Yes." Sair shifted, finding it hard to sit still. She didn't know what to expect. "Thadred is having a marriage contract drawn up."

"So I heard." Vespasia glanced to the stout young man who was still fresh from his lawyer's apprenticeship.

The young lawyer worked carefully over the lines of the document, making notations and crossing out sentences here and there.

Thadred sat across from the two women at a large desk, speaking with Major Caiden. The hunt for Caa Iss continued across the city, but there had been no trails found yet.

It seemed that the demon had disappeared into thin air. Sair wasn't sure whether to be relieved or not. A fleeing Caa Iss meant a weak Caa Iss. The demon would not risk a confrontation unless he was sure he could win.

Sair had changed out of her soaked dress, wearing a fresh evening gown. The dress was one Ketsia had gifted her, designed for the coastal empire.

Vespasia and Sair sat on a settee, eating a light supper. It seemed that Vespasia had not wanted to join her mother and younger brother for the evening meal any more than the rest of them. Dinner was a light clam soup with bread rolls and sweet wine.

Sair sipped at it carefully, trying to stop herself from chugging it in her nervousness.

Thadred had shaved and dressed in clothes that befitted an imperial gentleman. He was all manners and grace again, his blackthorn cane with the silver cap leaning against his chair.

"Lord Thadred has threatened to make me regent of the province," Vespasia said, dropping her voice.

Sair wasn't surprised. "I imagine you would be well-suited to the role."

Vespasia chirped a laugh with an edge of sardonicism. "My mother would hate me for it, of course. Like she hates me now."

"Darling." Sair rested a hand on the younger woman's arm.

"Don't worry about me." Vespasia cast Sair a smile that had no mirth in it. "My mother already hated me. I'm repeating her mistakes, she says."

Sair exhaled slowly. She didn't know how to help the younger woman. It didn't seem anything would be helpful at a time like this.

Vespasia looked to Sair. "How is your son?"

Sair's heart warmed at mention of Rhis—safe and secure within the mansion. "Surrounded by guards with the others," she said. "He's quite taken with that girl, Maëlys."

"The late baron's daughter?"

"Yes." Sair smiled sadly.

Vespasia looked down. "Have you told her yet?"

Sair shook her head. "After all she's been through…the poor child is barely speaking as it is."

"Will you leave her in our charge when you go?"

Sair looked at Thadred who was pointing to a map of Iandua, speaking to the major. "It depends. I imagine we will stay until Caa Iss is eradicated." However long that took.

Thadred would hunt the monster to the ends of the earth if he had to, never mind how far. And Sair would stay with him.

It might be safer back on the mainland, but Sair wouldn't risk leaving him. Her place was with Thadred, no matter what happened, and her son's place was with her.

The major and Thadred finished speaking and the officer straightened, preparing to go. He paused beside the billiard table currently being used to display a lengthy scroll. All contracts in the empire were meant to be a continuous scroll to prevent addition or subtraction at the edges.

The major glanced to the document, then to Thadred. "A contract, sir?"

"My marriage contract," Thadred answered, as if it was nothing at all. "I want special care taken at the docks. I'd be looking to escape by sea if I was a demon on the run."

"Your marriage contract?" The major's usual calm façade cracked, revealing his surprise.

"Yes. Did you hear me?"

The major recovered himself and nodded. "Yes, sir."

"Excellent." Thadred walked the major to the door, their voices carrying out into the hall. "Leave ten men here and two messengers. The rest of you head into the city to continue the search. Our best chance to catch them will be at the docks or city gates. Remember to keep an eye on your horses. Animals will be the first to react to the cythraul's presence."

Sair finished the last of her clam soup, wiping the bowl with a piece of bread.

Thadred returned and looked over the document. "Everything appears to be in order."

The clerk shuffled nervously. "Yes, sir. Just finishing up final details."

"Good." Thadred gestured for Sair. "Come, love." He gestured to the document. "Anything you want included? Or excluded, I suppose."

Sair's heart beat faster as she joined Thadred by the table. She looked over the document.

It appeared to be fairly standard for an imperial marriage contract, not that she had seen too many of those. There were clauses stating Thadred would be required to provide her a lifestyle comparative to his own, that she would become executor of his estate in the event of his death. Sair tried not to think too hard on that possibility.

The document listed Thadred's landholdings and assets. Sair found her brows rising as she read. She hadn't realized just how much land Thadred had been granted by the emperor.

Sair had never been more aware of how little she owned until she saw her own assets listed beside Thadred's. They came down to the belongings within her home back in the Haven and her station as the empress's advisor.

The contract stated that Sair owed Thadred fidelity, something she planned anyway. She could see several marks where Thadred had added an addendum requiring the same from him. Sair hadn't expected him to put that in writing, but it did warm her heart to see it.

Sair swallowed.

"What do you think?" Thadred rested a hand on the small of her back.

"One thing." Sair looked up to him.

"Name it."

"If we should have daughters, I want them to take my surname." Among the Istovari, all Sair's children would take her surname, so this seemed like a good compromise.

Thadred considered it. "Fine, but Rhis takes mine."

Sair's spine stiffened straight. Hot anger prickled the back of her neck. She opened her mouth, then closed it before she said something she would regret.

Thadred seemed to realize that he had overstepped. "I didn't mean it that way. It's just that…" Thadred exhaled. "He will be the oldest son."

Sair frowned and looked back to the document, finding the section on successors to the estate. "You're making Rhis your heir?"

"Well, yes." Thadred cleared his throat. "Why wouldn't I?"

Sair's chest clenched at that with several emotions at once. Thadred hadn't left any provisions for another son—one of his own blood—to come ahead of Rhis in succession. According to this document, Rhis would be the legal heir of everything Thadred owned as soon as Thadred and Sair were married.

There were a few provisions for additional sons and substantial dowries guaranteed for any daughters, but Rhis would be the main beneficiary.

"I'm not trying to take the place of your first husband," Thadred said. "I know better than that, but the world is unkind to boys without fathers." He exhaled a long breath. "Even if it is only a stepfather, there are certain advantages to having a nobleman claim you."

Sair realized Thadred would know that better than anyone. He was trying to protect Rhis in his own way. He was trying to spare her son what he'd gone through as a bastard in the imperial court. It wasn't quite the same situation, but Sair was willing to trust that Thadred knew the court better.

Sair touched his arm. "We let Rhis decide. Perhaps in a few years."

Thadred nodded. A compromise.

The clerk began rewriting that portion of the document.

"I don't know how to do this," Thadred said quietly. "I'm trying."

Sair squeezed his hand. "We'll figure it out together. The three of us."

Thadred smiled at that.

Vespasia came up beside Sair's other side, looking the document over as the clerk rewrote it into a brand-new sheaf of parchment. "I suppose this is why I am here? To witness?"

"Yes." Thadred cleared his throat. "I also need your permission."

Vespasia blinked. "My permission?"

Thadred nodded to Sair.

"Among the Istovari, all we need for a marriage is the permission of the bridegroom's family." Sair looked up to Thadred. "My mother is gone, and I am a widow. I can speak for myself, but…we need a woman of his family to give her consent."

Vespasia frowned at that. "What strange customs." She inhaled. "Oh, you were waiting for me? Yes, I'm fine with it." She glanced between them. "Is that all I need to say?"

Sair chuckled. "Yes, that will do."

Thadred caught the side of Sair's face, pulling her around to him. He claimed her mouth, drawing an arm around her and kissing her to make her head spin. She should have been worried about the indecency, but she leaned into it, feeling she could melt against him.

Brick let off a cough and Vespasia giggled.

Thadred ended their kiss, resting his forehead against hers. "You're mine now," he whispered in the space between them. He watched her like she was the only person in the room, the only woman to ever exist. "All mine."

"Yours," Sair whispered back. "But you're mine, too."

"Of course." Thadred's mouth curled mischievously at the edges. "But I think I came out ahead in this bargain."

Sair shook her head. He still saw himself as unworthy. They would need to work on that, but for now she smiled up at him, enjoying the possessive reverence of his embrace.

The clerk cleared his throat. "Just a few final steps, my lord. My lady."

Thadred kissed the top of Sair's head—one last quiet show of affection.

The clerk proffered the document and Thadred signed, then Sair signed it after. Vespasia signed beneath both their names as a witness, then Brick, and lastly the clerk.

When that was done, the clerk folded the document carefully and sealed it with wax before tucking it into an oilskin pouch. That pouch would be delivered to the imperial register when Thadred and Sair returned to Mynadra. Then it would be sent to Daindreth for either his approval or disapproval.

Thadred had a title and lands from the crown and as such, any changes to his estate, will, or other holdings had to be approved by the imperial authority. The emperor would also have final say as to whether Rhis would be allowed to become Thadred's heir.

Not that Sair worried about Daindreth approving. He was like a younger brother. If nothing else, Amira would be on her side, she was sure of that.

Thadred turned to see to a few final messages from across the city. The search for Caa Iss was still underway.

Sair and Vespasia left him, heading to check on Rhis and the other children one last time. As Sair stepped out into the hallway, she realized what she had done.

She was married to Lord Thadred Myrani, High Inquisitor of Erymaya.

After more than a year of pining, waiting, sidestepping, and repressed desire, he was hers. He'd married her in both the imperial and the Istovari way, just to make sure. It felt…strange.

There had been a time Sair had never thought she could consider loving again, much less remarrying. Her life had become something she could never have imagined. She still wasn't sure what the future might hold, but she knew she wanted Thadred in it. She knew Thadred was good for her, good for Rhis, even without setting her son up for life.

Rhis would never have to worry about anything ever again. His education, his future, all of it was paid for. Her son would be an aristocrat, along with any other children she and Thadred might have.

"I suppose congratulations are in order?" Vespasia offered hesitantly.

"Yes," Sair smiled awkwardly.

"It's not exactly the kind of wedding I'm used to," Vespasia said.

There wasn't any reason not to marry in this way. Imperial weddings were meant to impress people. Sair and Thadred had no one to impress.

"We don't know how long we will be hunting the cythraul in Iandua," Sair answered. "We could be here a week or a year. However long it takes. Though I doubt we will stay in this mansion if it takes so long."

The two women reached the suite of rooms where the children were being kept. Rhis had insisted on staying with the others.

Inside, they found several maids clearing away the remains of a meal off the apartment's table as well as the carpet.

It seemed that the children didn't all possess table manners, but they had all been bathed, fed, and dressed in clean if ill-fitting clothes.

Rhis sat with two of the younger boys, showing them how to balance a set of blocks into an archway. One of the other boys was asleep on the couch while the other was engrossed in some sort of puzzle box.

Maëlys, the girl, sat quietly on the couch, watching Rhis and the other two boys. The girl seemed exhausted and in a way beyond her years. It made Sair's heart twist. They still hadn't told Maëlys she was an orphan.

Her father had left a robust will and Maëlys would hardly be destitute, but it was one thing to have money and another entirely to have a family.

25

SAIR

Sair stayed with the children for hours after that, telling them stories, braiding Maëlys's hair, and shuffling all of them off into their separate pallets around the fire. Vespasia had to leave to manage the servants elsewhere in the house, but a few of Count Flavius's former nurses had been conscripted into service and they helped tend the small gaggle with the patience of experienced veterans.

"Mama?" Rhis asked as Sair was tucking him in. He was too old for it, or so he said, but had agreed to humor her just for tonight.

"Yes, son?" Sair studied him by the flickering fire. His face was round and soft, childlike, and earnest. He was so much like the boy his father had been before soldiers took his eyes.

"Will we live with Thadred now?"

"Yes. In the palace, most likely."

Rhis pursed his lips, considering. "Can Maëlys come, too?"

Sair smiled sadly, looking over to where the young girl was curled on her side, her back to them. "We'll have to see, alright?"

Rhis sat up. "There's room in the palace. I remember there's lots of rooms. I can ask the emperor. He likes me."

"Yes, Rhis, the emperor likes you." Sair nudged her son to lie back down. "It's just that Maëlys has a home here."

Rhis flopped on his back with a frustrated sound.

Sair brushed the hair from his forehead. She hoped he was truly as unaffected as he acted. It seemed he had spent his captivity focusing on the other children, Maëlys in particular.

"Rhis…" Sair wasn't sure how to ask this next question. "You know that Thadred asked me to marry him?"

Rhis chewed his lip. "I know."

"Do you…do you have any questions about that?"

Rhis inhaled a slow breath, then let it out again. He stayed silent. "Thadred likes me."

"He does." Sair smiled a little at that. Thadred had risked his life for Rhis and had made the boy a noble. It seemed a bit of an understatement.

"Will you have more babies?"

Sair did her best not to cough at that. "Probably. At some point."

Rhis chewed his lip. He stared past Sair, looking at the ceiling. "Will you love them more?"

"No." Sair smoothed his forehead with her thumb. "No, I will love you all the same. I promise."

Rhis nodded. "Thadred will love them more."

"Why do you say that?"

Rhis shrugged, as if it was obvious. "They'll be his babies."

Sair exhaled a long breath. "I don't know what will happen. Thadred and I might not have babies for all I know. But I know Thadred loves you." She smiled down at her son. "I wouldn't be marrying him if he didn't."

Rhis nodded, but his brow furrowed slightly.

"And I know he will do his best. It will be a change and we'll make mistakes, but we will always love you. Just like Papa loved you."

Rhis swallowed, nodding a little stiffly.

Sair brushed his cheek with her fingertips. "I know it's a lot."

Rhis didn't look at her, still staring at the ceiling. "I don't remember Papa," he said quietly. "I know what you told me and what Uncle Tapios told me, but I don't…" Tears welled in Rhis's eyes. "I'm sorry, Mama. I don't remember."

Pain lanced through Sair's chest. Rhis had been young,

barely three years old, when his father had died. Rhisiart had adored his son and Sair desperately hoped the boy would remember.

When Sair had been pregnant, Rhisiart would rest his cheek on her belly and sing to their child. When he held his son for the first time, Rhisiart had sobbed, cradling baby Rhis like he was the most precious thing in the world.

Rhisiart deserved to be remembered and Sair had long hoped her son would remember his father. But it seemed the boy had been too young.

"It's alright, Rhis." Sair brushed the tears from his face. "It's not your fault."

Rhis sniffled, scrubbing at his face.

"Papa would understand," Sair said. "He would." Sair pulled her son into her arms, cradling him as if he was a baby again.

As she spoke the words, Sair knew they were true. Rhisiart would have understood why Rhis couldn't remember him. And he would have understood Sair falling in love with Thadred.

Rhisiart would have wanted her to find love again. He would have wanted his son to have a father figure and he would have approved of Thadred. Damn it all, but he would have.

Sair squeezed her eyes shut against her own tears. She imagined what her late husband would have said if he could have seen them now, if he could have met Thadred.

He would have probably made some joke about her always going for cripples. But he would have approved. She was sure of that.

Thadred had fought for their son, fought for her. Thadred had been willing to risk his life for Sair even when they were enemies. He was a good man, for all he would have the world think otherwise. Not to mention, he had just drawn up a marriage contract that made Rhis his heir and Sair co-owner of everything he had.

Be happy—that was what Rhisiart would have said.

Sair held onto her son until he pulled away, tucking him back into the blankets.

"It's going to be alright, Rhis," Sair whispered.

Rhis nodded, his eyes red, but the tears were done. "Good night, Mama."

"Good night, sweetling. The servants can find me if you need anything." Sair kissed his forehead one final time before leaving.

Sair shut the door behind her. She leaned against the wall, taking a deep breath. Thadred had said that he didn't know how to do this, but she didn't know how to do this, either.

She took a moment, collecting herself. Rhisiart was gone. There was not a time she could remember when she had not either loved him or mourned him. But he wouldn't have wanted her to mourn him any longer.

She closed her eyes. For just another moment, she was Rhisiart's widow. Then she opened her eyes, and she was Thadred's wife.

She pushed off the wall and headed to Thadred's room. He might still be working late into the night, but she knew where he would be eventually.

The mansion was quiet. It seemed the hustle and bustle of the day had worn out everyone and most of the household had retired early.

Sair's footsteps were the only sound as she made her way down the short hallway to where Thadred was staying. She rounded the corner, and her heart skipped a beat.

A familiar figure headed toward her, leaning on a cane. "Sair?" Thadred's face was lit partially by the lamp in a nearby sconce.

"I was just seeing to Rhis."

"How is he?" Thadred took another step toward her.

Sair swallowed. "Better than I expected."

"The kid is made of stern stuff." Thadred nodded. Was it her imagination, or was that a note of pride in his tone?

Sair laughed a little. "He seems to be." Her heart fluttered, warmth curling through her.

Thadred came a step closer.

Sair drew nearer to Thadred, her heart rattling in her chest. Desire swelled, hot and needy through her, flushing her cheeks and coiling deep in her core.

She hadn't been with a man in years, not since…

Thadred reached out to her. Her throat tightened and she was as nervous as a maiden as she took his hand.

The lamps burned low, leaving languid shadows on the ground. It was a darkness meant for whispers and secrets, a darkness meant for lovers.

Sair followed Thadred back into his apartments. She had come here earlier today full of boldness and confidence, but that had been a few hours ago.

She was married to Thadred now, except in the unlikely event the emperor decided to dissolve their marriage. It had all happened so fast and yet a part of her felt it should have happened a long time ago.

Excitement coursed through her. She couldn't believe this was happening. It seemed almost too good to be true, like a trap.

"Are you alright, darling?" Thadred's voice reached her as he shut the door to his apartment, cloistering them in his sitting room.

"Yes," Sair answered, her voice coming out shaky.

Thadred set his cane down by the door and pulled her around to face him. Several lamps had been left burning, casting amber shadows over them both. "You're trembling, love." He stroked over the back of her hands. He traced the small ridges in her skin, the scars from over a year ago.

"I think I'm nervous." Even as she said it, Sair leaned into him, pressing against him. He was warm, solid, and muscle rippled under his coat.

Thadred rested his forehead to hers. "There's no need to be nervous." His thumb brushed her chin. He kissed the tip of her nose, making her giggle.

"That tickles."

Thadred cast her a wicked grin. "You're ticklish?"

"No," Sair answered hastily. "I am not."

"Hmm." Thadred didn't sound convinced. "I will have to test that at some point." He pressed his mouth to hers, teasing her lips apart with his tongue. His kiss was sensual and slow as he gently urged her to open for him.

A moan escaped her as Sair gripped his jacket, dragging him closer. Thadred's hands drifted down her back, pressing her against him.

Sair found the laces at the front of his shirt and fumbled to undo them. Thadred obliged, peeling off his jacket and draping it over the nearby chair.

Sair helped him pull his shirt over his head. She had seen him naked earlier today, but she still wasn't prepared. Lamplight shone over lean muscle and Sair's mouth went suddenly dry. He was beautiful. Absolutely beautiful. How had she married this?

Thadred seemed to know what she was thinking. He smiled and caught her wrists, pressing her hands to his chest.

Sair touched him with wonder, tracing the firm slopes and lines of his chest, shoulders, and abdomen. He was sculpted like an artist's fondest fantasy, like Sair's daydreams brought to life.

Thadred reached behind her to undo the laces of her dress. He untied them easily.

He kissed her shoulder, her neck, his tongue leaving swirls on her skin. Sair kissed him back, her hands groping him, exploring eagerly.

Thadred stripped her down, peeling her out of her corset and underthings. Sair had pinned her hair up and neatly tucked it under a kerchief. That went next.

In moments, Thadred had her hair loose and ran his fingers through it. He took his time, fanning the strands over her back. Her hair shone like liquid gold in the lamplight.

"Beautiful," Thadred whispered against her ear. "Beautiful creature."

Sair fumbled toward the bedroom, tugging him after her. He followed, pulling her back around to keep their kiss.

Sair reached the door leading to the bedroom, but Thadred grabbed her waist. He picked her up and she was a little surprised at how strong he was.

A narrow, decorative table with a vase stood at waist height on one side of the door. Thadred set her on top of it, bringing her closer to eye level. The polished wood was cool under Sair's bare skin, but not cold.

"Don't you want to go to the bed?" Sair asked, a little out of breath.

"In a moment." Thadred pulled her to the edge, one hand stroking up her bare thigh.

Sair shivered under his touch, her whole body vibrating with anticipation. "Thadred," she rasped, "how long will you make me wait?"

Thadred pressed closer, grinning ever so wickedly. "Are you getting impatient, my love?"

He slid an arm around her and Sair tilted her head up as he stroked up and down her back. Sair stretched, savoring the pleasant sensation. If she was a cat, she might have purred.

"Now, what was it you showed me the other night?" Thadred stroked the outside of her breast, magic tingling through her in the wake of his touch.

Pleasure shot through her, so intense it was almost painful. Sair whimpered, biting her lip to keep from screaming. Her whole body hummed and the space between her legs throbbed.

"Thadred, please!" Sair dug her nails into his shoulder. Her grip was tight, so tight she feared breaking the skin, but Thadred only smiled.

"Please, what?" Thadred traced a swirl around the outside of her breast, spiraling torturously close to her nipple. "What do you want?"

Everything. Nothing. Sair's mind scrambled and sitting in front of him, naked, with him between her knees and his hands on her, she could barely think straight. "You," Sair panted. "I want you."

"Mmm." Thadred's other hand trailed down her side. He gripped her thigh, thumb flicking over her hip bone.

Sair tilted her head back, pressing harder against him. She reached for his belt, but he pushed her hand away.

"Not yet," he whispered, nipping lightly at her ear. His fingers slid down between her thighs, far slower than she would have liked. "Mmm." Thadred chuckled with satisfaction as his fingers slid into her. "You're so wet." He kissed her cheek. "You really do want me, don't you?"

"I want you inside me," Sair panted, pulling him closer.

Thadred's fingers moved in and out of her, tantalizingly slow. "I am inside you."

"Please," Sair whimpered against his neck. "Please."

Thadred's fingers withdrew, but he found the apex of her entrance. Fingers still slick with her arousal, he stroked her. Pleasure radiated through her whole body, building up from her core.

Sair inhaled a sharp breath, pressing her forehead against his shoulder. "Thadred."

He wrapped his other arm around her, pulling her toward him. "Look at me, love. Look at me."

Sair looked up to him. She knew her eyes would be glazed with pleasure and her mouth open as she panted.

Thadred grinned down at her. "You're enjoying this." It was like he could see in her face just how close she was to release. "What about this?"

For a moment, Sair feared he would stop. Then magic tingled into her sex as he kept stroking her.

The pressure building in her core rose to new heights. Warm pressure fluttered up from between her legs, shooting through her whole body. It rose like a tide, dragging her into its current. She was going to climax, and she couldn't stop it even if she had wanted to.

Sair gasped, writhing against him. Teaching him that spell had been a mistake. A wonderful mistake. Thadred could make her helpless any time he wanted. He would have far too much power over her now that—

Sair's release came hard. She fought to smother her scream as waves wracked her body. She pulled Thadred's hand away from her newly tender sex and he wrapped his arms around her. Sair shivered. For a long set of heartbeats, she was helpless as the ecstasy took her over.

"Good girl." Thadred held her against him, cradling her head in the crook of his neck. "So lovely." He stroked her naked back, letting her whimper in his embrace.

Sair panted, clinging to him. "That was…that was amazing."

"You expected less?" Thadred's voice flushed with male pride.

She giggled, heady and drunk with delight. "You're arrogant."

"Rightfully so, wouldn't you say?" Thadred kissed her neck. *"Now* we go to the bed." He stepped back, lifting her off the table and setting her on the ground.

Sair was unsteady on her feet and stumbled.

Thadred caught her. "Have I given you a limp, too?"

Sair smacked his arm, but she couldn't stop laughing. "I just need a moment."

Thadred pulled her flush against him, cradling her backside and pressing one thigh between her legs. He kissed her, deep and slow. Gentle.

Sair scratched her fingers through the dark hair on his chest, sure she would never tire of touching him.

She thought he was going to pick her up again, but then she supposed carrying people would be difficult, no matter how strong he was.

"Steady?"

"Yes." Sair was still soaking in the afterglow of pleasure, but if the way Thadred looked at her was any indication, they were just getting started.

Thadred pushed the door open to the bedroom. Inside, a fire had been stoked in the hearth and the bed freshly made.

Thadred tugged her inside and shut the door after them. He went to the bed, the hitch in his gait not as pronounced as it had been earlier today, but still noticeable.

Concern flickered in Sair's chest. He was still recovering.

Thadred sat down and set to removing his boots. He got the first one off easily enough, but he remained stiff on his bad side.

Sair knelt to help him, her knees hitting the rug.

Thadred let her, eyes drinking her in.

Sair had almost forgotten she was naked. A flush crept up the back of her neck, but then she caught sight of Thadred's expression—dark, hungry. He wanted her and he didn't have to say it out loud.

Sair finished removing his boot and Thadred stood back up. He slipped his hand around to rest on the small of her back as she set to unbuckling his belt.

He watched her, silent and intent as a stalking beast. Sair's heart did that little fluttering in her chest as she moved to the laces of his trousers.

Thadred grabbed her upper arms and spun her around so her back was to the bed. He pushed her down until she was seated on the edge, then pressed her down onto her back.

Sair let him, kissing his neck, his shoulder, anything she could.

Thadred pulled back, standing straight and Sair almost whimpered at the loss of him. She propped herself up on her elbows as he sloughed off his trousers, leaving him as naked as her.

The firelight cast him in golden shadows, illuminating him like a bronze god. Dark hair fanned down his chest and tight abdomen, growing thicker around his considerable manhood.

Sair licked her lips. "This is a bit more than I was expecting."

Thadred grinned at that, like she thought he would. "Perhaps I should have warned you."

Sair shook her head, not taking her eyes off his impressive length. "It wouldn't change anything."

Thadred grabbed her legs behind the knees, dragging her to the edge of the bed. "Are you going to be able to take me, pretty girl?"

Sair scoffed at that. "I've given birth, Thadred. A whole child fit through—"

Thadred shoved into her. He must have taken her words as a challenge.

Sair bit off a cry, gritting her teeth. Perhaps she had spoken too soon.

Thadred pulled out. "Sair?" He looked concerned. "Was that too much?"

Sair breathed, willing her body to relax. Through a clenched jaw, she said, "On second thought, it has been a long time."

"I'm sorry." Thadred rubbed his thumb back and forth on her thigh. "I should have gone slower."

"It's alright." Sair hadn't thought she'd be so tight, either.

"Come here." Thadred pulled her to her feet. He sat down on the bed and guided her in front of him so that they were switched. He patted his thigh, beckoning.

Sair straddled him, her knees on the bed and his arms around her.

Thadred kissed her, gentle, sweet. He ran his hands up and down her back but didn't make a move to pull her toward him. "When you're ready, love."

Sair took his erection in her hand, stroking along the length of him. He was hard, rigid, and swollen under her touch.

Thadred groaned, shifting under her.

Sair eased him to her entrance and rocked her hips, carefully pushing him deeper. She eased him inside her little by little, her body adjusting to the size of him.

Thadred bit his lip and looked to the ceiling. He swore under his breath but didn't push her. "Gods, Sair." He rested his forehead at the crook of her shoulder and neck.

He wanted her. He had to be aching for her. Sair could see his fraying composure in the tight lines of his face. But he let her take her time.

"Do you want me?" Sair asked, breathing in his ear.

Thadred snorted, voice strained. "What do you think?"

"I want to hear you say it."

"I want you, Sair," Thadred panted. "I want you so badly it hurts."

A thrill rippled through Sair at that. "You do?"

"I've wanted you since the Cursewood, when you showed me how to use my magic." Thadred pressed his forehead to hers.

"How do you want me?" Sair rasped. "Tell me how you imagined it."

Thadred chuckled at that. "I've imagined you under me, on top of me, in my arms, screaming my name." He groaned as she finally eased down, fitting him fully inside her. "I've pictured you on your back, on all fours, against the wall." He pushed back her hair, studying her by the firelight. "I thought it would pass, but it never did. Ever since I met you, my fantasies, my dreams, have been consumed with you. Only you."

Sair kissed him, kneading her hands on his shoulders. "I love you," she whispered between kisses. "I love you so much."

She rocked her hips, slowly at first and then faster as she adjusted to him. She rode him, enjoying how he tilted his head back, eyes partly closed.

At first, there was discomfort as her body stretched and long-neglected muscles remembered their purpose. Then she began to slide back into the familiar movements. Thadred's size pushed her to her limits, but she enjoyed the feeling of being filled, of having him take up every inch of her.

Sair moaned, arching her back. Thadred felt good inside her. He felt right.

"Finish me, Sair," he rasped, his voice a plea. "Please finish me."

Thadred Myrani had seduced and charmed his way through court. His exploits were legendary and yet here he was, begging her.

Sair couldn't have smiled any broader at the sense of triumph and pride that swelled through her.

Mine, she thought to herself. *He's mine.*

Sair rocked faster, her thighs burning with the effort. Thadred growled and gripped her hips, driving her harder against him. He slammed her up and down on his cock, almost desperately.

Sair matched his rhythm, speeding toward a crescendo.

She watched his face as he strained, reaching for his own release.

Thadred climaxed with a roar, wrapping his arms around her. He panted, clutching her to him, cradling the back of her head.

"Sair," he gasped, chest heaving. "Sair, you beautiful creature. You pretty girl." He kissed her cheek, her lips, her eyes, her temple. "You do me so well."

Thadred collapsed, pulling her on top of him. He kissed the

top of her head, rubbing her back.

Sair curled against him, nuzzling his chest as they lay panting with the effort. A sheen of sweat coated them both, though Sair didn't remember when either of them had started sweating. Thadred murmured endearments and praises, his hands still stroking up and down her back.

She pressed her ear to Thadred's chest, listening as his racing heart slowed and relaxed. She breathed in the smell of his bare skin, enjoying the warmth of him pressed against her naked body.

Sair giggled, snuggling closer to Thadred.

Thadred shifted under her. "What's funny?"

"Nothing," Sair said. "I'm just happy."

Thadred chuckled at that, shifting her to lie next to him. He tucked her into his arms, keeping her flush against his side. "I'm happy, too."

Sair laid against him, closing her eyes. She sank into a sense of peace, of contentment. She would be glad to spend the rest of her life like this, held in Thadred's arms. "That was amazing," she whispered, resting her cheek on his shoulder, one hand on his chest. "I enjoyed that."

"I enjoyed it, too." Thadred shifted. "But bold of you to assume we're done."

"What?" Sair cocked her head even as her heart fluttered in excitement.

Thadred squeezed her backside. "Sit on my face."

Sair wasn't sure she'd heard correctly. "What?"

"I want you to sit on my face." Thadred tugged her up. "Here. I'll show you."

26

THADRED

Lying in bed with Sair, Thadred watched as she slept. The fire had died down, plunging them into near darkness.

She nestled against his side, her breathing level and peaceful. The stress and strain of the past weeks were gone. Thadred knew she wouldn't have been this peaceful without the assurance her son was safe in the next room, but he also liked to think she wouldn't have been this peaceful without him.

He loved how she giggled after sex, too happy to contain herself. And he loved how she snuggled in his arms and fell asleep.

Thadred listened to the sounds of the mansion, feeling for *ka* nearby. He could sense the guards outside their window. He could feel the presence of several sleeping forms down the hall, probably Rhis and the other children, judging by their excess of magic.

Thadred was aware of several shapes still moving about, most likely servants. Farther out, he could feel the rest of the mansion. His senses got less precise the farther he reached, but he was at a point where he could feel the general location of people.

He looked down to Sair again, feeling her more than seeing her. He could just make the outline of her face, her bare shoulder peeking out from under the covers. He touched her lightly, her soft skin like silk under his fingers.

My wife.

The thought felt both momentous and surprisingly normal. Marrying her might be the most impulsive and reckless thing he had done, but it didn't feel that way.

When she had asked him to wait for her, he should have at least asked for an engagement. Even if they still had their separate obligations, he should have married her before she headed to Hylendale.

A whole year. He supposed it wasn't much in the grand scheme of things, but that was one year less that he would get to spend nights like this—lying next to her with her scent on his skin and the taste of her lingering in his mouth.

Thadred exhaled. He might have taken too long to figure things out, but he had fixed the problem. Sair was his wife and he'd adopt Rhis as his son. That would immediately set the succession of his estate and if he and Sair had children, particularly if they had a daughter first, it would avoid any more questions about whether daughters could inherit ahead of sons. Thadred didn't want to deal with that for his own estate on top of the imperial throne.

Thadred brushed a strand of hair back from Sair's face. She was so beautiful it made his chest ache.

Thadred pressed his face into her hair and breathed her in. Everything was beautiful, peaceful, content. He felt himself slipping back to sleep.

But what had awakened him in the first place?

That thought niggled at the back of his mind. Why was he awake at all?

A shriek ripped the air, faint, but loud enough that Thadred recognized it. Lleuad?

Thadred sat up. The kelpie was angry.

Thadred reached out with his magic again. Sick, poison *ka* flared into Thadred's awareness.

Thadred threw back the covers, grabbing Sair's arm. "Sair!"

Sair jolted awake. "Thadred?"

"Caa Iss is here." Thadred snatched his trousers off the

floor, fumbling them on.

Sair was out of bed, scrambling to his side. She wore one of his shirts that hung just below her hips.

Thadred would like to see her wear it again sometime when their lives weren't in danger. He yanked his boots back on.

"Caa Iss?" Sair's voice croaked with sleep, but she was fully awake, magic flaring around her as she prepared to work spells.

"Unless there's another demon come to call." Thadred straightened, pouring magic into his bad hip. It was always stiff after sleeping.

Thankfully, he'd been sleeping on a bed this time and the consequences weren't as bad, but he still limped badly on the way to the bedroom door, Sair in tow.

They came to the sitting room and Sair yanked her dress on, fumbling with the laces at the back.

"Here." Thadred tossed her his coat as he snatched up his cane.

Sair pulled the coat over her hastily tied laces, preserving her modesty.

Thadred didn't see his shirt, the lamps having burned out hours ago. No time for it, then.

Thadred grabbed his cane sword, glad he at least remembered where he had put that. He shoved the door into the hallway open, Sair at his back.

He looked left and right, even though his senses told him the demon was still some distance away. The hall was empty.

"Brick!" Thadred called into the darkness.

Brick should have slept in the servants' quarters adjoining Thadred's suite, but he had dismissed the manservant for tonight. He had intended to bed Sair and hadn't planned to do it quietly.

"Rhis." Sair was breathless at Thadred's back, anxiety making her voice shake.

"Get him and the others. But try to keep quiet for now." Thadred nodded, pushing her in the direction of the children down the hall. "I'll be right behind you."

Sair ran much faster than Thadred could have, rushing into

the room.

Thadred could sense the demon coming closer. He might have other sources of *ka* with him, possibly the other Kadra'han, but at this distance, Thadred couldn't tell for sure.

"Sir!" Brick came stumbling out of one of the other rooms, jacket askew, yanking his shoes on as he hopped.

"Brick!" Thadred leaned on his cane. "Rouse the guards. Wake the household. We're under attack."

"Attack, sir?"

"Caa Iss is here." Thadred cocked his head, focusing on the point of toxic magic that was the demon. "Somewhere on the cliff side of the mansion, possibly scaling up."

The side with the cliff was the one side they had not guarded. It was meant to be perfectly defensible—to a human enemy.

The empress, Amira, had a suit etched with runes that had once allowed her to use magic to crawl upside down along the inside of a stone culvert. The magic existed, but Amira was the only sorceress they knew of powerful enough to use it.

Thadred hadn't considered someone else could use magic to do the same because none of the Kelamora Kadra'han had been strong enough. But if Caa Iss fed on enough sorcerer's blood…

That explained the *how*, but not the *why*.

Thadred waited as Sair came running toward him, herding the sleepy-eyed and frightened children in front of her.

Thadred's mind raced. Why would Caa Iss be here? They had assumed the cythraul was running away. Caa Iss feared being sent back to the Dread Marches. It was why Thadred had sent Major Caiden and most of his men to guard the docks and watch the city gates. He had only twelve soldiers here at the estate and two of them were messenger boys.

Rhis reached Thadred first, clutching the hand of Maëlys. Rhis looked up to him then back to Sair.

"This way." Thadred's training said to secure the children— presumably, that was what the demon was after. But the cythraul and his Kadra'han had already surprised him several times thus far.

Thadred led the way, Brick racing ahead. Thadred pulled at

the air around him, drawing *ka* to himself. He would need every drop of magic he could procure. Power. He needed more power.

They reached the central stairwell of the house, where they had agreed to rally if anything went wrong.

Brick had already fetched several of the officers and a few soldiers.

"Lieutenant Ákos," Thadred singled out a young man with red hair that remained curly no matter how close he cropped it to his skull. "We're being attacked from the south side, the cliff face."

"The cliff face, sir?"

Thadred nodded. "I can sense a cythraul nearing that direction. I think the demon has come for a confrontation."

The soldier nodded curtly. "What are your orders?"

Thadred considered it. What did the demon want? This made no sense. None at all.

Caa Iss should have fled. Why was he here?

Thadred straightened, putting more weight on his cane. It didn't matter. Caa Iss wanted a fight and that was fine. They wouldn't have to hunt him. "Send both messengers to Major Caiden, then prepare for an attack," Thadred said to the lieutenant. "Gather all the soldiers we have here. We'll have to let the dowager's men guard the outside."

The soldier rushed to do Thadred's bidding.

Thadred looked to Sair, shushing several of the children. Rhis watched Thadred, silent and calm, the same way he had looked to Thadred when they were captives.

Rhis didn't appear worried at all. Fear, Thadred could have handled. Even anger or blame. That unshakeable confidence? That was much harder to bear.

Don't put your faith in me, kid, Thadred wanted to say. *I make a poor savior.*

"Lord Thadred?" Vespasia rushed down the stairs, her hair disheveled, a dressing gown tied hastily over her nightdress. She looked first to Sair and appeared to count the children before looking back to Thadred.

"We're under attack," Thadred explained. "Or we're about

to be."

Vespasia swallowed, fear flickering across her face in the lamplight. "What should we do?"

Shouts rose from the edges of the estate. Hounds barked and horses squealed. Most animals avoided cythraul. They must sense the demon.

Thadred cursed under his breath. From inside the mansion and away from the windows, he couldn't see what was happening, but he could guess. He turned to his sister. "Get your mother and brother down here. If they won't come, leave them."

Vespasia nodded hastily, then rushed back up the stairs, her maids in tow.

Thadred scratched the stubble on his jaw, feeling the cythraul's presence creep closer.

This choice left Caa Iss vulnerable. Except the demon never left himself vulnerable, not willingly, which meant there had to be a reason.

Thadred turned to his wife. "Sair."

Sair shook her head. "Thadred, if anything happens to you—"

"I'm not dying, my dear," Thadred grinned at her with a confidence he didn't feel. "The gods love me too much."

Sair forced a smile back, tears shining at the edges of her eyes. She was afraid. Terribly afraid. She'd lost one husband. To lose another one after mere hours...

Well, she wouldn't be losing him. He decided that.

He pulled on a coat that Brick brought for him, letting his valet button it up the front. It seemed Brick's sense of decency remained stronger than Thadred's.

"You and the children should stay here." The stairwell was the strongest room in the house with multiple escape routes. It was why they had retreated here in the first place.

Sair nodded, though it seemed from her face that she wanted to argue. Sair and Thadred were the only adult sorcerers here. He was needed to lead his men and that left Sair to protect her son and the others.

"I want to go with you," Rhis protested. "I can use magic,

too. I can fight!"

Every second was precious, but Thadred stopped to grip the boy's shoulder. "Protect your mother for me. Can you do that?"

Rhis hesitated and swallowed, seeming to realize for the first time that Thadred was worried.

"Please, Rhis."

The boy nodded, suddenly serious.

"Good lad." Thadred clapped his shoulder. "Thank you." When Thadred looked back to Sair, there were tears in her eyes.

Thadred hated that. He pulled her to him one last time, clutching her to his chest, trying to memorize the shape of her, the warmth of her. Sair clung to him, her nails digging into his back.

Then the soldiers came rushing into the stairwell with Lieutenant Ákos at their head. Thadred counted all ten men. It was time to go.

He almost kissed Sair on the mouth, then remembered Rhis was watching. He kissed her forehead instead.

Sair made a muffled whimpering sound as he pulled away. It tore at his heart, worse than the fear of facing a demon.

Thadred and his soldiers headed for the south wing of the mansion as Vespasia appeared at the top of the stairs alongside the dowager and the sleepy young count.

"Get your guards to secure the mansion," Thadred ordered. He looked straight to Vespasia. "Make her do it. This is no time for games."

Vespasia nodded. She would do her best.

Thadred spared one last glance for Sair before heading down the hallway.

Sair stood with the girl Maëlys against one side and holding the straw-haired boy on the other. She watched him with unshed tears shining in her eyes, Rhis looking between her and Thadred with something like confusion.

Thadred hated leaving her, hated leaving them, but he had to.

Even if Thadred died—which he wouldn't—Sair and Rhis would be fine. Rhis had already been designated as his heir. The two of them would be fine.

He just needed to deal with this cythraul and send the thing back to the Dread Marches where it belonged.

Thadred's soldiers fell in around him, closing ranks. He couldn't help but feel a little excited.

This was what Thadred had been trained for. It was his duty to serve the emperor and defend the empire.

He considered having Lleuad freed from the stables. Perhaps he should have told Sair to do that, but the kelpie was still recovering and Thadred didn't think he'd do well in the tight spaces of the mansion.

Thadred directed his men to the dining room where the balcony let out onto the ridge overlooking the cliff and the city below. The room was dark, everything set in perfect order. Nothing would appear amiss if Thadred hadn't had a sorcerer's senses.

If he was correct, Caa Iss was headed straight up the cliff face and would climb onto the balcony.

Thadred signaled to his men to form a defensive line. He gestured the two crossbowmen forward, perched on the edges of the formation. "Wait until the creature is fully in view then shoot. I want to verify we kill it. But if it tries to run or attacks sooner, shoot. Do you understand me?" He kept his voice low, hoping the demon didn't have supernatural hearing.

The men signaled their understanding, weapons at the ready.

Thadred focused on breathing even and steady. This was the hardest part of battle—the waiting. It was much easier to engage an enemy than to wait for one to show itself. But this was where battles were won—in the waiting.

There were a thousand stories of battles that had been lost because impatient men had broken ranks. Every general knew that unity was the greatest discipline to master.

The men locked shields as they had been trained to do. Their leather sections touched, linking them together. Thadred touched the backs of two of them and let his power slide into the linked shields. It would help the shields withstand an attack, even one against magic. The men wouldn't be able to break apart as quickly, but hopefully that wouldn't be necessary.

Thadred reinforced them with a surge of power, making the shields glow to his sorcerer's senses. He wondered if the men could tell the difference. Regardless, it would make their shields that much harder to break, even for a demon.

That done, Thadred drew his cane sword, though he didn't anticipate having to use it. Two rows of men with shields stood in front of him. He was a proper general now—too important to be put in any real danger.

The men waited, Thadred pushing *ka* into their shields even as he drew more of it to himself. If they could kill Caa Iss here, if they could stop him once and for all, it would be done.

Thadred and Sair wouldn't have to be looking over their shoulders for the cythraul. Daindreth could rest easy in his crown and he and Amira could welcome their child unburdened by the fear of that demon returning to torment them.

A kind of dreadful anticipation overcame Thadred. There was something of a thrill to combat, not unlike the feeling of charging down the lysts in a joust.

Thadred felt the demon drawing closer up the cliff face. Thadred crouched lower to signal readiness to his men.

The figure appeared slowly, red eyes glowing in the darkness. Tension rippled through the men, but they remained still, silent and ready.

The cythraul crawled up to the railing, hands gripping the edge of the balcony. Red eyes glowed like windows into the pits of the Dread Marches.

Thadred steeled himself.

The demon's head spun toward them, malice and hate glittering out from that ruby gaze. Caa Iss had seen them.

"Loose," Thadred ordered.

Bows twanged, but not before Thadred felt their target's *ka* change. The miasmic presence of a demon winked out, leaving behind an ordinary man with the golden noose of a Kadra'han curse around his neck.

The crossbow bolts smacked into the human vessel, iron ripping into flesh. The man yelled and fell backwards, hurtling toward his death. If the bolts hadn't been enough to kill him, the fall certainly would.

"Did we hit him?" one of the officers asked.

"You did." Thadred grimaced. He looked over his shoulder. "Good shots, men."

"What's wrong, sir?"

Thadred's tone must have given it away. "The demon fled before his host was struck." The knight cursed. "We didn't get him." He exhaled sharply, then froze.

At his back, the demon's presence burst into his awareness.

Thadred spun around, realization hitting him like a sack of bricks. Cythraul were reluctant to abandon hosts because they could only inhabit people with the proper permissions. But Caa Iss had an entire order of sorcerers who had no choice but to obey him.

Caa Iss could force them to do anything he wanted. Caa Iss could force them to allow possession at will.

Horror flooded Thadred and for the first time that night, he felt true and unadulterated fear.

"Back to the staircase!" he ordered his soldiers. "Back to the staircase now!"

They had left the household guards to watch the outside of the mansion. They'd had no choice.

Thadred had assumed the dowager's men were competent, but he would appear to be wrong. They must have allowed the Kadra'han assassins inside—somehow.

And Caa Iss was with them.

27

SAIR

Sair's magic had been growing stronger in the days since the Elder Mother's death. She wasn't yet where she had been and she might never be at Amira's level, but she was growing stronger.

Huddled with Rhis by her side, Sair tried to keep her awareness of Thadred as he ventured to the south wing of the mansion. She closed her eyes, begging Eponine for his protection.

Sair had just found happiness again. She had just found peace again.

How could this end so soon? What if she lost everything tonight?

"Thadred will stop them," Rhis said.

For a moment, Sair thought he was talking to her, but when she opened her eyes, he was speaking to Maëlys, crouched beside the girl protectively.

"Lord Thadred is the best knight in Erymaya. He's fought cythraul before and he's never lost."

Sair wanted to smile. Rhis had so much faith in Thadred, in the world. She wished she had half as much.

Vespasia spoke with her maids. From the way she touched their arms and smiled reassuringly, Sair guessed she was trying to stop them from fleeing into the night.

"Lady Sairydwen." Zeyna faced down Sair, back straight, holding the hand of her youngest son.

Sair schooled her face into one of respect, lowering her head slightly. "Dowager."

"What is the meaning of this?" the countess demanded. She showed indignation, far more than she had shown to Thadred.

She fears Thadred, Sair realized. *But she thinks she can bully me.*

"Why have my children and I been dragged from our beds at this hour?" Zeyna took in Sair's disheveled state, probably drawing obvious conclusions from Sair wearing Thadred's coat.

"Lord Thadred fears we are under attack from a cythraul. He and his men are dealing with it." Sair glanced at Rhis, who was still consoling Maëlys and two of the younger boys. It made her heart twist in her chest with equal parts dread and pride. She hoped everything he said was true, that Thadred would easily overcome the cythraul and return to her.

"Cythraul?" Zeyna's outrage left at that. She looked to Vespasia, seeking confirmation.

"Yes," Vespasia said. "But Lord Thadred is the High Inquisitor. He will know—"

"Cythraul? On our doorstep?"

"Scaling the cliff face, Lord Thadred believes," Sair answered.

"We must leave at once." Zeyna wasted no time. "Vespasia, we must go. Summon the household guards. We are leaving."

"There could be a trap," Sair protested. "They could be trying to flush us out. You could be fleeing into an ambush."

"I will not stay here and allow those creatures to prey on us, not again." Zeyna's voice rose to a shrill pitch. She squeezed her son's arm, clutching him to her side.

"Thadred is dealing with the cythraul," Sair said. "He will tell us if—"

"We are leaving now!" Zeyna whirled on one of the servants. "Have all the household guards come to protect my children and me. Now!"

This was wrong. Sair knew a break in the defensive line when she saw it.

"You cannot do this," Sair protested, rising to her feet. "You will leave your servants defenseless? You will leave these children? Your—" Sair almost reminded the other woman that Thadred was her son, then thought better of it. "The representatives of your emperor?"

"The emperor did nothing to prevent the sacking of this city the first time," Zeyna cried. "And these servants all fled and abandoned me before." Zeyna didn't seem to care that at least ten of those servants were now listening from around the room. "We are leaving!"

"You are to stay," Vespasia ordered the household guards, stomping in front of one of the helmeted men. "Lord Thadred speaks with the authority of the empire and I—"

Zeyna's hand flew, slapping the girl mid-sentence.

Vespasia clutched at her cheek, whirling on her mother. From her look of shock, Sair would guess that had never happened before.

Zeyna clutched a hand to her own mouth the next instant, as if she was shocked, too. She reached for her daughter. "Vespasia, I'm sorry, I—"

Vespasia batted her mother's hand aside. "Don't touch me." Her eyes watered as she stepped back, out of her mother's reach.

"Vespasia, we don't have time for this. We must flee."

"I fled last time," Vespasia said, her voice shaky. "And the man I loved died for it."

Zeyna hesitated, glancing to Sair and then away, as if she had been hoping for help and then remembered which sides they were on.

"You want to run?" Vespasia was determined. "Then run. But I'm not leaving my brother."

Zeyna looked to Flavius, clinging anxiously to his mother. Gone was the demanding young despot from a few nights ago. This was just a frightened little boy. "Your brother is right here."

"My *older* brother." Vespasia faced down Zeyna, her cheek still red from Zeyna's handprint, but defiance in her stance, shoulders back and fists clenched at her sides.

Zeyna looked about to argue.

"My lady, the carriage is ready," one of the soldiers said. "But the grooms are having trouble with the horses. We must move quickly."

Zeyna looked to the guard, then back to her daughter. She reached for Vespasia. "Dearest—"

Vespasia jerked out of her reach again. She looked to Sair. "Lady Sairydwen?"

Sair swallowed. Fear threatened to claw its way up her throat. Rhis and the other children were staring at her. A part of her wanted to flee. A part of her wanted to get her son and herself as far away from that thing as she could, but she trusted Thadred, and more than that, she wouldn't leave him. The words came out steadier than she felt. "We stay. We follow Thadred's instructions."

Sair couldn't keep all the children safe from Caa Iss and his Kadra'han by herself. She didn't have enough soldiers either. Still, instinct told her this was the best course of action.

Vespasia nodded curtly, seeming to take courage from Sair's resolve. "I stay with them."

"Mama, I want to go," Flavius wept. "I want to leave."

Zeyna looked to the guards. "Bring Lady Vespasia."

Vespasia was having none of it. "If even one of your men lays a hand on me, I will tell Lady Marciana everything. *Every*thing."

Zeyna's eyes went wide. "Vespasia…"

"Do it, I dare you," Vespasia said.

Sair didn't know who this Lady Marciana was, but it seemed her name was enough to break the dowager's will. Zeyna let off a cry of anguish and rushed from the entryway, bustling out with her son at her side.

Sair watched as Zeyna left, taking the count and all the guards with her, leaving the rest of them to fend for themselves.

Vespasia looked back to Sair. "What should we do now?"

Brick also looked to Sair. He stood straight, hands behind his back, but he seemed pale in the lantern light, his posture too rigid, too stern.

"Mama." Rhis shifted on the step.

Everyone was looking at her.

Sair had to stay composed. "We stay here for as long as we can, or until Thadred returns." Sair ran her hand through Rhis's hair. "We wait." She was proud that her voice didn't tremble.

Sair sat on the stairs, watching the doorway where the countess and her retinue had fled. Oddly, Sair didn't feel the need to watch her back. Thadred was at her back.

As word spread that the dowager countess was fleeing in the middle of the night with all the household guards, panic began to catch. Sair could hear servants shouting, people rushing through the house.

Someone screamed and Sair jumped, but then the commotion died down. She breathed easier, smiling at the frightened children around her feet.

"I want my papa," Maëlys whimpered. "I just want to go home."

Vespasia sat on the stairs beside Sair and pulled Maëlys into her lap, speaking softly to the girl.

Sair kept her attention on the others, soothing the little blond boy, the youngest of them. "It will be alright," Sair said. "It will be—"

Another scream rent the air.

Sair forced herself to remain calm. This was the safest place in the house, the sturdiest room with the most escape routes.

Sair flinched the instant that toxic, poisonous *ka* flared into her awareness. Caa Iss was close, at her back. She could feel him creeping closer from the south side of the mansion.

Her heart raced and her scalp tingled. Something deep and primal told her to run. She wanted to flee after Zeyna and get far away from this place.

In that moment, she couldn't blame Zeyna for fleeing. The dowager had seen her city ravaged, her husband lost to the demons, and her family torn apart. Even her son had been possessed at one point, if reports were true.

Sair focused on breathing and not panicking. She mustn't show fear. The children needed her to be strong. Vespasia needed her to be strong. Thadred was counting on her.

Caa Iss's presence winked out. Sair couldn't sense him. For just a moment, relief flooded her chest. Had Thadred killed the thing?

Then the cythraul's presence flared to life in front of her. Caa Iss had moved too quickly. He'd drawn Thadred and the soldiers away, leaving the children exposed.

Sair bolted to her feet.

Vespasia jumped, still holding onto Maëlys. "What is it?"

"Caa Iss." Sair found herself looking at Rhis, a squeezing sensation in her chest. "Caa Iss is in the north wing of the mansion. Somehow."

"What?" Vespasia's voice was a rasp. "Lord Thadred said he was scaling the south cliff."

"He was." Sair reached for Rhis. "He must have switched hosts." That was the only explanation, unless there were other cythraul.

Vespasia's eyes widened, and she looked toward the doorway. "Mama…"

Then the screaming started.

A woman's voice rang out and men shouted. Horses squealed. Sair could feel their *ka* as a jumble of sources, mixing and mingling and churning in chaos.

"Fall back," Sair said. "Get back to Thadred and the soldiers. This way. Come!" The sorceress grabbed Rhis with one hand, though he was already helping to shoo the other children back down the hall. Brick and Vespasia followed close behind, leading Maëlys.

"Quickly." Sair could feel the demon headed their direction, closing in.

Besides the cythraul, more sources of human *ka* trailed in his wake, probably the Kadra'han. Zeyna had taken the guards from the perimeter, giving them an opening. People would die for this.

From the screaming, people had already died.

Sair herded the others in front of her through the hallway, heart racing. She closed the hallway doors after them and began weaving spells. Sair couldn't stop all the Kadra'han and certainly not the demon, but she could slow them down.

Beneath the gilding and the bright polish, the wood of the doors remembered what it was to be alive. The doors soaked up her spells, letting her link them together with loops of *ka* at the center like sutures.

"Go!" Sair ordered, looking to Vespasia. "Find Thadred."

Rhis came up beside her. He raised his hands, working his own magic in the wake of hers, the way she had taught him.

"Rhis, go!" Sair said. "Follow them!"

"I'm supposed to protect you!"

Sair wanted to scream. She could feel the cythraul had reached the room with the staircase. Caa Iss and his Kadra'han were on the other side of the door and time was running out.

She heard men's voices shouting at her back. Thadred and the soldiers were close, but they wouldn't reach her before the cythraul did. "Rhis, go!" Sair was practically begging. "Please!"

Something struck the doors—hard. The hinges of the doors splayed, buckling under the force.

Whatever was on the other side, it was coming through.

"Rhis, get out of here now!" Sair dropped all pretense, her panic showing in her desperation. "Find Thadred—go!"

Voices cried out at her back. Male voices came closer. Thadred was almost here and that made it worse.

Power surged on the other side of the door. Tainted, demonic spells smashed into the wood, singeing her hands and pulsing with heat. She wasn't going to hold him for much longer.

Everything she loved was in the direct path of the demon.

The door cracked and splintered, breaking under the onslaught of power from the other side.

Sair let go of the door and took a step back. She dropped her defense and the demon tore the remains of the door to splinters in a blink, just as Sair wove an offensive spell. After not using it for decades, here she was using it twice in one day. She only hoped she had enough of her power back to cast it on her own.

Sair traced a line of *ka* through the air, stringing it diagonally across the hall. Some sorceresses had been able to weave dozens of these strands, but even a single one could be deadly.

Sair shaped the strand of *ka* narrow in the front and thicker in the back, so that the line of power formed a wedge. The difficult part was to make the front of the wedge tight, condensing *ka* into a narrow point—a sharpened edge.

Her work was messy and haphazard, but she finished it just as the first Kadra'han stepped through the ruined door.

As he charged into the spell, he screamed, his skin burning, then giving way. He was unarmored and moving too fast to stop as he collided with Sair's line of death.

The spell sliced off the man's right leg just above the knee, leaving behind a bloody stump. He collapsed, shrieking.

Someone hurled a knife for her chest, and she had to duck. The blade missed, but Sair lost her concentration, dropping the spell.

Caa Iss was coming. She could feel him.

The remains of the doors crumpled before the demon.

"Mama!" Rhis grabbed for her arm. The boy's face was white with horror as he gagged at the sight of the mutilated man on the floor.

Sair shoved her son ahead of her even as she retreated, demonic power blossoming once again.

"Well, that's a shame," the demon's voice rumbled. Caa Iss came into view, eyes burning bright red as he took in his screaming Kadra'han. "Wilman was a good servant. Obedient."

Sair didn't look at the man. She couldn't. If she looked, she would think about what she had done. That man had been attacking them, but he probably hadn't had a choice. He was bound in a Kadra'han's curse.

Caa Iss looked down at the sobbing man even as the other Kadra'han closed ranks around the cythraul. They had no shields, but they carried swords and were armored in leather.

Sair noticed that there appeared to only be eight or so, counting the whimpering man on the ground.

"I had to kill two of them to have enough blood for this encounter." Caa Iss tsked, like a man examining a stain on a favorite doublet. "And there was also Meko, who so obligingly served as my temporary host as I climbed up that cliff face."

Sair retreated even as she wove more defensive spells. She created a shield, one that wouldn't stop something like an arrow or a crossbow bolt, but it would be strong enough to stop thrown knives or more spells. At least Sair thought it would stop the demon's spells. She didn't know how powerful Caa Iss might be now, or any of his Kadra'han.

"Please, master," the wounded man, Wilman, whimpered. "I can still serve you."

Caa Iss leaned over the screaming man and dipped his fingers into the pools of blood on the floor. "Yes, you can still serve me."

Sair gagged as the cythraul licked the man's blood from his fingers. The blood turned golden as it met the demon's tongue, like he was sucking the power from it.

"Sair!" Thadred's voice boomed through the hallway. The knight and his men were close, they should have found Vespasia and the others.

Caa Iss had turned his attention to Sair. "I remember you. You are a friend of my former host." Caa Iss must mean the emperor. "And his bitch of a wife." Caa Iss licked his lips and grinned. Blood stained his teeth. "I am going to enjoy this."

Caa Iss raised his hands, clasping them together as if in prayer.

Sair wove faster, pouring power into her shield until she felt sweat beading on her brow.

"You think that will stop me?" Caa Iss sounded genuinely amused.

Sair had no idea, but she had to try.

The Kadra'han at his sides circled Caa Iss defensively. At the cythraul's left, Sair recognized Iasu, the man who had killed the Elder Mother and stolen her child in the first place. She wished her spell had hit him instead of Wilman.

Caa Iss gathered power to himself in torrents. How much power did he have? Sair felt like a candle compared to his inferno. His power struck her shield. His spell didn't touch her, but the impact did.

Sair flew backward. She smacked into the wall and slumped

down, the wind knocked out of her. She gasped, heaving for breath.

She had been thrown down the length of the hall to the adjoining parlor. Motion from the corner of her eye told her Vespasia and the children were already here.

"Rhis," she croaked. "Rhis!"

Her son lay beside her several steps away. He'd also been caught in the surge of power. Thankfully, her shield appeared to have kept him from being directly hit by the demon's magic.

"Mama." He rolled onto his stomach, voice little more than a squeak. "I landed on my arm."

Sair looked down to her son's arm to see it was in one piece. That would have to do for now. She grabbed him by his collar. "We need to move." She barely had her own voice back. "Sweetling, we need to move."

Caa Iss was storming down the hallway, his Kadra'han in front and behind. He came like a harbinger of doom, promising wrath and retribution.

Caa Iss had been denied rulership of the empire. He blamed Amira and Daindreth, but Amira and Daindreth weren't here. Sair, Rhis, and Thadred would have to do.

Sair got Rhis to his feet as the cythraul and his men burst into the sitting room. The Kadra'han fanned out around the demon like a vanguard, Iasu at his side.

All of them were using magic, but they appeared weakened. Despite the cythraul claiming he had killed a few of his Kadra'han for power, Sair expected that some of the living had given him blood as well.

Sair shoved Rhis ahead of her, not bothering to be gentle. She needed to get him away from that thing.

Caa Iss laughed. "Chasing sorceresses through the dark. How this brings back memories!"

Sair turned around, racing down another hallway and into a large atrium of some sort with large pillars supporting the arched ceiling. The line of soldiers rushed toward her. Thadred and the imperials had reached them. Vespasia, Brick, and the other children huddled behind them at the far side.

The soldiers closed ranks around Sair, forming a protective wall between her and the oncoming monster.

"Sair!" Thadred reached them. His limp had slowed him down, but he grabbed Rhis and pulled them both behind a couch in what appeared to be a sitting area.

"My shoulder hurts," Rhis whimpered, still dazed by the pain.

"You were very brave. Hang on, kid," Thadred said. He looked to Sair. "Take them and get out."

Sair swallowed. "You need my help."

Thadred shook his head. "Damn it, woman. Get out of here."

Caa Iss was bearing down on them. The soldiers had some protections against magic, but none of them were sorcerers.

Sair gripped his arm. "Two Istovari stand a better chance against him than one." Either they could face certain death by splitting up, or they could fight Caa Iss together and hope.

She saw the struggle flash across his face. He had to know she was telling the truth. That thing had just torn through Zeyna's guards as if they were nothing. Sair was still not back up to her full power, but she was stronger than she had been in decades, and she had the skill. Thadred had years of faithful service to the emperor. Together, they might be able to give Caa Iss a real fight. Together, they might be able to win.

Thadred looked to Brick. "Take the kid." He nodded to Rhis. "Then go."

Obediently, Brick stepped forward to pick up Rhis.

Vespasia held a child in either hand and the rest clustered around her, frightened. She looked to Thadred. "I—"

"Now, Vespasia!" Thadred shouted.

Dragging the children after her with Brick carrying Rhis, Vespasia rushed for the exit at the far end.

"Can you keep Caa Iss from escaping his host again?" Thadred asked. "Is there any way we can do that?"

Sair nodded, licking her lips. She remembered some of the curse they had used, at least in principle. A single sorceress couldn't force a demon into a host, but perhaps she could contain one that was already in possession.

Caa Iss and his Kadra'han were coming. They had maybe twenty seconds to prepare.

Sair didn't have a circle of sorceresses or enough blood to write the spells, but if Thadred helped her, maybe she could still make it work. They didn't necessarily have to write the spells, they just needed something that could hold them.

"The wool rug." Sair gestured hastily to the massive rug between the two couches. "For the spells!"

Thadred didn't question her. "Kess. Landric. Do as she says. Now."

Two soldiers stepped from the back of the formation and rushed to obey. They moved much faster than Thadred could have, grabbing the large rug and smacking it in front of the line of soldiers at Sair's direction.

Sair crouched at the edge of the rug, letting her magic ripple into it. Wool was less workable than leather, but it too had once been alive. Sair sent her magic into the rug in a concentric circle, flowing out into a spiraling pattern that grew narrower at the center. The spell formed a cyclone, designed to draw the demon into a single point. *Ka* soaked into the rug, infusing it

Thadred rested a hand on her shoulder and she felt his additional power flow into her. The feeling was heady, almost intoxicating, like inhaling too much air.

"Quickly, love," Thadred muttered.

Sair's heart raced and her hands shook, but she completed the spell, keeping herself connected by a long strand of *ka* so she could keep feeding power into it.

Thadred dragged her back behind the line of shields moments before Caa Iss burst into the atrium, surrounded by his Kadra'han.

"Iasu, Blyst, bring me the children," Caa Iss rumbled. "Alive." He slid his tongue over his lips. "I will enjoy making your son my slave, sorceress. I won't wait to make him take the vows this time. I will cut little pieces off him until he complies. Children never last long."

Sair inhaled a deep breath. Her heart hammered. The whole

world seemed to be moving too fast and at the same time painfully slow.

Caa Iss grinned, red-stained teeth flashing. He marched toward the line of soldiers surrounded by his Kadra'han.

Thadred stood at Sair's side, rigid, but with his jaw set. Determined. "Steady." Sair wasn't sure if that was for her or the soldiers. Maybe all of them.

Caa Iss came closer. Closer.

Sair could barely take it. She was sure he would sense the trap. But the demon walked straight over the rug.

Sair didn't question her good luck. She whipped her spell up, pouring all her terror, her desperation, and wrath into the strand of *ka* that spiraled through the woolen threads.

The spell snaked upward, lashing around Caa Iss like a net. The cythraul shrieked as the power enveloped him, roping him into his body.

If Caa Iss had been a human sorcerer, he could have countered by trying to wrest control of the spell from her. But the demon couldn't use *ka* in its pure form, he had to harvest it from blood.

Perhaps the Kadra'han could have helped them, but he either didn't trust them to use magic or they were too weak.

Caa Iss roared his outrage. "You think to bind me, sorceress?" he hissed. "Be careful what you wish for."

Sair gulped. She could keep him in this body, but she wasn't sure that would be enough.

Caa Iss raised hands covered in the gore of a dead man. A blast of fire tore into the line of shields.

The men in front cried out, shoving back. Heat licked up, singing their armor and warping the shields.

The spells Thadred had poured into the shields kept the flames from reaching the soldiers, but not enough to fully stop the heat.

"Behind the pillars!" Thadred shouted, dragging Sair to the nearest one.

The men obeyed, ducking back as Caa Iss loosed another torrent of flame.

The heat made Sair's eyes water, but she held her spell. She was connected to Caa Iss, if only by a tendril of magic.

One thing at a time. She needed to keep Caa Iss from fleeing this body. That was the only way they could hope to kill him.

Sair held onto the spell, clinging to it as Caa Iss gathered his strength for another attack.

28

Thadred

Caa Iss was powerful. Too powerful.

He might be even stronger than Amira right now, if only temporarily. The cythraul had glutted himself on the blood of his sorcerers. Their only hope was to survive long enough to wear him down and kill him.

Thadred reached for Sair, heat buffeting them from all sides. "Are you alright?"

Sair nodded hastily, hair falling around her face.

Thadred jerked his head toward the cythraul on the other side of the pillar. "Can you hold him?"

She nodded again. "For a while, at least."

"That's my girl." Thadred looked past her, to his men crouched by the nearby pillars. "Good?"

Several helmeted heads nodded, including the men who had been in front.

"A bit toasty, but ready to fight, sir."

Thadred's magicked shields seemed to be working, at least in part. Though even a layer of tenebrous steel wouldn't stop heat.

Two figures broke off and raced down the hallway—Iasu and the man who was apparently Blyst. They chased after where Vespasia, Brick, and the children had gone.

Sair's face twisted in anguish, but she whirled back to

317

Thadred. "How do we kill him?"

If they killed Caa Iss, they could deal with the Kadra'han far easier. One fight at a time.

Thadred reached out for *ka,* counting the sources besides the demon. "He has five men left. We outnumber them." Thadred had ten soldiers with him and though his men were bruised and might have minor burns from the sound of it, none appeared too badly hurt.

A familiar twang went off—one of the crossbowmen had loosed. A cry rent the air.

Thadred grimaced, not optimistic enough to hope that the demon had been hit.

A surge of power was the only warning before the crossbowman spattered across the room in several pieces. The soldier had loosed, missed, and Caa Iss retaliated.

Thadred exhaled sharply. Mikhail had been a good soldier.

He had nine left.

"Come out, little mice," Caa Iss rumbled. "Come out and play."

Thadred leaned against the pillar, drawing power to himself. "Sair, that spell you used on that man yesterday, can you cast it again?"

Sair shook her head. "Maybe, but it's hard to aim at what I can't see. I need a distraction."

"I can smell you," Caa Iss purred. "The air is ripe with your fear. How I have missed this!" The demon's footsteps came closer, the other Kadra'han shuffling around him.

Thadred had been practicing with shields of magic, but he wasn't quite good enough to block knives or swords just yet. But he might be good enough to block magic—or at least redirect it. "You need me to take his mind off you?"

From her face, Sair didn't like the idea of him serving as bait, but she only said, "That would help."

Caa Iss lumbered toward them, laughing. Sair's spell didn't keep him immobile, just in that body.

Thadred looked to his soldiers, the men in sight who were close enough to see. He waved to signal their intentions.

"Even if you can't hit Caa Iss, see if you can hit one of the Kadra'han," Thadred whispered. Bodies kept their *ka* for some time after death. If they could force Caa Iss to stay near the corpses of his men, it would at least limit his movement.

Still, the demon was confident he could win. As frightened as Caa Iss was, he had come here to—what? Make a point? Take revenge?

"What's your plan, Caa Iss?" Thadred called to the creature.

"Plan?" Caa Iss crooned, sounding amused.

"You have to know that the emperor will hunt you to the ends of the earth."

Caa Iss chuckled. "Maybe I look forward to it."

Thadred readied his shield of power even as Sair wove her own spells. If they could just keep the demon talking …

"Killing you will hurt Daindreth," Caa Iss purred. "Especially when he hears you died screaming."

Thadred grunted. "You're risking your life over dramatics?"

"Death is an illusion," Caa Iss sneered, as if everyone knew that and Thadred was an idiot. "Even for humans. So attached to your bodies that you assume leaving them means an end to existence."

"Fair enough. I suppose you're risking the full weight of your mother's wrath. Which seems much worse."

Caa Iss growled. "You think I am afraid of anything?"

"You fear your mother," Thadred said. He looked to Sair and she nodded.

"*Your* mother died like a coward." Caa Iss bit out the words like a curse. "Weeping and begging."

Thadred froze. Zeyna was dead? He looked to Sair, but the sorceress just shook her head. She didn't know.

"She tried to run," Caa Iss said. "Tried to shield the boy. She need not have bothered. I wasn't interested in him."

The cythraul was trying to get to Thadred. Trying to taunt him.

"I cracked her skull on the steps of her verandah." Caa Iss laughed. "She tried to escape me, but only ran straight into my arms."

Thadred shook his head, clearing the thoughts away. Whether Zeyna was dead or not, it didn't change what he needed to do. "Ready?" he whispered to Sair.

Sair nodded.

Thadred motioned to his men. The moment they signaled their understanding, Thadred ripped away from Sair and cast a spell at the nearest Kadra'han.

It wasn't a lethal spell, just enough that the man felt it coming and ducked.

As Thadred did, the remaining crossbowman launched a bolt for Caa Iss. The demon evaded but whirled his attention in that direction.

Taking her cue, Sair lashed a golden band of power toward the demon. Her power surged like a whip of *ka,* flying straight for the cythraul.

Sair's lash of power cut into him, going for exposed skin. Her spell ripped through his face.

Thadred felt a jolt of elation, right before the demon let off a roar that shook the very tiles. Something instinctive in Thadred told him to run, told him to get away from this creature, but he couldn't give in to fear.

Red bloomed on Caa Iss's cheek and white teeth showed. Sair had struck him, but in moments the wound healed. Caa Iss recovered, dropping into a crouch as the remaining Kadra'han shielded him with their bodies. The cythraul was too strong.

Thadred felt the demon's power surge. "Get back!"

Sair and Thadred scrambled back behind the pillar just as a blast of fire hurled at them. Thadred grabbed Sair, doubling over her as the flames licked around the pillar.

The enamel coating shone like wax, the surface threatening to melt. Heat singed Thadred's forearms and sweat slicked his forehead and trickled down his back.

The cythraul had power the likes of which Thadred hadn't even imagined.

"Are you impressed?" Caa Iss rumbled, that perpetual sneer in his words.

Thadred's heart raced. He held onto Sair, still shielding her as best he could.

"You are mayflies!" Caa Iss taunted. "Maggots! You have no idea what is possible!"

Thadred hated that the creature was right. He hadn't even known sorcerers could create blasts of fire like that.

Maybe they didn't stand a chance of defeating Caa Iss, but they had to try.

29

IASU

Iasu had often thought himself clever. He was less sure of that now.

He'd been able to leave Myrani and the boy alive because Caa Iss had said to *see them both dead*. And Iasu had seen both Myrani's guards dead. Caa Iss had not been amused at the deliberate misinterpretation. Iasu had paid for his defiance with a beating and several new cuts over his body.

Myrani had insisted that a Kadra'han curse could be broken. Iasu had been wracking his mind for a way to do it.

Every curse could be broken, true enough, but it seemed the only thing that could break a Kadra'han's vows were death or the vows themselves.

Iasu still remembered the words of the vows. He had memorized them, recited them over and over, trying to find something in them that might allow him to defy Caa Iss for the sake of Caa Iss.

Under these circumstances, he'd thought of nothing.

He might have been raised to be the perfect warrior. He might have been trained in strategy, espionage, and combat by Anders Darrigan himself, but Iasu had still ended up enslaved to Caa Iss. He was helpless, impotent, and he hated it.

Iasu had respected the late Empress Vesha. She was shrewd,

strategic, and easy to respect. She was also fair to her Kadra'han and had treated them well, as far as Iasu's experience. He had been content to die in her service. It wasn't as if men like him could hope for any better.

But Iasu had outlived Vesha and the cythraul had weaseled his way into holding Iasu's vows on a technicality. Iasu had two choices—find a loophole or spend the rest of his likely short life being bled to give that creature power.

Iasu would have preferred to die, but Caa Iss had forbidden him from taking his own life.

Iasu ran beside Blyst, one of the Kelamora Kadra'han he didn't know particularly well. They were to fetch the escaped children and return them to Caa Iss.

Easy enough. The brats were guarded by a noblewoman and a servant. This would be easy. Pathetically easy.

The sounds of fighting echoed up the hallway. Caa Iss would make short work of Myrani, the sorceress, and their soldiers.

Blyst and Iasu caught up with the fleeing children in a gallery lined with gaudy portraits of nobles wearing too many layers.

The servant was at their head, leading several little ones behind him. He spun around at the sight of the Kadra'han, and the children screamed.

"Go!" the noblewoman shrieked.

"But Lady Vespasia—"

"No time, get the little ones!"

The servant turned and kept running, the sobbing, snotty gaggle of brats rushing after him.

Bring me the children.

That was the order from Caa Iss. There had been nothing in those orders about their adult companions—or Blyst.

The young noblewoman seized a bust from a tall platform, brandishing it like a weapon. It was the noblewoman from yesterday, the one who had arrived with the soldiers.

She blocked their path as the servant and the weeping children ran. Did she really think she stood a chance against two Kadra'han?

Then Iasu saw her face—eyes wide in fear, mouth pressed

in determination. No, she didn't think she stood a chance. She was sacrificing herself to buy the others time.

How interesting.

Blyst drew one of his long fighting daggers, face devoid of emotion. Iasu understood that. He tried not to feel anything himself these days.

Iasu rushed ahead of the other man, reaching the noblewoman first.

She swung the stone bust at him and Iasu grabbed it, but instead of snatching it away, he shoved sideways.

The marble shape arced up and smashed straight into Blyst's head. The other Kadra'han wasn't expecting Iasu's betrayal, and the stone battered into his temple.

Blyst collapsed, dagger skittering across the floor. The man went down and didn't move.

It wasn't anything personal, but Blyst would have stopped him from what he was about to do next.

Bring me the children.

Caa Iss's command grated against Iasu's throat, driving him to obey. But this woman was blocking his path. He had to deal with her first. He *had* to, or at least that was what he told his curse.

Iasu grabbed the woman by her forearms. She let off a cry as he shoved her against the wall.

She whimpered, trying to fight him, but she was unarmed and obviously untrained. Her eyes were wide, and her chest heaved with fear, but she didn't beg.

Iasu kept his grip on her forearms, squeezing tight as his Kadra'han vows compelled him to give chase, to bring those weeping children to the cythraul. Fighting the compulsion with every shred of will he had left, Iasu looked up to the woman he held pinned. Iasu gasped as Caa Iss's commands fluttered at his throat, his own vows threatening to strangle him if he delayed much longer.

The only thing strong enough to break the Kadra'han curse was the Kadra'han curse itself.

Iasu clamped his hands tighter on the woman, like she was

his anchor in a tempest. "Obedience unto death. Power unto life. My service for strength." Iasu croaked out the words, pouring what magic he had into them. "Your enemies are my enemies, and your friends are my friends. I will defend what you love and destroy what you hate. To you I give my allegiance, from now until death claims me."

30

THADRED

With his back to the pillar, the cythraul on the other side, and Sair in front of him, Thadred was running out of ideas.

Caa Iss was strong, but not strong enough to blast through the pillars. Thadred was grateful for small mercies.

Despite that, he'd lost three more men, down to six. Caa Iss was having his Kadra'han pick them off, attacking one pillar at a time while keeping the imperial soldiers divided with flames so no one could help those under attack.

Thadred was inexperienced at fighting with magic, but the closer something was to being alive, the easier it was to use magic on it. Magic could be deflected by stone, metal, and even by leather and cloth, though to a lesser extent. It was much like blades in that way. But it made no difference when Caa Iss used fire, which burned regardless of whether it touched skin or not.

Thadred couldn't cast a shield large or strong enough to protect them all from the blasts. His men were too spread out. Besides that, the carpets and walls had caught fire, and the flames were spreading. The heat had melted the enamel off the far wall and caught the wood behind it. Smoke filled the atrium.

They might just choke to death before burning.

At least Caa Iss couldn't make shields and attack at the same time. And he had not set the rug under his feet ablaze, though Sair's binding spell probably didn't need it anymore.

"Daindreth is going to make you pay for this," Thadred said, looking left and right, trying to think of *something*.

"No, he won't," Caa Iss purred back. "He's never going to find me."

"I don't know," Thadred answered, trying to sound nonchalant. "Amira might."

Caa Iss made an inhuman animal sound at that. It seemed Amira was still a sore topic.

The cythraul came closer, Thadred could feel his presence marching nearer to the pillar where he and Sair crouched.

Thadred squeezed Sair. "We have to attack him directly," he said to the soldier behind the nearest pillar. There wasn't time to wait for Caa Iss to run out of power.

"Thank you." Sair whispered, her voice cracking. "For everything."

Thadred thought his chest might break open. There was so much he wanted to say, but no time. A lifetime of never really belonging, of being left by every woman who had ever meant anything to him and now—one night? Was that all they got? It was downright cruel. "I love you." He kissed her, hard and quick. It was all they had time for.

Caa Iss was closing in.

"I'm going to cast a shield over Caa Iss," Thadred whispered, hoping the demon couldn't hear. Hopefully, Thadred could manage one strong enough since the shield wouldn't be too large. "It might be enough to contain his spells, or at least slow them down."

Sair nodded.

"But you need to hold him while the soldiers and I attack."

Sair didn't reply, but he could sense her hold on her spell binding the demon remained strong. She nodded solemnly.

Thadred began drawing power from the air to himself. He needed to create as strong a shield as possible. He still expected Caa Iss to attack him and probably blast him to cinders, but that would give the soldiers the opening they needed.

Some of them would probably die in the attack, but like Thadred, they had all known this might someday be expected of them. They had all agreed to pay this price.

Sair's eyes shone. She knew. She knew he was expecting to die. But he was grateful she didn't try to stop him.

Thadred signaled to the men behind the pillars, communicating his intentions. They signaled their understanding, passing his intent to their comrades.

Thadred paused, cradling the side of Sair's face, even as he began preparing for his final spell. "Be brave for me, pretty girl."

Sair nodded and Thadred braced himself.

"Master!" Iasu's voice rang out in the silence, startling them all.

Thadred could see the small man from this angle, returning from the direction he had chased after Vespasia, Brick, and the children.

Something was off. Iasu's neck burned with magic. Had his curse always been that bright? Thadred could swear the golden band had gotten larger. And the man was conspicuously alone.

"What?" Caa Iss demanded, whirling on the man.

Iasu stopped, panting heavily. Was he having some sort of attack? His breath wheezed in and out, unsteady and strained.

Thadred looked to Sair. She seemed to sense something was wrong, too.

"Where is Blyst?" Caa Iss demanded.

"Back that way." Iasu gestured down the hall.

"Where are the children?" Caa Iss growled. "Did I not order you to bring them back?"

Thadred was sure he had heard that exact order, too. What had happened?

"Rhis…" Sair's fearful gasp echoed Thadred's own worries.

Iasu nodded. "Yes, master. But there has been a complication."

"What complication?" Caa Iss growled. The cythraul shifted. Caa Iss was nervous, and his attention was on Iasu. Regardless of what had happened, now would be the time to strike.

Iasu didn't look in their direction, but Thadred felt him reach out with a tendril of magic, almost like a nudge. Iasu's power was weak, but Thadred was strong enough to see it. "I have orders to assist the High Inquisitor."

Caa Iss blinked at the man.

Thadred shook his head. What was happening?

"I never gave that order," Caa Iss growled.

Iasu winced, his breathing labored. "I know."

Caa Iss cocked his head to the side. "What have you done?"

Iasu laughed. It was a dark laugh, the laugh of a man looking an adder in the eyes and daring it to strike. His laugh devolved into a cough, his voice turning to a croak.

"Come here, Iasu," Caa Iss ordered.

"No."

Caa Iss paused for the briefest moment. *"What* did you say?"

Iasu coughed, but he wasn't on the ground choking like he should have been. The small man laughed maniacally. "I said *no."*

Caa Iss didn't seem to understand what was happening either, but he wasn't going to risk it. The cythraul whirled on Iasu, another blast of fire heading straight for the Kadra'han.

Thadred cast his shield, locking it around the demon. As he expected, Caa Iss's power ripped through the shield, but it knocked the blast off course, sending the fire pouring into the wall to Iasu's left.

Caa Iss dropped into a crouch. He sent a gust of air through the room, stoking the flames as the walls and furniture caught.

Sweat beaded Sair's forehead and she panted alongside Thadred. "I can keep holding him, but he's fighting me. Either we need to wear him down or end this soon."

"We'll have to do it the old-fashioned way," Thadred muttered. Exactly like he had been planning.

"Kill him!" Caa Iss singled out three of his remaining five Kadra'han—Thadred wasn't sure Iasu counted anymore. "Kill the knight and the sorceress."

Caa Iss was sending everything after Sair and Thadred, leaving himself undefended. But if Sair and Thadred were killed, nothing would stop the demon from slaughtering their soldiers and then anyone else who got in his way.

"Sword!" Thadred yelled. His cane sword wouldn't be enough for this.

"Sir!" A soldier tossed Thadred a longsword.

Caa Iss screeched, glaring at Iasu. "What have you done, you little rat? How are you defying me?"

The three Kadra'han sprinted for Thadred and Sair. Thadred couldn't see them, but he could feel them coming.

Something twanged, and one of the Kadra'han fell. Thadred's last crossbowman was doing his part, but it meant he'd had to step out of the protection of the pillar. Caa Iss sent a fire blast straight for the man and he went down screaming.

Thadred looked to Sair over his shoulder. "I'll do what I can and then pass them to you."

Thadred didn't have time to see Sair's reaction because the Kadra'han were on them. The first man led with his own longsword, stabbing for Thadred's chest.

The knight deflected and pushed up, locking their blades at the hilt before he wrenched, knocking the man off-balance. The second Kadra'han stabbed while Thadred recovered and Thadred blocked the second blade with his forearm. The blade was a dagger, lucky for Thadred, and though it bit deep through his coat sleeve and into his forearm, it stopped at the bone. Distantly, he was aware of pain shooting up his arm.

Thadred shoved the dagger down. He punched his elbow up into the man's face, then followed with a backhand from his sword hilt. The second Kadra'han went down.

The first Kadra'han recovered and spun to attack Thadred again. He seemed to have dismissed Sair as harmless. That was his mistake. He lunged for Thadred, but Sair grabbed him from behind. She must have gotten her hands on skin, because the man's neck ripped open.

Thadred felt the moment she pressed her hand to his bloody wound because her power surged. She tore the Kadra'han's *ka* out. There was no elegance to it, no finesse. Sair struck with all the precision of a street drunkard the morning after Maying Day, but precision wasn't necessary to kill.

The man went down.

Thadred turned back to the first. Despite being stabbed, the first Kadra'han whirled on Sair, blade raised.

Thadred couldn't stab him at these close quarters without risking Sair, so he punched the man full force in the back. The Kadra'han stumbled as Sair scrambled out of the way.

The other Kadra'han lay on the ground, drained and dead.

The remaining Kadra'han spun for Thadred, sword raised. The curse shone gold around his neck, driving him to do this. The wretch couldn't stop even if he wanted to.

He lunged for Thadred. The knight blocked again, driving their blades up over their heads and forcing his enemy's blade sideways. The enemy Kadra'han was clumsy, bleeding.

Still, the man recovered, blocking Thadred's counterattack. He skirted to the left, ducking out of reach.

Sair rested a hand on the dead Kadra'han's neck and blood seeped out. His heart had stopped beating and the blood came slower, but her gory work soaked the floor in red.

Thadred faced the remaining Kadra'han. He was blocking Sair's view, preventing her from using a spell to take him down, but he was also blocking the man's access to Sair.

One of the tenebrous steel shields had been dropped by a dead soldier—Ivo, a sergeant and the second son of a tailor in Mynadra.

Thadred leaned over to pick up the shield, keeping his sword up. As he expected, the Kadra'han took the opening and lunged.

Thadred blocked the enemy sword with his own and swung the shield up right after it, using the shield as a bludgeon.

He smashed the edge of the shield into the Kadra'han's shoulder. It knocked the man back hard enough that he stayed off balance for one precious heartbeat.

A heartbeat was all it took for Thadred to bring his sword back down and cleave the man's head free.

Behind them, Caa Iss hurled spells at the soldiers to keep them back and blasted at Iasu in a mad frenzy.

Sair locked eyes with Thadred, her nostrils flaring. He sensed her gathering power, pulling it from the dead man. She shot out from behind the safety of the pillar and lashed at Caa Iss.

Thadred grabbed her arm just as an answering spell hurled in her direction. He dragged her back as a blast of fire surged past them.

A roar filled the chamber.

Thadred dared a brief look.

Caa Iss's legs had been sheared off at the ankles. Not even he could heal from amputation. Sair hadn't killed his host, but she had weakened him.

"He put a shield on his upper body," Sair panted. "But this way he can't run."

Between Sair's attack and her spell still binding the demon, Caa Iss was trapped. They just had to find a way to get close and finish him off.

Thadred looked down to his bleeding right arm. He could feel the power leeching out of him.

Sair pressed a hand to the wound and Thadred winced. "I'm sorry," she grimaced. She peeled back the fabric of his sleeve, clearing it from the wound before she sent a shock of power through it.

Thadred gritted his teeth as his flesh knit back together. It was a sensation not unlike being sewn—stabbing pain as his body re-wove itself. It left a dull ache, but he could use his arm again.

Iasu fought beside the soldiers, though his movements were sluggish and strained. He was still fighting his Kadra'han curse. Whatever he had done, he wasn't completely free.

The soldier at the pillar to Thadred's left stumbled back as a spell from the cythraul caught him in the side. Thadred grabbed him by the back of his hauberk and yanked him behind the pillar just as another blast of fire from Caa Iss struck the space where he had been.

"Landric, damn it." Blood poured down the other man's side. It was like he had been gored by a bull. Thadred eased the soldier against the pillar. What spell had done this?

"Hold still." Sair crouched beside the wounded man.

"Sorry, my lord," the soldier grunted.

Thadred cursed as Sair pressed her hands over the man's wound. He could feel her pulling *ka* from the man's blood, using his own lost *ka* to heal him. That was a good idea, actually. One he'd have to remember.

Thadred crouched, taking much longer than anyone else would have. He braced his shield on the ground, using it for balance. He reached for the bodies of the two dead Kadra'han, their blood leeching onto the tiles. Thadred thought about how Caa Iss had taken blood, made it run up like it was alive.

As the knight knelt, he pictured that. He willed the fading power in these bodies to rise over his arm.

He felt the power rush up, but instead of drawing it into himself as he usually did with magic, he kept it outside himself, held just over his forearm. The power gathered much faster that way. Without taking the magic into his body, it didn't try to flow into his multitude of injuries, namely the permanent one in his hip.

His body throbbed and his joints ached, but he could pull power much faster if he skipped trying to draw it into himself first.

The *ka* slid up his arm, almost like a bracer. Curious, Thadred touched his shield and tried pulling more from the dead bodies. He drew their *ka* up, coating the front of the shield in a veneer. The spell withered wherever it touched the inner lining of tenebrous steel, so Thadred had to be careful to focus on the front.

Sair looked up from Landric and her eyes widened. "Thadred."

He had a shield coated entirely in the power of the dead men. He frowned as it flickered at the edges, requiring concentration to hold its shape.

"Take power from yourself," Sair said. "And use it to…coat the outside."

Thadred had never done this before, but Sair seemed to understand what he was doing. Following her instructions, he took some of his own power and sealed it around the power on the shield, like a glaze on a clay vase.

The shield of *ka* held around the metal shield, binding to some of the leather inlay as well. Thadred swallowed and looked up to Sair. "Can you keep holding him?" He jerked in the direction of Caa Iss.

Sair glanced at the dead corpses, fresh and still with power to spare. "I think so. At least for a few minutes."

More than Thadred needed. "Stay with him." Thadred nodded to the soldier between them.

Sair nodded. She looked as if she would argue but didn't.

Thadred rose, hobbling awkwardly with his bad hip.

Smoke filled the room. The flames were catching. Heat licked up as the smoke began to thicken. They couldn't stay here for much longer.

Thadred stepped out from behind the pillar, fully aware he might be stepping in the path of death.

Caa Iss didn't waste time. The cythraul launched a spell at him, a blast of power shaped like a spear.

Thadred caught the blast on his shield, knocking it aside like he would any other missile. The impact jarred up his arm and shoulder, making his teeth rattle—but the shield held.

Caa Iss roared, equal parts fear and wrath.

Thadred tried not to feel too satisfied. He marched past the pillar, toward the demon.

Caa Iss launched another blast of fire, aiming for his shins. The blasts were getting smaller.

Thadred sidestepped that one though heat singed along his trouser leg.

Caa Iss followed that up with a bolt sent for Thadred's head. Smart. He was probably hoping that Thadred wouldn't be able to raise his shield fast enough, but these tower shields were standard issue for a reason.

Thadred dropped the shield to the ground and crouched behind it just as Caa Iss predictably tried to take a shot at his feet an instant later. "For a thing that's been at it for thousands of years," Thadred grunted against the impact of another blast, "you're not very good at this, are you?"

Caa Iss let off a howl and scrambled back.

Thadred glanced over his shoulder. Sair was hidden from view—good—but he could feel her working magic, binding Caa Iss into his current body, keeping him from fleeing again.

Caa Iss had escaped the Witch War and he had escaped from the brothel. He wouldn't be escaping this mansion.

"Stop him!" Caa Iss ordered. "Kill him!"

The last two remaining Kadra'han leapt to obey. Thadred sensed their *ka* closing in on him from opposite sides. They had probably seen what happened to the others and decided that harrying him from both sides at once was the better plan.

Thadred couldn't fight them both from his left and right and worry about Caa Iss in front of him. Thadred gritted his jaw and braced himself as the two Kadra'han closed in.

The one coming at him from the right stopped, a third source of *ka* lunging at him.

Iasu attacked the Kadra'han to Thadred's left. The smaller man had picked up a longsword from one of Thadred's fallen soldiers and tore into his former comrade.

Not having time to wonder about it, Thadred lashed out for the Kadra'han attempting to circle his right.

A soldier threw something at the Kadra'han. It was just a piece of tile, and it went wide but the Kadra'han jumped, spinning to meet what he thought was a new attack.

The hesitation bought Thadred enough time to slice the man's shoulder. These Kadra'han were lightly armored, not used to fighting knights. Thadred was sure he saw a flash of white bone before the man's left arm went limp.

Still the Kadra'han raised his saber. It was a clean, slightly arched weapon, like the ones carried by light cavalry.

Thadred smacked the blade away with his shield and stabbed. He impaled the man through the ribs and yanked the blade out.

That wound would probably prove lethal, but for now the Kadra'han still didn't go down. He stumbled, trying to circle and force Thadred to turn his back to Caa Iss.

Thadred wasn't the lightest on his feet, but he skirted back. The Kadra'han seemed surprised at how fast Thadred moved.

The knight grinned. Crippled didn't mean helpless and many dead men had learned that the hard way.

From the corner of his eye, Thadred saw Iasu had won his

fight with the other Kadra'han.

Caa Iss cursed at Iasu, using words in that strange language that made Thadred's skin crawl. The demon sent a blast after Iasu and the Kadra'han ducked back behind one of the pillars.

That left Thadred with a single bleeding warrior between him and the cythraul.

The wounded man stumbled as blood soaked down his clothes.

Caa Iss shrieked, trying to claw free of his body, but Sair's trap held.

"Thadred!" Sair yelled, her voice desperate. "Quickly!"

Thadred shoved forward, smashing his shield into the face of the opposing Kadra'han. The man went down without any real resistance, losing his strength to blood loss. As Thadred raised his sword over his foe, he saw nothing but hopelessness in the stranger's face.

This man had accepted defeat a long time ago. He had probably known he was dead as soon as Caa Iss had taken over as grandmaster.

Thadred finished the man off with a sharp blow to the temple. The man's skull caved, crumpling under the force of the longsword.

Stepping over the body, Thadred marched onward to Caa Iss.

The demon mewled and howled, crawling across the floor dragging the ruined stumps of his legs behind him. He whined and hissed, blubbering incoherently.

Caa Iss sent another blast of power in Thadred's direction, but this one fizzled weakly. The demon had overextended himself and his Kadra'han were dead, out of reach.

The cythraul lunged at Thadred's shield, snarling and foaming at the mouth like a rabid animal. Thadred smashed the edge of his shield down on the creature's hands and the bones fractured before knitting back together without resetting. His hands came back up with knobs and crooked angles. The creature was still healing almost instantly, but his healing had gotten worse.

Crushing the edge of the shield below the creature's collarbone, Thadred pinned the cythraul to the tiles. He pressed against the demon's chest as the creature writhed and struggled.

"I can give you power!" the cythraul wheedled, clawing at the shield with ruined hands. "I am a prince of the Dread Marches! I can bring you wealth, fame, riches beyond your wildest—"

Thadred's lip curled in disgust. "You're just a coward, aren't you?"

"I am a prince of the Dread Marches. If you spare me, I will—"

"No," Thadred said, raising his sword again. Sweat poured down his face and soaked his arms and back. "No, I think you're done."

Thadred stabbed through the demon's mouth, the blade punching out the back of the host's throat. This time, the shape of the demon rippled free, mutilated, misshapen features twisted in horror. His translucent shape turned to mist and vanished, slipping into the Dread Marches.

The presence of demonic *ka* winked out, leaving behind the brutalized body of a dead man in Thadred's grasp.

The knight stared down at the poor wretch. Maybe he had volunteered to be Caa Iss's host. But being bound in a Kadra'han curse was to put oneself wholly at the mercy of whoever held your vows. Daindreth had always held his bonds loosely, but Thadred was still technically bound in this same curse. He was just lucky that he served a good man.

Thadred pulled his sword free. He looked around him at the piles of dead Kadra'han as the smoke rose.

"My lord!" Several of his soldiers came out from behind the pillars.

Thadred counted four still on their feet and breathing. They'd lost five and there was the man behind the pillar with Sair.

A dark laugh came from Thadred's left. The laugh grew louder, almost hysterical.

Iasu lay on his back, staring up at the ceiling. He looked like a madman, lying there covered in blood, with smoke and flames rising at the edges of the room, the bodies of his former comrades strewn around him.

"Zahn?" Thadred snapped. "Are we going to have problems?"

Iasu lolled his head in Thadred's direction. "I owe you a drink, Myrani."

Thadred cocked his head, studying the golden band around the man's neck—only one now. "You're still bound in a Kadra'han's vows." The knight shot a glance at the corpses around him. "The new grandmaster?"

"The order is gone," Iasu said, rolling upright so that he was sitting cross-legged. "Dead and gone. And it should stay gone."

"Then who holds your vows?"

Iasu shrugged. "I'm not sure."

Sair emerged from behind the pillar. She looked over Thadred and there was visible relief on her face before she looked back to Iasu.

"What do you mean?" Thadred demanded.

Iasu looked at Sair just a little too long for Thadred's liking. "It seems you were right." Iasu turned back to Thadred, face unreadable. "The only thing that can resist the Kadra'han curse is itself."

"Who holds your vows?" Thadred put himself between Sair and Iasu. He had just sent Caa Iss back to the Dread Marches and he'd be damned if he let one little stray Kadra'han hurt her.

Iasu gestured vaguely back in the direction he had come from, the same direction that Vespasia and Brick had gone with the children. "I don't know her name. She came at me with a statue." Iasu's face wrinkled with something like intrigue. "I've never been attacked with a statue before."

"Vespasia?" Thadred felt his blood going hot as an alien protectiveness surged through him. "If you've hurt my sister, I swear—"

"She's fine," Iasu muttered. He stood, wiping his bloody hands on his thighs. "We should probably get out of this mansion." Iasu gestured to the fire spreading around the gallery.

"Wouldn't you agree?"

"I'm not letting you out of my sight." Thadred kept his sword leveled at Iasu.

The Kadra'han simply rolled his eyes but didn't protest.

Thadred lowered his shield. "Sair?"

As if she had been waiting for permission, she ran to him.

Thadred dropped his shield to catch her hand, using the one that wasn't leveling a sword at Iasu. "Ready?" he called back to his soldiers. He could sense their *ka* lining up behind him as the wounded were collected by their fellows.

"Ready, sir," one of the soldiers replied.

Thadred nodded to Iasu. "I'm guessing my sister took the children outside to safety?"

"Probably," Iasu agreed.

"Take us to them. Now."

Iasu's nostrils flared, but he turned back around and led them through the maze of the mansion. Thadred's soldiers came behind them. Landric limped between two other men. Others were also injured, but they were still able to walk on their own.

Thadred kept track of their surroundings and yes, Iasu was leading them in the general direction of the exit. They left the burning atrium and smoking remains of the hall behind.

Iasu took them into a portrait gallery and past the body of a dead Kadra'han, the other man who had followed Iasu after the children but had never come back. Beside the corpse lay a bloody marble bust.

Either Vespasia had become superhuman, or Iasu had turned on his fellow Kadra'han.

Thadred could believe that Iasu had sworn a new set of vows to Vespasia to circumvent his vows to Caa Iss. It was the sort of desperate, foolhardy thing he might have tried himself.

But Iasu had been so quick to turn on his friends. What kind of man resorted to murdering his fellow soldiers for his own chance at freedom?

Perhaps Thadred should kill Iasu. The empress would probably do as much if Thadred knew Amira. Dain wouldn't like it, though.

Was it worth the risk to leave Iasu alive? If he really was sworn to Vespasia now, he might be an invaluable asset.

Kadra'han had been officially outlawed in the empire and those currently held were supposed to be released, but Thadred doubted anyone would sleep easy with Iasu on the loose.

The man had served Vesha the Usurper faithfully and had most recently been mastered by Caa Iss. That was not a good history to have when petitioning the empire's mercy.

By the time Iasu led them outside, Thadred had still not figured out what to do.

They found themselves in a garden. At their backs, the mansion smoked and burned, and a bucket chain was starting as servants rushed inside to put out the flames before they spread.

Thadred looked left and right, Sair on one arm and sword still drawn in the other. "There." He jerked his chin to a spot down the hill. He singled out two of his men. "Watch him," he pointed to Iasu. "If he tries anything, stab him. Repeatedly."

Iasu folded his arms across his chest, glaring at Thadred.

Thadred took the rest of the men down the hill toward where he sensed the grouping of bodies. At his side, Sair was rigid. He could feel her fear in how she gripped him, her worry in how she kept shifting her hold on his arm.

"Brick?" Thadred called. "We're alive. We won." Thadred still didn't lower his sword. "Brick?"

"Here, sir." Brick appeared from behind a row of hedges. "We're here. All of us."

A shape appeared behind Brick. Vespasia in her white dressing gown. "Thadred?"

"Hello, sister." Thadred glanced up the hill to where Iasu stood guarded by two soldiers. "I hear you got yourself a Kadra'han?"

"He helped you like I told him?"

"Ah," Thadred nodded. "I should have known he wouldn't do that on his own."

"Mama!" Rhis leapt up from behind the hedges, rushing straight for Sair.

"Rhis!" Sair caught him, crushing him up in her embrace.

"Oh, my baby. My sweet boy." She kissed his hair, her shoulders shaking. She put her hand on his injured arm, easing her power into it to speed the healing. It was probably just badly bruised.

Rhis held on tight to her. He didn't cry, but he clung to her for dear life, face buried in her shoulder.

Thadred put an arm around Sair, not sure if he was welcome in this moment or not. Sair turned into him, still clutching Rhis and Thadred tucked both her and Rhis beneath his chin. Thadred's sword still hung in his grip, soaked in the blood of Caa Iss.

Thadred closed his eyes. For just a moment, he basked in the moment. It had cost them dearly in the lives of his men, but Sair and Rhis were safe.

And Caa Iss had been sent back to the Dread Marches.

Thadred was holding the woman he loved and her child. They were going to be a family. Maybe they already were.

Thadred didn't know the first thing about being a family, but he was willing to learn.

After a long set of heartbeats, Rhis lifted his head. The light from the burning mansion illuminated his face and Thadred saw he had been crying after all.

"Did you get him?" Rhis asked, his voice barely more than a squeak.

Thadred nodded. "We got him."

31

SAIR

Lleuad had not become any more amenable to ships, it seemed.

Sair watched Thadred wrestle with the kelpie, spewing curses and insults at the beast. She couldn't help but smile as she pulled her red cloak tighter against the wind on the docks. It was the same one Thadred had given her—his courting gift.

"That kelpie is magically bound to Thadred, you say?" Vespasia had come to see them off, standing beside Sair on the pier.

"He is," Sair replied. "A gift from Eponine herself."

Vespasia frowned, watching her brother use increasingly inventive oaths as the pony refused to set foot on the ramp. "I thought a magically gifted steed would be less…that."

Sair shrugged. "Being magically bound doesn't mean they get along. At least not all the time."

Vespasia's eyes slid back a short distance down the pier to where Iasu stood guard. He faced away from them, watching the rest of the docks. "I suppose not."

Sair exhaled. No one was sure what to do with him now.

Kadra'han were illegal, but Iasu had willingly sworn himself to Vespasia. Even if he had done it without her permission.

Thadred had debated hauling them both back to Mynadra to face Daindreth—or more specifically, Amira. In the end,

Thadred had written out a list of commands for Iasu and Vespasia had delivered them.

Iasu had not seemed pleased, but the commands had been straightforward enough. He was forbidden from harming Vespasia in any way—he had actually laughed at that one—as well as a list of other basics that would keep him from conspiring against the empire.

"Are you sure you don't want us to take him back to Mynadra?" Sair asked. None of them knew exactly what might happen to him there, but Sair was sure Amira would have some use for him in her ever-growing network of spies.

When they had asked Iasu what he wanted, he had simply said that he had sworn himself to Vespasia and would do what she wanted.

Vespasia shook her head. "I…I feel responsible for him."

"You don't have to be," Sair said. The wind whipped up, tugging at Sair's red cloak. "He vowed himself to you against your will."

"I know, but…" Vespasia swallowed. "With you and Thadred leaving, I need someone my mother can't influence."

Sair nodded solemnly. "I understand."

Dowager Countess Zeyna was not, in fact, dead as Caa Iss had said. Zeyna had a few bruises, but no other injuries. But she had blamed Thadred and Vespasia for everything, by her actions if not her words. She refused to speak directly to either of them since the events of that night and had insisted on relaying her words through Sair or servants.

"I'm sure your mother will come around."

Vespasia inhaled a long breath. "I hope so."

Sair caught the younger woman's hand. "You can always come to court, my dear." She nodded to where Thadred had stopped trying to drag the kelpie onto the ship and appeared to be reasoning with him. "Your brother will welcome you. I will welcome you."

"We'll see if my mother allows it."

"Well, if nothing else." Sair looked to where Iasu stood guard like a hound outside a money changer's shop. "That one knows how to travel with an alias. He could probably take you anywhere that you asked."

Vespasia laughed a little, but it sounded forced. "Good to know."

Finally, Brick brought Thadred what appeared to be a raw pork chop and backed away.

Lleuad sniffed it, then lunged for the slab of meat. He gobbled it down, then leaned back hard on the lead rope.

"Glue!" Thadred vowed. "I will turn you into glue!"

Lleuad swallowed and stepped gingerly onto the deck.

"What devilry is this?" Thadred demanded as the pony walked up the wooden planks.

Lleuad allowed himself to be taken below, suddenly acting like a perfect knight's horse.

Sair's eyes narrowed. Sure enough, as soon as they were out of sight, she heard a squeal and a crash followed by Thadred bellowing a fresh string of curses.

"Is he alright?" Vespasia looked past Sair.

The sorceress waited, just a little concerned. She didn't think Lleuad would actually harm Thadred, but…

Thadred staggered back into view, muttering and gripping his bad hip. He clambered across the deck, exchanging low words with the crew.

Several wooden boxes were carried onto the decks by the soldiers, two men to each. Each box was draped with the insignia of the empire. Each one carried a soldier who had fallen in these past days.

Silence descended as Thadred and the other officers stopped, standing at attention. It was a solemn procession with a kind of grim reverence.

Vespasia cleared her throat softly at Sair's side. "I'm sorry those men died."

"I am, too," Sair said. "Just like I am sorry that those other Kadra'han died." Sair was not sure they had been good men, but they had been at the mercy of Caa Iss. No one deserved that.

Vespasia inhaled deeply. "I will have to come and visit you and my brother. Once you are settled back in Mynadra. You'll be having to set up your household first, of course. My sister has told me the early months of marriage are the most hectic."

Sair nodded, almost forgetting that. It was surreal. Last time, there was no household to set up. It had just been her and Rhisiart in their barrow.

Thadred was an imperial lord. He had servants and retainers, and she would need maidservants and Rhis would need tutors and—those were all problems for another day.

The coffins were carried below decks to be secured in the cargo hold. The solemn air on the deck cleared, though Sair noticed less chatter amongst the sailors.

Thadred headed toward the two women, his cane returned to his side. He smiled at the sight of Sair. "Have everything you need, my love?" He rested a hand on the small of her back as he came to stand beside her.

"Yes," Sair answered softly as she cupped his cheek. "Yes, I have everything I need." She had Thadred and she had her son. She didn't need anything else.

Rhis was already on board the ship, at the front of the deck. Several of the boys they'd rescued from the Kadra'han as well as the young Count Flavius crouched around the ship's helm. They all appeared fascinated with something in the water, pointing and calling to one another.

It would be an adventure to keep that lot contained all the way across the Jaunty Straits back to Mynadra.

Thadred looked to his sister. "Come to Mynadra soon. Or I'll be forced to send an imperial order demanding it."

Vespasia smiled, sensing the jest in his words. "I'll keep that in mind."

Thadred nodded curtly. "And if that one gives you any trouble—" He jabbed his cane in the direction of Iasu. "—just send word and I'll come back to knock some sense into him."

If Iasu heard Thadred's threat, he ignored it. The smaller man kept staring out like a sentinel. At least he seemed to take his duty to Vespasia seriously.

Thadred cleared his throat, shooting a brief glance to Sair. "And if you ever need anything, anything at all, you had best let me know. If I have to find out from the empress's spies that you're ever in trouble and you didn't tell me—"

Vespasia flung her arms around Thadred.

Thadred went stiff at the sudden gesture then he hugged her back, lowering his head to bow over her.

"Thank you," Vespasia said. "Thank you so much."

"I feel like I should be thanking you," he said. "I'd probably be dead without you."

"I'm sure you could have managed." Vespasia kissed his cheek before ending their embrace.

Thadred shouted past her to Iasu. "If you give my sister any trouble at all, I will be back to beat the shit out of you, hear?"

Iasu made a rude gesture in Thadred's direction, not turning his head.

Vespasia giggled, clamping a hand over her mouth to keep it down. "Thank you."

Sair embraced Vespasia next, squeezing her sister-in-law tight. "And thank you. For everything."

Vespasia nodded, clearing her throat again as they broke apart.

Thadred inhaled a deep breath through his nose, looking toward the open water. "Ready?"

Sair nodded, hooking her arm through his. The two of them walked up the ramp of the ship. They moved slower thanks to Thadred's limp, but Sair didn't mind. She hugged close to his side as the wind whipped up again.

They joined the boys near the prow of the vessel as the anchor raised.

The sailors called to one another, the soldiers arranged trunks and bags in the hold while others worked on final checks for their horses.

Vespasia waved to them from the pier. Iasu had stepped closer to her, but he still faced away from her, as if he dared any of the sailors or passersby to just try something.

"She'll have her hands full with that one," Thadred muttered. "I'm not sure I should leave him with her."

"Your sister will be fine," Sair said. "She's made of stronger stuff than anyone gives her credit for."

"You're right." Thadred leaned over and kissed the top of Sair's head. "You're always right."

"Mama!" Rhis ran up to her. "Did you see the anchor?"

"Yes," Sair said, crouching down.

"It's bigger than me!" Rhis said, eyes wide. "And I think we saw a shark! Have you ever seen a shark?"

"I don't think I have."

"Well, I think we saw one, but it's gone now."

The sails unfurled, dropping down with a rippling, snapping roar. Several of the boys jumped, spinning around. Most of them had probably never seen a ship of this size before.

Flavius sat to one side, unimpressed. Thadred was making good on his threat to have Flavius serve as a squire for the next few years and the boy was none too happy about it.

Zeyna had begged, pleaded, and threatened, but in the end, there was nothing she could do about it. Thadred was an imperial minister. He could do what he wanted in this case. Zeyna had shrieked about the cruelty of it, but Thadred was right.

Flavius was going to rule this province one day. The fates of tens of thousands would be in his hands. Yes, he was just a boy, but he needed discipline and a good dose of humility if he didn't want to run this province into ruin in ten, twenty, or thirty years.

This was about the future government, not just a mother and her child.

"Why couldn't Maëlys come with us?" Rhis asked, looking back toward the pier. "Everyone else has."

Sair brushed Rhis's hair back. "Maëlys has a house here. Her papa made sure she had enough money to last her the rest of her life. She'll be fine, Rhis. Didn't you see what a big house she has?"

The boy shook his head. "But she's alone."

Sair didn't know what to say to that. It was true the girl was now an orphan, even if she would hardly be poor.

Vespasia had promised to look in on the child now and again, but as far as Sair had been able to tell, Maëlys's father had planned incredibly well for his own death.

Several of the boys shouted, pointing at something as the ship began to shift and glide away from the docks. Rhis dashed off to see, on his tiptoes, as he and the others tried to lean over the railing.

"Not so far!" Thadred shouted. "Heels on the deck." As soon as he said it, he shot an unsure look to Sair.

She nodded, agreeing. "Heels on the deck!"

The boys reluctantly obeyed, standing on the flats of their feet.

Sair and Thadred had talked about it, but they still needed to sort out discipline and rules with Rhis. This was new for all of them.

Rhis had started challenging Thadred, testing his boundaries even in the past week since they had been here.

Thadred had been patient so far, but Sair could see it frustrated him. Rhis liked Thadred, but he still seemed determined to put her new husband through his paces.

"I don't know what I'm doing," Thadred admitted, his voice low enough that the wind carried it away from the boys. "I've never been a stepfather before."

"Rhis has never been a stepson before."

Thadred ran a hand through his hair. "I guess not."

Sair pulled Thadred tighter against her side.

"You know I'm going to muck this up," Thadred said. "Sooner or later, I'm going to make a terrible mistake."

"You will," Sair agreed. "And then you'll make amends, learn from it, and we'll move on."

Thadred heaved a long breath. "I'm not sure that is comforting."

Sair laughed a little at that. "There are no perfect parents, my love."

"I'll take your word for it." Thadred kissed the top of her head again. "My wise wife."

The ship made its way out of the harbor, drifting toward the open water. Vespasia became a speck on the docks, staying until they faded into the distance.

Thadred remained beside Sair, watching as Rhis and the other boys ran back and forth across the deck. They kept to the front half, out of the way of most the sailors as the men guided the ship toward the sea.

"Things might get rough ahead," Thadred said. He might have been talking about the Jaunty Straits in their path, but he watched Rhis as he said it.

Sair nodded. "It probably will."

"But you're worth it." Thadred looked at her.

She met his gaze she saw he was being earnest. There was a kind of nervousness in the way he shifted, the way he watched her almost fearfully.

"Both of you. You're worth it." He looked down to where Sair's hand was wrapped around his arm. "I hope I can make it worthwhile for you."

"*You* are worth it." Sair slipped her hand up, fingers tracing the outline of his jaw. "*We* are worth it. All three of us."

Thadred leaned down and kissed her. It was a stolen kiss, begun and over while Rhis's back was turned.

Thadred slid his arm around Sair, holding her against his side as the ship made its way out of the harbor and back toward Mynadra.

There was a whole new life to begin once they reached the city. Sair wasn't fully sure yet what it would look like. There were still many unknowns and unanswered questions, but she was full of hope and quiet confidence that everything would work out.

Sair rested her head against Thadred's shoulder as the ship carried them toward home.

AUTHOR'S NOTE

I never intended for Thadred to get his own book.

In the original draft of the *Daindreth's Assassin* series, Thadred died tragically in book 3. But shortly after the publication of book 1, an unexpected thing happened—I got a boyfriend.

Not only did I get a boyfriend, but for the first time ever, I had a boyfriend who showed an interest in my writing. Said boyfriend read book 1 of *Daindreth's Assassin* and soon decided that Thadred was his favorite character.

If I'd had more reader feedback, I might have known that Thadred would be the best-loved character in the *Daindreth's Assassin* series, but I was a nobody and had very few readers at the time. Luckily, I couldn't bring myself to off my boyfriend's favorite character. I quietly rewrote Thadred's fate, sparing him so he could fulfill his destiny as a fan favorite. The need for a spinoff became undeniable.

As Thadred continued to thrive in later books, he soon developed remarkable chemistry with a certain widowed sorceress. I still tried to shoehorn Thadred into another story because of reasons (there's this idea about a magical banking mafia I've wanted to write). But no matter how hard I tried, the story refused to work.

Finally, I accepted that Thadred and Sair are meant for each other and there's nothing I can do to change that.

I am not sure how much credit I can take for a story that seems to exist in spite of me. All the same, thank you so much for reading and I hope you love Sair and Thadred's story as much as I do.

Most of all, thank you to Christian, who has since been upgraded from boyfriend to husband. Everything is better with you.

Thank you for reading!

You can expect more soon in the world of Erymaya, and from Vespasia and Iasu.

Visit my website elisabethwheatley.com for latest news, updates, and early bird sign-ups.

ABOUT THE AUTHOR

Elisabeth Wheatley is the author of High Fantasy with Epic Romance. She lives in Austin, TX with her husband Christian and her geriatric Jack Russell Terrier, Schnay.

You can find her at elisabethwheatley.com

www.ingramcontent.com/pod-product-compliance
Lightning Source LLC
Chambersburg PA
CBHW022002310726
48972CB00006B/1486